CARTOON HANGOVER

BRAVEST WARRIORS

CREATED by PENDLETON WARD

VOLUME ONE

ROSS RICHIE CEO & Founder • MATT GAGNON Editor-in-Chief • FILIP SABLIK VP-Publishing & Marketing • LANCE KREITER VP-Licensing & Merchandising • PHIL BARBARO Director of Finance • BRYCE CARLSON Managing Editor
DAFNA PLEBAN Editor • SHANNON WATTERS Editor • ERIC HARBURN Editor • CHRIS ROSA Assistant Editor • ALEX GALER Assistant Editor • WHITNEY LEOPARD Assistant Editor • JASMINE AMIRI Assistant Editor • STEPHANIE GONZAGA Graphic Designer
KASSANDRA HELLER Production Designer • MIKE LOPEZ Production Designer • DEVIN FUNCHES E-Commerce & Inventory Coordinator • VINCE FREDERICK Event Coordinator • BRIANNA HART Executive Assistant

BRAVEST WARRIORS Volume One — July 2013. Published by KaBOOM!, a division of Boom Entertainment, Inc. Based on "Bravest Warriors" © 2013 Frederator Networks, Inc. Originally published in single magazine form as BRAVEST WARRIORS 1-4. Copyright © 2012, 2013 Frederator Networks, Inc. All rights reserved. KaBOOM!™ and the KaBOOM! logo are trademarks of Boom Entertainment, Inc., registered in various countries and categories. All characters, events, and institutions depicted herein are fictional. Any similarity between any of the names, characters, persons, events, and/or institutions in this publication to actual names, characters, and persons, whether living or dead, events, and/or institutions is unintended and purely coincidental. KaBOOM! does not read or accept unsolicited submissions of ideas, stories, or artwork.

A catalog record of this book is available from OCLC and from the KaBOOM! website, www.kaboom-studios.com, on the Librarians Page.

BOOM! Studios, 5670 Wilshire Boulevard, Suite 450, Los Angeles, CA 90036-5679. Printed in China. First Printing. ISBN: 978-1-60886-322-8

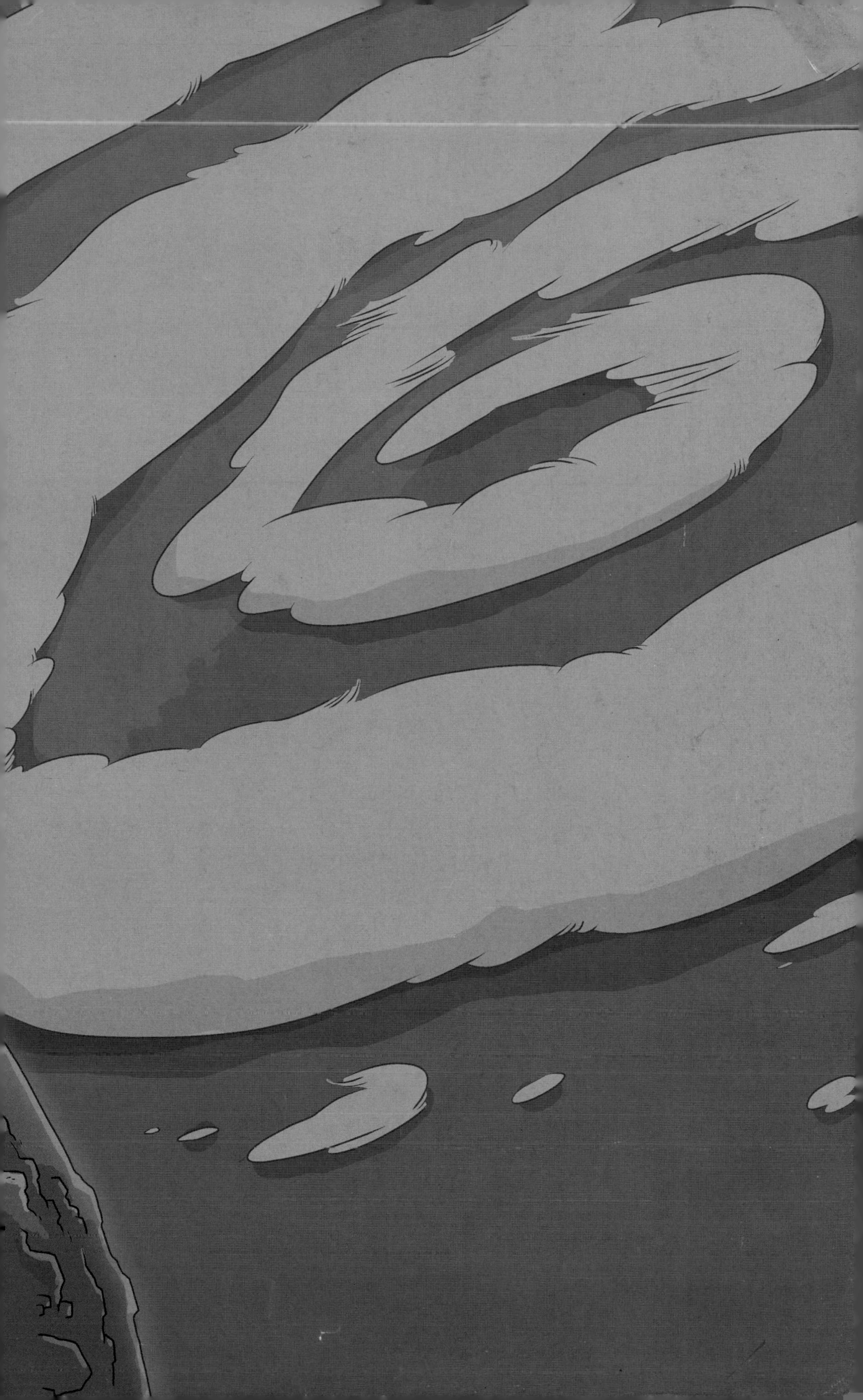

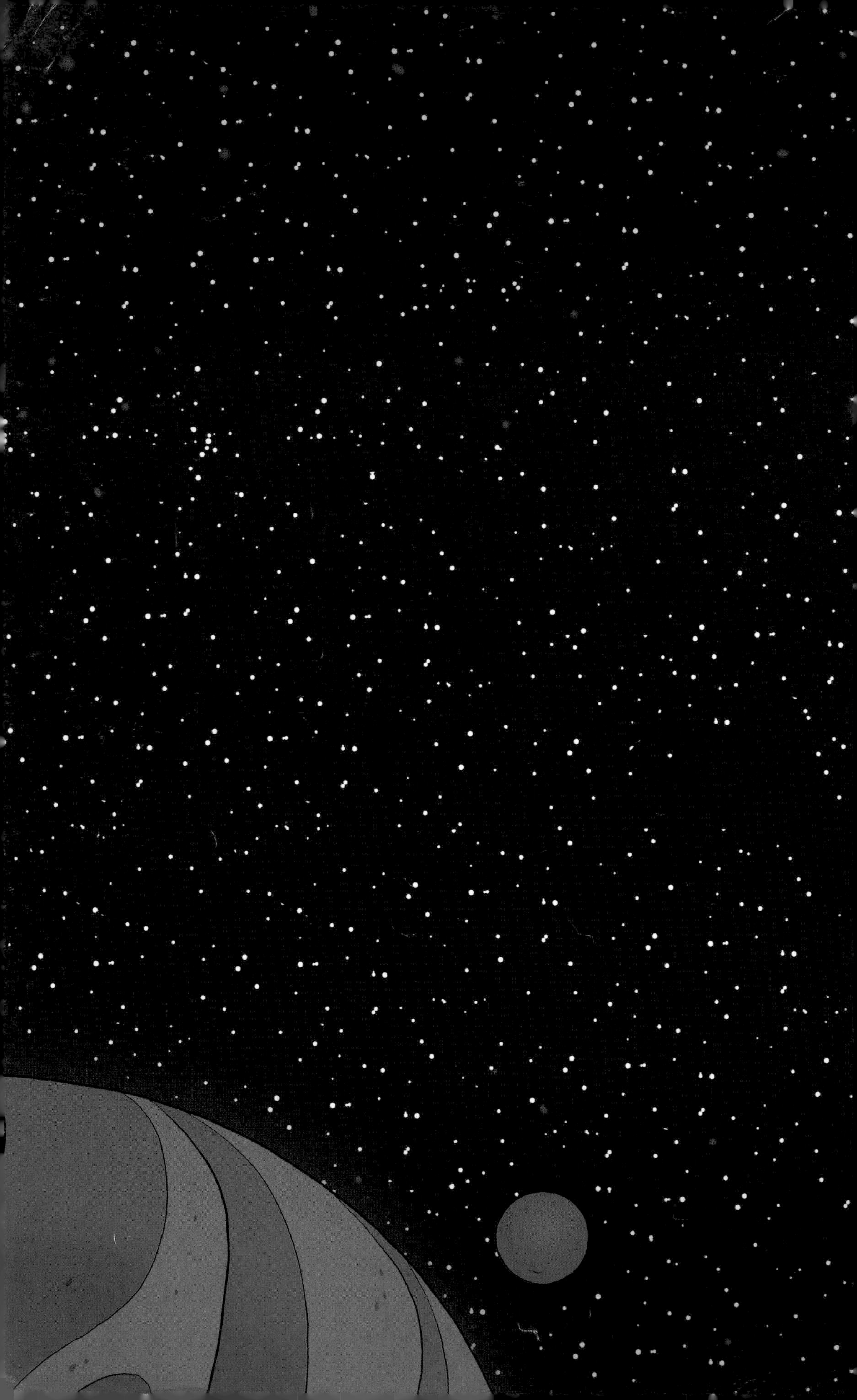

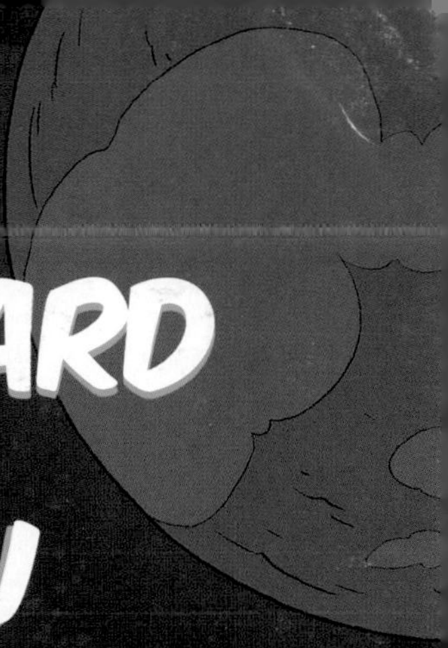

CREATED BY
PENDLETON WARD

WRITTEN BY
JOEY COMEAU

ILLUSTRATED BY
MIKE HOLMES

COLORS BY
ZACK STERLING

LETTERS BY
STEVE WANDS

COVER BY
TYSON HESSE

ASSISTANT EDITOR
WHITNEY LEOPARD

EDITOR
SHANNON WATTERS

DESIGNER
KASSANDRA HELLER

SHORT MISSIONS
WRITTEN & ILLUSTRATED BY
RYAN PEQUIN

"LASER SUNDAY"
AND
"TRIVIAL REALITY"
COLORS BY **MIRKA ANDOLFO**

"SPACE FLU"
COLORS BY **STUDIO PARLAPÁ**

"BRAVEST WARRIOR (BY DANNY)"
COLORS BY **LISA MOORE**

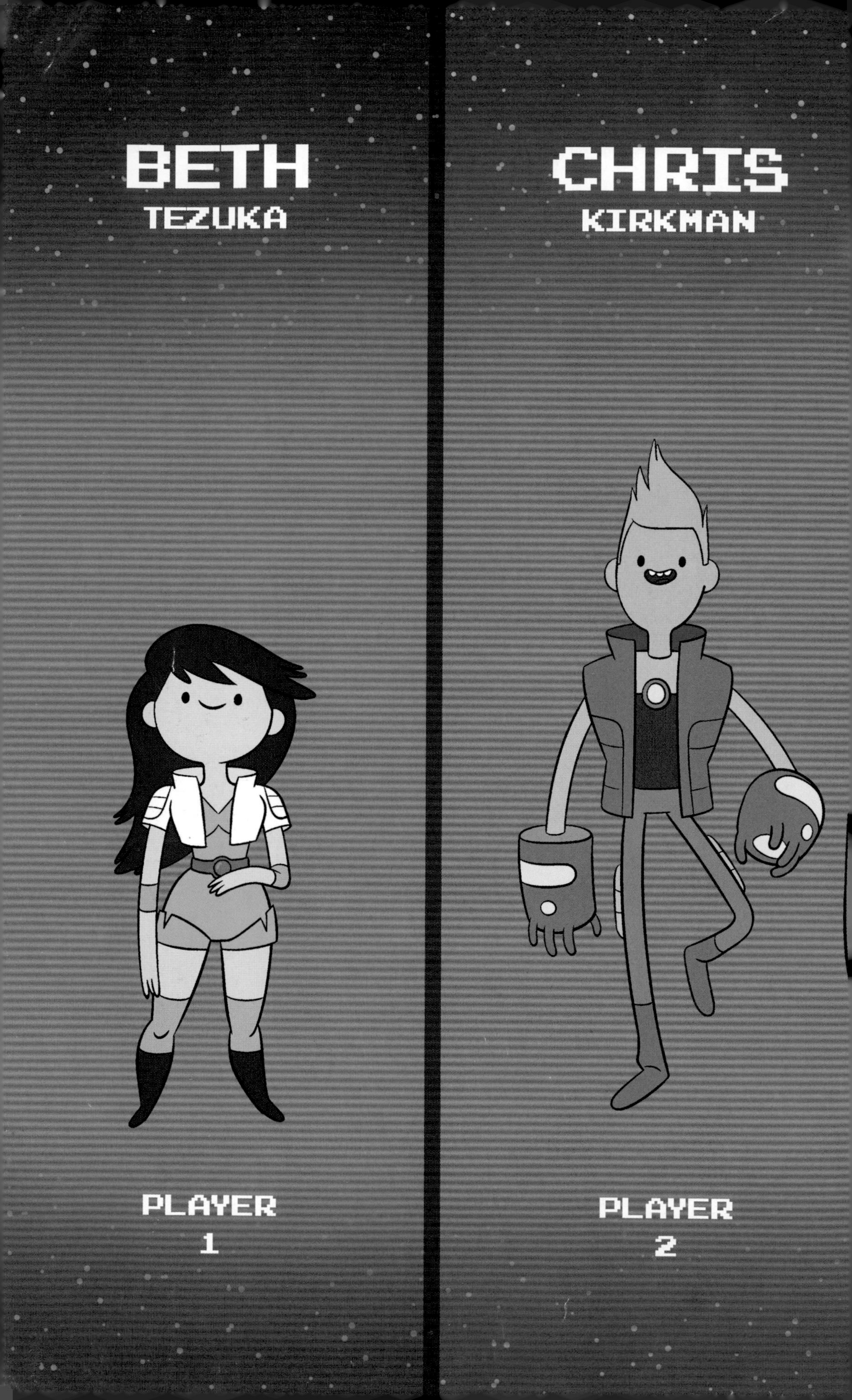
BETH
TEZUKA
PLAYER
1
CHRIS
KIRKMAN
PLAYER
2

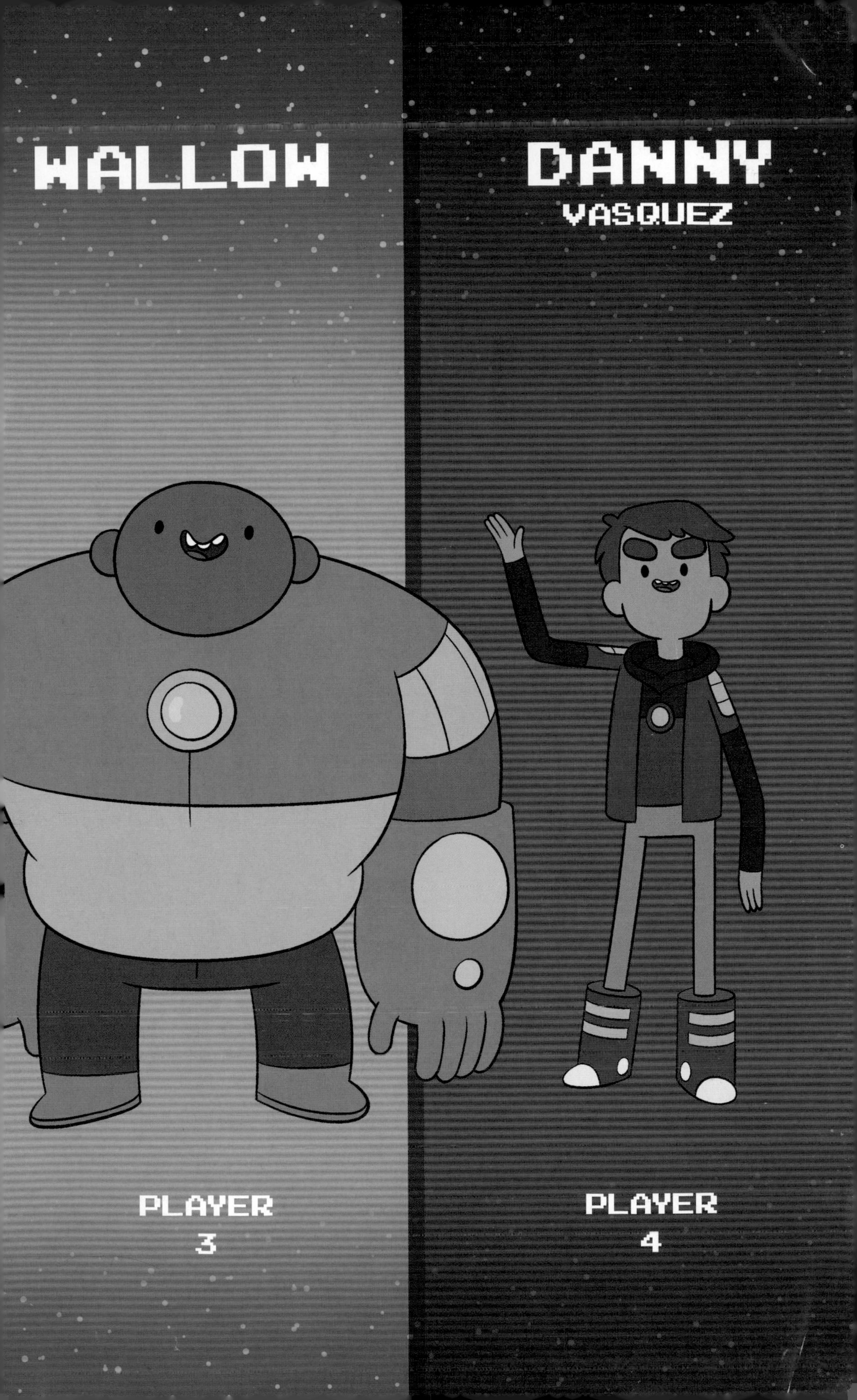
WALLOW
DANNY
VASQUEZ
PLAYER
3
PLAYER
4

CHAPTER
ONE

CONTINUE?

Somewhere in the quaint suburbs of space...

WHY HAVE YOU NOT YET SOLVED OUR CIVILIZATION'S PROBLEM OF GENDER INEQUALITY? *WHY DOES SEXISM STILL EXIST?!*

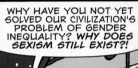

QUIT SWEATING IT, AMBASSADOR. THESE ARE NEW CARPETS.

I DO NOT UNDERSTAND, BRAVEST WARRIORS. WE HAVE TOLERATED YOUR IRREVERENCE FOR *DAYS* NOW...

HERE. PULL MY FINGER.

OH NO, OH NO NO NO. THIS WAS A MISTAKE. OUR PLANETS ARE DOOMED TO ENDLESS CIVIL WAR BECAUSE I FOOLISHLY TRUSTED A GROUP OF DINGBAT TEENS TO SOLVE SEXISM...

WHOA WHOA WHOA. HOLD ON THERE, MADAM AMBASSADOR. WE WOULD NOT ASK YOU TO PULL BETH'S FINGER UNLESS IT WAS *ABSOLUTELY NECESSARY.* YOU BETTER BELIEVE *THAT.*

I HAD A NIGHTMARE LIKE THIS, ONCE.

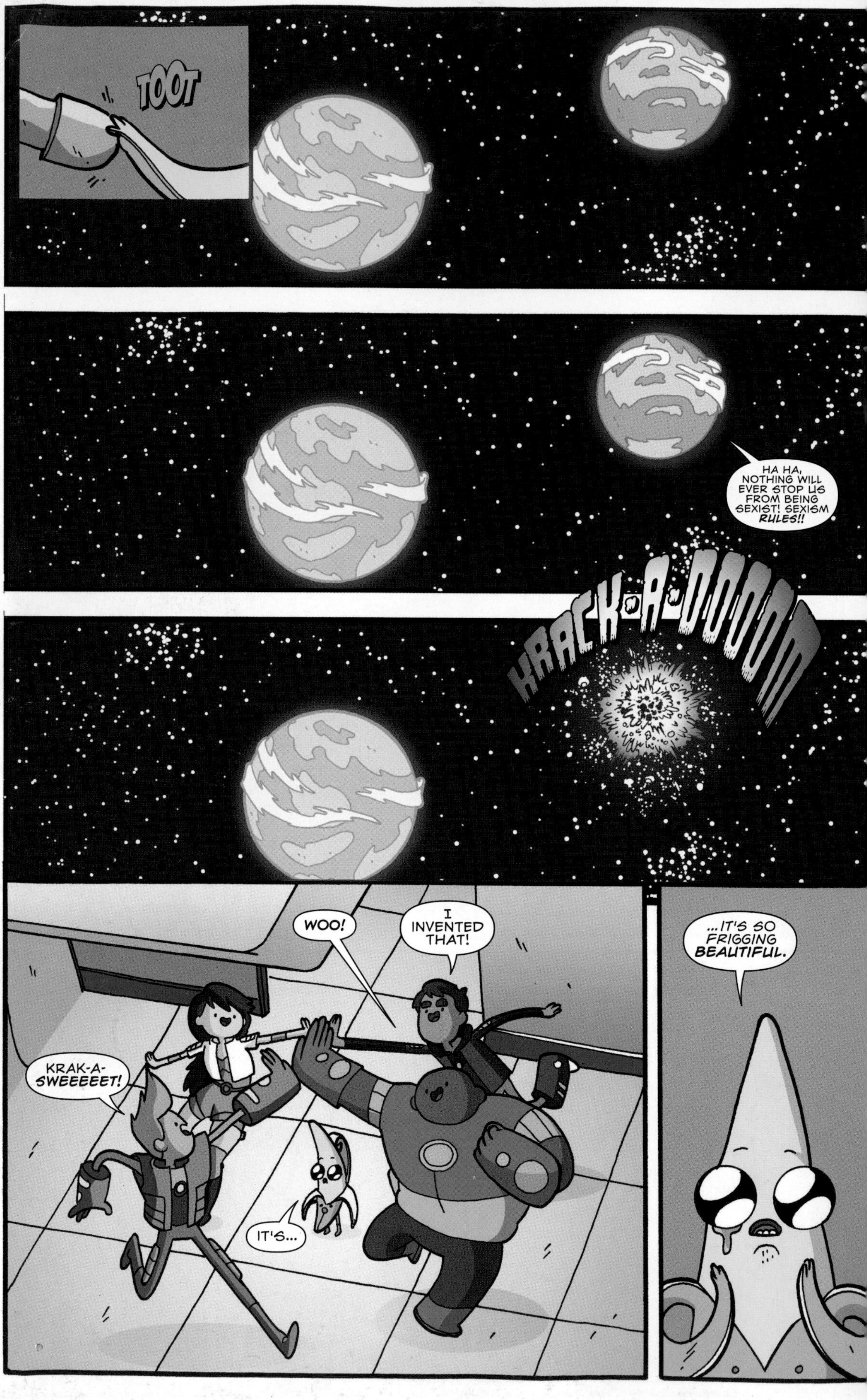
TOOT
HA HA, NOTHING WILL EVER STOP US FROM BEING SEXIST! SEXISM RULES!!
KRACK-A-DOOOM
WOO!
I INVENTED THAT!
KRAK-A-SWEEEEET!
IT'S...
...IT'S SO FRIGGING BEAUTIFUL.

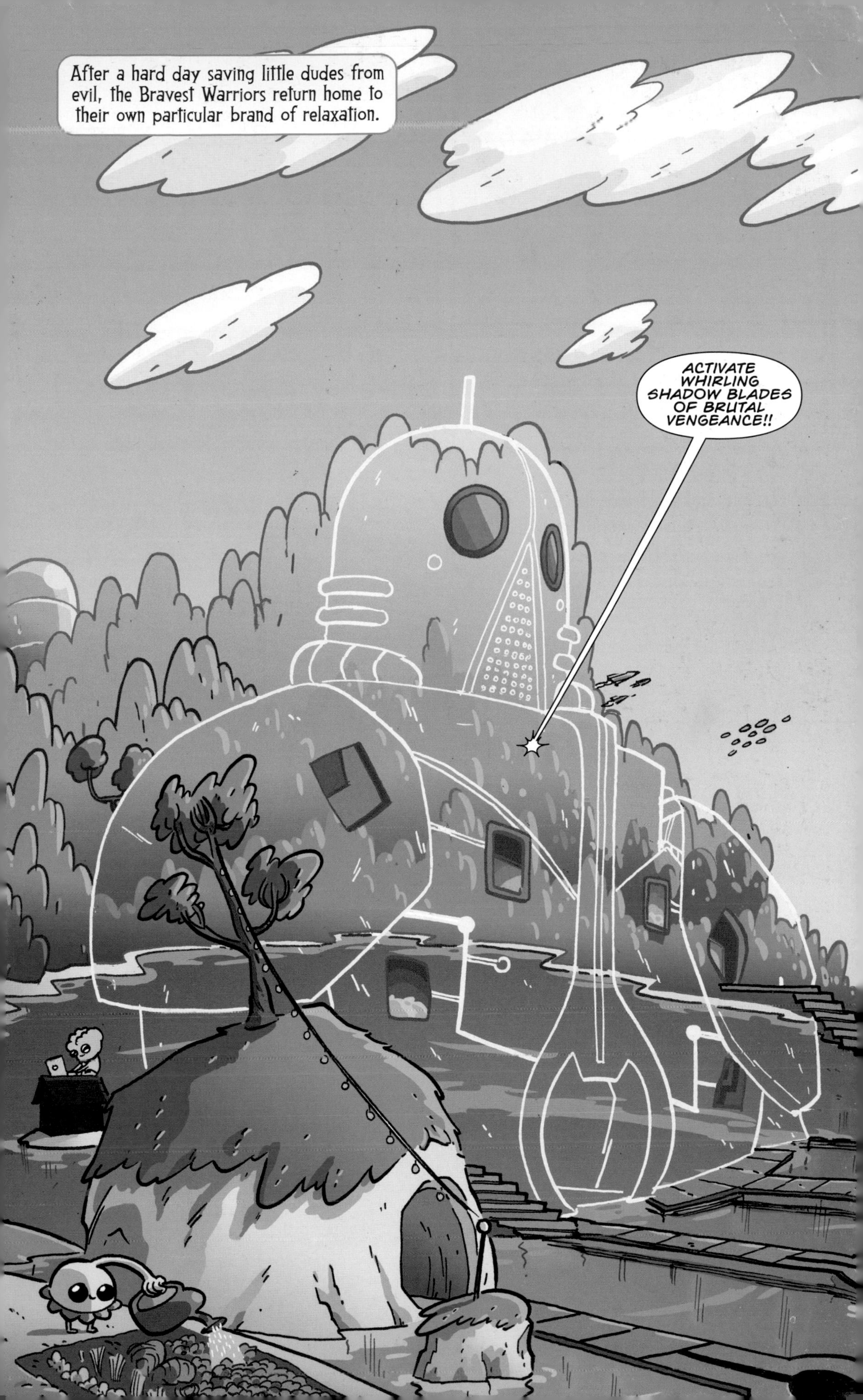
After a hard day saving little dudes from evil, the Bravest Warriors return home to their own particular brand of relaxation.
ACTIVATE WHIRLING SHADOW BLADES OF BRUTAL VENGEANCE!!

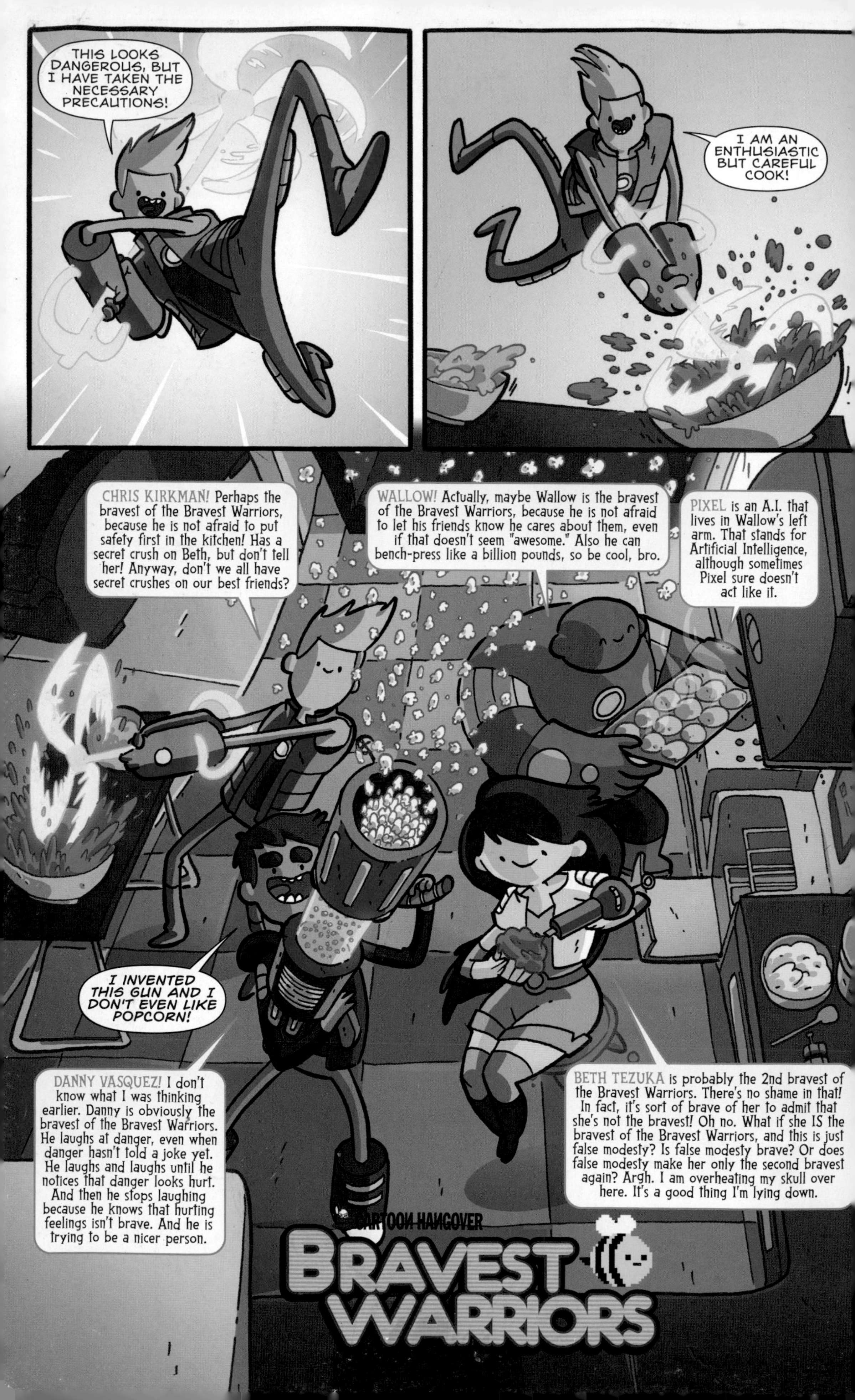

THIS LOOKS DANGEROUS, BUT I HAVE TAKEN THE NECESSARY PRECAUTIONS!
I AM AN ENTHUSIASTIC BUT CAREFUL COOK!
CHRIS KIRKMAN! Perhaps the bravest of the Bravest Warriors, because he is not afraid to put safety first in the kitchen! Has a secret crush on Beth, but don't tell her! Anyway, don't we all have secret crushes on our best friends?
WALLOW! Actually, maybe Wallow is the bravest of the Bravest Warriors, because he is not afraid to let his friends know he cares about them, even if that doesn't seem "awesome." Also he can bench-press like a billion pounds, so be cool, bro.
PIXEL is an A.I. that lives in Wallow's left arm. That stands for Artificial Intelligence, although sometimes Pixel sure doesn't act like it.
I INVENTED THIS GUN AND I DON'T EVEN LIKE POPCORN!
DANNY VASQUEZ! I don't know what I was thinking earlier. Danny is obviously the bravest of the Bravest Warriors. He laughs at danger, even when danger hasn't told a joke yet. He laughs and laughs until he notices that danger looks hurt. And then he stops laughing because he knows that hurting feelings isn't brave. And he is trying to be a nicer person.
BETH TEZUKA is probably the 2nd bravest of the Bravest Warriors. There's no shame in that! In fact, it's sort of brave of her to admit that she's not the bravest! Oh no. What if she IS the bravest of the Bravest Warriors, and this is just false modesty? Is false modesty brave? Or does false modesty make her only the second bravest again? Argh. I am overheating my skull over here. It's a good thing I'm lying down.
CARTOON HANGOVER
BRAVEST WARRIORS

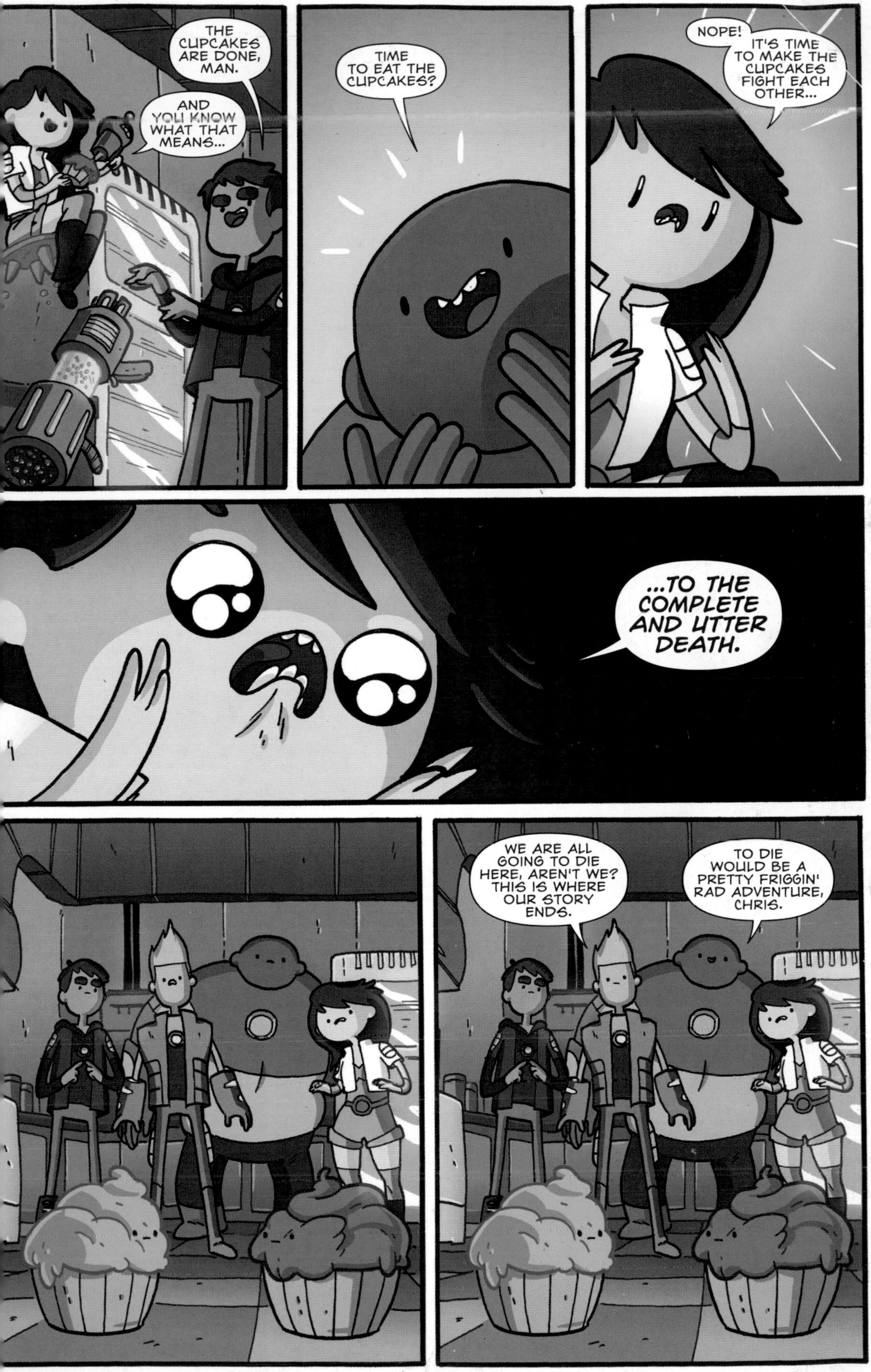
THE CUPCAKES ARE DONE, MAN.
AND YOU KNOW WHAT THAT MEANS...
TIME TO EAT THE CUPCAKES?
NOPE!
IT'S TIME TO MAKE THE CUPCAKES FIGHT EACH OTHER...
...TO THE COMPLETE AND UTTER DEATH.
WE ARE ALL GOING TO DIE HERE, AREN'T WE? THIS IS WHERE OUR STORY ENDS.
TO DIE WOULD BE A PRETTY FRIGGIN' RAD ADVENTURE, CHRIS.

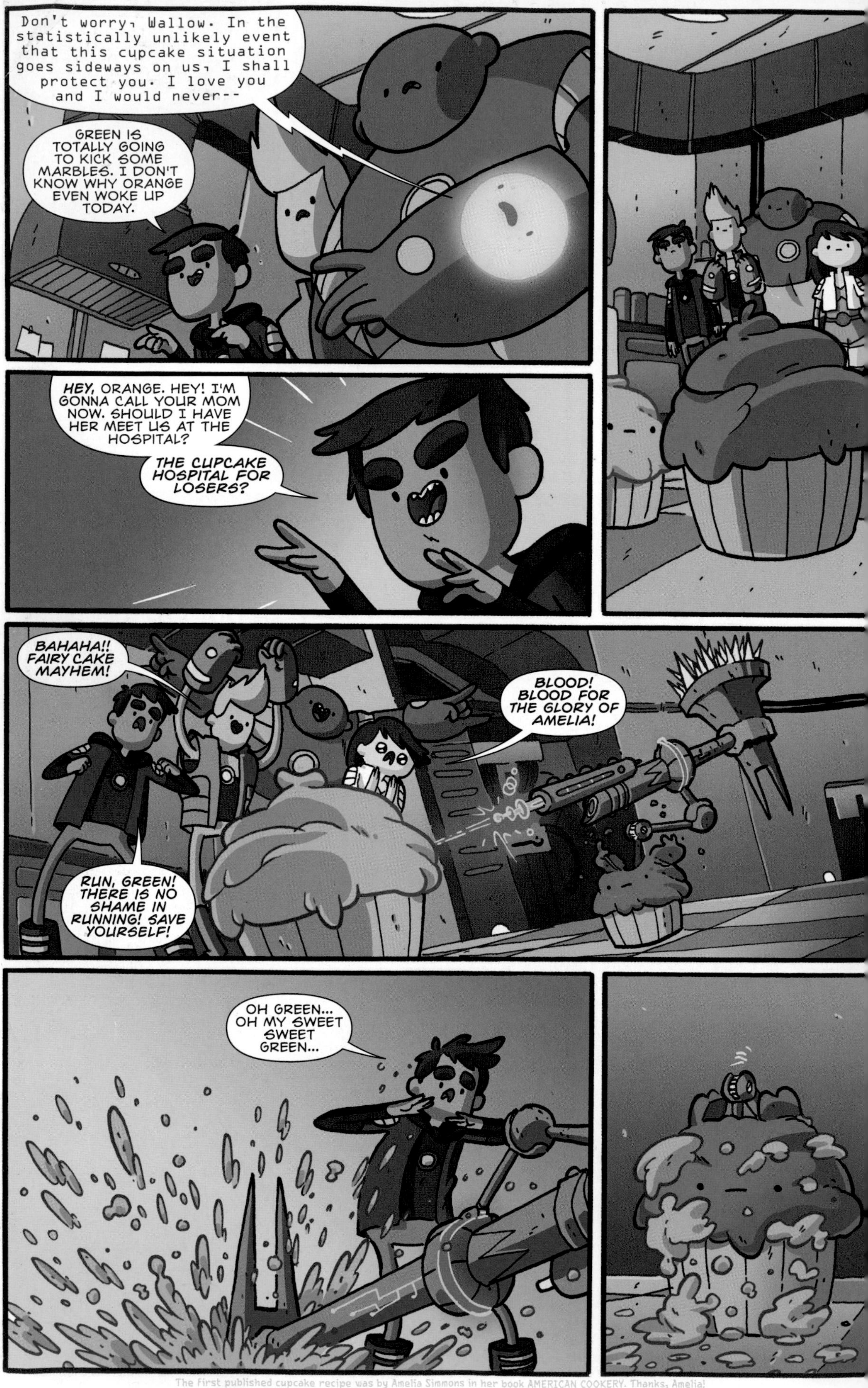
Don't worry, Wallow. In the statistically unlikely event that this cupcake situation goes sideways on us, I shall protect you. I love you and I would never--
GREEN IS TOTALLY GOING TO KICK SOME MARBLES. I DON'T KNOW WHY ORANGE EVEN WOKE UP TODAY.
HEY, ORANGE. HEY! I'M GONNA CALL YOUR MOM NOW. SHOULD I HAVE HER MEET US AT THE HOSPITAL?
THE CUPCAKE HOSPITAL FOR LOSERS?
BAHAHA!! FAIRY CAKE MAYHEM!
BLOOD! BLOOD FOR THE GLORY OF AMELIA!
RUN, GREEN! THERE IS NO SHAME IN RUNNING! SAVE YOURSELF!
OH GREEN... OH MY SWEET SWEET GREEN...

The first published cupcake recipe was by Amelia Simmons in her book AMERICAN COOKERY. Thanks, Amelia!

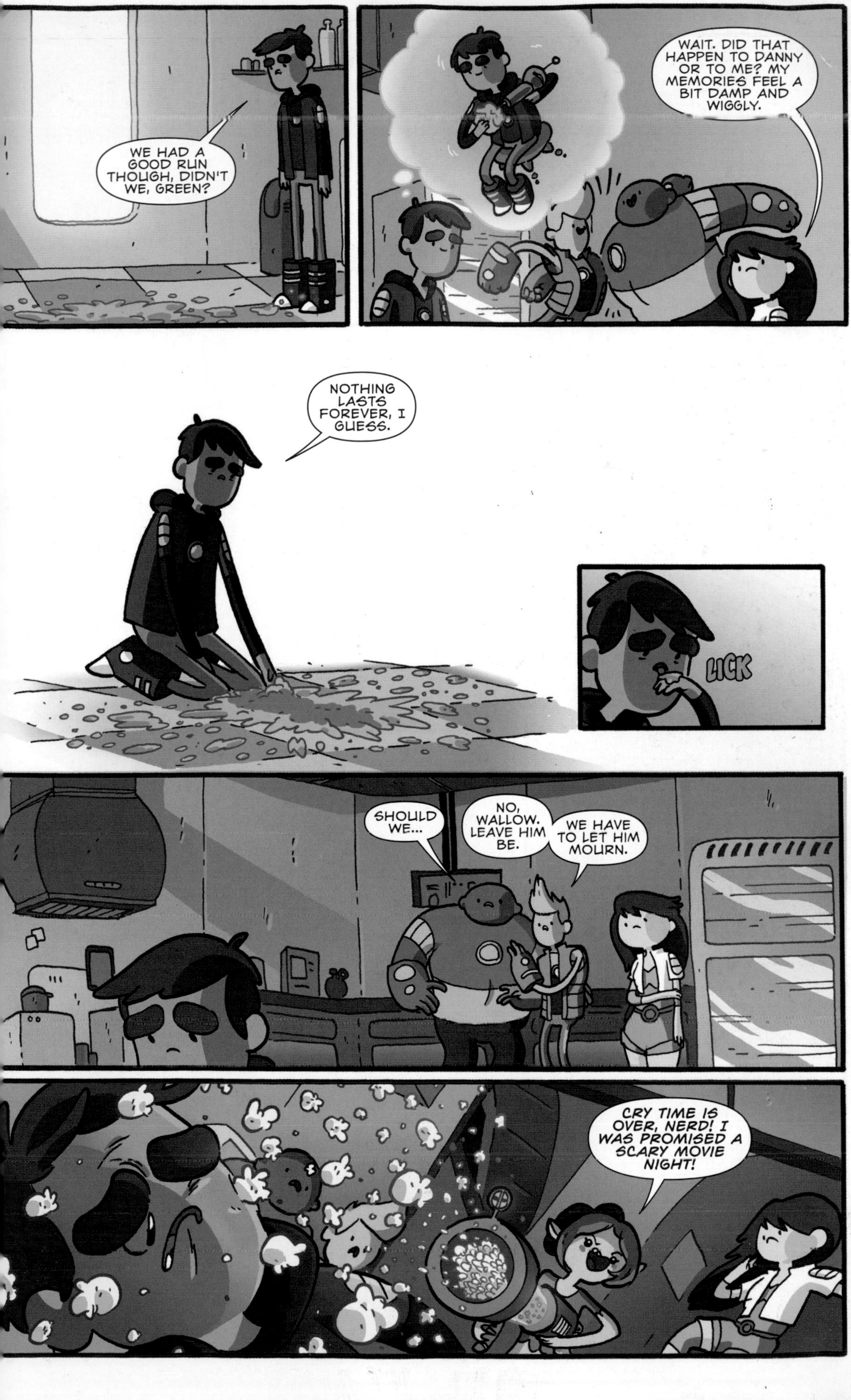
WE HAD A GOOD RUN THOUGH, DIDN'T WE, GREEN?
WAIT. DID THAT HAPPEN TO DANNY OR TO ME? MY MEMORIES FEEL A BIT DAMP AND WIGGLY.
NOTHING LASTS FOREVER, I GUESS.
LICK
SHOULD WE...
NO, WALLOW. LEAVE HIM BE.
WE HAVE TO LET HIM MOURN.
CRY TIME IS OVER, NERD! I WAS PROMISED A SCARY MOVIE NIGHT!

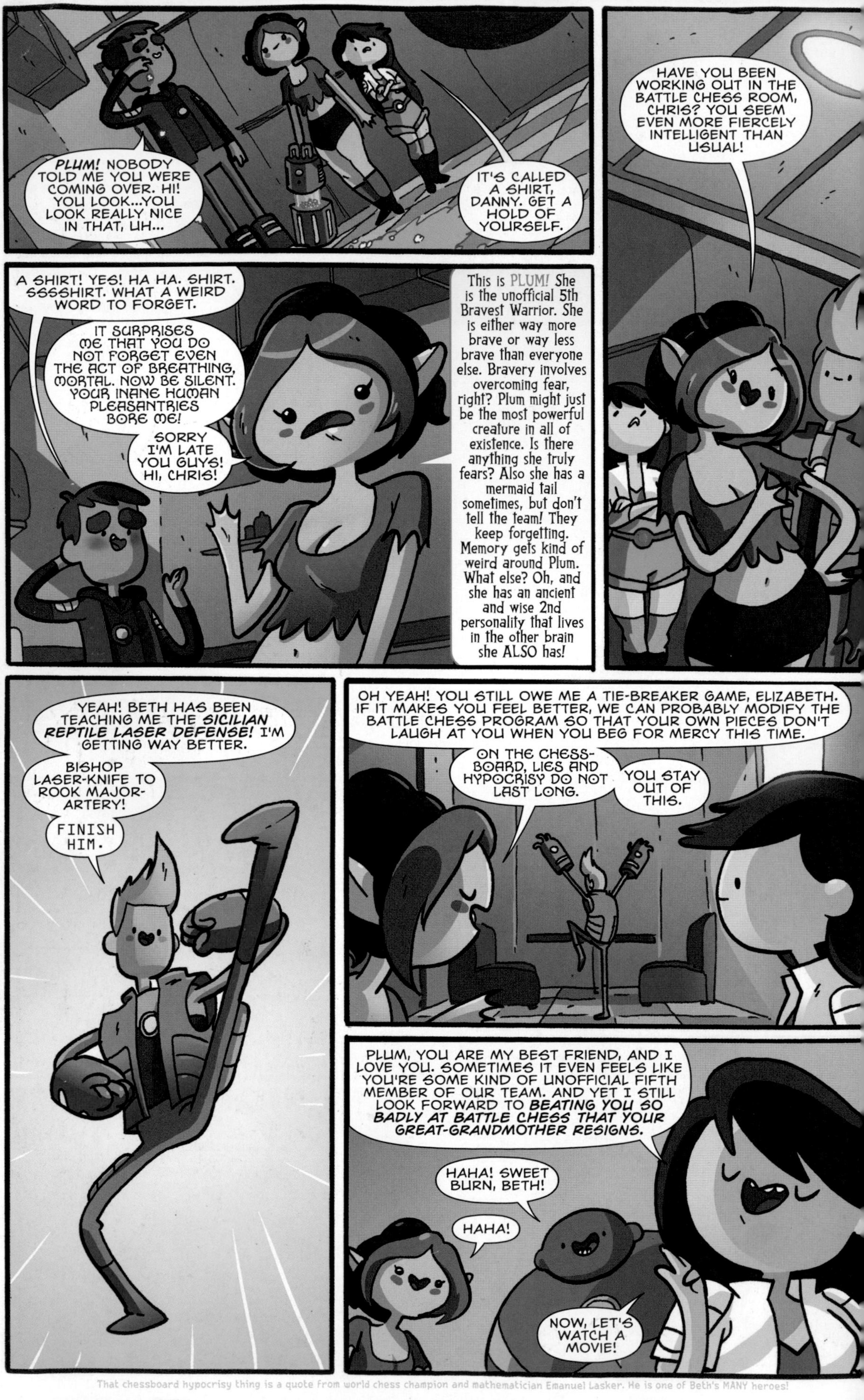
PLUM! NOBODY TOLD ME YOU WERE COMING OVER. HI! YOU LOOK...YOU LOOK REALLY NICE IN THAT, UH...
IT'S CALLED A SHIRT, DANNY. GET A HOLD OF YOURSELF.
HAVE YOU BEEN WORKING OUT IN THE BATTLE CHESS ROOM, CHRIS? YOU SEEM EVEN MORE FIERCELY INTELLIGENT THAN USUAL!
A SHIRT! YES! HA HA. SHIRT. SSSSHIRT. WHAT A WEIRD WORD TO FORGET.
IT SURPRISES ME THAT YOU DO NOT FORGET EVEN THE ACT OF BREATHING, MORTAL. NOW BE SILENT. YOUR INANE HUMAN PLEASANTRIES BORE ME!
SORRY I'M LATE YOU GUYS! HI, CHRIS!
This is PLUM! She is the unofficial 5th Bravest Warrior. She is either way more brave or way less brave than everyone else. Bravery involves overcoming fear, right? Plum might just be the most powerful creature in all of existence. Is there anything she truly fears? Also she has a mermaid tail sometimes, but don't tell the team! They keep forgetting. Memory gets kind of weird around Plum. What else? Oh, and she has an ancient and wise 2nd personality that lives in the other brain she ALSO has!
YEAH! BETH HAS BEEN TEACHING ME THE SICILIAN REPTILE LASER DEFENSE! I'M GETTING WAY BETTER.
BISHOP LASER-KNIFE TO ROOK MAJOR-ARTERY!
FINISH HIM.
OH YEAH! YOU STILL OWE ME A TIE-BREAKER GAME, ELIZABETH. IF IT MAKES YOU FEEL BETTER, WE CAN PROBABLY MODIFY THE BATTLE CHESS PROGRAM SO THAT YOUR OWN PIECES DON'T LAUGH AT YOU WHEN YOU BEG FOR MERCY THIS TIME.
ON THE CHESS-BOARD, LIES AND HYPOCRISY DO NOT LAST LONG.
YOU STAY OUT OF THIS.
PLUM, YOU ARE MY BEST FRIEND, AND I LOVE YOU. SOMETIMES IT EVEN FEELS LIKE YOU'RE SOME KIND OF UNOFFICIAL FIFTH MEMBER OF OUR TEAM. AND YET I STILL LOOK FORWARD TO BEATING YOU SO BADLY AT BATTLE CHESS THAT YOUR GREAT-GRANDMOTHER RESIGNS.
HAHA! SWEET BURN, BETH!
HAHA!
NOW, LET'S WATCH A MOVIE!

That chessboard hypocrisy thing is a quote from world chess champion and mathematician Emanuel Lasker. He is one of Beth's MANY heroes!

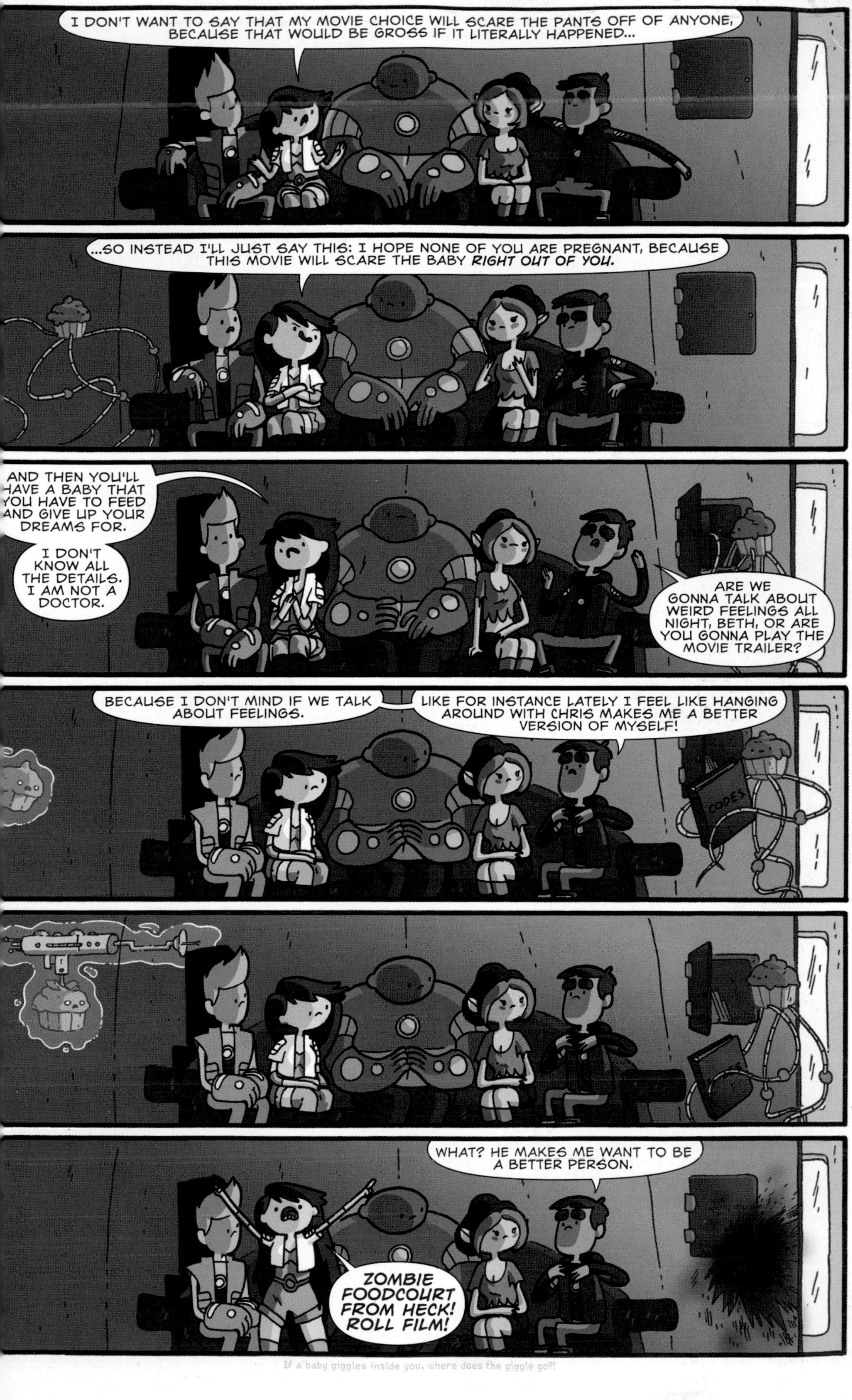
I DON'T WANT TO SAY THAT MY MOVIE CHOICE WILL SCARE THE PANTS OFF OF ANYONE, BECAUSE THAT WOULD BE GROSS IF IT LITERALLY HAPPENED...
...SO INSTEAD I'LL JUST SAY THIS: I HOPE NONE OF YOU ARE PREGNANT, BECAUSE THIS MOVIE WILL SCARE THE BABY RIGHT OUT OF YOU.
AND THEN YOU'LL HAVE A BABY THAT YOU HAVE TO FEED AND GIVE UP YOUR DREAMS FOR.
I DON'T KNOW ALL THE DETAILS. I AM NOT A DOCTOR.
ARE WE GONNA TALK ABOUT WEIRD FEELINGS ALL NIGHT, BETH, OR ARE YOU GONNA PLAY THE MOVIE TRAILER?
BECAUSE I DON'T MIND IF WE TALK ABOUT FEELINGS.
LIKE FOR INSTANCE LATELY I FEEL LIKE HANGING AROUND WITH CHRIS MAKES ME A BETTER VERSION OF MYSELF!
CODES
WHAT? HE MAKES ME WANT TO BE A BETTER PERSON.
ZOMBIE FOODCOURT FROM HECK! ROLL FILM!

If a baby giggles inside you, where does the giggle go?!

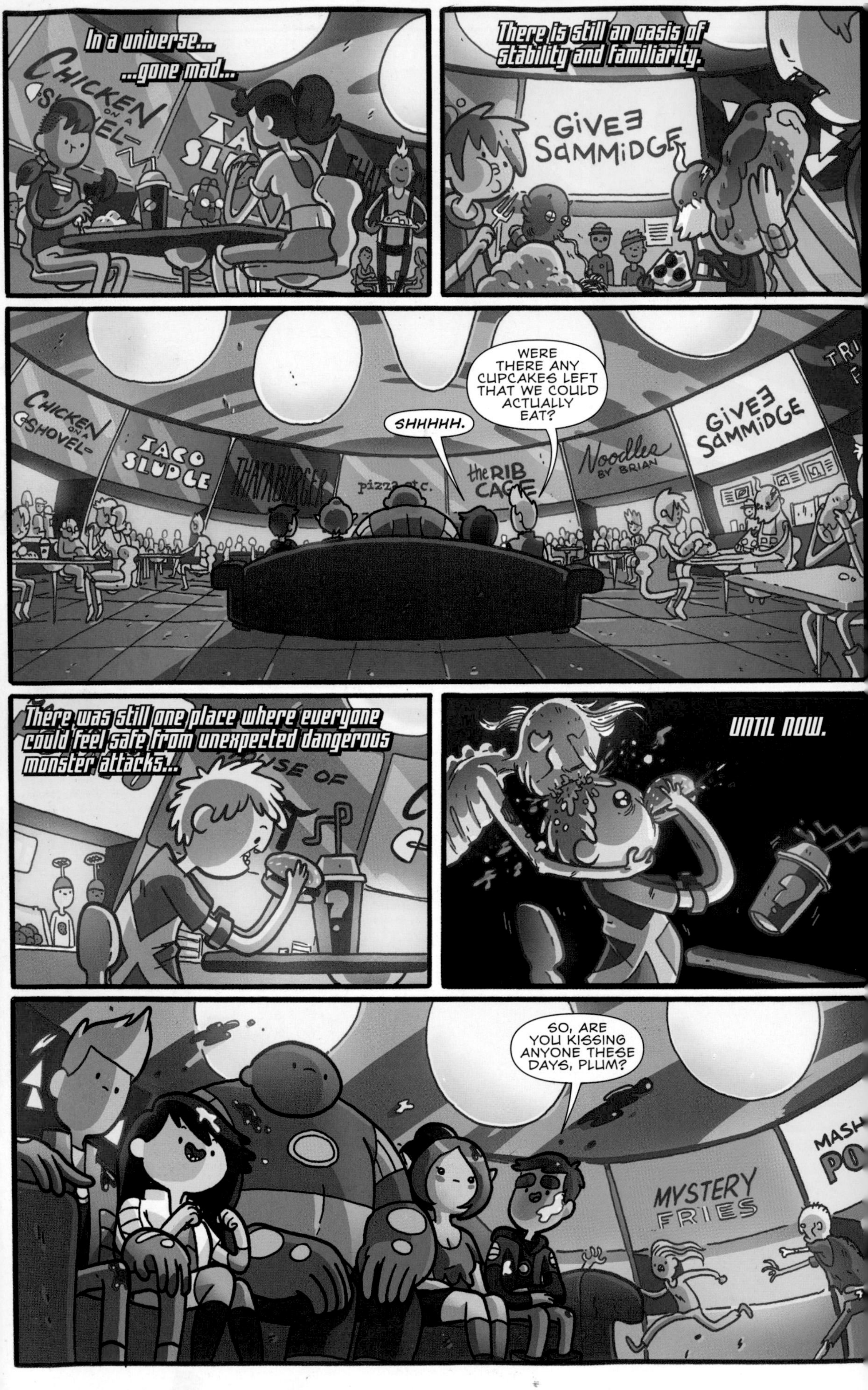
In a universe...
...gone mad...
CHICKEN ON A SHOVEL
There is still an oasis of stability and familiarity.
GIVE∃ SAMMIDGE
CHICKEN ON A SHOVEL
TACO SLUDGE
THATABURGER
pizza etc.
the RIB CAGE
Noodles BY BRIAN
GIVE∃ SAMMIDGE
SHHHHH.
WERE THERE ANY CUPCAKES LEFT THAT WE COULD ACTUALLY EAT?
There was still one place where everyone could feel safe from unexpected dangerous monster attacks...
UNTIL NOW.
SO, ARE YOU KISSING ANYONE THESE DAYS, PLUM?
MYSTERY FRIES

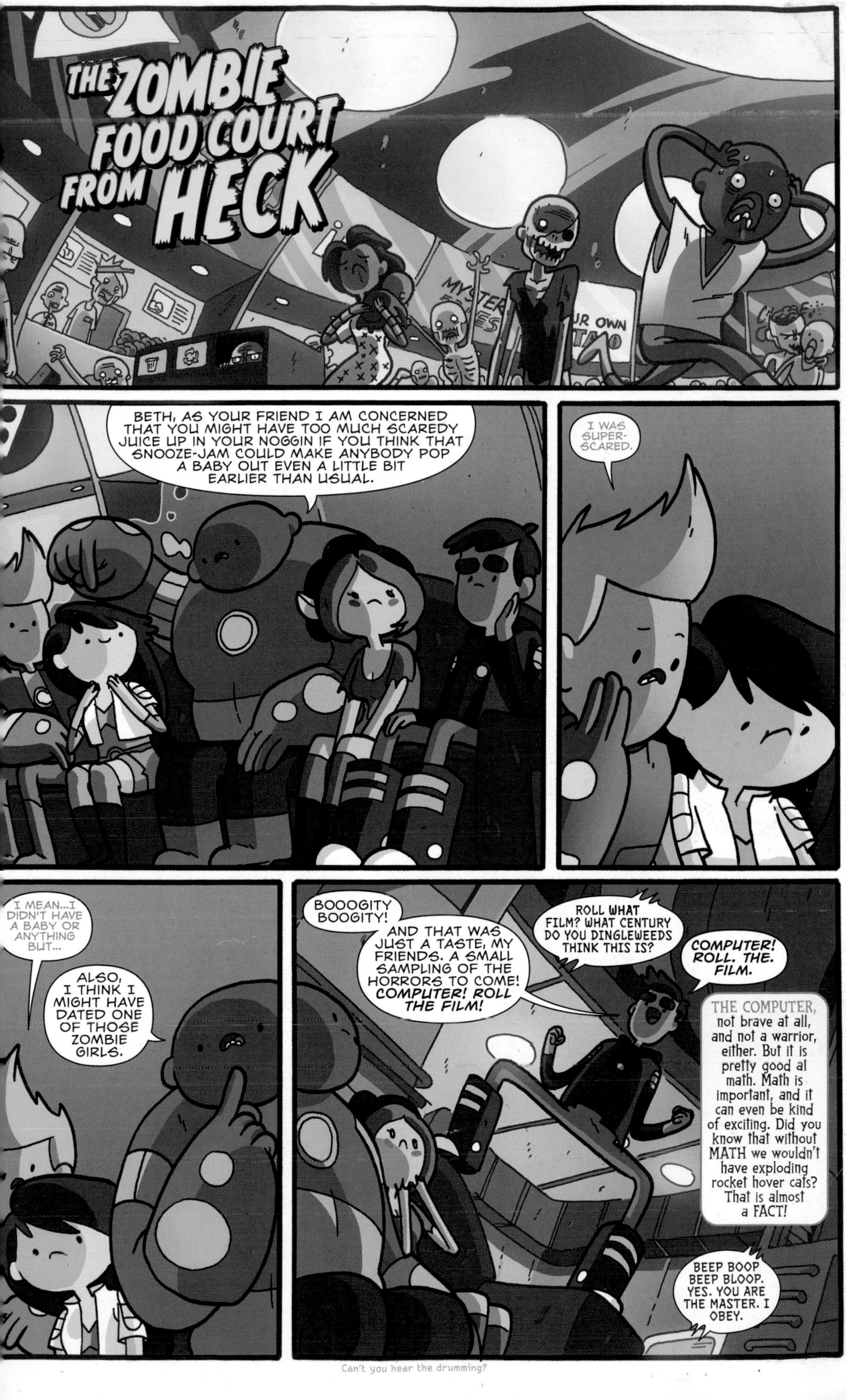
THE ZOMBIE FOOD COURT FROM HECK
BETH, AS YOUR FRIEND I AM CONCERNED THAT YOU MIGHT HAVE TOO MUCH SCAREDY JUICE UP IN YOUR NOGGIN IF YOU THINK THAT SNOOZE-JAM COULD MAKE ANYBODY POP A BABY OUT EVEN A LITTLE BIT EARLIER THAN USUAL.
I WAS SUPER-SCARED.
I MEAN...I DIDN'T HAVE A BABY OR ANYTHING BUT...
ALSO, I THINK I MIGHT HAVE DATED ONE OF THOSE ZOMBIE GIRLS.
BOOOGITY BOOGITY!
AND THAT WAS JUST A TASTE, MY FRIENDS. A SMALL SAMPLING OF THE HORRORS TO COME! *COMPUTER! ROLL THE FILM!*
ROLL WHAT FILM? WHAT CENTURY DO YOU DINGLEWEEDS THINK THIS IS?
COMPUTER! ROLL. THE. FILM.
THE COMPUTER, not brave at all, and not a warrior, either. But it is pretty good al math. Math is important, and it can even be kind of exciting. Did you know that without MATH we wouldn't have exploding rocket hover cats? That is almost a FACT!
BEEP BOOP BEEP BLOOP. YES. YOU ARE THE MASTER. I OBEY.

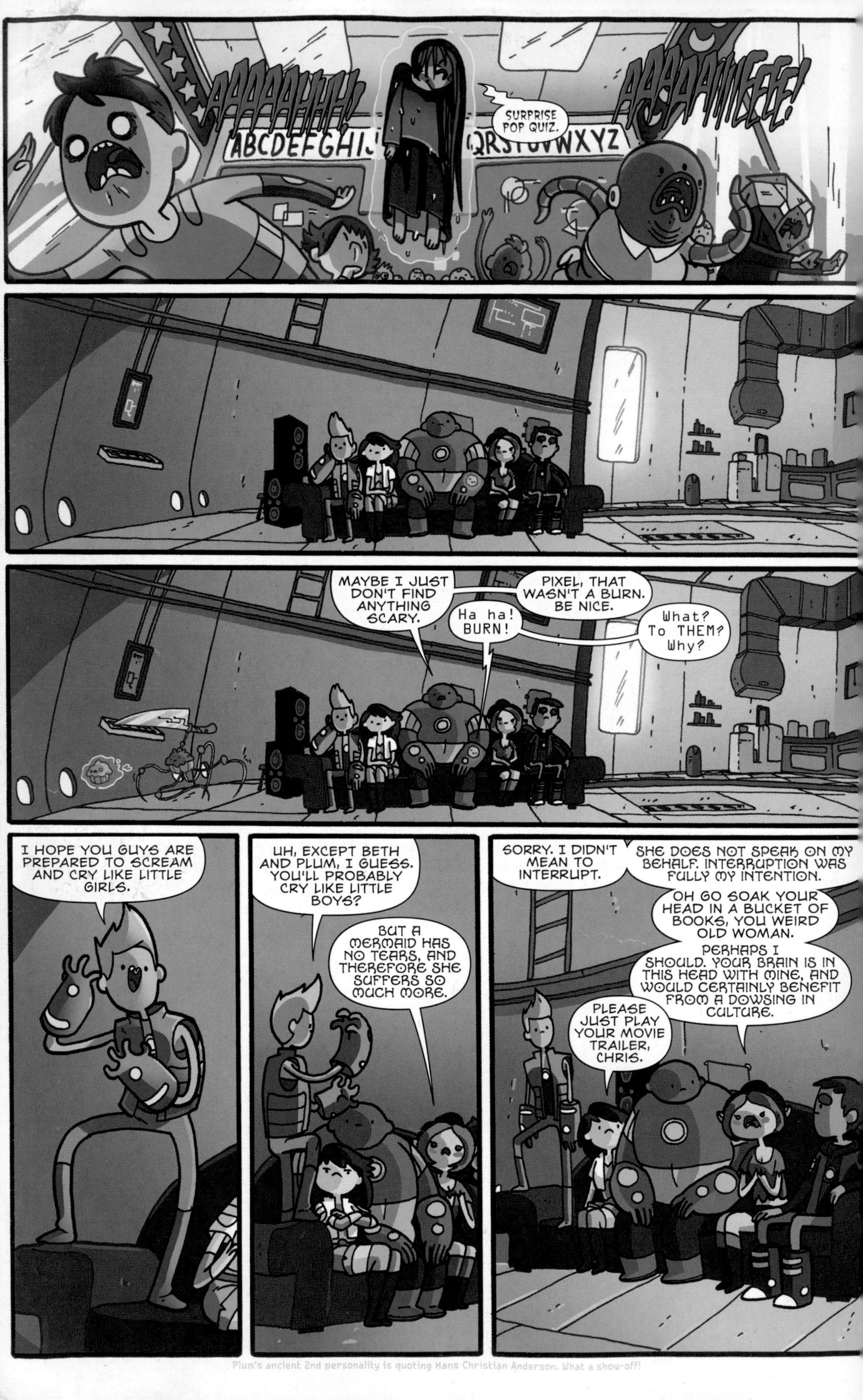

AAAAAHHH!
ABCDEFGHI
SURPRISE POP QUIZ.
QRSTUVWXYZ
AAAAAIIIEEEE!
MAYBE I JUST DON'T FIND ANYTHING SCARY.
Ha ha! BURN!
PIXEL, THAT WASN'T A BURN. BE NICE.
What? To THEM? Why?
I HOPE YOU GUYS ARE PREPARED TO SCREAM AND CRY LIKE LITTLE GIRLS.
UH, EXCEPT BETH AND PLUM, I GUESS. YOU'LL PROBABLY CRY LIKE LITTLE BOYS?
BUT A MERMAID HAS NO TEARS, AND THEREFORE SHE SUFFERS SO MUCH MORE.
SORRY. I DIDN'T MEAN TO INTERRUPT.
SHE DOES NOT SPEAK ON MY BEHALF. INTERRUPTION WAS FULLY MY INTENTION.
OH GO SOAK YOUR HEAD IN A BUCKET OF BOOKS, YOU WEIRD OLD WOMAN.
PERHAPS I SHOULD. YOUR BRAIN IS IN THIS HEAD WITH MINE, AND WOULD CERTAINLY BENEFIT FROM A DOWSING IN CULTURE.
PLEASE JUST PLAY YOUR MOVIE TRAILER, CHRIS.

Plum's ancient 2nd personality is quoting Hans Christian Anderson. What a show-off!

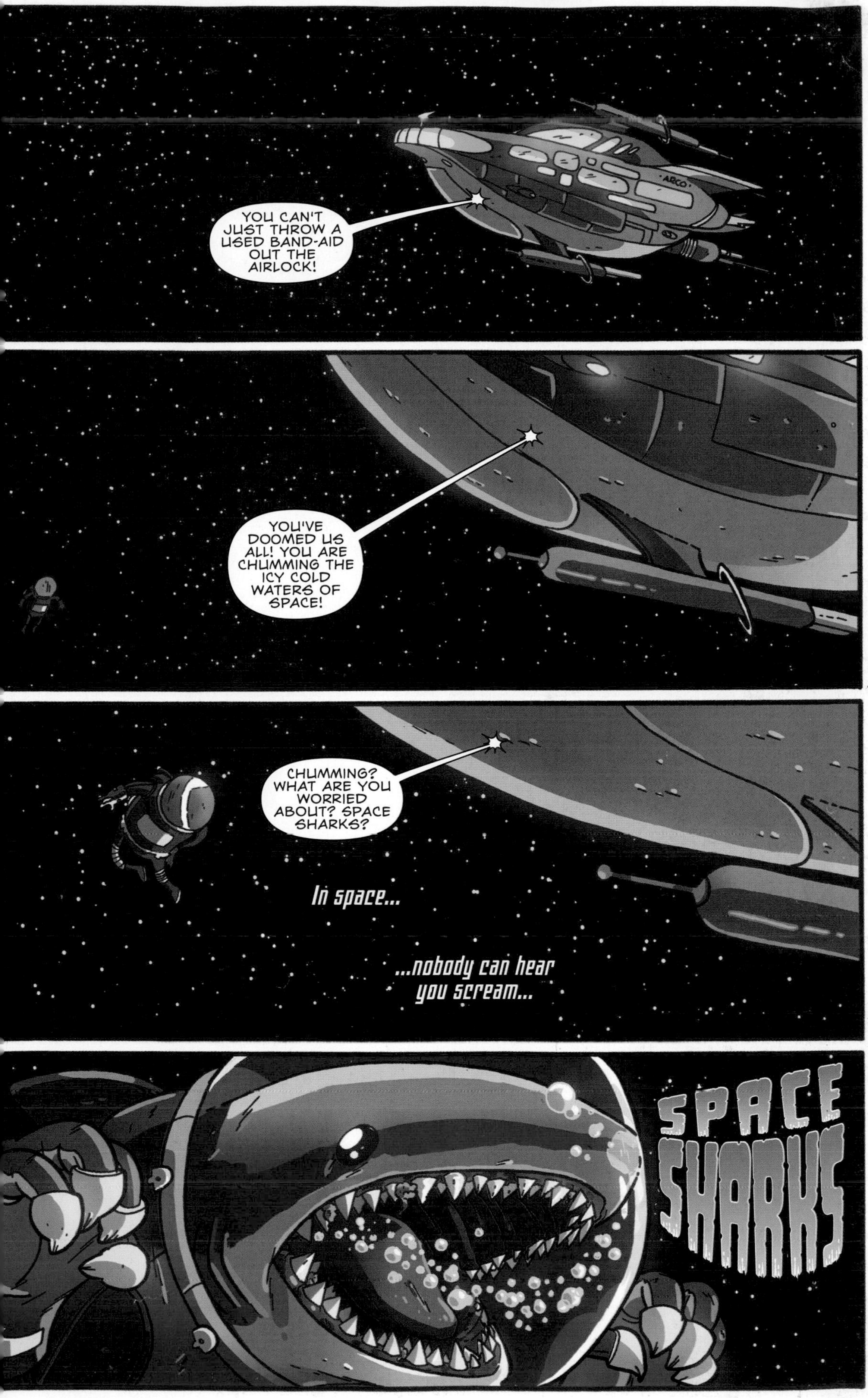

YOU CAN'T JUST THROW A USED BAND-AID OUT THE AIRLOCK!
YOU'VE DOOMED US ALL! YOU ARE CHUMMING THE ICY COLD WATERS OF SPACE!
CHUMMING? WHAT ARE YOU WORRIED ABOUT? SPACE SHARKS?
In space...
...nobody can hear you scream...
SPACE SHARKS

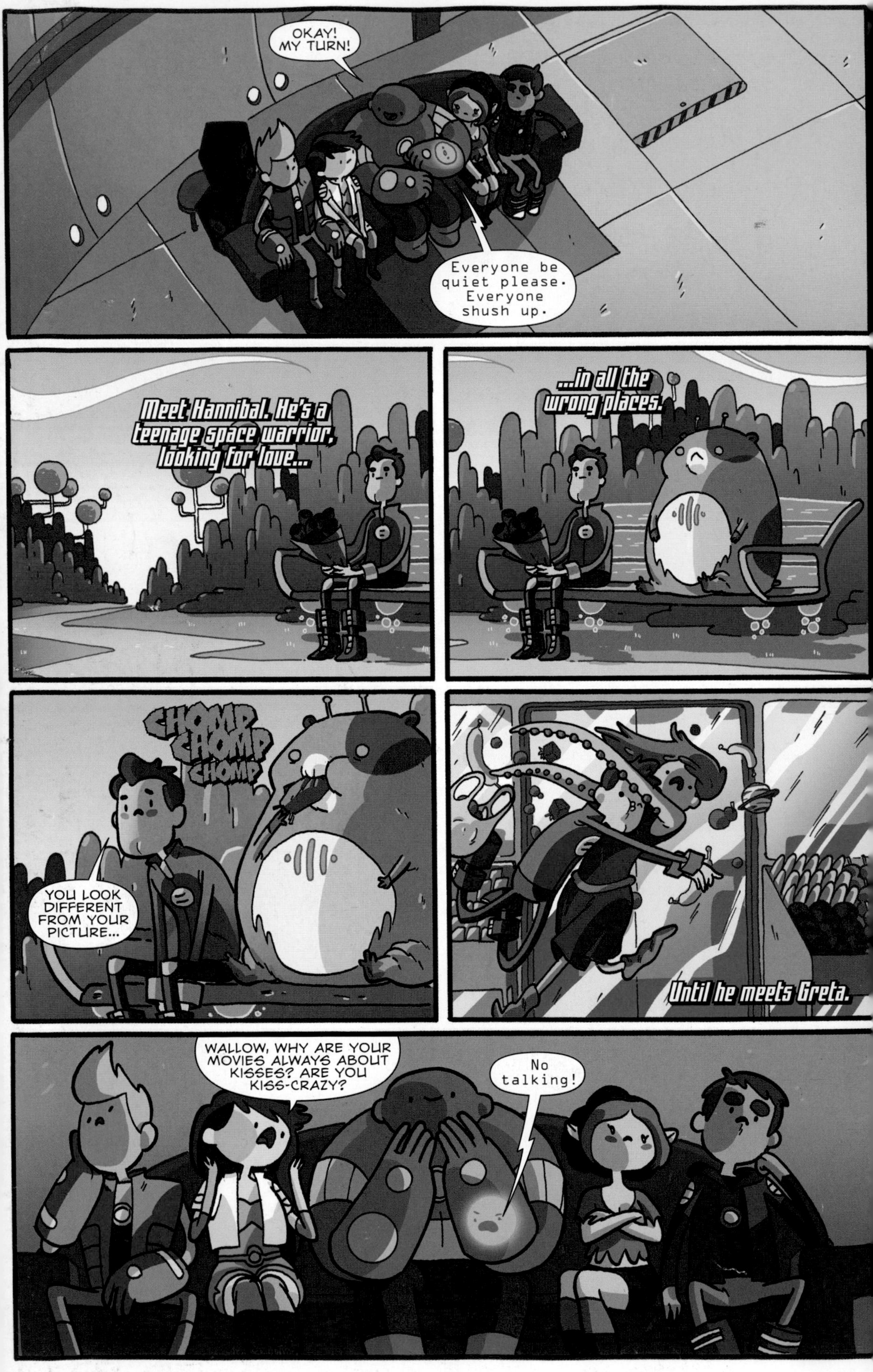

OKAY! MY TURN!
Everyone be quiet please. Everyone shush up.
Meet Hannibal. He's a teenage space warrior, looking for love...
...in all the wrong places.
CHOMP CHOMP CHOMP
YOU LOOK DIFFERENT FROM YOUR PICTURE...
Until he meets Greta.
WALLOW, WHY ARE YOUR MOVIES ALWAYS ABOUT KISSES? ARE YOU KISS-CRAZY?
No talking!

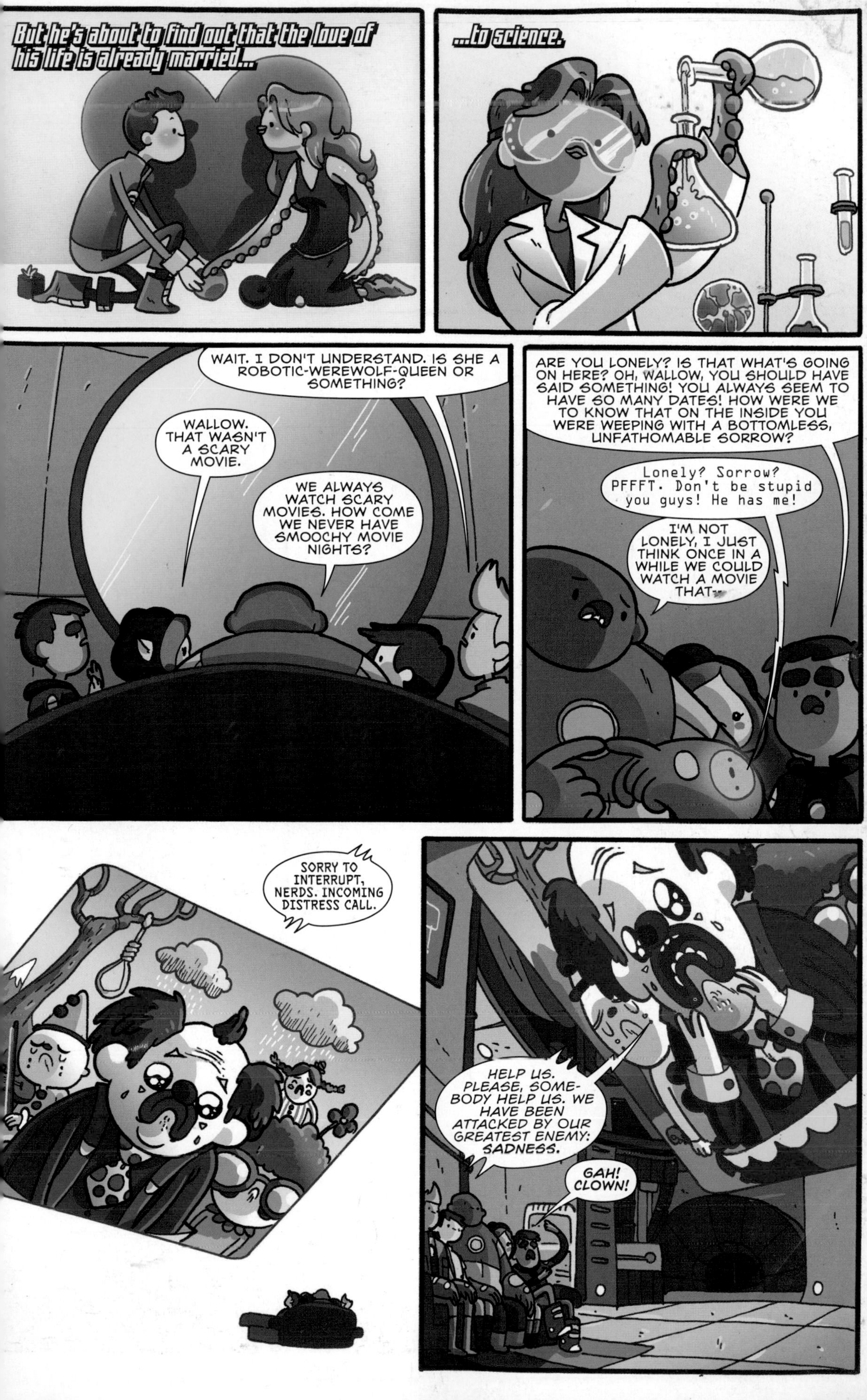
But he's about to find out that the love of his life is already married...
...to science.
WAIT. I DON'T UNDERSTAND. IS SHE A ROBOTIC-WEREWOLF-QUEEN OR SOMETHING?
WALLOW. THAT WASN'T A SCARY MOVIE.
WE ALWAYS WATCH SCARY MOVIES. HOW COME WE NEVER HAVE SMOOCHY MOVIE NIGHTS?
ARE YOU LONELY? IS THAT WHAT'S GOING ON HERE? OH, WALLOW, YOU SHOULD HAVE SAID SOMETHING! YOU ALWAYS SEEM TO HAVE SO MANY DATES! HOW WERE WE TO KNOW THAT ON THE INSIDE YOU WERE WEEPING WITH A BOTTOMLESS, UNFATHOMABLE SORROW?
Lonely? Sorrow? PFFFT. Don't be stupid you guys! He has me!
I'M NOT LONELY, I JUST THINK ONCE IN A WHILE WE COULD WATCH A MOVIE THAT–
SORRY TO INTERRUPT, NERDS. INCOMING DISTRESS CALL.
HELP US. PLEASE, SOMEBODY HELP US. WE HAVE BEEN ATTACKED BY OUR GREATEST ENEMY: SADNESS.
GAH! CLOWN!

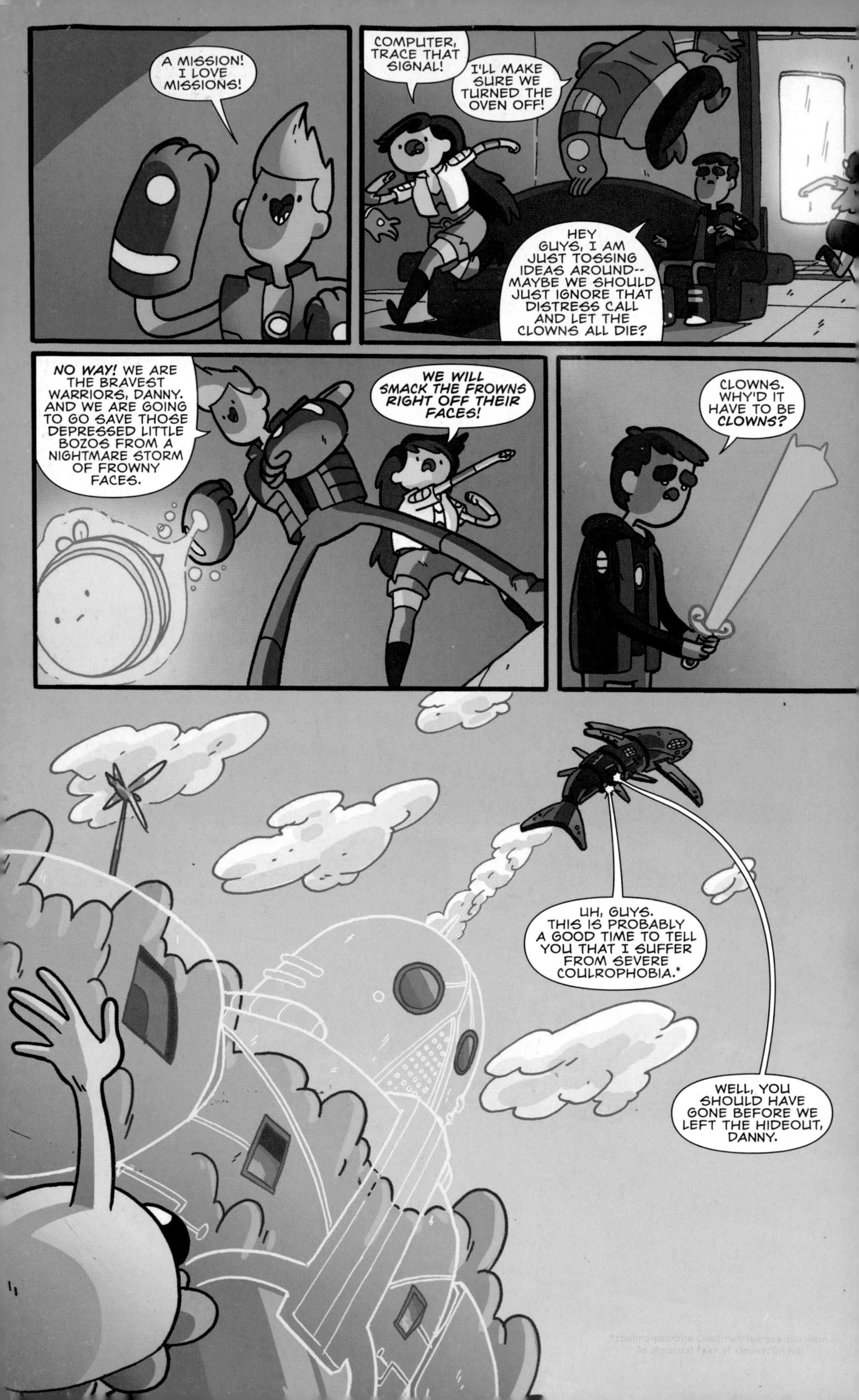
A MISSION! I LOVE MISSIONS!
COMPUTER, TRACE THAT SIGNAL!
I'LL MAKE SURE WE TURNED THE OVEN OFF!
HEY GUYS, I AM JUST TOSSING IDEAS AROUND-- MAYBE WE SHOULD JUST IGNORE THAT DISTRESS CALL AND LET THE CLOWNS ALL DIE?
NO WAY! WE ARE THE BRAVEST WARRIORS, DANNY. AND WE ARE GOING TO GO SAVE THOSE DEPRESSED LITTLE BOZOS FROM A NIGHTMARE STORM OF FROWNY FACES.
WE WILL SMACK THE FROWNS RIGHT OFF THEIR FACES!
CLOWNS. WHY'D IT HAVE TO BE CLOWNS?
UH, GUYS. THIS IS PROBABLY A GOOD TIME TO TELL YOU THAT I SUFFER FROM SEVERE COULROPHOBIA.*
WELL, YOU SHOULD HAVE GONE BEFORE WE LEFT THE HIDEOUT, DANNY.

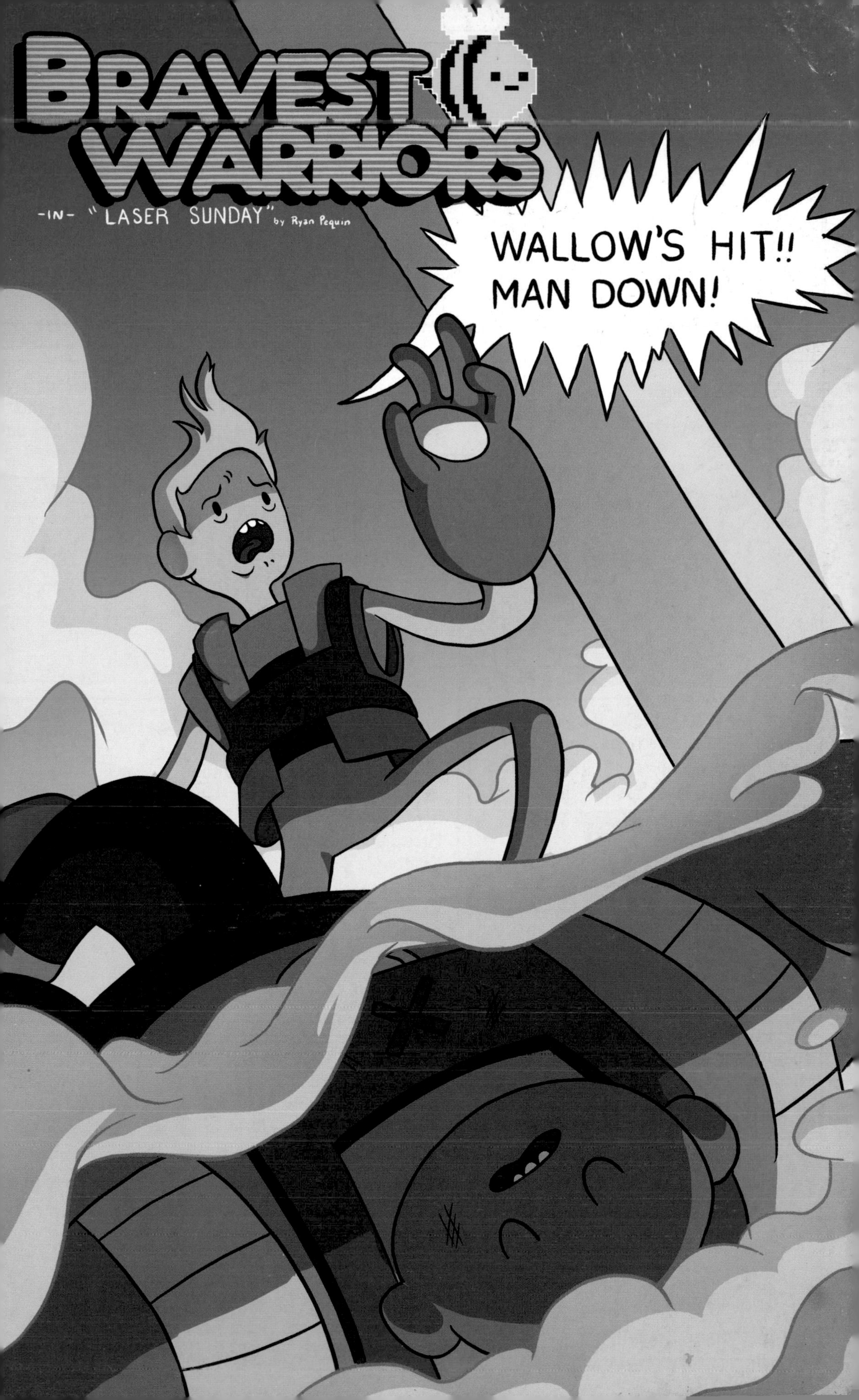
BRAVEST WARRIORS
-IN- "LASER SUNDAY" by Ryan Pequin
WALLOW'S HIT!! MAN DOWN!

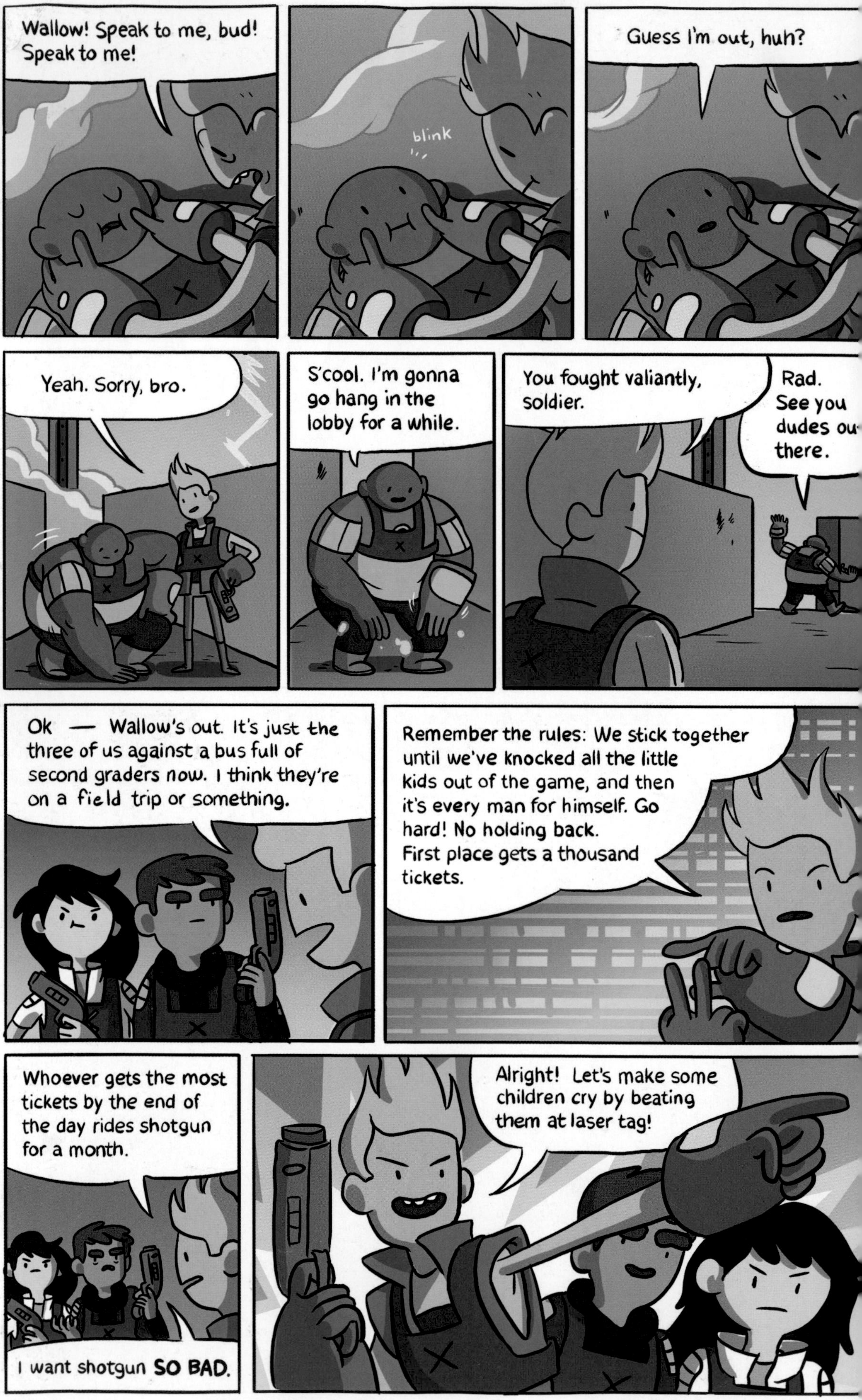
Wallow! Speak to me, bud! Speak to me!
blink
Guess I'm out, huh?
Yeah. Sorry, bro.
S'cool. I'm gonna go hang in the lobby for a while.
You fought valiantly, soldier.
Rad. See you dudes ou there.
Ok — Wallow's out. It's just the three of us against a bus full of second graders now. I think they're on a field trip or something.
Remember the rules: We stick together until we've knocked all the little kids out of the game, and then it's every man for himself. Go hard! No holding back. First place gets a thousand tickets.
Whoever gets the most tickets by the end of the day rides shotgun for a month.
I want shotgun SO BAD.
Alright! Let's make some children cry by beating them at laser tag!

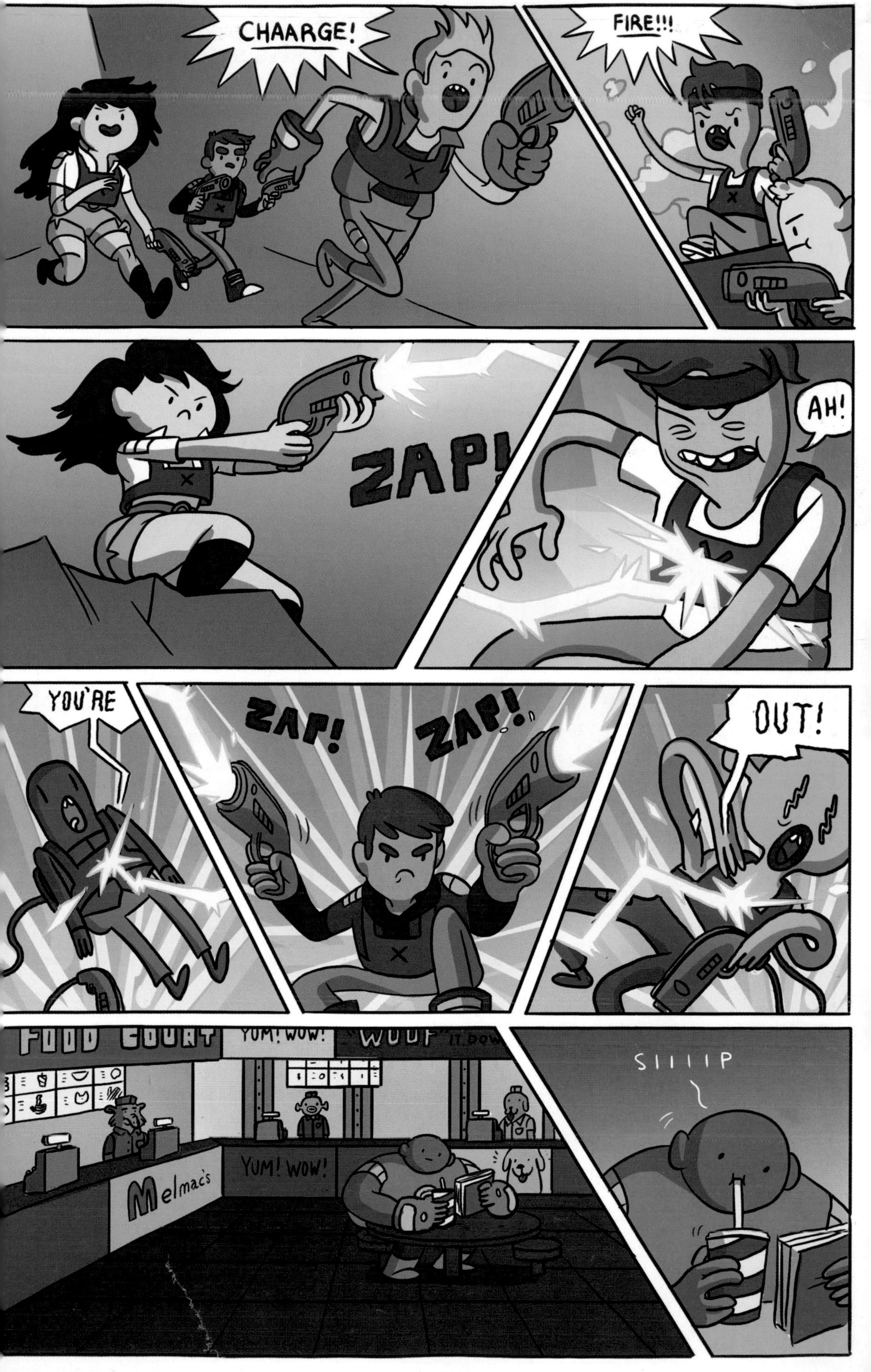
CHAARGE!
FIRE!!!
ZAP!
AH!
YOU'RE
ZAP!
ZAP!
OUT!
FOOD COURT
YUM! WOW!
YUM! WOW!
Melmac's
SIIIIP

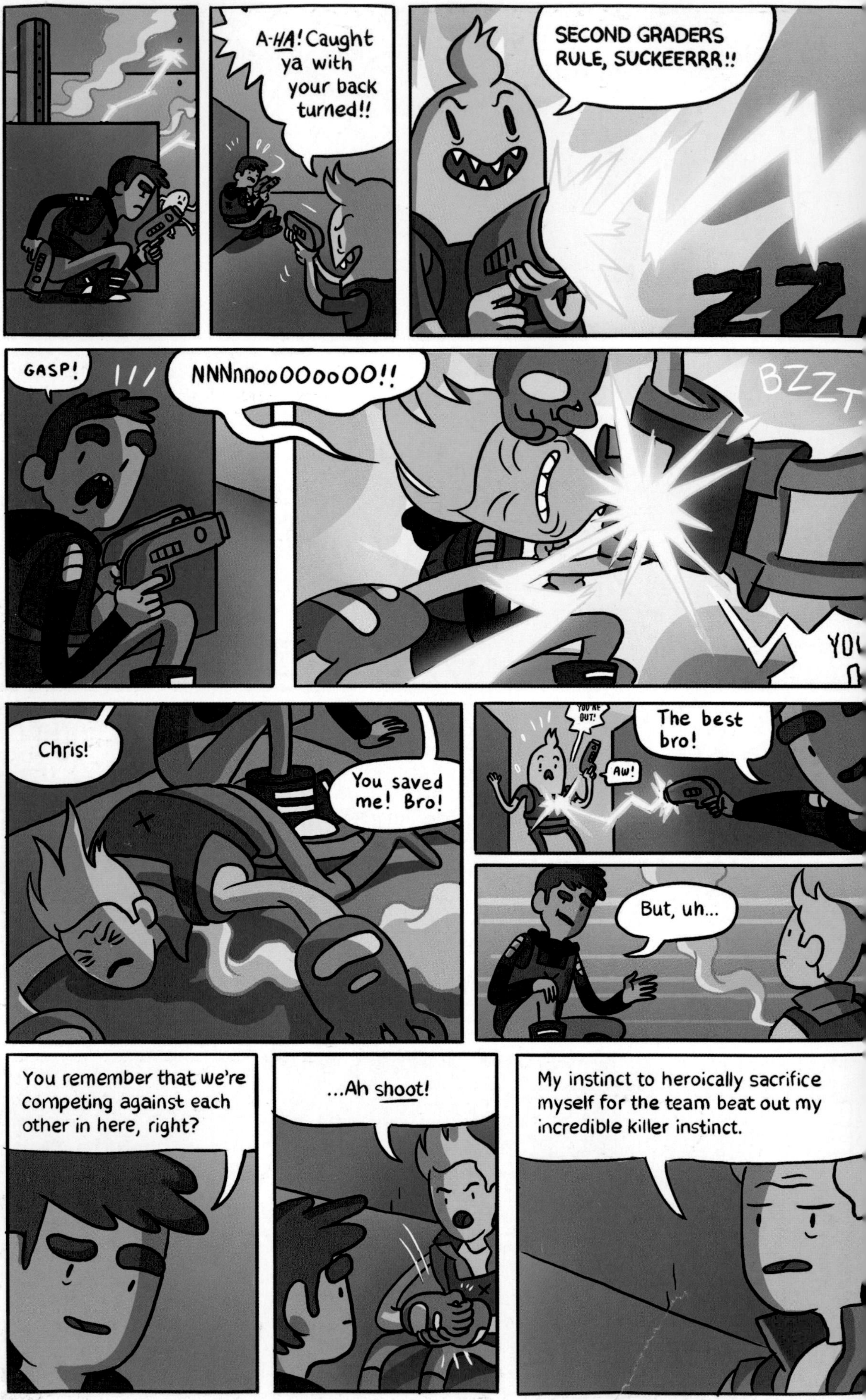
A-HA! Caught ya with your back turned!!
SECOND GRADERS RULE, SUCKEERRR!!
ZZ
GASP!
NNNnnooOOOooOO!!
BZZT
Chris!
You saved me! Bro!
YOU'RE OUT!
AW!
The best bro!
But, uh...
You remember that we're competing against each other in here, right?
...Ah shoot!
My instinct to heroically sacrifice myself for the team beat out my incredible killer instinct.

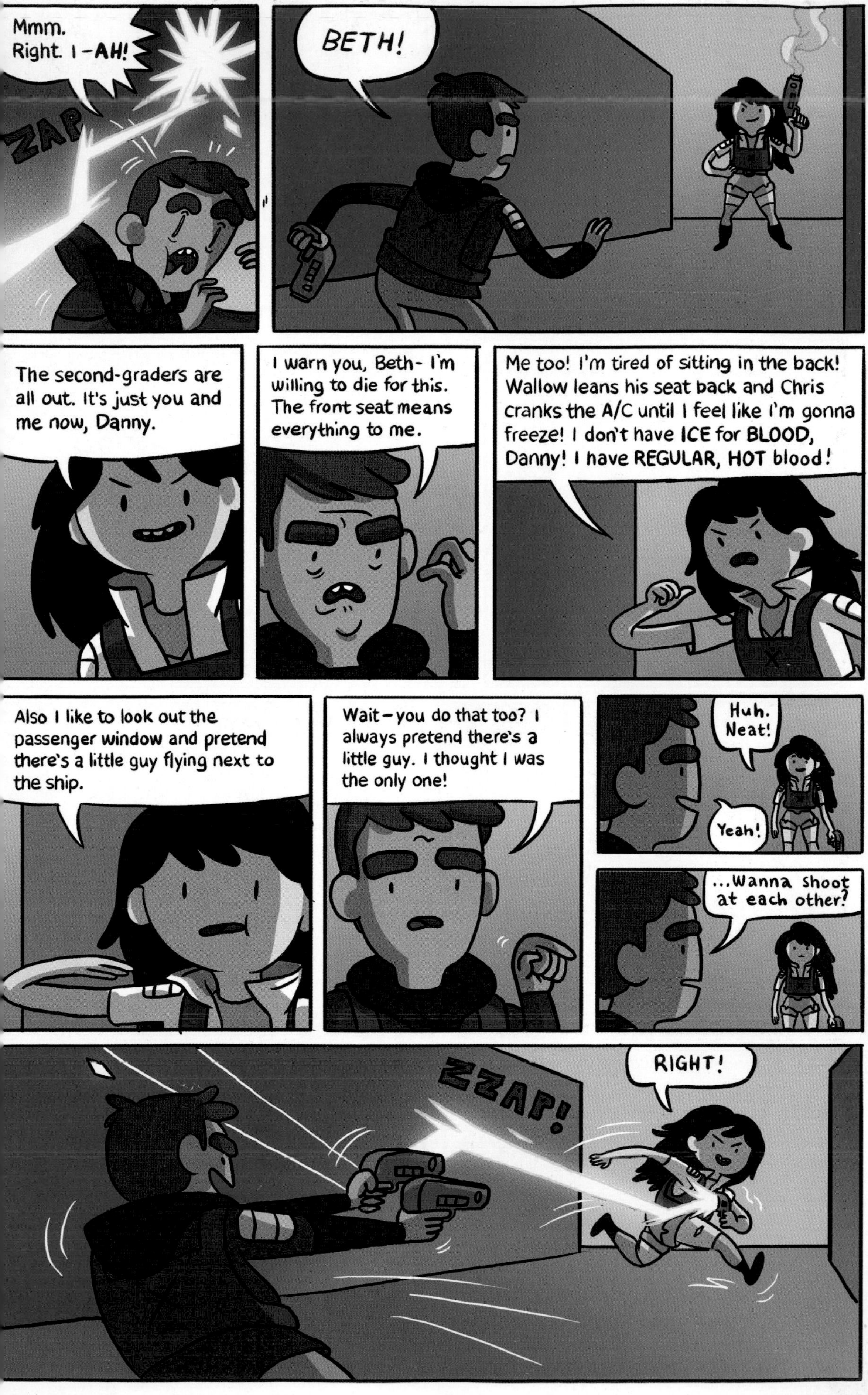
Mmm. Right. I—AH!
ZAP
BETH!
The second-graders are all out. It's just you and me now, Danny.
I warn you, Beth- I'm willing to die for this. The front seat means everything to me.
Me too! I'm tired of sitting in the back! Wallow leans his seat back and Chris cranks the A/C until I feel like I'm gonna freeze! I don't have ICE for BLOOD, Danny! I have REGULAR, HOT blood!
Also I like to look out the passenger window and pretend there's a little guy flying next to the ship.
Wait—you do that too? I always pretend there's a little guy. I thought I was the only one!
Huh. Neat!
Yeah!
...Wanna shoot at each other?
ZZAP!
RIGHT!

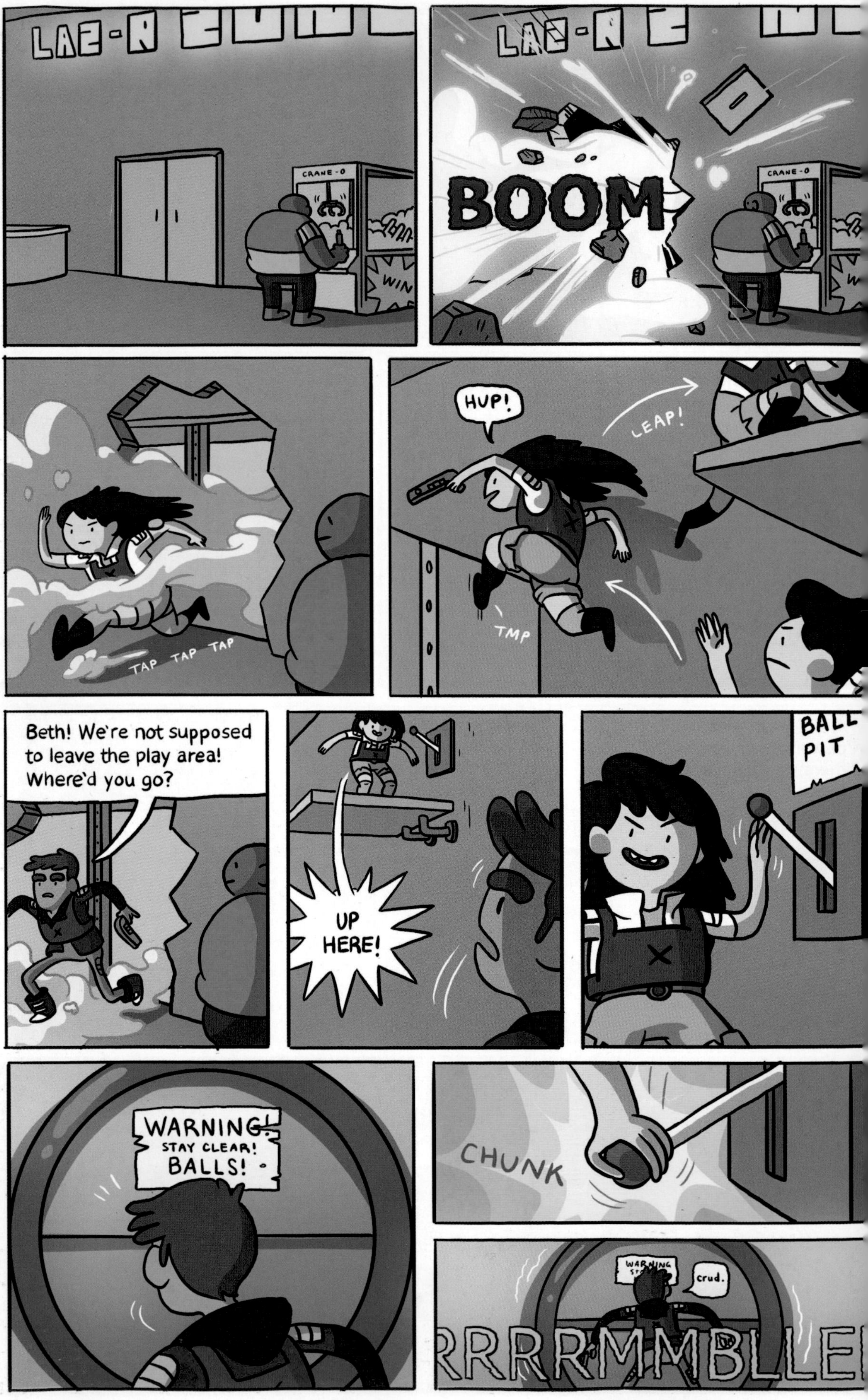
LAZ-R
CRANE-O
WIN
BOOM
TAP TAP TAP
HUP!
LEAP!
TMP
Beth! We're not supposed to leave the play area! Where'd you go?
UP HERE!
BALL PIT
WARNING!
STAY CLEAR!
BALLS!
CHUNK
crud.
RRRRMMBLLE

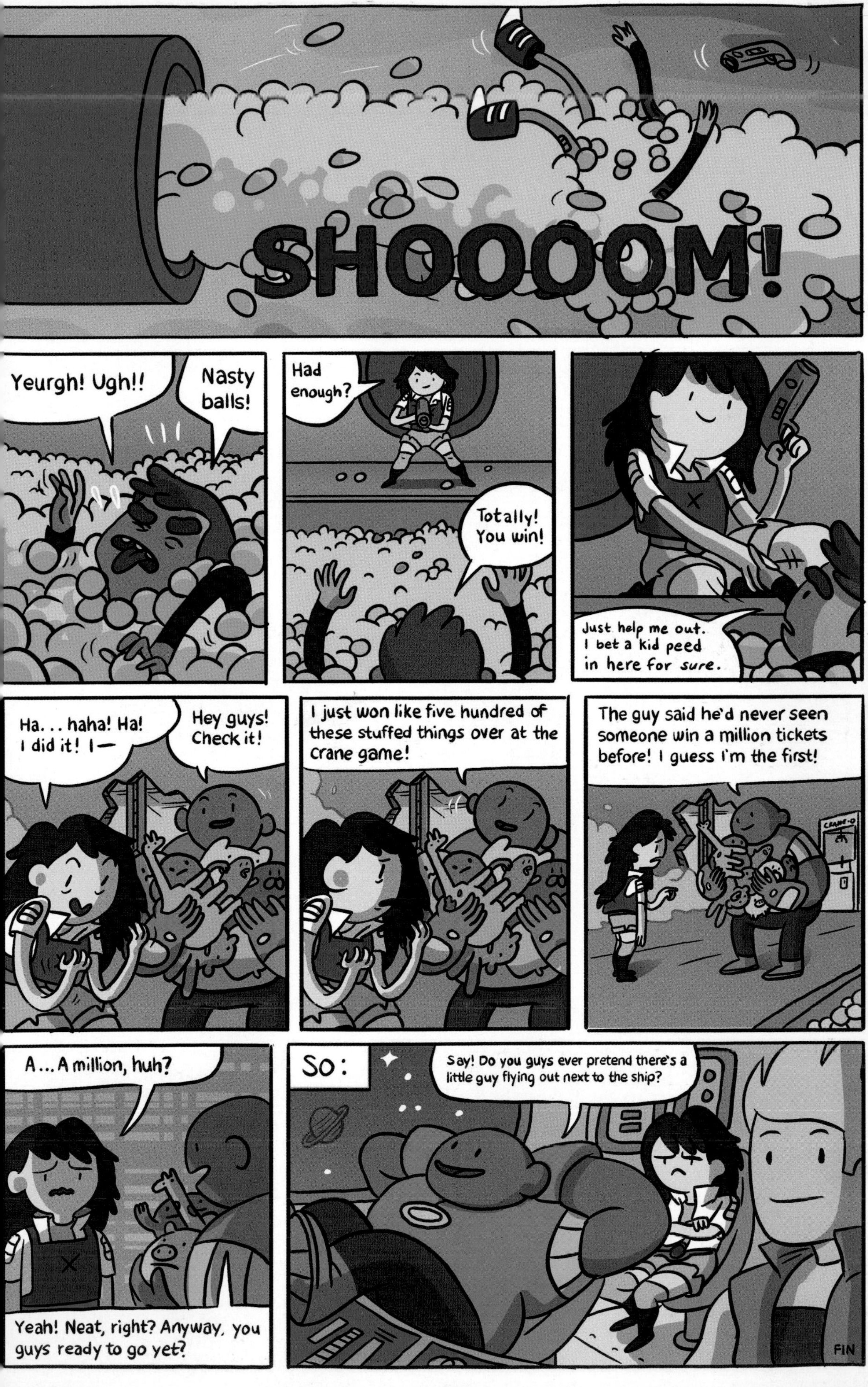
SHOOOOM!
Yeurgh! Ugh!!
Nasty balls!
Had enough?
Totally! You win!
Just help me out. I bet a kid peed in here for sure.
Ha... haha! Ha! I did it! I—
Hey guys! Check it!
I just won like five hundred of these stuffed things over at the crane game!
The guy said he'd never seen someone win a million tickets before! I guess I'm the first!
CRANE-O
A... A million, huh?
Yeah! Neat, right? Anyway, you guys ready to go yet?
So:
Say! Do you guys ever pretend there's a little guy flying out next to the ship?
FIN

CHAPTER
TWO

CONTINUE?

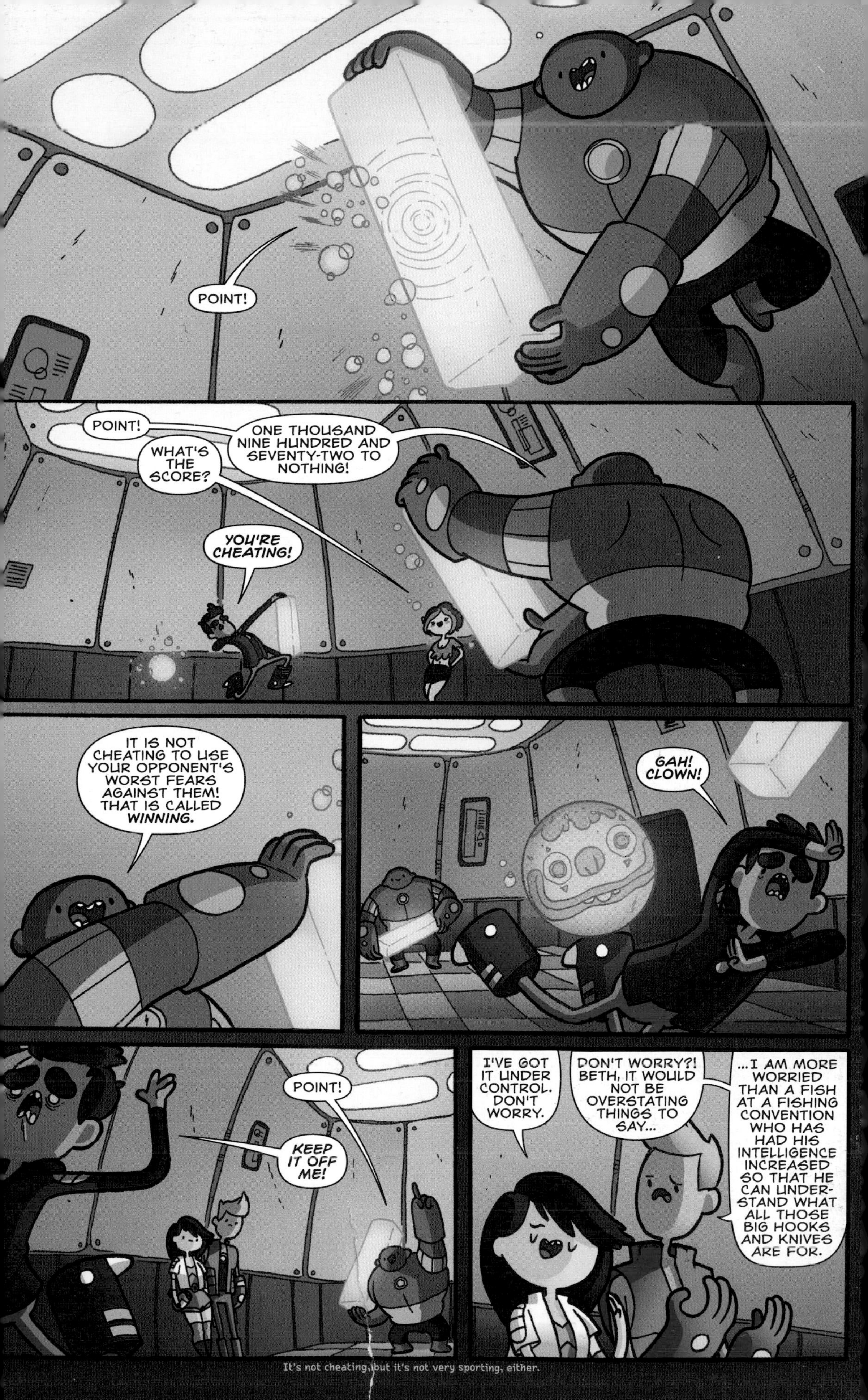
POINT!
POINT!
WHAT'S THE SCORE?
ONE THOUSAND NINE HUNDRED AND SEVENTY-TWO TO NOTHING!
YOU'RE CHEATING!
IT IS NOT CHEATING TO USE YOUR OPPONENT'S WORST FEARS AGAINST THEM! THAT IS CALLED WINNING.
GAH! CLOWN!
POINT!
KEEP IT OFF ME!
I'VE GOT IT UNDER CONTROL. DON'T WORRY.
DON'T WORRY?! BETH, IT WOULD NOT BE OVERSTATING THINGS TO SAY...
...I AM MORE WORRIED THAN A FISH AT A FISHING CONVENTION WHO HAS HAD HIS INTELLIGENCE INCREASED SO THAT HE CAN UNDERSTAND WHAT ALL THOSE BIG HOOKS AND KNIVES ARE FOR.

It's not cheating, but it's not very sporting, either.

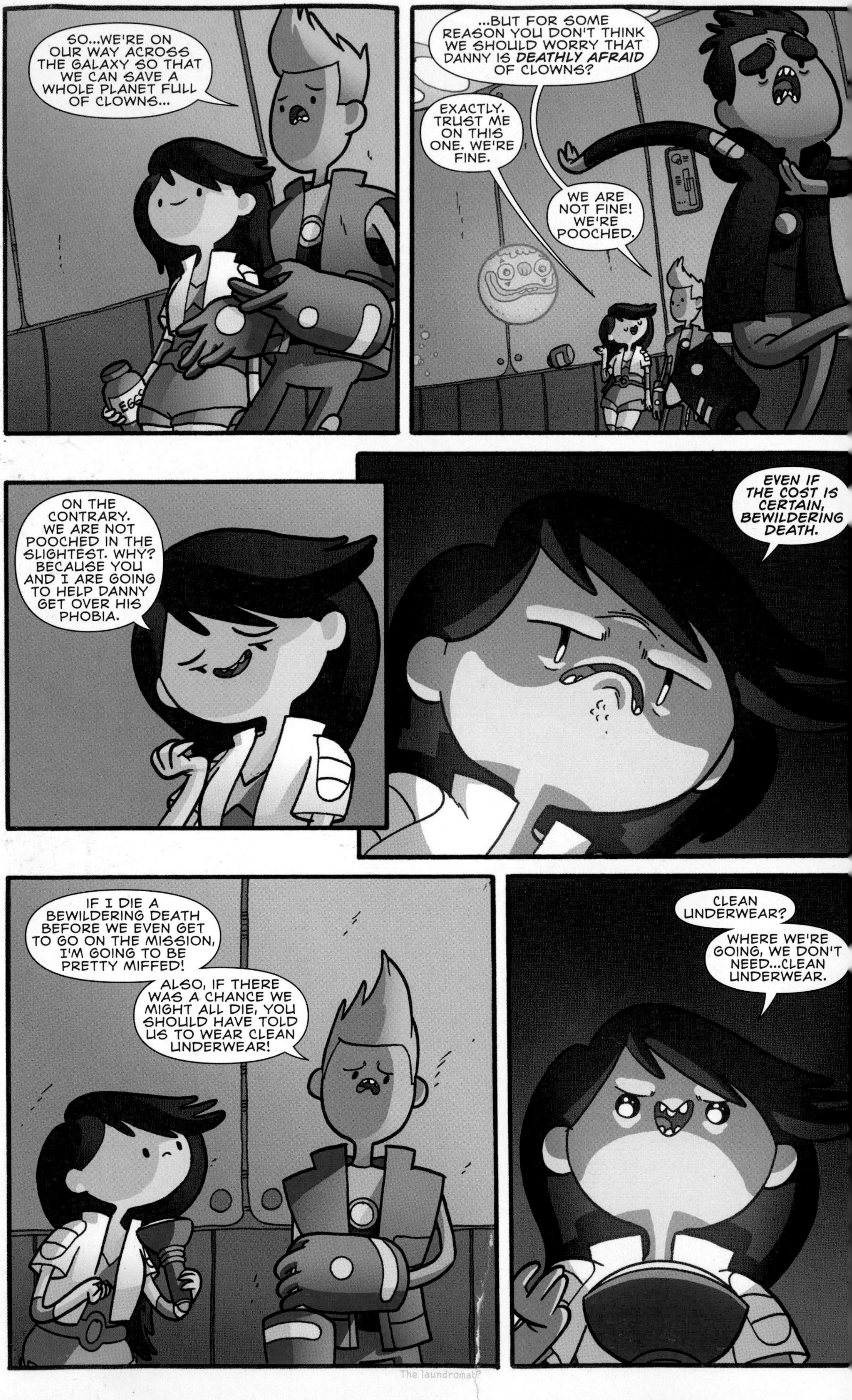
SO...WE'RE ON OUR WAY ACROSS THE GALAXY SO THAT WE CAN SAVE A WHOLE PLANET FULL OF CLOWNS...
EGGS
...BUT FOR SOME REASON YOU DON'T THINK WE SHOULD WORRY THAT DANNY IS *DEATHLY AFRAID* OF CLOWNS?
EXACTLY. TRUST ME ON THIS ONE. WE'RE FINE.
WE ARE NOT FINE! WE'RE POOCHED.
ON THE CONTRARY. WE ARE NOT POOCHED IN THE SLIGHTEST. WHY? BECAUSE YOU AND I ARE GOING TO HELP DANNY GET OVER HIS PHOBIA.
EVEN IF THE COST IS CERTAIN, BEWILDERING DEATH.
IF I DIE A BEWILDERING DEATH BEFORE WE EVEN GET TO GO ON THE MISSION, I'M GOING TO BE PRETTY MIFFED!
ALSO, IF THERE WAS A CHANCE WE MIGHT ALL DIE, YOU SHOULD HAVE TOLD US TO WEAR CLEAN UNDERWEAR!
CLEAN UNDERWEAR?
WHERE WE'RE GOING, WE DON'T NEED...CLEAN UNDERWEAR.

The laundromat?

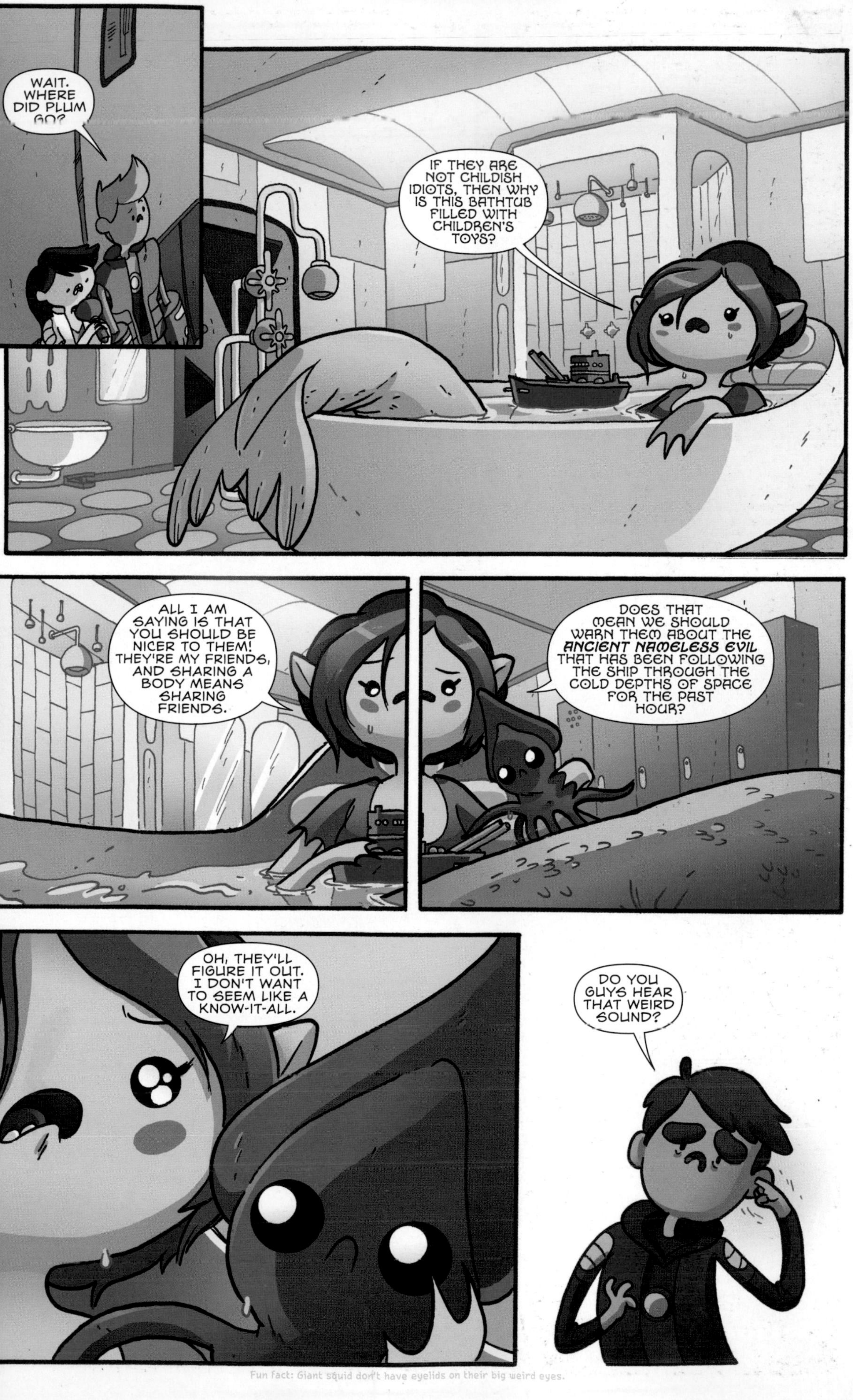
WAIT. WHERE DID PLUM GO?
IF THEY ARE NOT CHILDISH IDIOTS, THEN WHY IS THIS BATHTUB FILLED WITH CHILDREN'S TOYS?
ALL I AM SAYING IS THAT YOU SHOULD BE NICER TO THEM! THEY'RE MY FRIENDS, AND SHARING A BODY MEANS SHARING FRIENDS.
DOES THAT MEAN WE SHOULD WARN THEM ABOUT THE ANCIENT NAMELESS EVIL THAT HAS BEEN FOLLOWING THE SHIP THROUGH THE COLD DEPTHS OF SPACE FOR THE PAST HOUR?
OH, THEY'LL FIGURE IT OUT. I DON'T WANT TO SEEM LIKE A KNOW-IT-ALL.
DO YOU GUYS HEAR THAT WEIRD SOUND?

Fun fact: Giant squid don't have eyelids on their big weird eyes.

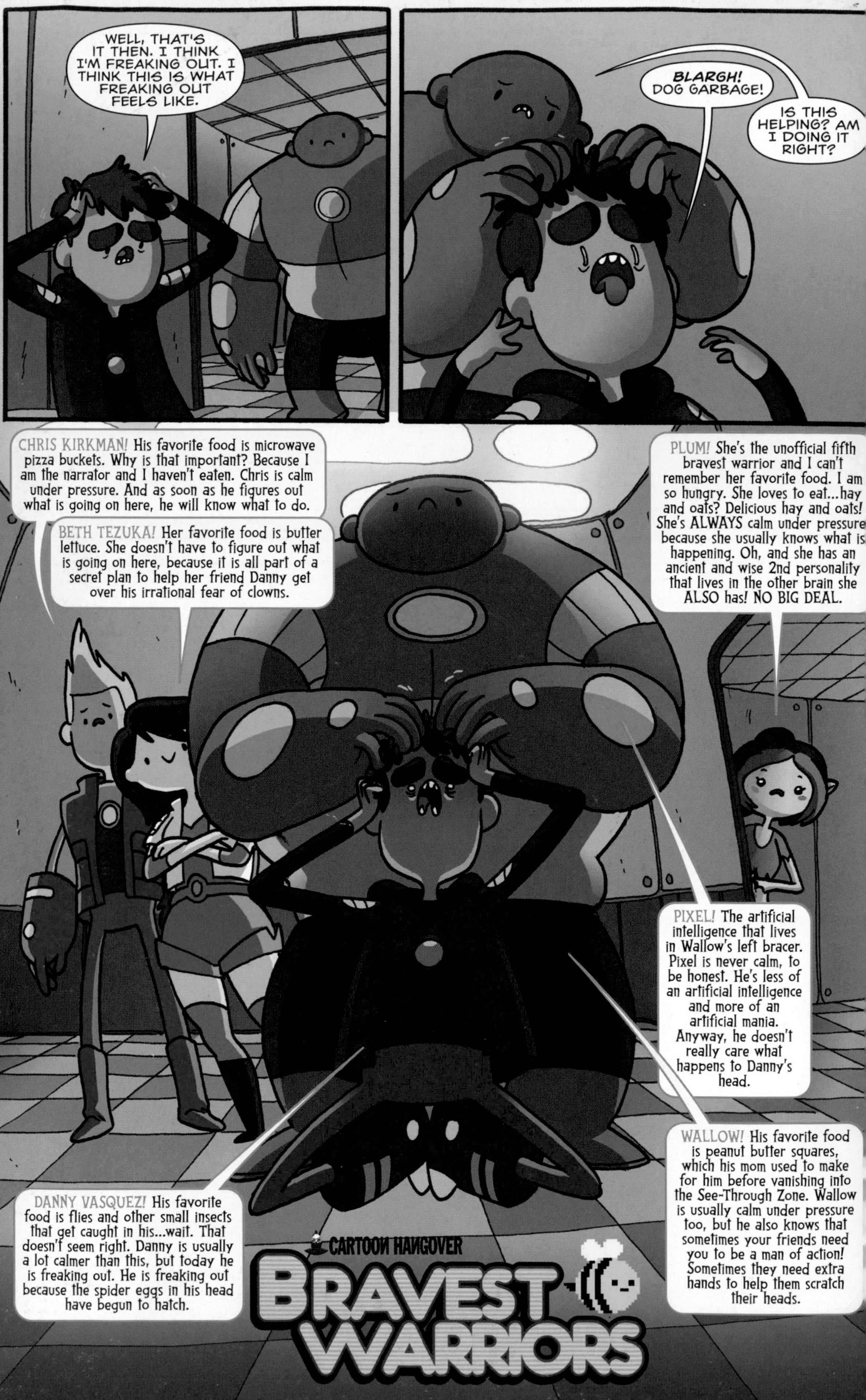
WELL, THAT'S IT THEN. I THINK I'M FREAKING OUT. I THINK THIS IS WHAT FREAKING OUT FEELS LIKE.
BLARGH! DOG GARBAGE!
IS THIS HELPING? AM I DOING IT RIGHT?
CHRIS KIRKMAN! His favorite food is microwave pizza buckets. Why is that important? Because I am the narrator and I haven't eaten. Chris is calm under pressure. And as soon as he figures out what is going on here, he will know what to do.
BETH TEZUKA! Her favorite food is butter lettuce. She doesn't have to figure out what is going on here, because it is all part of a secret plan to help her friend Danny get over his irrational fear of clowns.
PLUM! She's the unofficial fifth bravest warrior and I can't remember her favorite food. I am so hungry. She loves to eat...hay and oats? Delicious hay and oats! She's ALWAYS calm under pressure because she usually knows what is happening. Oh, and she has an ancient and wise 2nd personality that lives in the other brain she ALSO has! NO BIG DEAL.
PIXEL! The artificial intelligence that lives in Wallow's left bracer. Pixel is never calm, to be honest. He's less of an artificial intelligence and more of an artificial mania. Anyway, he doesn't really care what happens to Danny's head.
WALLOW! His favorite food is peanut butter squares, which his mom used to make for him before vanishing into the See-Through Zone. Wallow is usually calm under pressure too, but he also knows that sometimes your friends need you to be a man of action! Sometimes they need extra hands to help them scratch their heads.
DANNY VASQUEZ! His favorite food is flies and other small insects that get caught in his...wait. That doesn't seem right. Danny is usually a lot calmer than this, but today he is freaking out. He is freaking out because the spider eggs in his head have begun to hatch.
CARTOON HANGOVER
BRAVEST WARRIORS

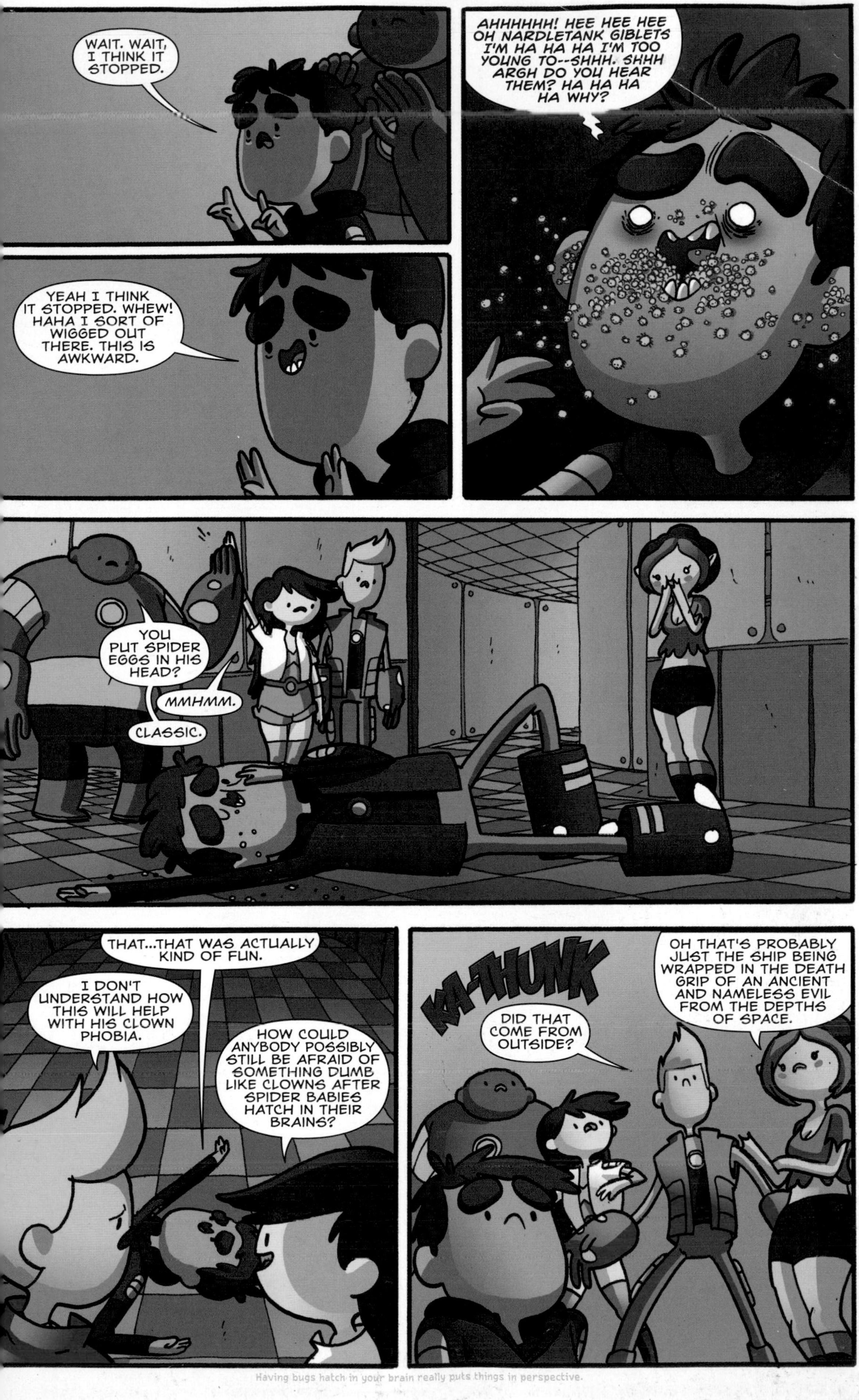
WAIT. WAIT, I THINK IT STOPPED.
AHHHHHH! HEE HEE HEE OH NARDLETANK GIBLETS I'M HA HA HA I'M TOO YOUNG TO--SHHH. SHHH ARGH DO YOU HEAR THEM? HA HA HA HA WHY?
YEAH I THINK IT STOPPED. WHEW! HAHA I SORT OF WIGGED OUT THERE. THIS IS AWKWARD.
YOU PUT SPIDER EGGS IN HIS HEAD?
MMHMM.
CLASSIC.
THAT...THAT WAS ACTUALLY KIND OF FUN.
I DON'T UNDERSTAND HOW THIS WILL HELP WITH HIS CLOWN PHOBIA.
HOW COULD ANYBODY POSSIBLY STILL BE AFRAID OF SOMETHING DUMB LIKE CLOWNS AFTER SPIDER BABIES HATCH IN THEIR BRAINS?
KA-THUNK
DID THAT COME FROM OUTSIDE?
OH THAT'S PROBABLY JUST THE SHIP BEING WRAPPED IN THE DEATH GRIP OF AN ANCIENT AND NAMELESS EVIL FROM THE DEPTHS OF SPACE.

Having bugs hatch in your brain really puts things in perspective.

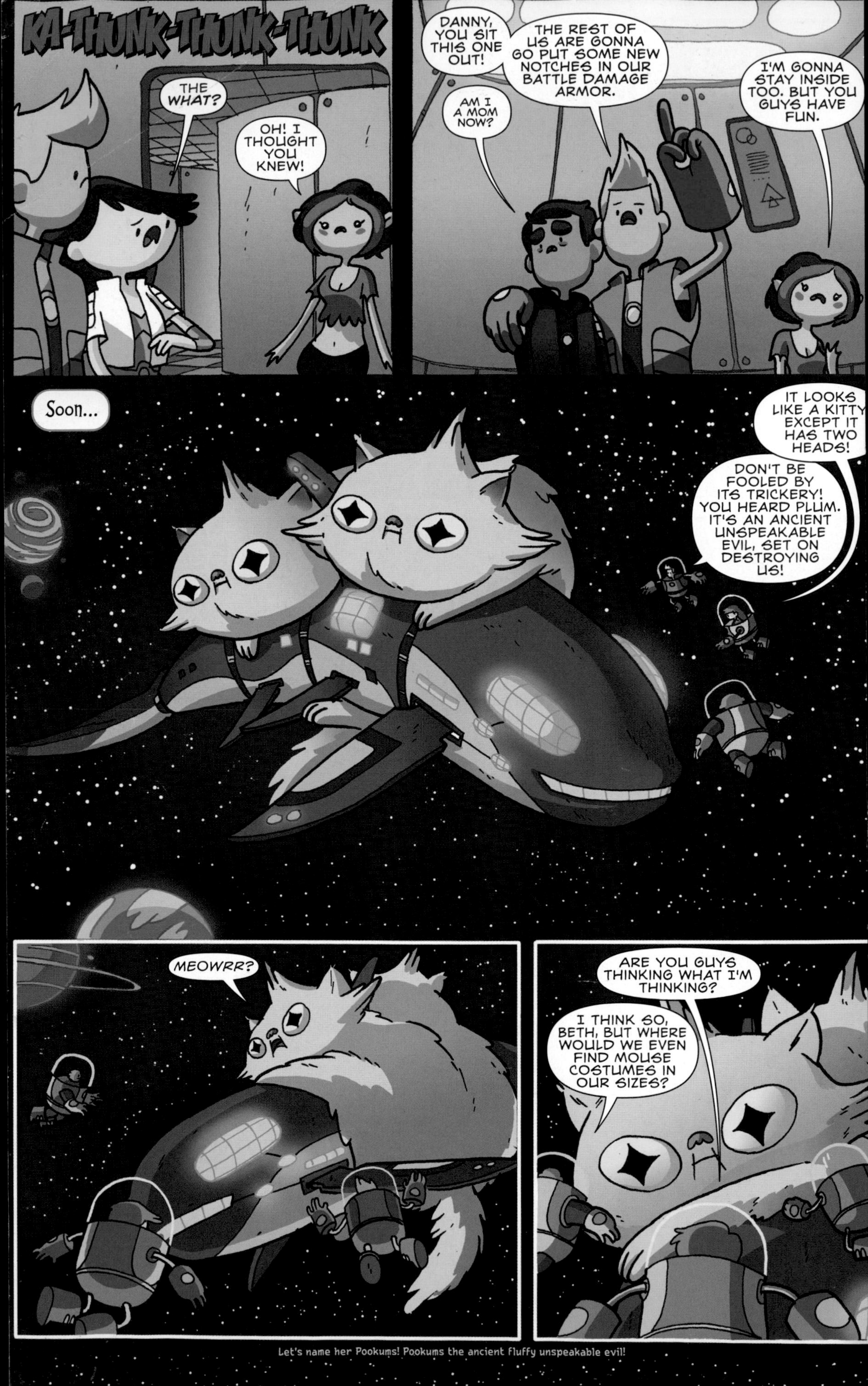

KA-THUNK-THUNK-THUNK
THE WHAT?
OH! I THOUGHT YOU KNEW!
DANNY, YOU SIT THIS ONE OUT!
THE REST OF US ARE GONNA GO PUT SOME NEW NOTCHES IN OUR BATTLE DAMAGE ARMOR.
AM I A MOM NOW?
I'M GONNA STAY INSIDE TOO. BUT YOU GUYS HAVE FUN.
Soon...
IT LOOKS LIKE A KITTY EXCEPT IT HAS TWO HEADS!
DON'T BE FOOLED BY ITS TRICKERY! YOU HEARD PLUM. IT'S AN ANCIENT UNSPEAKABLE EVIL, SET ON DESTROYING US!
MEOWRR?
ARE YOU GUYS THINKING WHAT I'M THINKING?
I THINK SO, BETH, BUT WHERE WOULD WE EVEN FIND MOUSE COSTUMES IN OUR SIZES?

Let's name her Pookums! Pookums the ancient fluffy unspeakable evil!

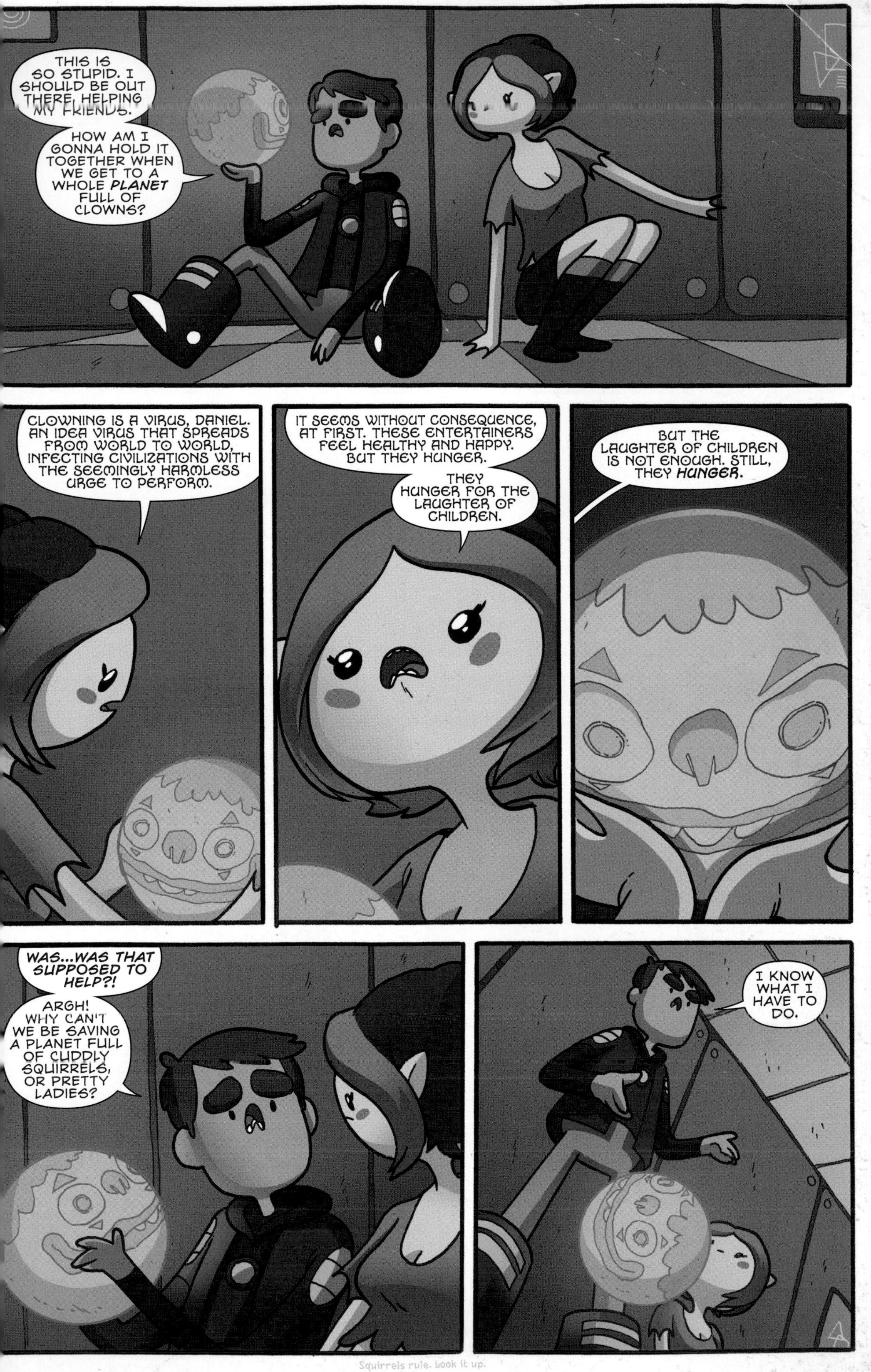
THIS IS SO STUPID. I SHOULD BE OUT THERE, HELPING MY FRIENDS.
HOW AM I GONNA HOLD IT TOGETHER WHEN WE GET TO A WHOLE *PLANET* FULL OF CLOWNS?
CLOWNING IS A VIRUS, DANIEL. AN IDEA VIRUS THAT SPREADS FROM WORLD TO WORLD, INFECTING CIVILIZATIONS WITH THE SEEMINGLY HARMLESS URGE TO PERFORM.
IT SEEMS WITHOUT CONSEQUENCE, AT FIRST. THESE ENTERTAINERS FEEL HEALTHY AND HAPPY. BUT THEY HUNGER.
THEY HUNGER FOR THE LAUGHTER OF CHILDREN.
BUT THE LAUGHTER OF CHILDREN IS NOT ENOUGH. STILL, THEY ***HUNGER.***
WAS...WAS THAT SUPPOSED TO HELP?!
ARGH! WHY CAN'T WE BE SAVING A PLANET FULL OF CUDDLY SQUIRRELS, OR PRETTY LADIES?
I KNOW WHAT I HAVE TO DO.

Squirrels rule. Look it up.

MRRRR?

RRRRRRR...

HE'S TOYING WITH US!

OR SHE.

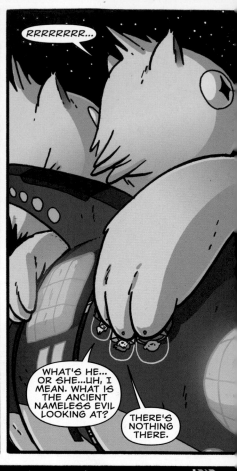

SNIFF SNIFF SNIFF

MAYBE IT ISN'T A BOY OR A GIRL. IT'S OBVIOUSLY NOT LIKE REGULAR KITTIES. OH NO AND NOW I KEEP SAYING 'IT.' I FEEL LIKE A REAL JERK HERE YOU GUYS.

SHOULD WE ASK? IS THAT POLITE?

HEY KITTY. WHAT PRONOUN DO YOU PREFER?

WHAT'S HE... OR SHE...UH, I MEAN. WHAT IS THE ANCIENT NAMELESS EVIL LOOKING AT?

THERE'S NOTHING THERE.

RRRRR RRRRRR RRRR...

RRRRRRR RRRRRRRR RRRRRRR...

WELL, THIS IS UNSETTLING.

WHAT WOULD DANNY DO IF HE WERE HERE? SOMETHING FANCY AND HI-TECH, I BET. I THINK I CAN ACTIVATE MY SUIT'S HIGH-VOLTAGE-ELECTRO-GIGGLE-STUN-SHIELD! WALLOW, CAN YOU BE READY TO--

I HAVE A PLAN.

HEY GOOD-LOOKING! I DON'T MEAN TO SOUND FORWARD, BUT...ARE YOU CURRENTLY DATING ANYONE?

There's NOTHING THERE. Cats are weird.

THANK YOU FOR SAVING US, WALLOW! AND I AM SURE YOU WILL HAVE A VERY NICE TIME ON YOUR DATE.

YEAH! THAT WAS SOME QUICK THINKING. THANKS, MAN.

I STILL DON'T UNDERSTAND IF THAT WAS A BOY CAT OR A GIRL CAT.

THE PROBLEM WITH CALLING AN ANCIENT NAMELESS EVIL FOR A DATE IS THE WHOLE NAMELESS PART. WHO DO I ASK FOR ON THE PHONE?

DANNY?

HEY GUYS.

HEY, YOU'RE BACK! WHAT HAPPENED? DID YOU BREAK THE ANCIENT CURSE BY FINALLY GIVING THE CREATURE A NAME?

WERE...WE SUPPOSED TO DO THAT?

WHAT'S WITH THE SILLY-LOOKING CHAPEAU ON YOUR NOGGIN?

THIS IS MY *CLOWN CENSOR*. IT WILL FILTER OUT ANY CLOWNS I SEE BEFORE THE IMAGE REACHES MY EYES, AND MAKE THEM LOOK LESS FRIGHTENING.

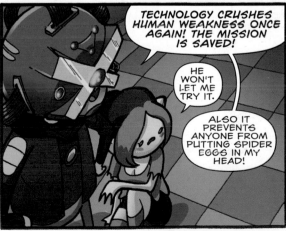

TECHNOLOGY CRUSHES HUMAN WEAKNESS ONCE AGAIN! THE MISSION IS SAVED!

HE WON'T LET ME TRY IT.

ALSO IT PREVENTS ANYONE FROM PUTTING SPIDER EGGS IN MY HEAD!

Wait, did I break the curse by accident when I named the kitty Pookums?

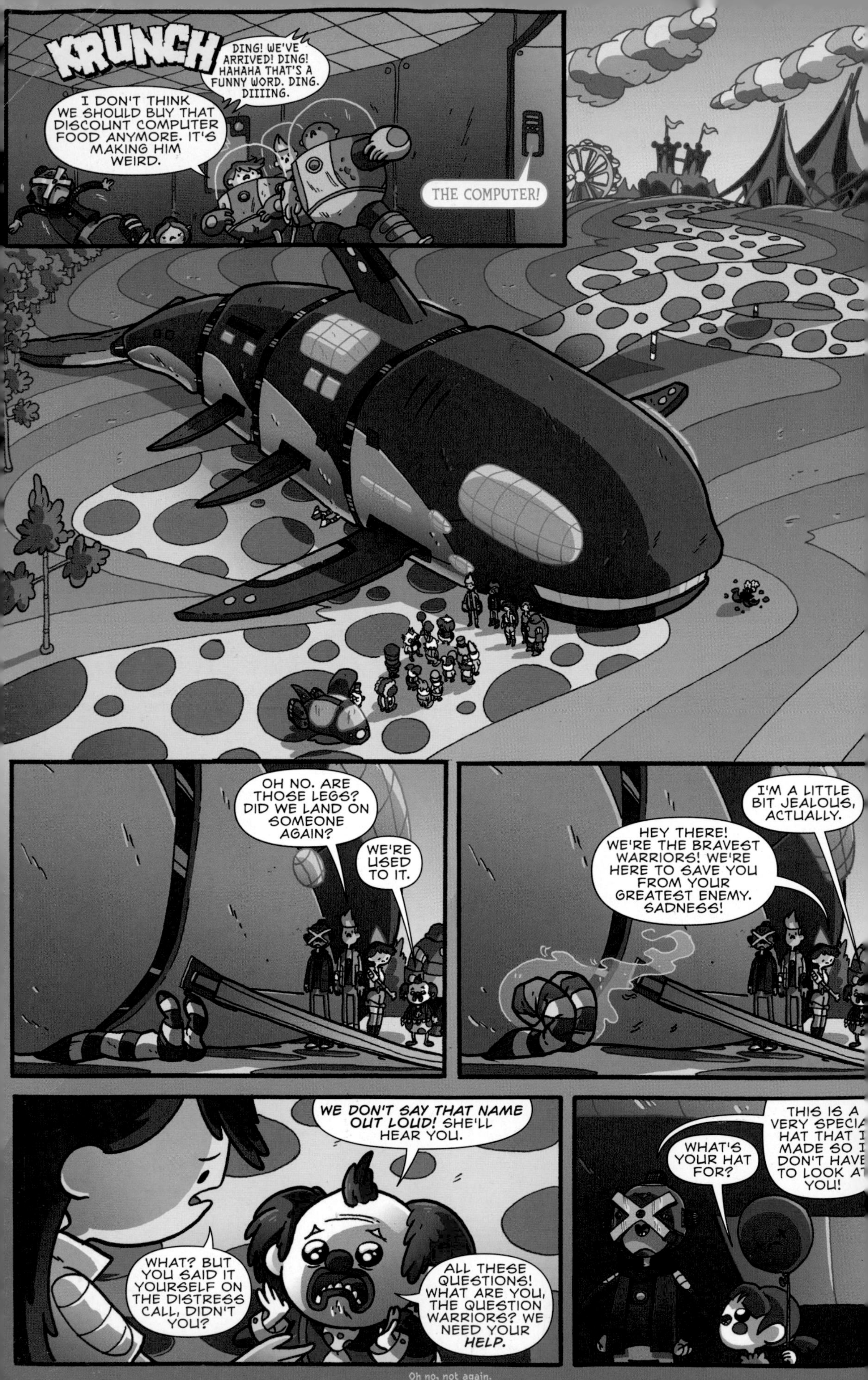
KRUNCH
DING! WE'VE ARRIVED! DING! HAHAHA THAT'S A FUNNY WORD. DING. DIIIING.
I DON'T THINK WE SHOULD BUY THAT DISCOUNT COMPUTER FOOD ANYMORE. IT'S MAKING HIM WEIRD.
THE COMPUTER!
OH NO. ARE THOSE LEGS? DID WE LAND ON SOMEONE AGAIN?
WE'RE USED TO IT.
I'M A LITTLE BIT JEALOUS, ACTUALLY.
HEY THERE! WE'RE THE BRAVEST WARRIORS! WE'RE HERE TO SAVE YOU FROM YOUR GREATEST ENEMY. SADNESS!
WE DON'T SAY THAT NAME OUT LOUD! SHE'LL HEAR YOU.
WHAT? BUT YOU SAID IT YOURSELF ON THE DISTRESS CALL, DIDN'T YOU?
ALL THESE QUESTIONS! WHAT ARE YOU, THE QUESTION WARRIORS? WE NEED YOUR HELP.
WHAT'S YOUR HAT FOR?
THIS IS A VERY SPECIA HAT THAT I MADE SO I DON'T HAVE TO LOOK AT YOU!

Oh no, not again.

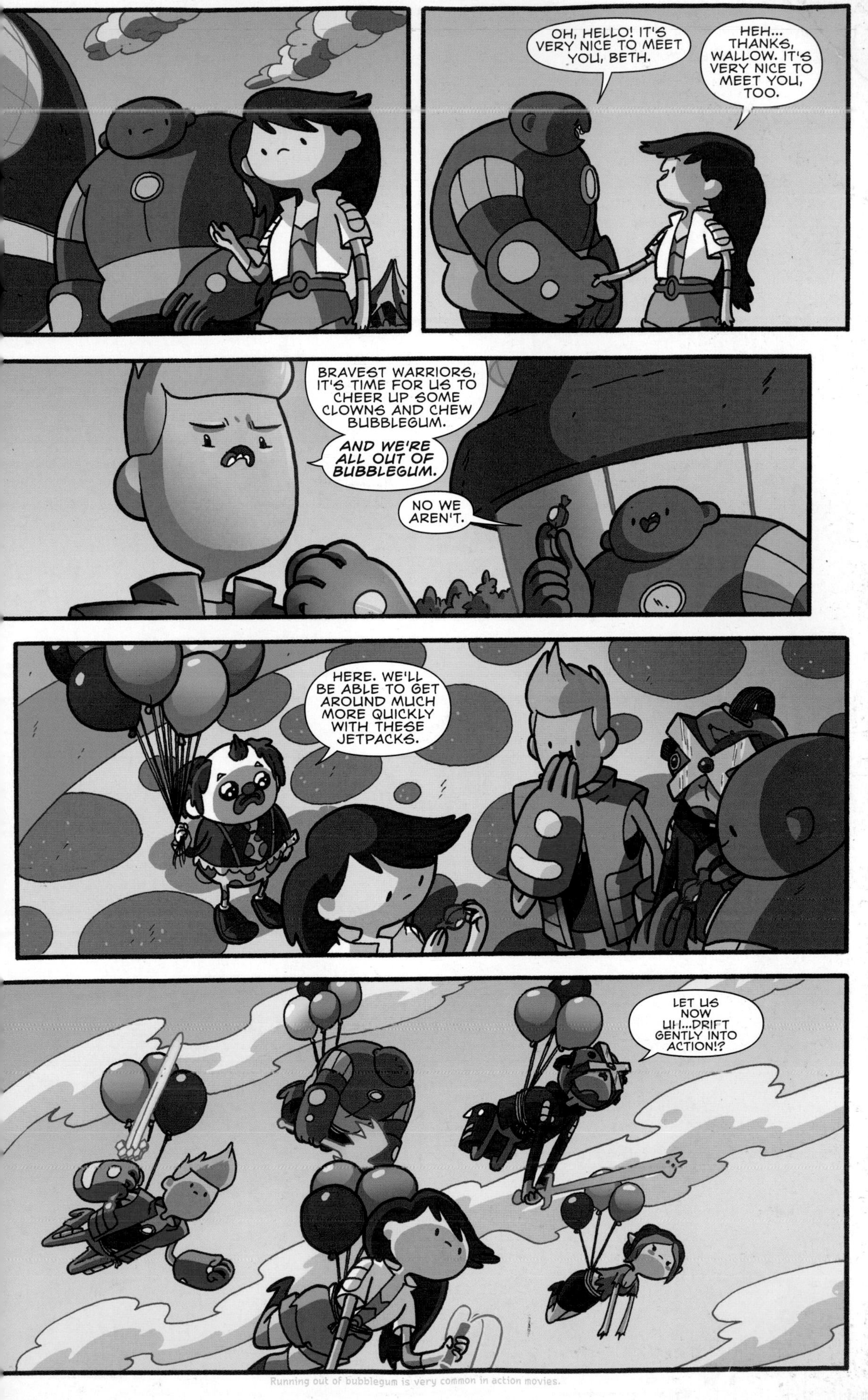
OH, HELLO! IT'S VERY NICE TO MEET YOU, BETH.
HEH... THANKS, WALLOW. IT'S VERY NICE TO MEET YOU, TOO.
BRAVEST WARRIORS, IT'S TIME FOR US TO CHEER UP SOME CLOWNS AND CHEW BUBBLEGUM.
AND WE'RE ALL OUT OF BUBBLEGUM.
NO WE AREN'T.
HERE. WE'LL BE ABLE TO GET AROUND MUCH MORE QUICKLY WITH THESE JETPACKS.
LET US NOW UH...DRIFT GENTLY INTO ACTION!?

Running out of bubblegum is very common in action movies.

And so our intrepid heroes begin their work...

FIRST OF ALL, LET'S THROW THESE DEPRESSING VIOLINS INTO THE "VIOLIN HOLDER"...

...WHICH IS WHAT I CALL THE GARBAGE CAN!

VIOLIN HOLDER!
Favorite food: Violins.

NONE OF YOUR TIRE-SWINGS HAVE TIRES IN THEM!

BUT--

THERE WE GO!

BETH, YOU ARE MY BEST FRIEND, AND MY LIFE IS RICHER WITH YOU IN IT, BUT I HAVE TO DISAGREE WITH YOU ON THIS.

MUSIC CAN BRING BEAUTY TO EVEN THE BLEAKEST OF DAYS, AND BRING HOPE TO THE DARKEST OF HEARTS.

SO MAYBE THE SOLUTION ISN'T THROWING THE VIOLINS AWAY, MAYBE WE JUST NEED...

"I could crawl into the space between the notes and curl my back to loneliness." - Maya Angelou

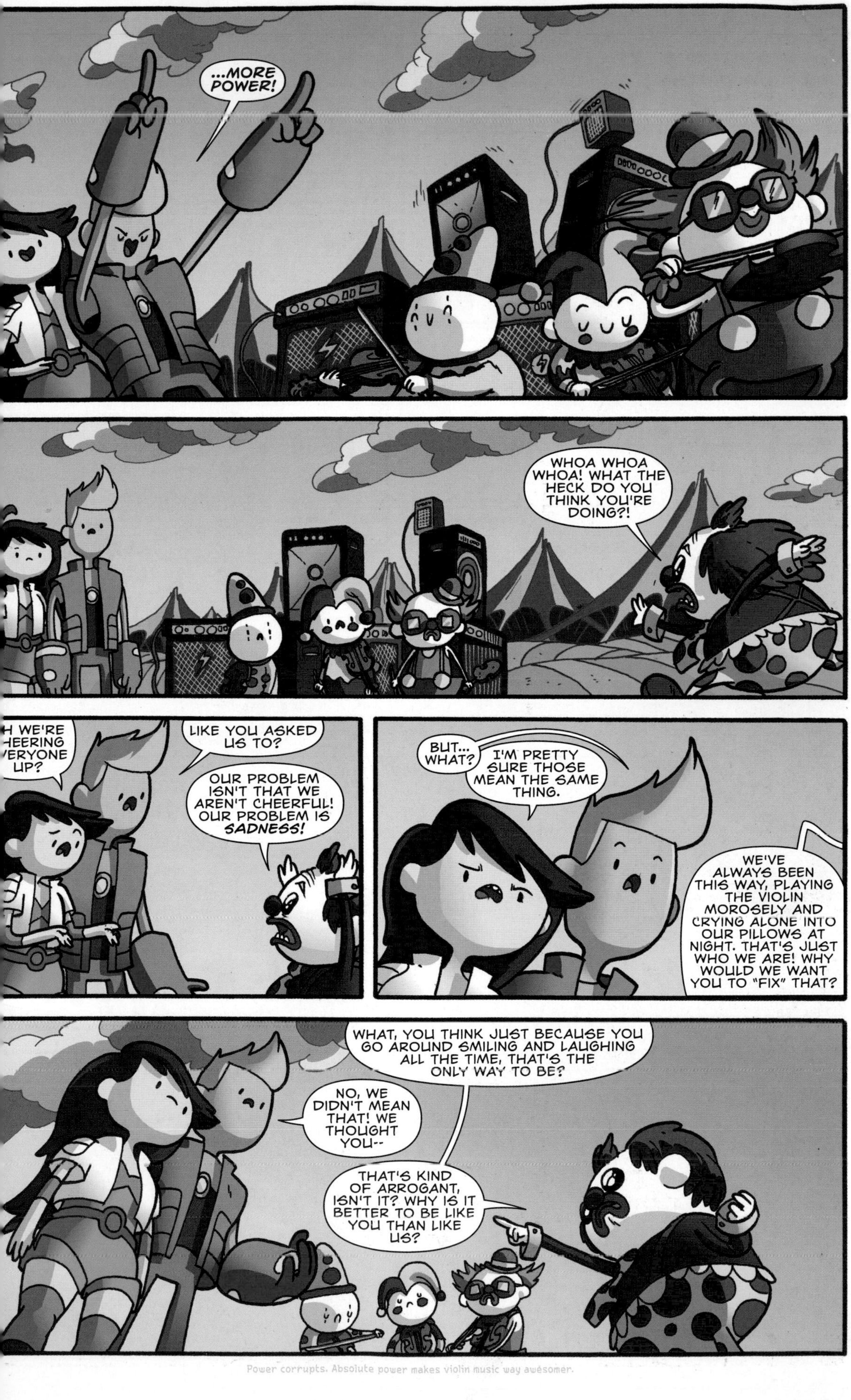
...MORE POWER!
WHOA WHOA WHOA! WHAT THE HECK DO YOU THINK YOU'RE DOING?!
H WE'RE HEERING VERYONE UP?
LIKE YOU ASKED US TO?
OUR PROBLEM ISN'T THAT WE AREN'T CHEERFUL! OUR PROBLEM IS SADNESS!
BUT... WHAT?
I'M PRETTY SURE THOSE MEAN THE SAME THING.
WE'VE ALWAYS BEEN THIS WAY, PLAYING THE VIOLIN MOROSELY AND CRYING ALONE INTO OUR PILLOWS AT NIGHT. THAT'S JUST WHO WE ARE! WHY WOULD WE WANT YOU TO "FIX" THAT?
WHAT, YOU THINK JUST BECAUSE YOU GO AROUND SMILING AND LAUGHING ALL THE TIME, THAT'S THE ONLY WAY TO BE?
NO, WE DIDN'T MEAN THAT! WE THOUGHT YOU--
THAT'S KIND OF ARROGANT, ISN'T IT? WHY IS IT BETTER TO BE LIKE YOU THAN LIKE US?

Power corrupts. Absolute power makes violin music way awesomer.

Meanwhile...

AND EVENTUALLY WE REALIZED THAT THE WHOLE PLANET WAS GIVING OFF STRANGE RADIATION THAT MADE PEOPLE ACT MEAN TO ONE ANOTHER. SO DO YOU KNOW WHAT WE DID THEN, BOYS AND GIRLS?

DID YOU GO HOME AND CRY?

NO.

DID YOU WRITE A POEM ABOUT HOW YOU WANTED TO CRY BUT FELT LIKE YOU HAD RUN OUT OF TEARS?

NO, WE DIDN'T DO THAT, EITHER.

DID YOU HIT YOURSELF IN THE HEAD AGAIN AND AGAIN BECAUSE YOU WERE SUCH A DUMMY THAT NOBODY WOULD EVER LOVE YOU?

WHAT?! NO!

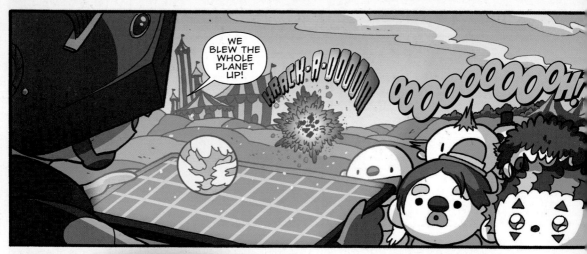

WE BLEW THE WHOLE PLANET UP!

KRACK-A-DOOOM

OOOOOOOOOH!

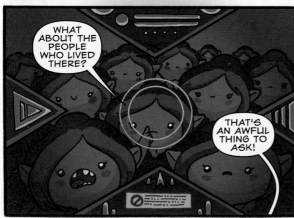

WHAT ABOUT THE PEOPLE WHO LIVED THERE?

THAT'S AN AWFUL THING TO ASK!

NOW, BEFORE I GO, LET'S PLAY ONE MORE GAME. IT'S CALLED "DID YOU EVER THINK ABOUT HOW BIG THE UNIVERSE IS...

...AND HOW WE'R ALL SO SMALL AN MEANINGLESS AN NOBODY WILL REMEMBER US WHEN WE'RE GONE?"

I think about that sometimes!

WHY ARE ALL THOSE KIDS CRYING?

OH, WHO KNOWS WHY LITTLE KIDS DO ANYTHING. WHAT HAPPENED TO YOU?

I GOT IN A FIGHT WITH A TIRE SWING.

WE'VE NEVER NEEDED A WORD TO DESCRIBE HOW WE FEEL. WE ALWAYS FEEL THIS WAY, SO WE DON'T REALLY EVER TALK ABOUT IT.

I DON'T UNDERSTAND. THEN WHY DID YOU SEND US THAT DISTRESS SIGNAL?

I TOLD YOU! WE NEED YOUR HELP! OUR GREATEST ENEMY HAS RETURNED. SADNESS!

DID I MISS SOMETHING?

WAIT...SO SADNESS IS A PERSON?

NO, NOT A PERSON. A GOD. SADNESS IS THE GOD OF FEAR, AND SHE HAS BEEN SENDING HORRIBLE NIGHTMARE CREATURES INTO OUR WORLD.

THAT'S A REALLY STUPID NAME FOR A GOD OF FEAR.

WHAT KIND OF HORRIBLE NIGHTMARE CREATURES ARE WE TALKING HERE?

TH...THOSE KIND!

SWEET POTATOES ALMIGHTY!

The anticipation is terrible, I hope it lasts.

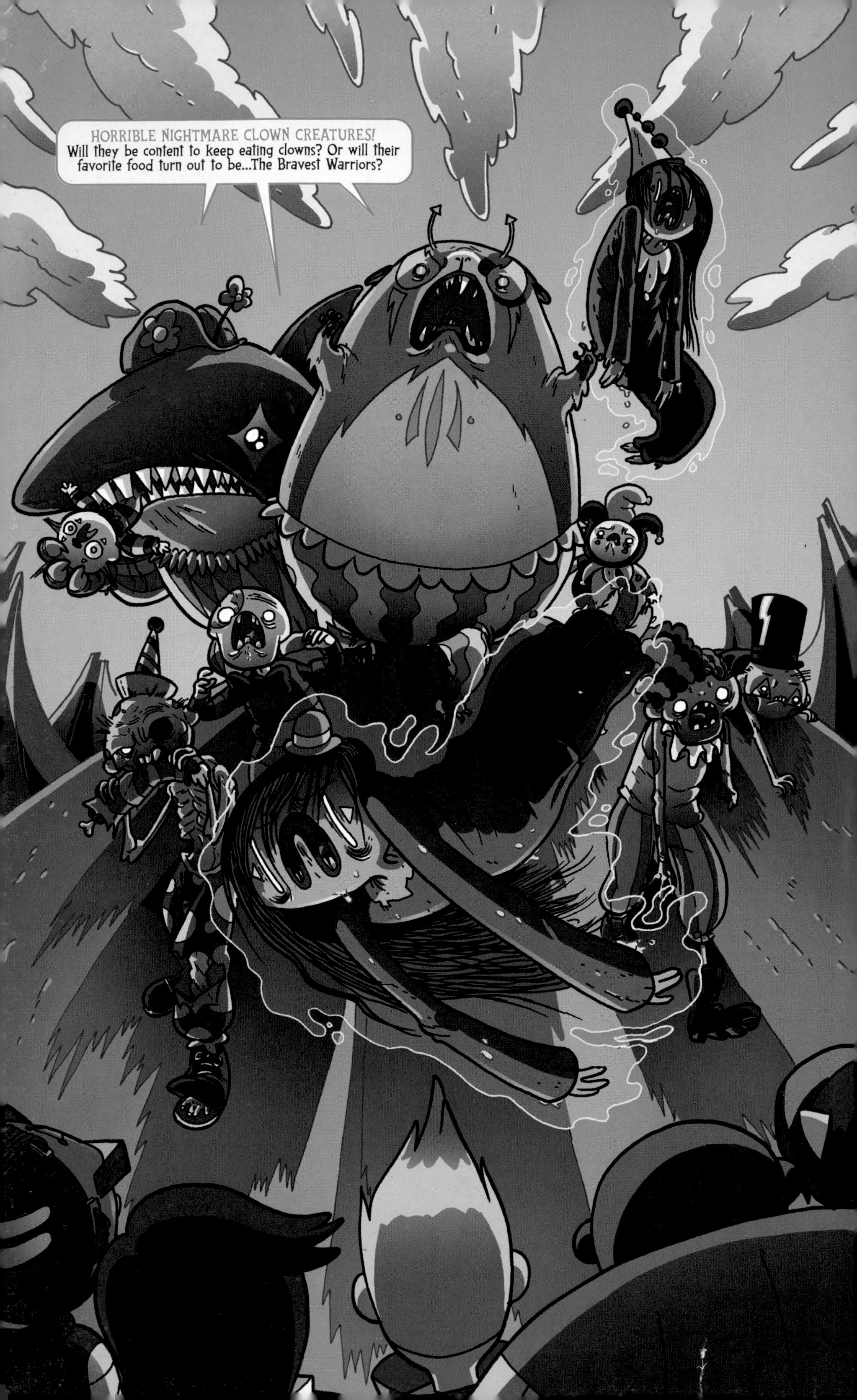
HORRIBLE NIGHTMARE CLOWN CREATURES!
Will they be content to keep eating clowns? Or will their favorite food turn out to be...The Bravest Warriors?

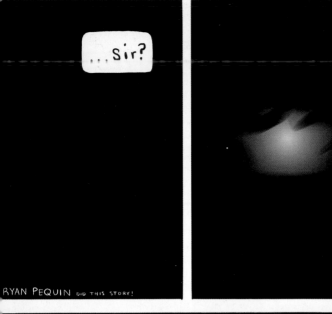

...sir?

Mr. Warrior? You awake?

RYAN PEQUIN DID THIS STORY!

I brought you some soup.

I emptied out your barf bucket too.

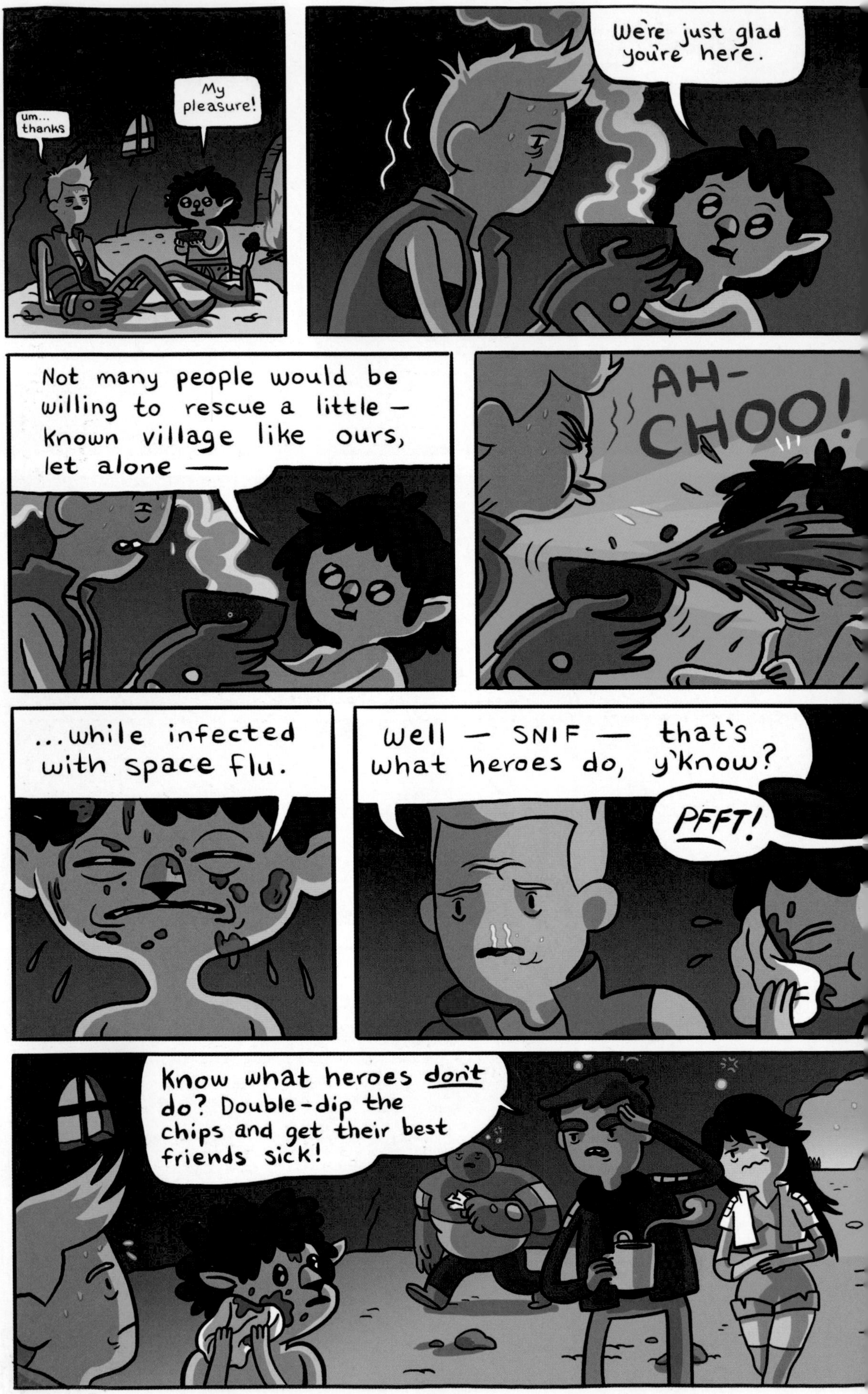
um... thanks
My pleasure!
We're just glad you're here.
Not many people would be willing to rescue a little-known village like ours, let alone —
AH-CHOO!
...while infected with space flu.
Well — SNIF — that's what heroes do, y'know?
PFFT!
Know what heroes don't do? Double-dip the chips and get their best friends sick!

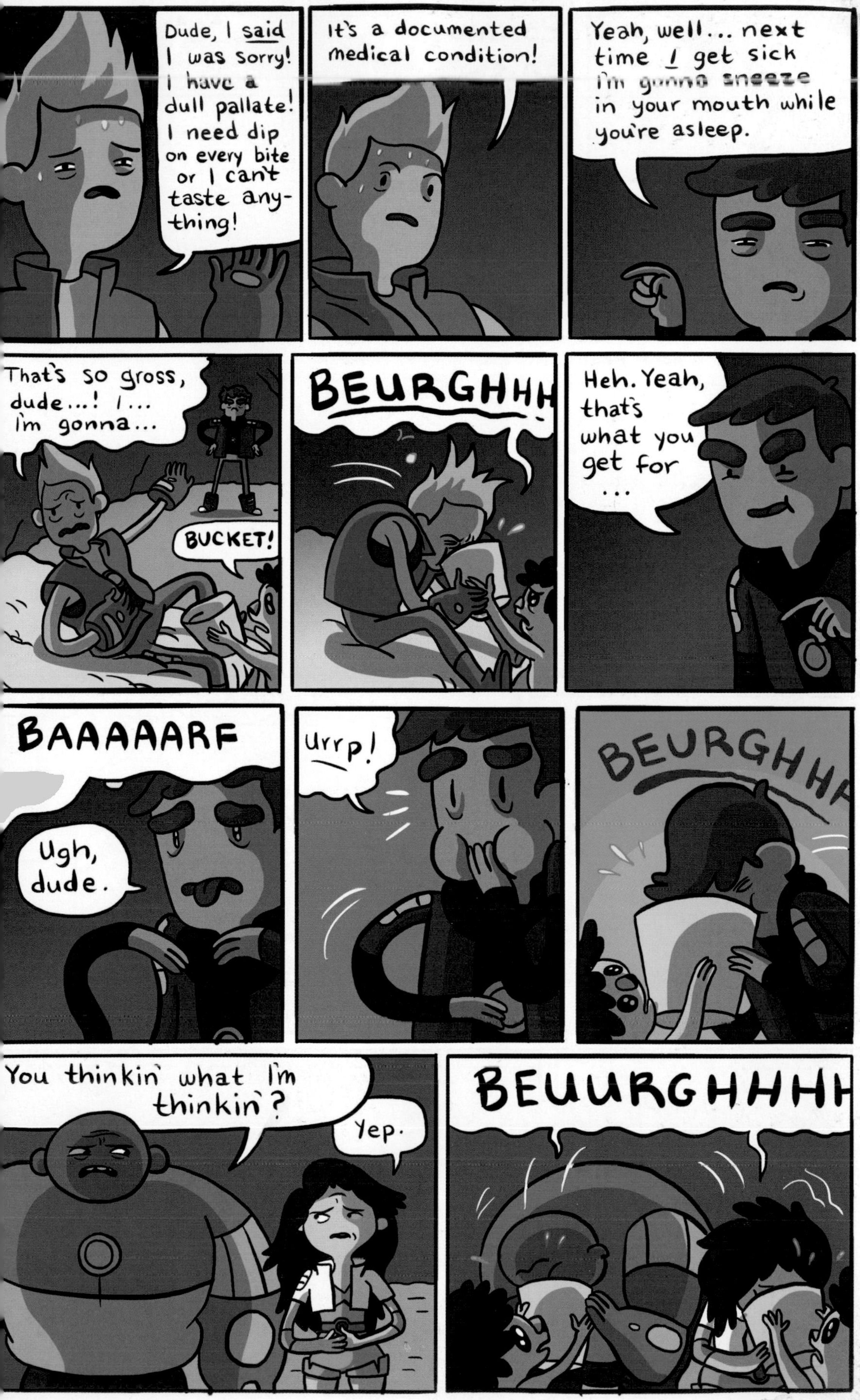
Dude, I said I was sorry! I have a dull pallate! I need dip on every bite or I can't taste anything!
It's a documented medical condition!
Yeah, well... next time I get sick I'm gonna sneeze in your mouth while you're asleep.
That's so gross, dude...! I... I'm gonna...
BUCKET!
BEURGHHH
Heh. Yeah, that's what you get for ...
BAAAAARF
Ugh, dude.
Urrp!
BEURGHHH
You thinkin' what I'm thinkin'?
Yep.
BEUURGHHHH

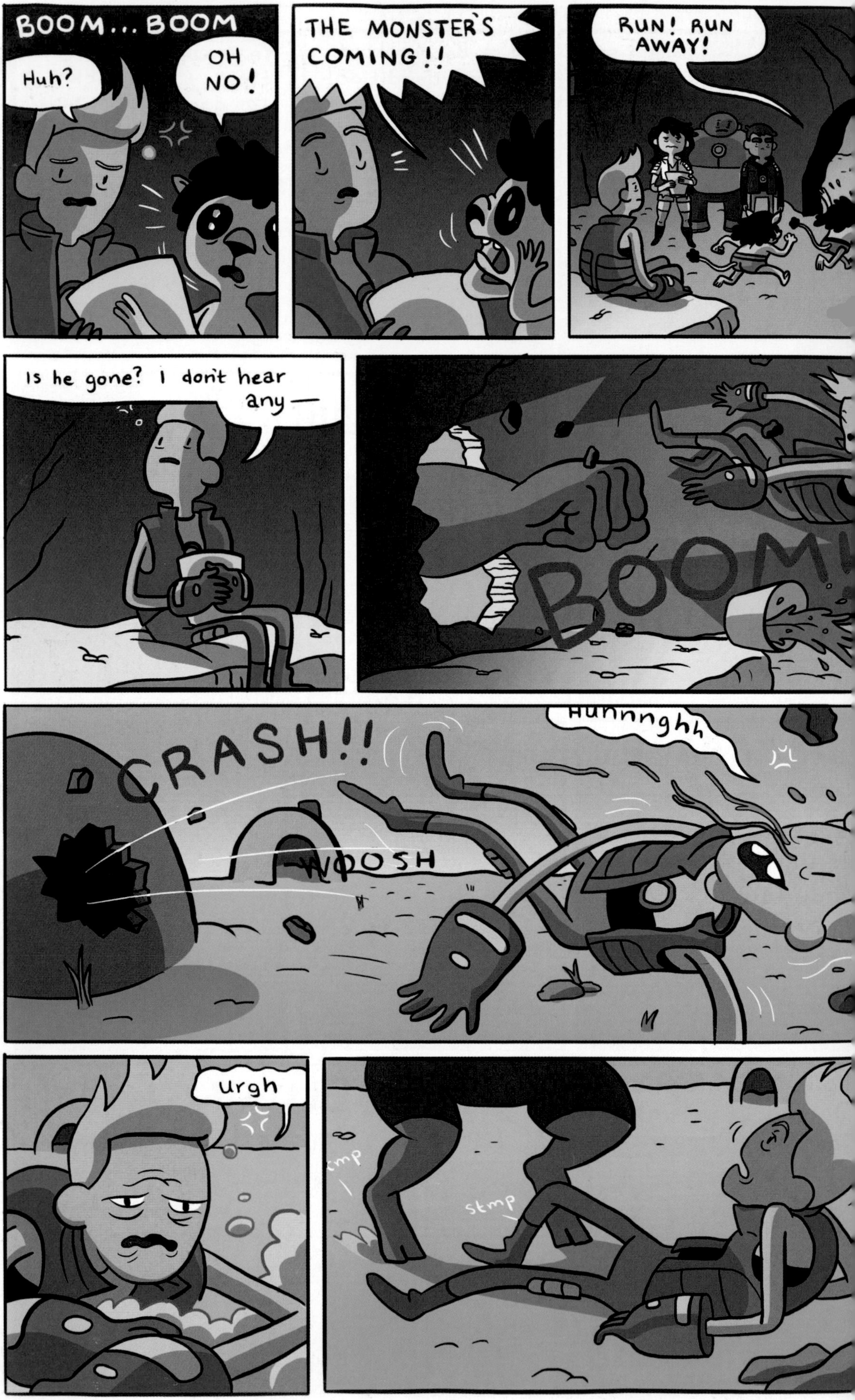
BOOM... BOOM
Huh?
OH NO!
THE MONSTER'S COMING!!
RUN! RUN AWAY!
Is he gone? I don't hear any—
BOOM!
CRASH!!
WOOSH
Hunnnghh
urgh
stmp

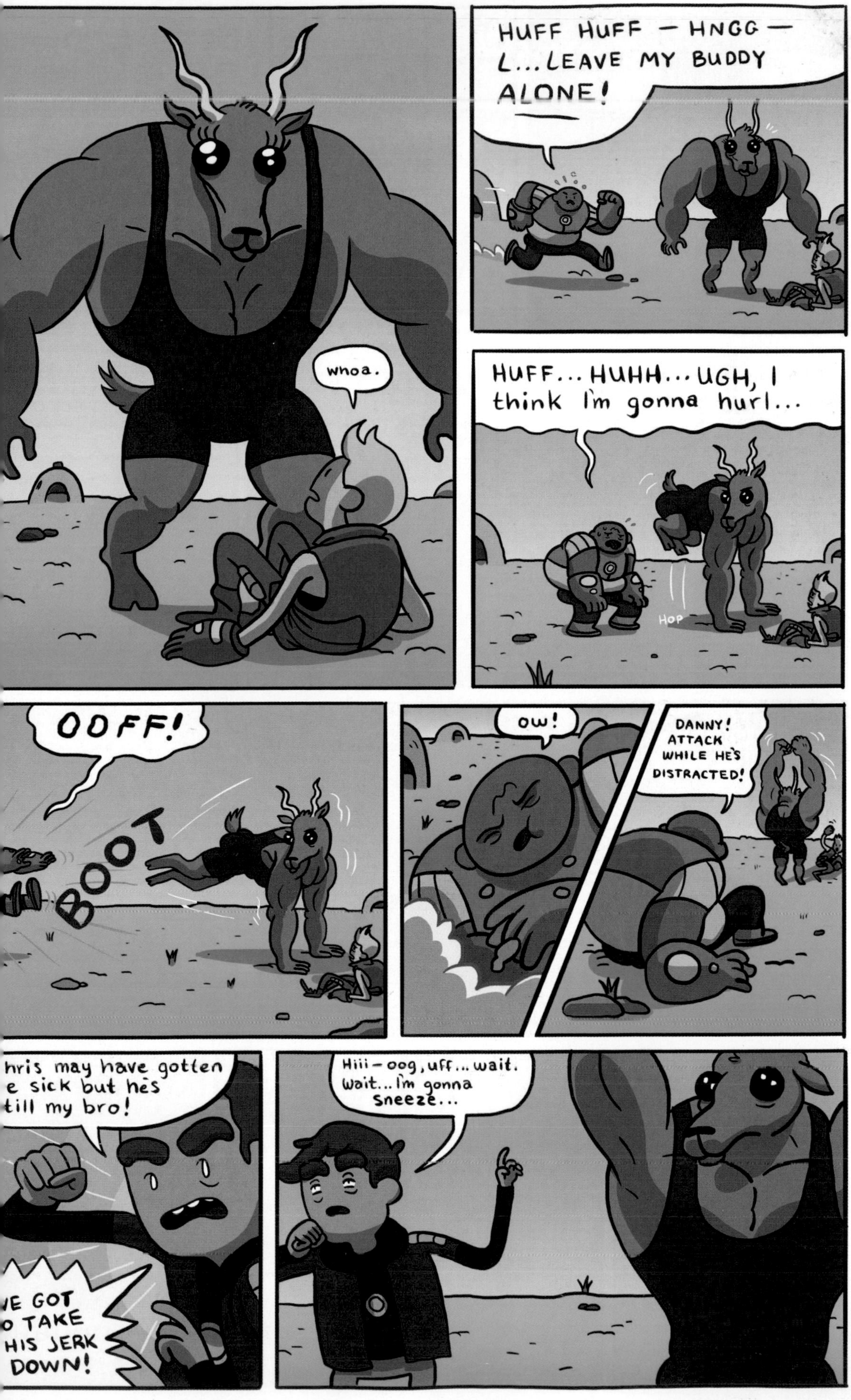
whoa.
HUFF HUFF — HNGG — L...LEAVE MY BUDDY ALONE!
HUFF... HUHH... UGH, I think I'm gonna hurl...
HOP
OOFF!
BOOT
OW!
DANNY! ATTACK WHILE HE'S DISTRACTED!
hris may have gotten e sick but he's till my bro!
VE GOT O TAKE HIS JERK DOWN!
Hiii-oog, uff... wait. Wait... I'm gonna sneeze...

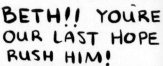

SMACK

Ugh! He slapped my boogers all over me!

BETH!! YOU'RE OUR LAST HOPE RUSH HIM!

But:

BLUHHHH

HOIST

This guy is kickin' our butts! I can't let him pick on these lion dudes...

Gotta go all out

SQUEEZE

SMOOCH

HEE

UH

UUUGHH

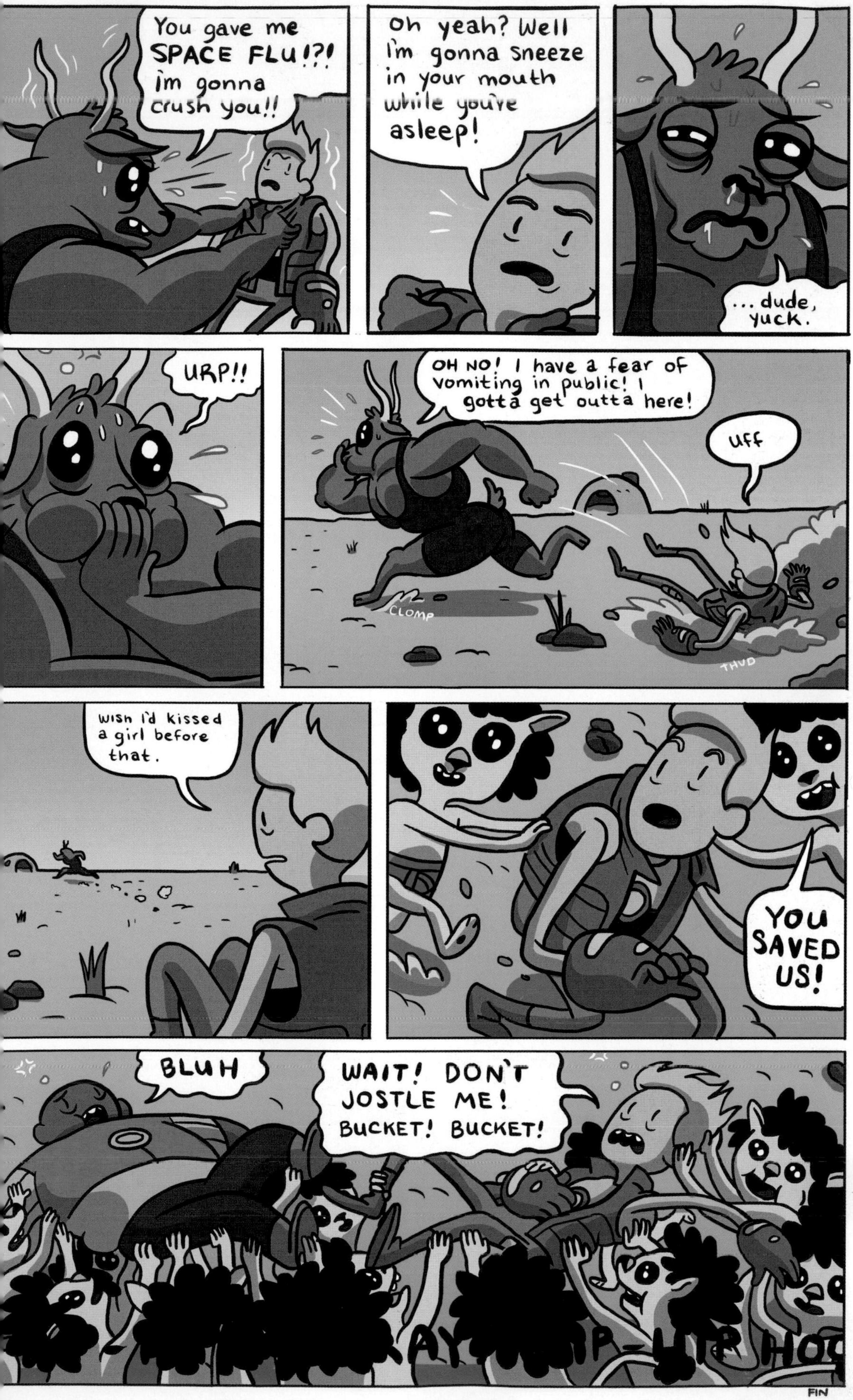
You gave me SPACE FLU!?! im gonna crush you!!
Oh yeah? Well I'm gonna sneeze in your mouth while you're asleep!
...dude, yuck.
URP!!
OH NO! I have a fear of vomiting in public! I gotta get outta here!
UFF
CLOMP
THUD
wish I'd kissed a girl before that.
YOU SAVED US!
BLUH
WAIT! DON'T JOSTLE ME! BUCKET! BUCKET!

FIN

CHAPTER
THREE

CONTINUE?

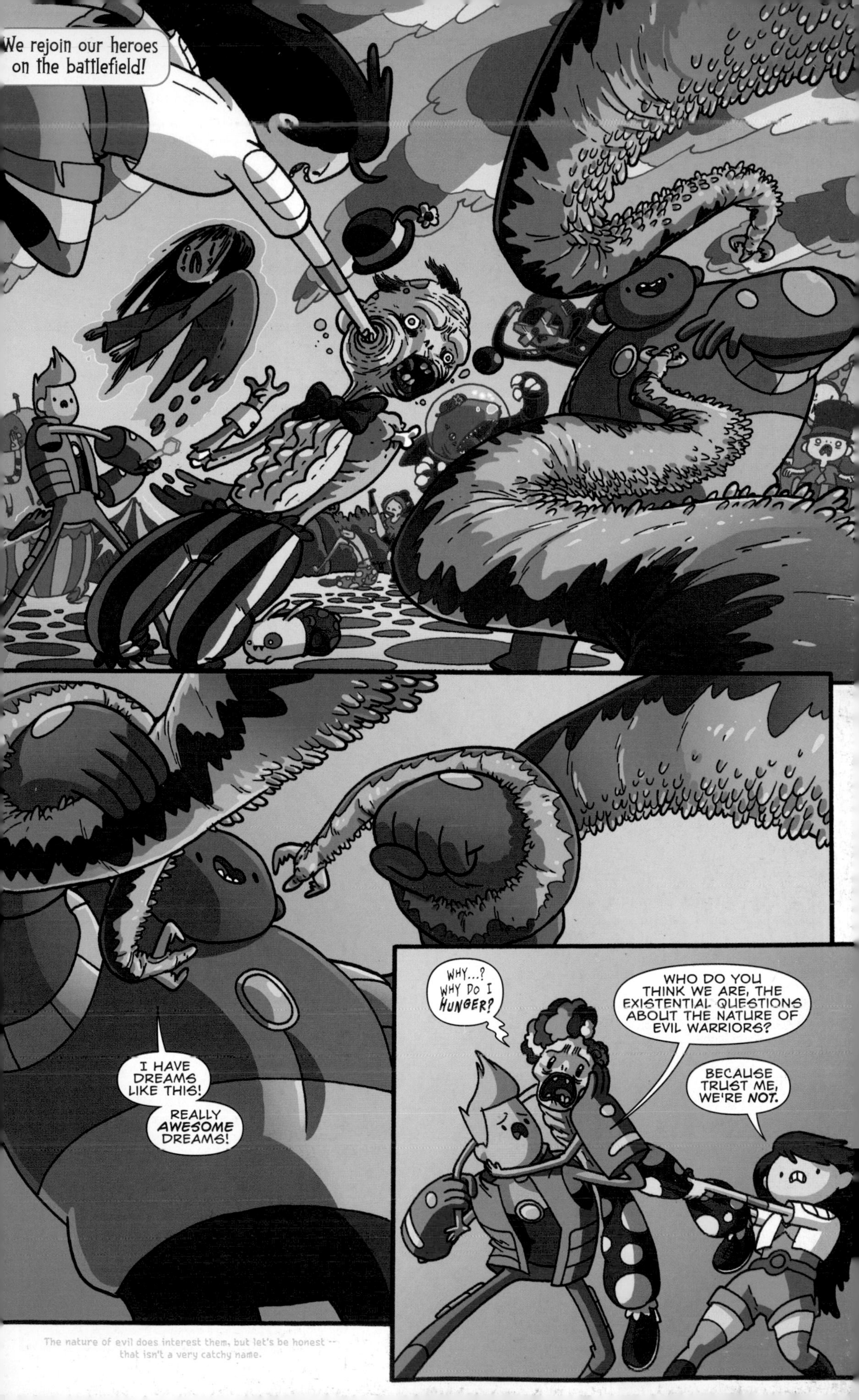
We rejoin our heroes on the battlefield!
I HAVE DREAMS LIKE THIS!
REALLY AWESOME DREAMS!
WHY...? WHY DO I HUNGER?
WHO DO YOU THINK WE ARE, THE EXISTENTIAL QUESTIONS ABOUT THE NATURE OF EVIL WARRIORS?
BECAUSE TRUST ME, WE'RE NOT.

The nature of evil does interest them, but let's be honest -- that isn't a very catchy name.

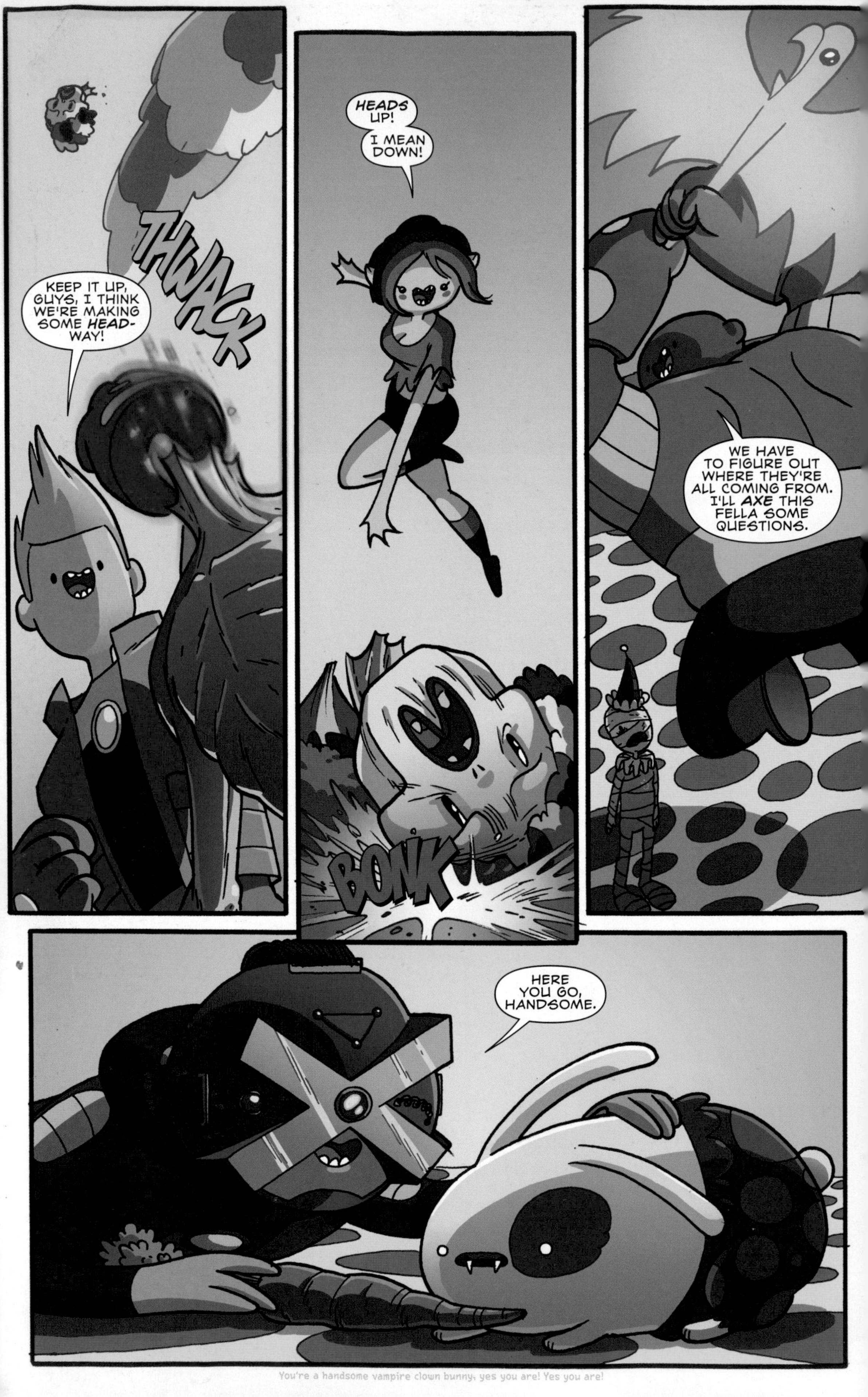
THWACK
KEEP IT UP, GUYS, I THINK WE'RE MAKING SOME HEAD-WAY!
HEADS UP!
I MEAN DOWN!
BONK
WE HAVE TO FIGURE OUT WHERE THEY'RE ALL COMING FROM. I'LL AXE THIS FELLA SOME QUESTIONS.
HERE YOU GO, HANDSOME.

You're a handsome vampire clown bunny, yes you are! Yes you are!

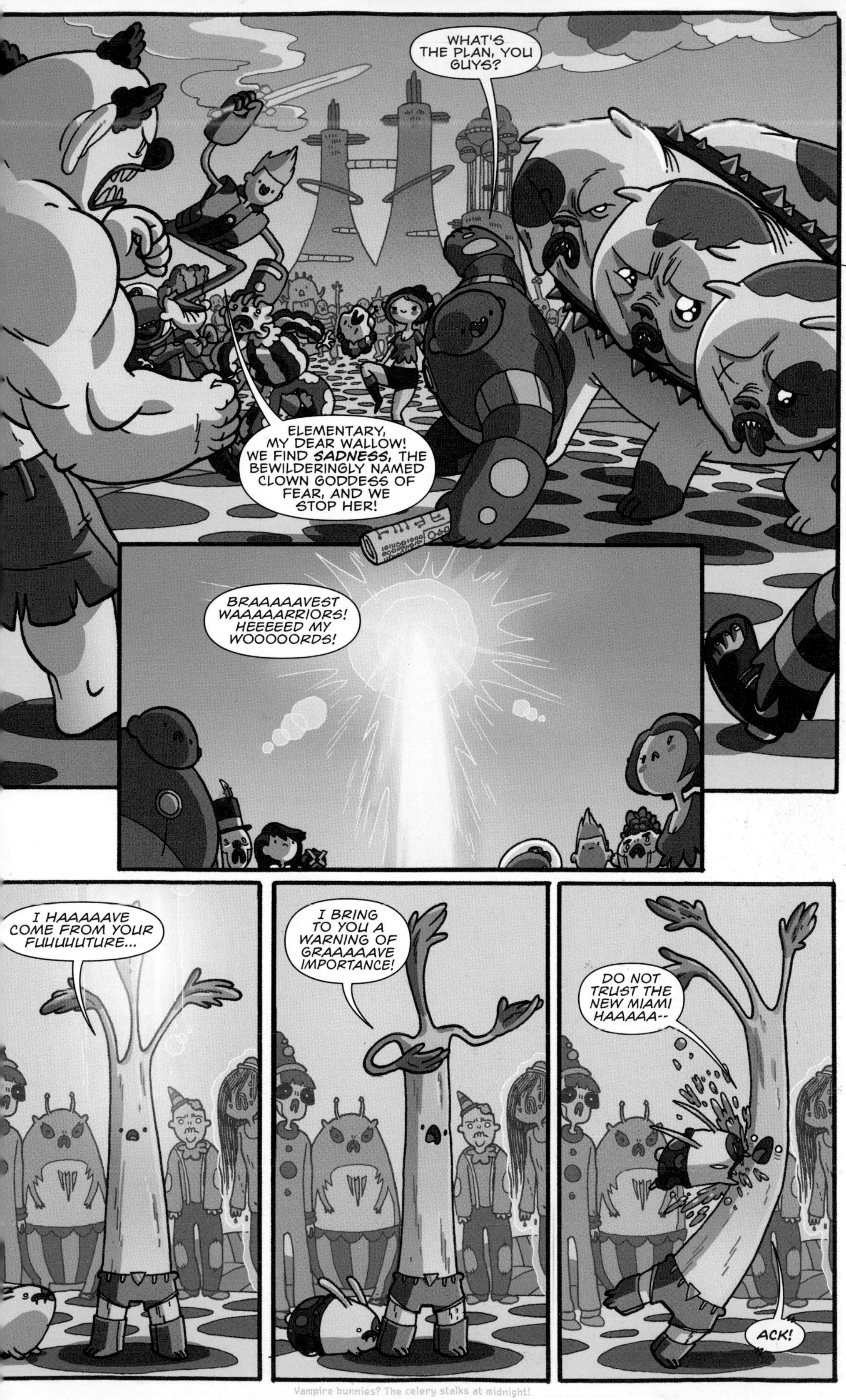
WHAT'S THE PLAN, YOU GUYS?
ELEMENTARY, MY DEAR WALLOW! WE FIND SADNESS, THE BEWILDERINGLY NAMED CLOWN GODDESS OF FEAR, AND WE STOP HER!
BRAAAAAVEST WAAAAARRIORS! HEEEEED MY WOOOOORDS!
I HAAAAAVE COME FROM YOUR FUUUUUTURE...
I BRING TO YOU A WARNING OF GRAAAAAVE IMPORTANCE!
DO NOT TRUST THE NEW MIAMI HAAAAA--
ACK!

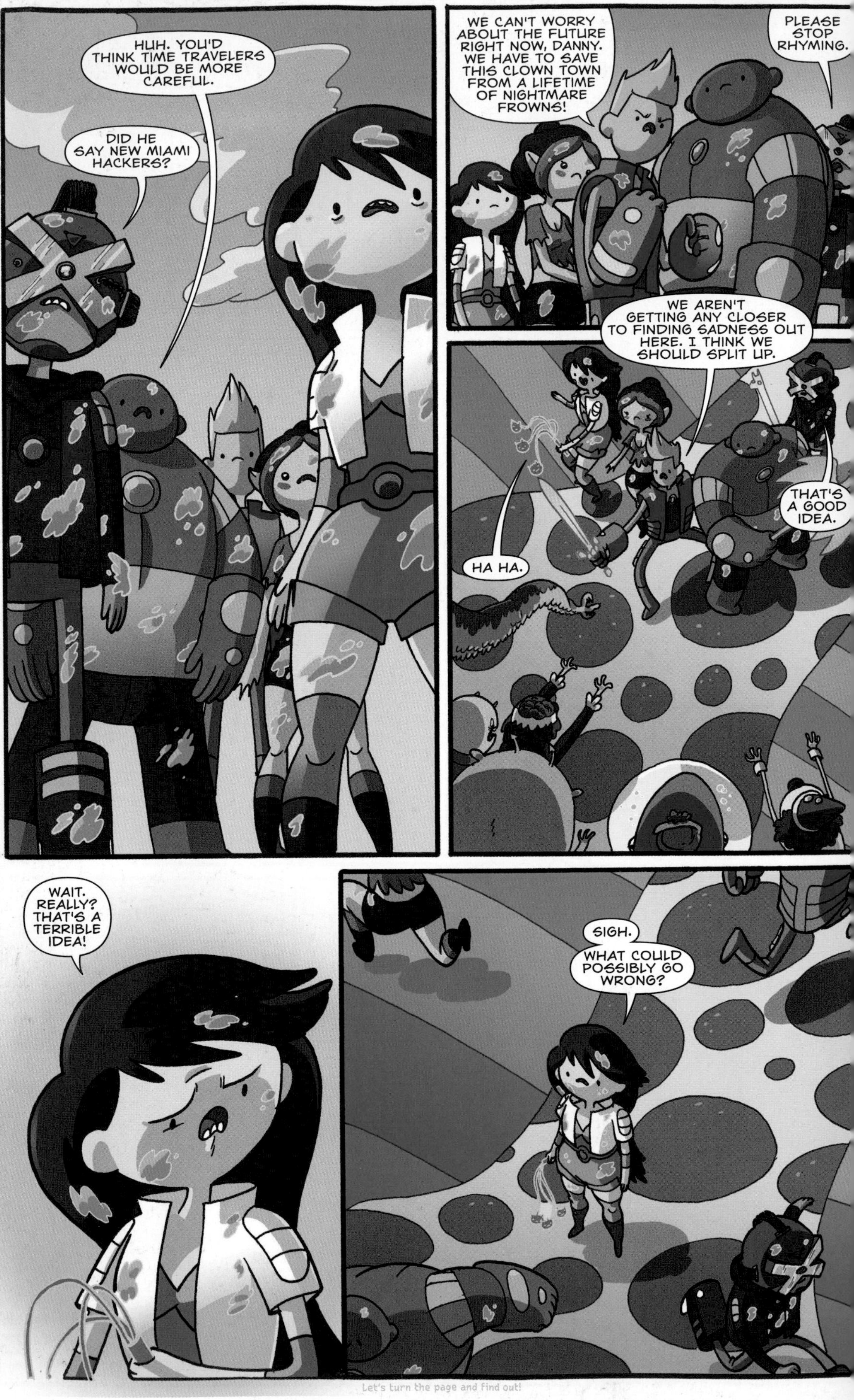
HUH. YOU'D THINK TIME TRAVELERS WOULD BE MORE CAREFUL.
DID HE SAY NEW MIAMI HACKERS?
WE CAN'T WORRY ABOUT THE FUTURE RIGHT NOW, DANNY. WE HAVE TO SAVE THIS CLOWN TOWN FROM A LIFETIME OF NIGHTMARE FROWNS!
PLEASE STOP RHYMING.
WE AREN'T GETTING ANY CLOSER TO FINDING SADNESS OUT HERE. I THINK WE SHOULD SPLIT UP.
THAT'S A GOOD IDEA.
HA HA.
WAIT. REALLY? THAT'S A TERRIBLE IDEA!
SIGH.
WHAT COULD POSSIBLY GO WRONG?

Let's turn the page and find out!

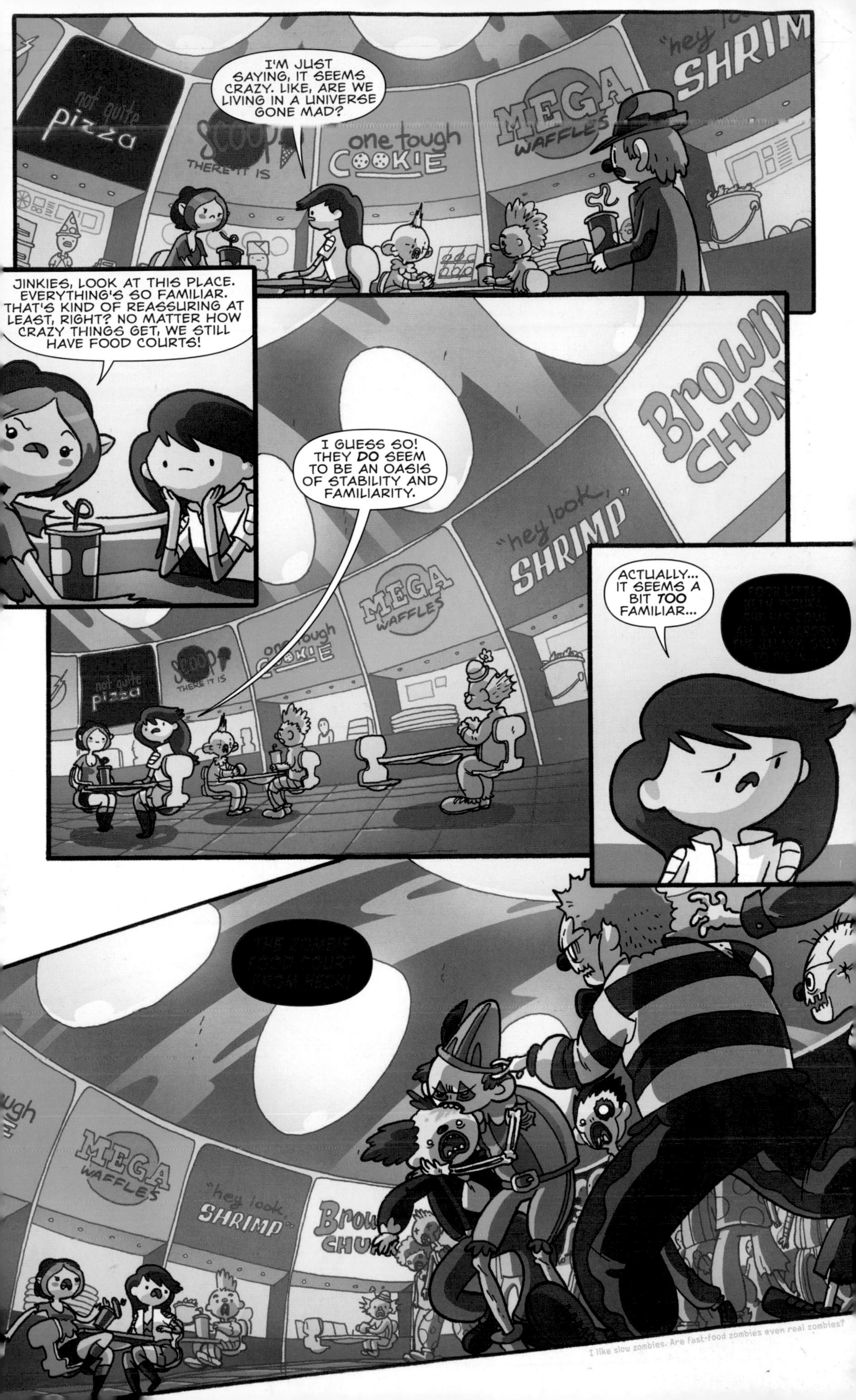
I'M JUST SAYING, IT SEEMS CRAZY. LIKE, ARE WE LIVING IN A UNIVERSE GONE MAD?
not quite pizza
SCOOP THERE IT IS
one tough COOKIE
MEGA WAFFLES
"hey look, SHRIMP"
JINKIES, LOOK AT THIS PLACE. EVERYTHING'S SO FAMILIAR. THAT'S KIND OF REASSURING AT LEAST, RIGHT? NO MATTER HOW CRAZY THINGS GET, WE STILL HAVE FOOD COURTS!
I GUESS SO! THEY DO SEEM TO BE AN OASIS OF STABILITY AND FAMILIARITY.
Brown CHUN
ACTUALLY... IT SEEMS A BIT TOO FAMILIAR...
[redacted]
[redacted]

I like slow zombies. Are fast-food zombies even real zombies?

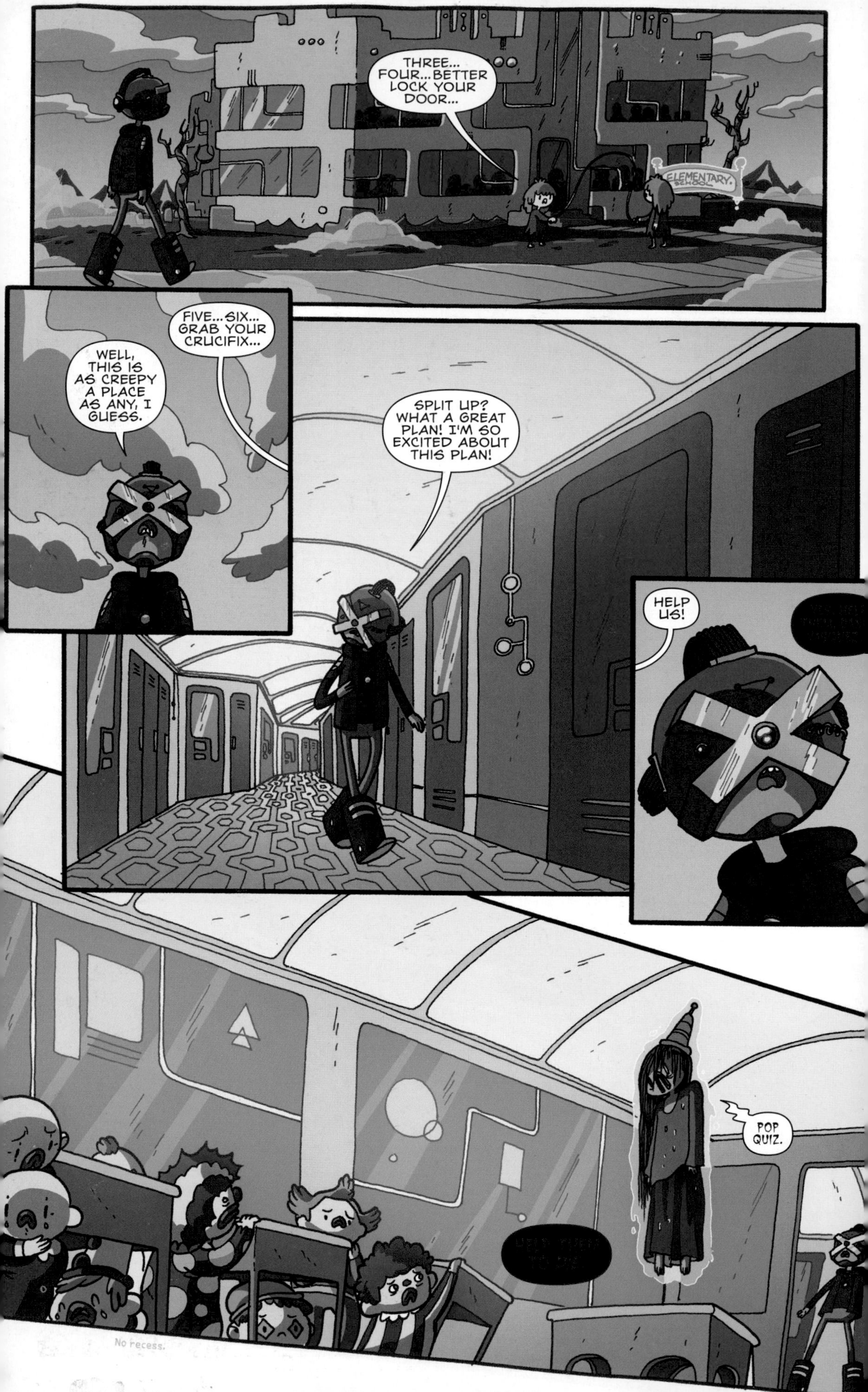
THREE... FOUR...BETTER LOCK YOUR DOOR...
FIVE...SIX... GRAB YOUR CRUCIFIX...
WELL, THIS IS AS CREEPY A PLACE AS ANY, I GUESS.
SPLIT UP? WHAT A GREAT PLAN! I'M SO EXCITED ABOUT THIS PLAN!
HELP US!
ELEMENTARY SCHOOL
POP QUIZ.
No recess.

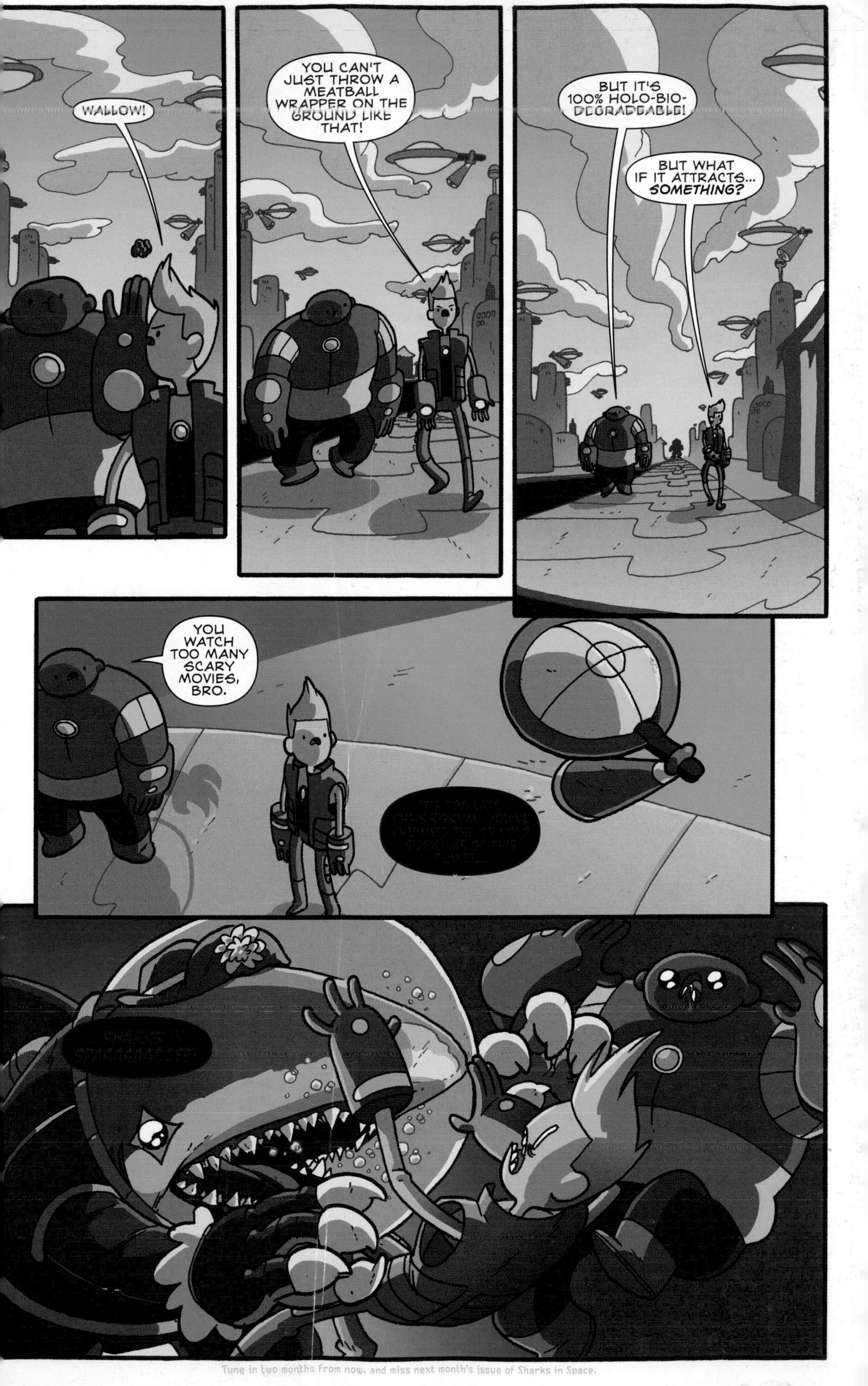
WALLOW!
YOU CAN'T JUST THROW A MEATBALL WRAPPER ON THE GROUND LIKE THAT!
BUT IT'S 100% HOLO-BIO-DEGRADABLE!
BUT WHAT IF IT ATTRACTS... SOMETHING?
YOU WATCH TOO MANY SCARY MOVIES, BRO.

Tune in two months from now, and miss next month's issue of Sharks in Space.

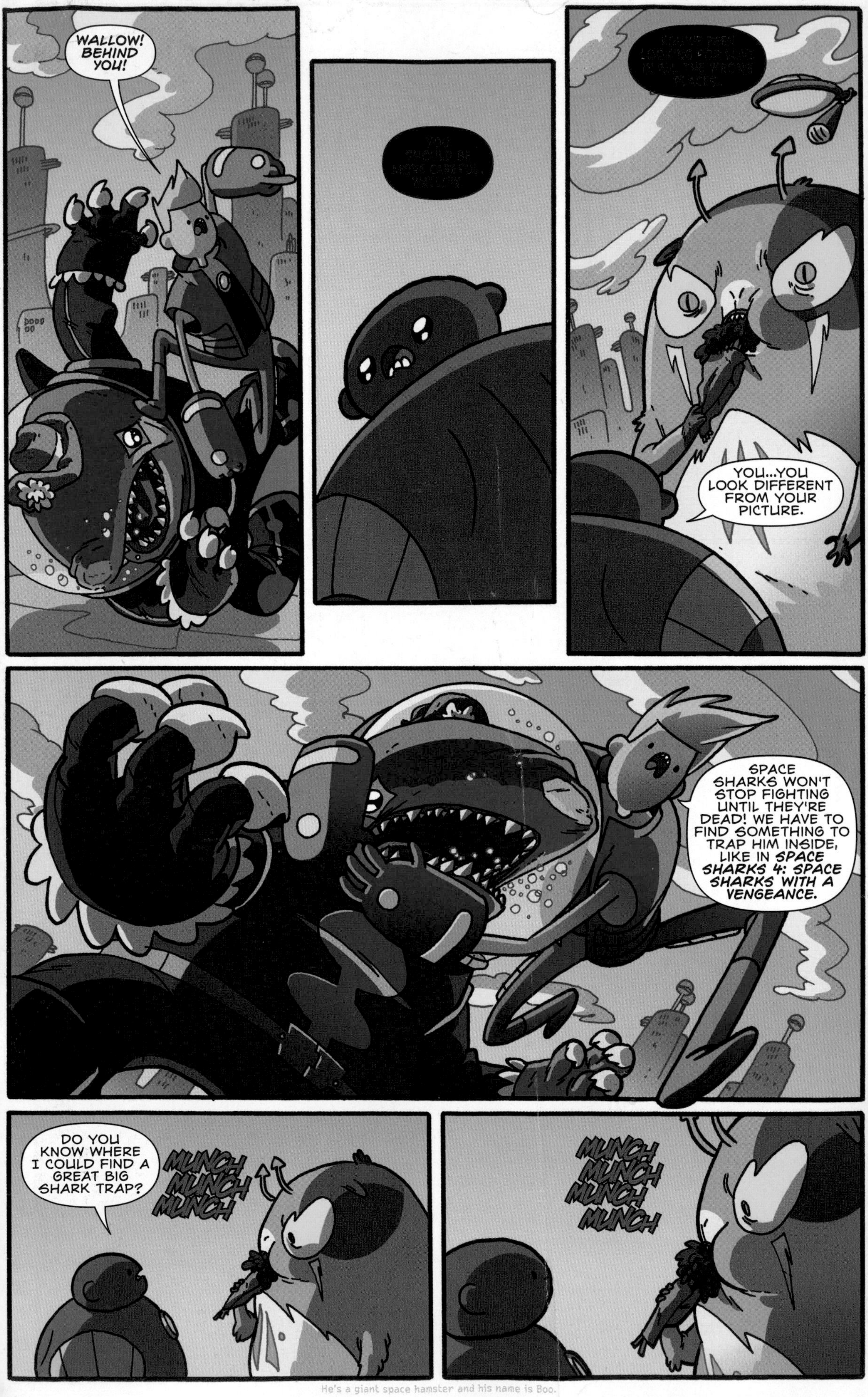
WALLOW! BEHIND YOU!
YOU SHOULD BE MORE CAREFUL, WALLOW!
YOU'VE BEEN LOOKING FOR IN ALL THE WRONG PLACES.
YOU...YOU LOOK DIFFERENT FROM YOUR PICTURE.
SPACE SHARKS WON'T STOP FIGHTING UNTIL THEY'RE DEAD! WE HAVE TO FIND SOMETHING TO TRAP HIM INSIDE, LIKE IN *SPACE SHARKS 4: SPACE SHARKS WITH A VENGEANCE.*
DO YOU KNOW WHERE I COULD FIND A GREAT BIG SHARK TRAP?
MUNCH MUNCH MUNCH
MUNCH MUNCH MUNCH MUNCH

He's a giant space hamster and his name is Boo.

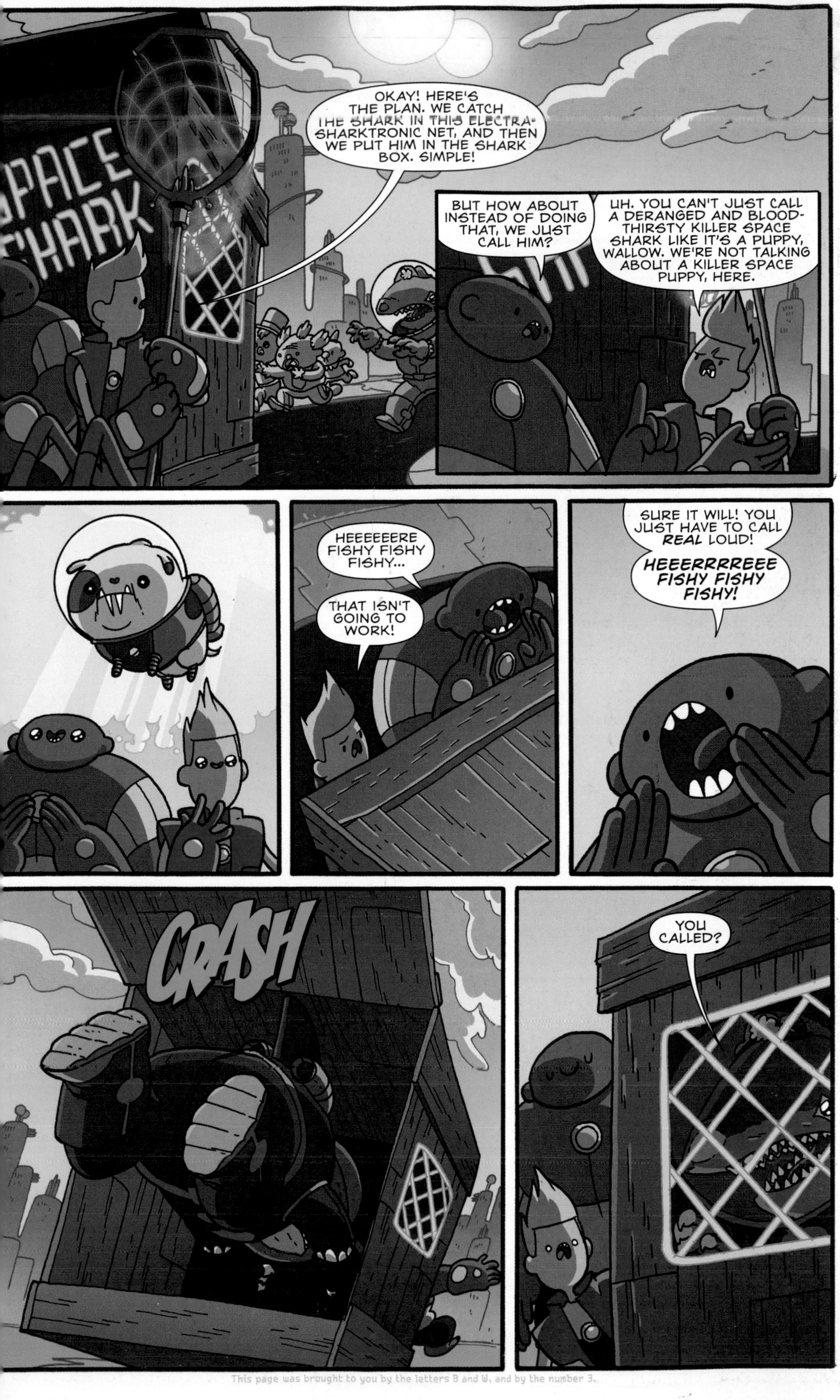
SPACE SHARK
OKAY! HERE'S THE PLAN. WE CATCH THE SHARK IN THIS ELECTRA-SHARKTRONIC NET, AND THEN WE PUT HIM IN THE SHARK BOX. SIMPLE!
BUT HOW ABOUT INSTEAD OF DOING THAT, WE JUST CALL HIM?
UH. YOU CAN'T JUST CALL A DERANGED AND BLOOD-THIRSTY KILLER SPACE SHARK LIKE IT'S A PUPPY, WALLOW. WE'RE NOT TALKING ABOUT A KILLER SPACE PUPPY, HERE.
HEEEEEERE FISHY FISHY FISHY...
THAT ISN'T GOING TO WORK!
SURE IT WILL! YOU JUST HAVE TO CALL *REAL* LOUD!
HEEERRRREEE FISHY FISHY FISHY!
CRASH
YOU CALLED?

This page was brought to you by the letters B and W, and by the number 3.

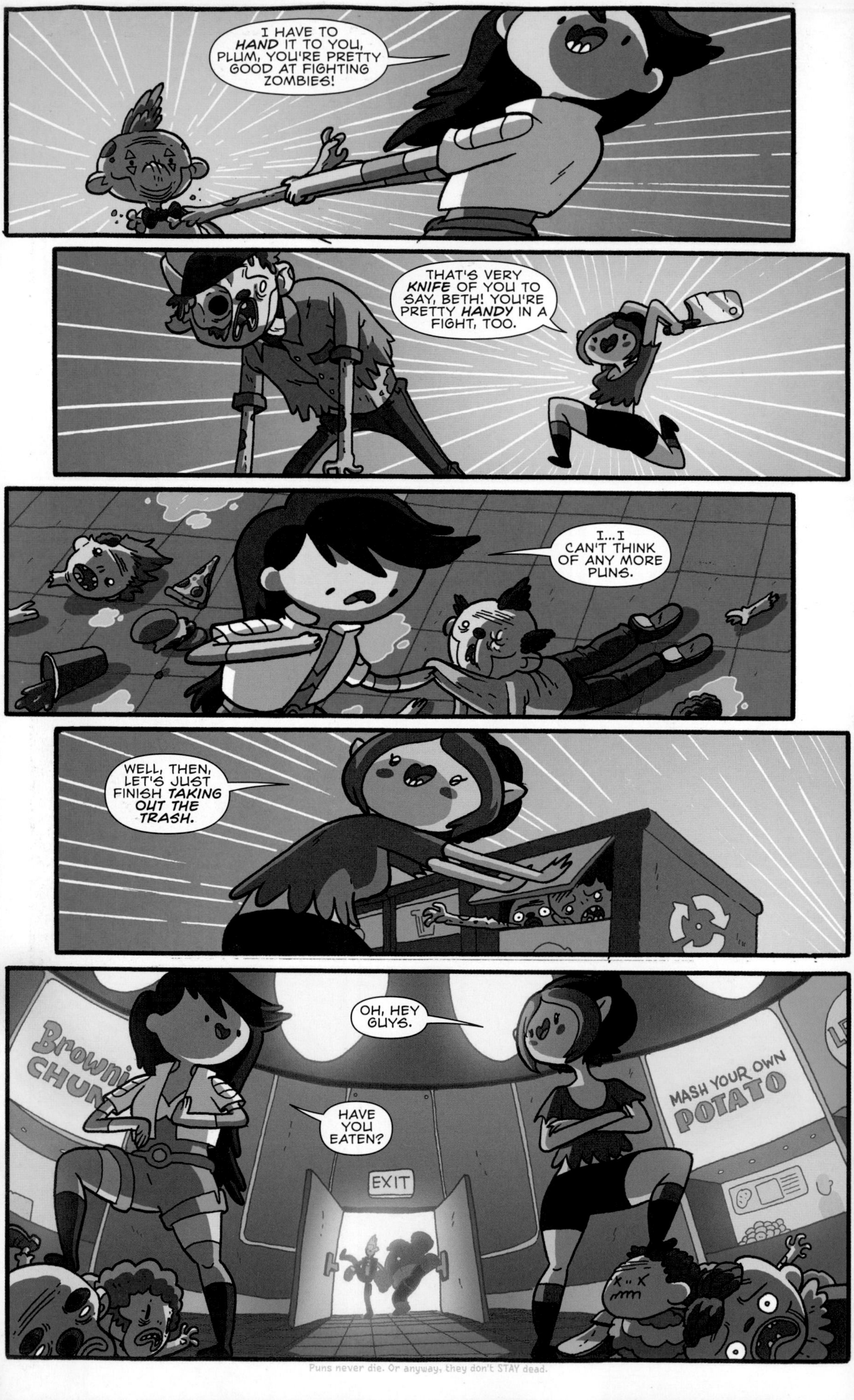
I HAVE TO HAND IT TO YOU, PLUM, YOU'RE PRETTY GOOD AT FIGHTING ZOMBIES!
THAT'S VERY KNIFE OF YOU TO SAY, BETH! YOU'RE PRETTY HANDY IN A FIGHT, TOO.
I...I CAN'T THINK OF ANY MORE PUNS.
WELL, THEN, LET'S JUST FINISH TAKING OUT THE TRASH.
Browni
CHUN
OH, HEY GUYS.
MASH YOUR OWN POTATO
HAVE YOU EATEN?
EXIT

Puns never die. Or anyway, they don't STAY dead.

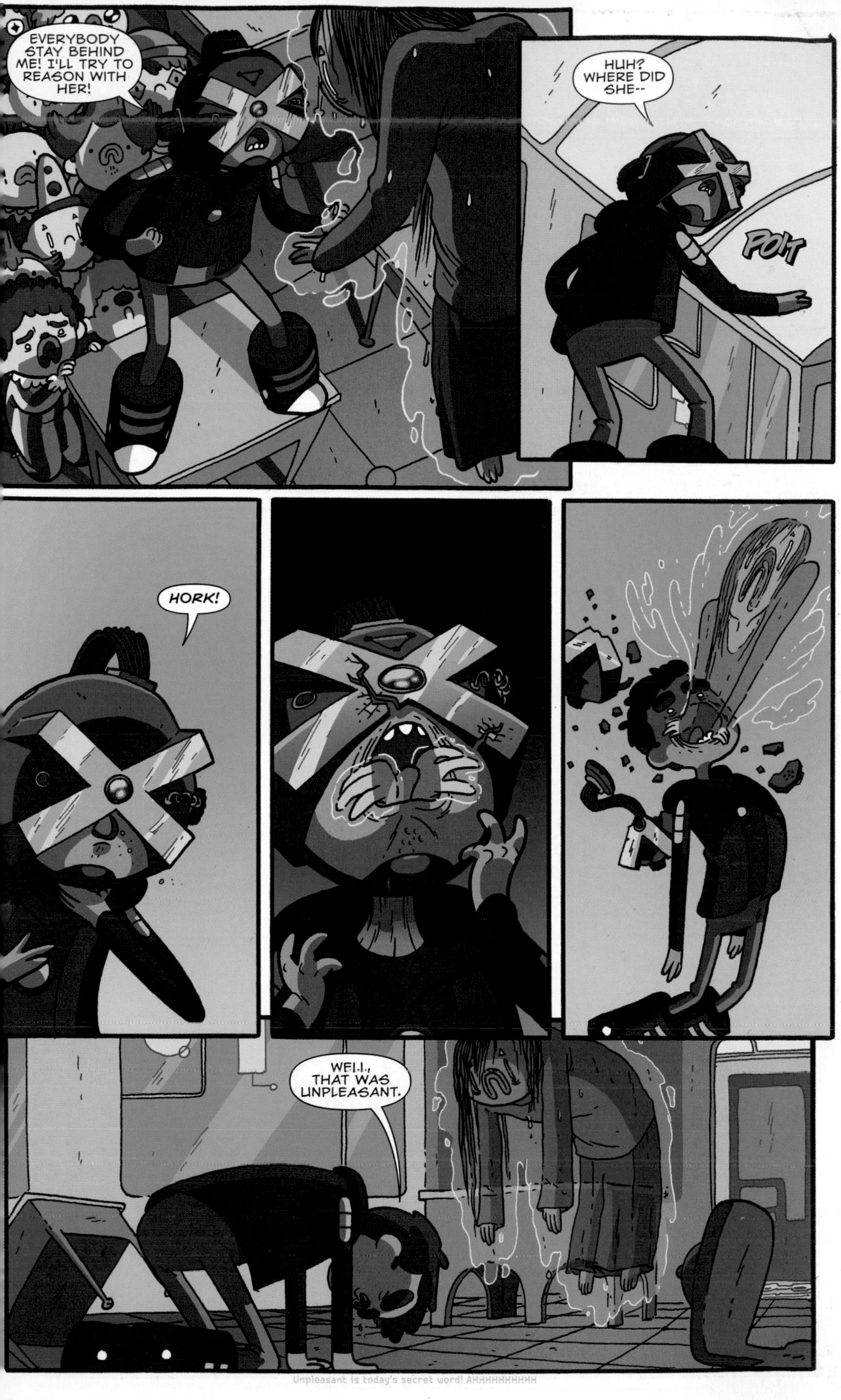

EVERYBODY STAY BEHIND ME! I'LL TRY TO REASON WITH HER!
HUH? WHERE DID SHE--
POIT
HORK!
WELL, THAT WAS UNPLEASANT.

Unpleasant is today's secret word! AHHHHHHHHHH

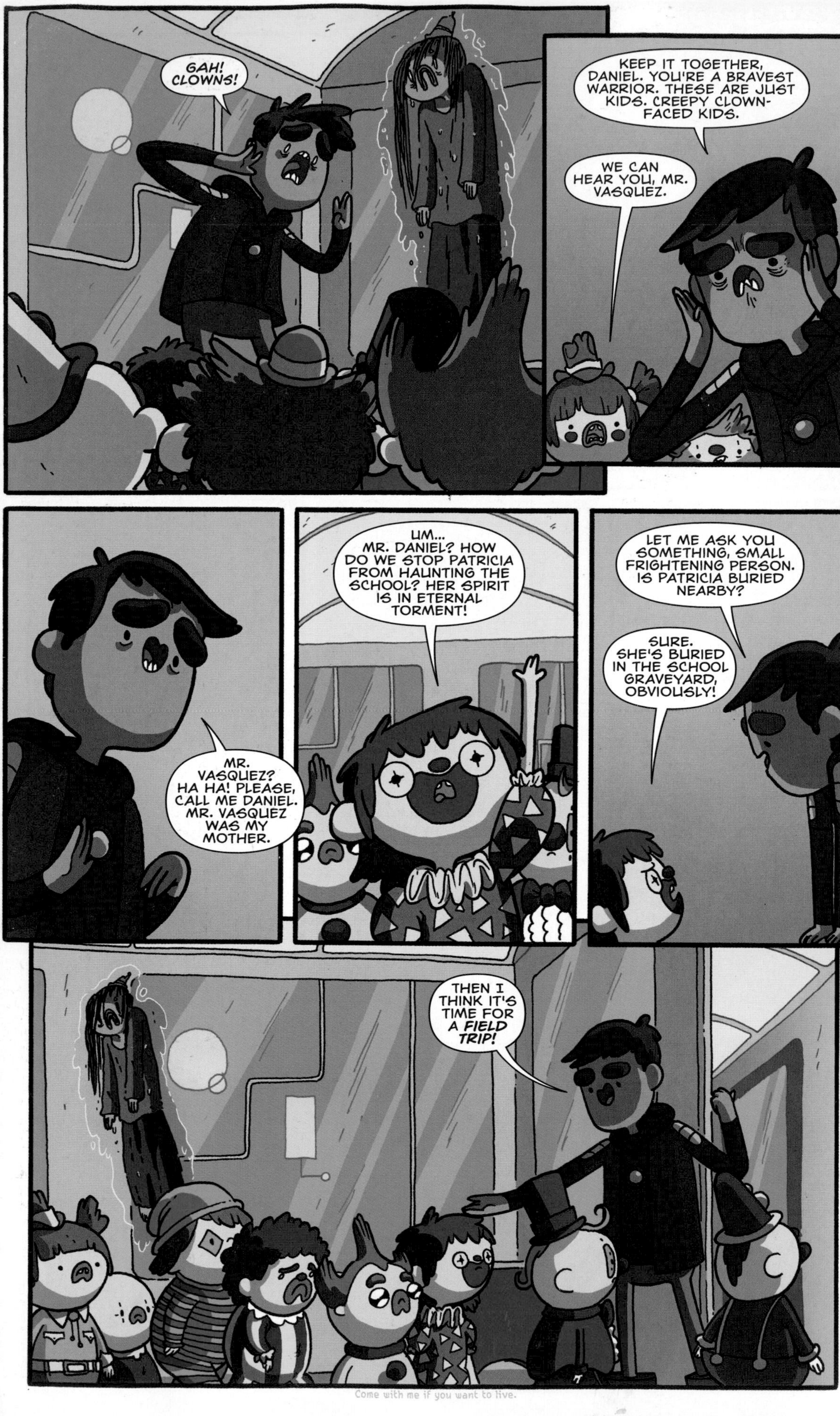
GAH! CLOWNS!
KEEP IT TOGETHER, DANIEL. YOU'RE A BRAVEST WARRIOR. THESE ARE JUST KIDS. CREEPY CLOWN-FACED KIDS.
WE CAN HEAR YOU, MR. VASQUEZ.
MR. VASQUEZ? HA HA! PLEASE, CALL ME DANIEL. MR. VASQUEZ WAS MY MOTHER.
UM... MR. DANIEL? HOW DO WE STOP PATRICIA FROM HAUNTING THE SCHOOL? HER SPIRIT IS IN ETERNAL TORMENT!
LET ME ASK YOU SOMETHING, SMALL FRIGHTENING PERSON. IS PATRICIA BURIED NEARBY?
SURE. SHE'S BURIED IN THE SCHOOL GRAVEYARD, OBVIOUSLY!
THEN I THINK IT'S TIME FOR A *FIELD TRIP!*

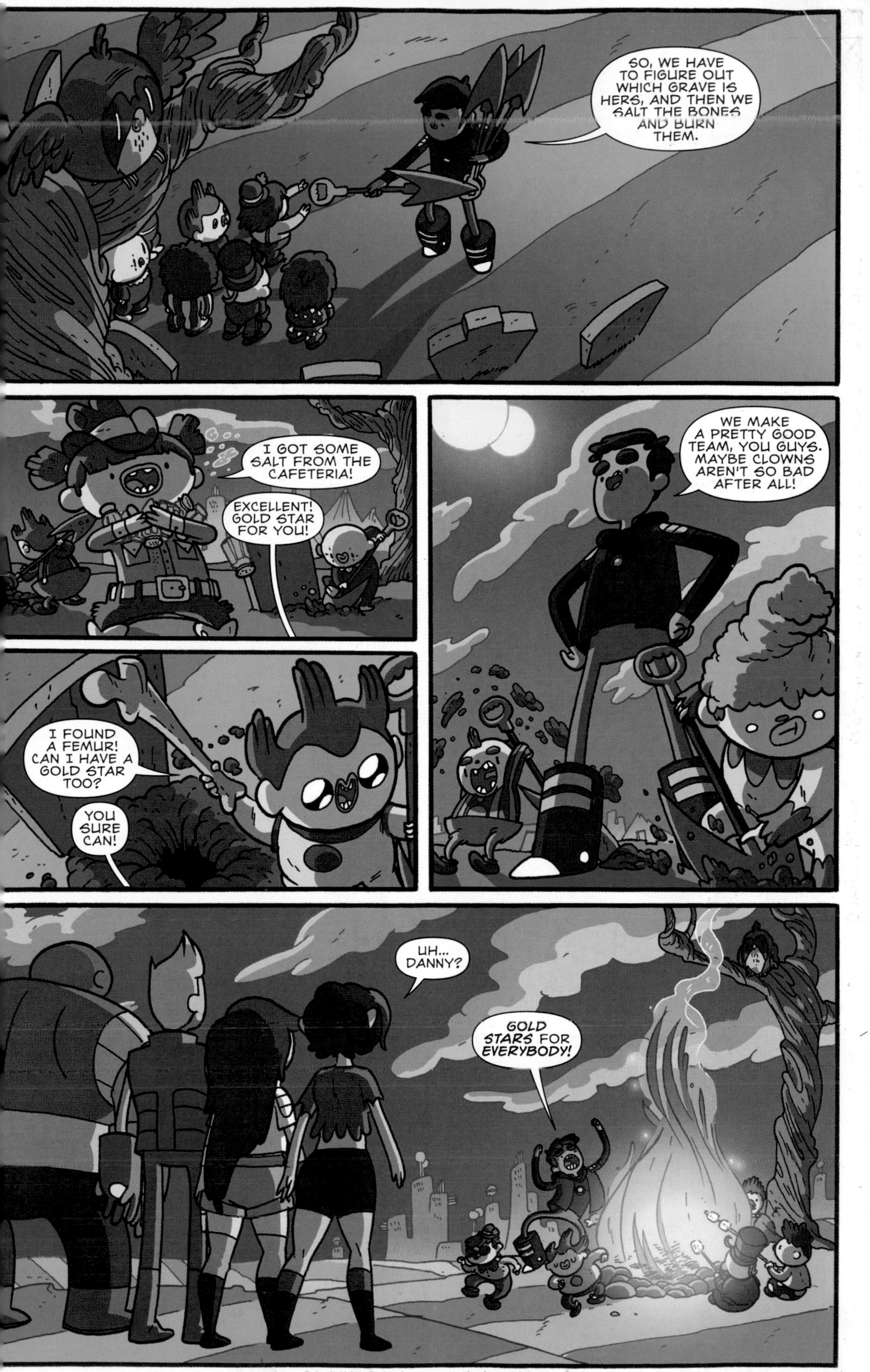
SO, WE HAVE TO FIGURE OUT WHICH GRAVE IS HERS, AND THEN WE SALT THE BONES AND BURN THEM.
I GOT SOME SALT FROM THE CAFETERIA!
EXCELLENT! GOLD STAR FOR YOU!
WE MAKE A PRETTY GOOD TEAM, YOU GUYS. MAYBE CLOWNS AREN'T SO BAD AFTER ALL!
I FOUND A FEMUR! CAN I HAVE A GOLD STAR TOO?
YOU SURE CAN!
UH... DANNY?
GOLD STARS FOR EVERYBODY!

I don't think Danny is a very good role model.

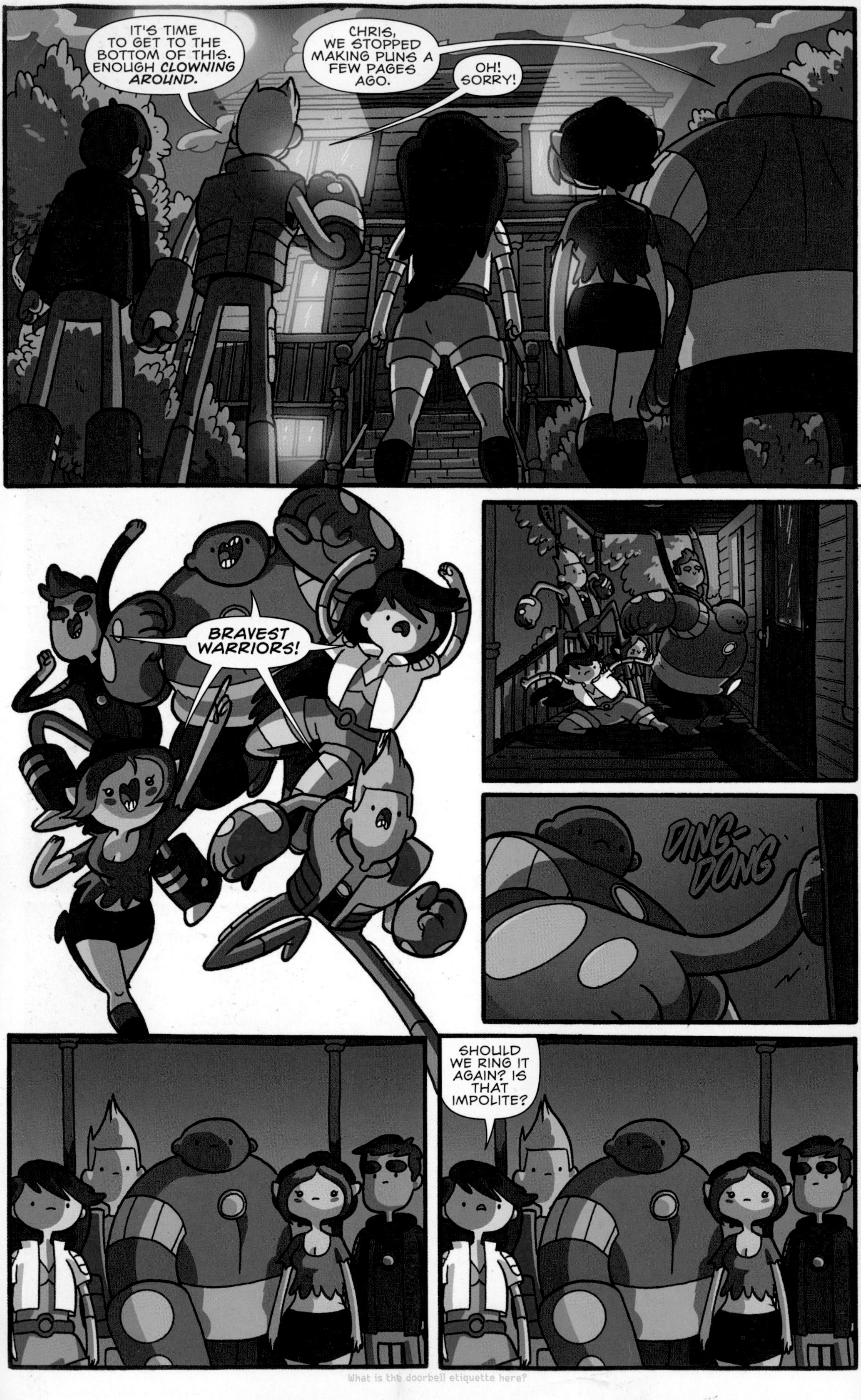
IT'S TIME TO GET TO THE BOTTOM OF THIS. ENOUGH **CLOWNING AROUND.**
CHRIS, WE STOPPED MAKING PUNS A FEW PAGES AGO.
OH! SORRY!
BRAVEST WARRIORS!
DING-DONG
SHOULD WE RING IT AGAIN? IS THAT IMPOLITE?

What is the doorbell etiquette here?

UH, WE'RE THE BRAVEST WARRIORS, MA'AM. WE'RE LOOKING FOR...
IS...IS SHE BONKING HERSELF ON THE HEAD IN THERE?
I THOUGHT THAT WAS OUR JOB!
HEY. ARE YOU OKAY IN THERE?
HEY! STOP BONKING YOUR HEAD OR WE'LL COME IN THERE AND BONK IT FOR YOU.

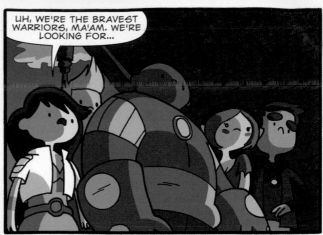

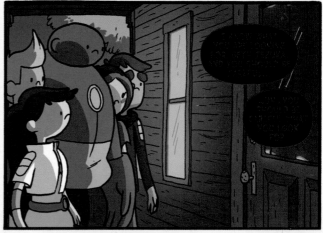

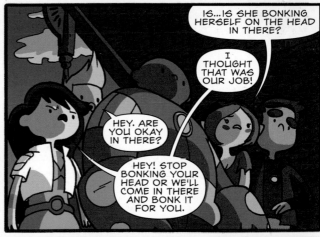

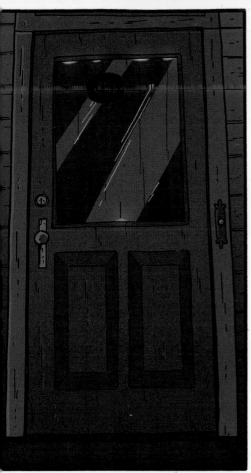

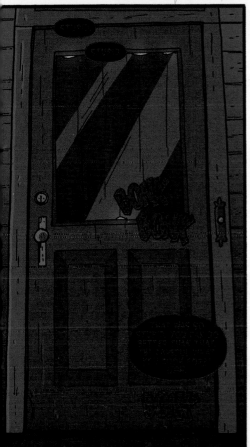

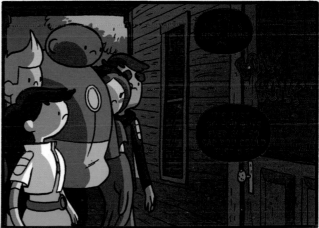

BETH IS NOT THE BEST NEGOTIATOR.

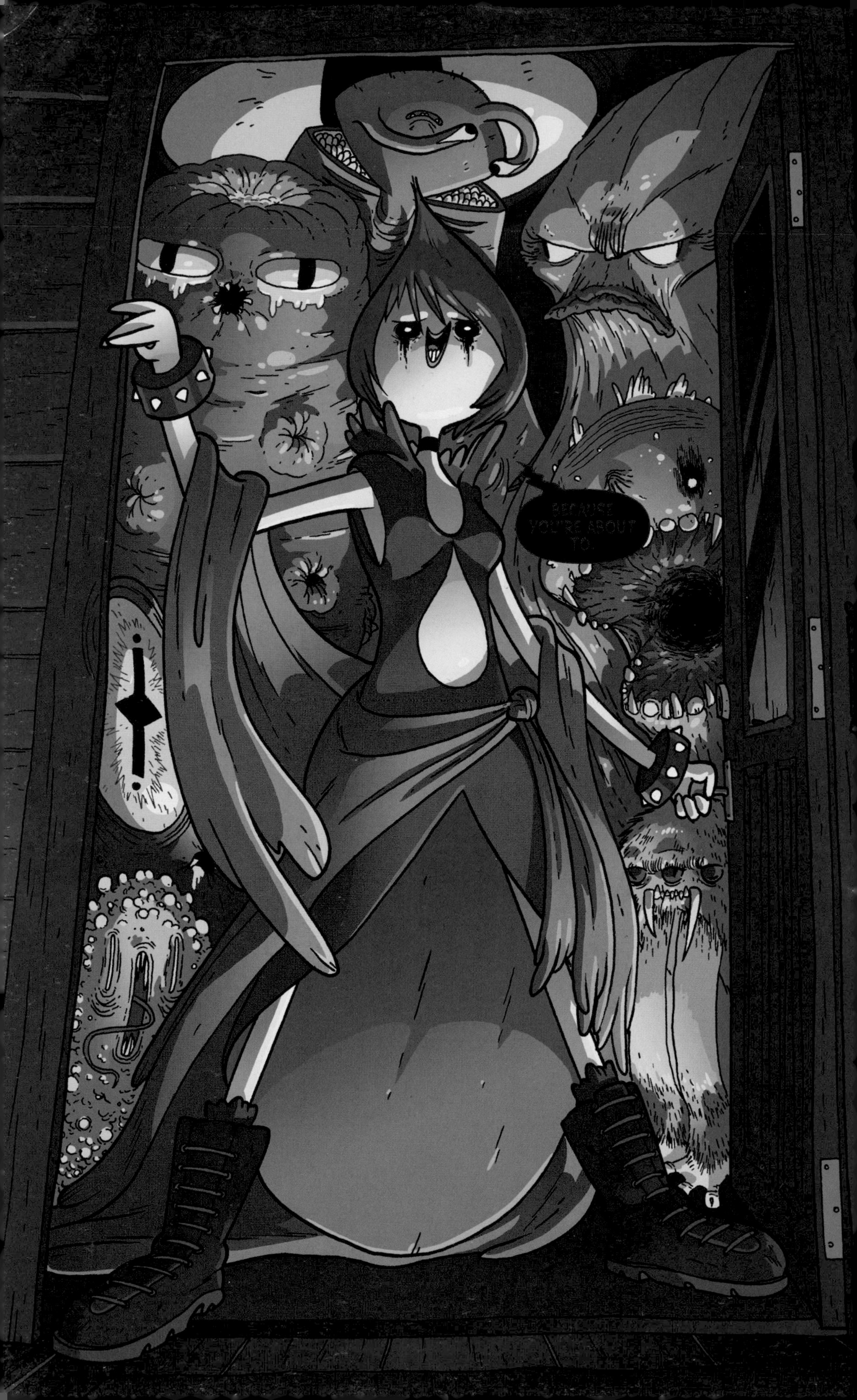
BECAUSE YOU'RE ABOUT TO.

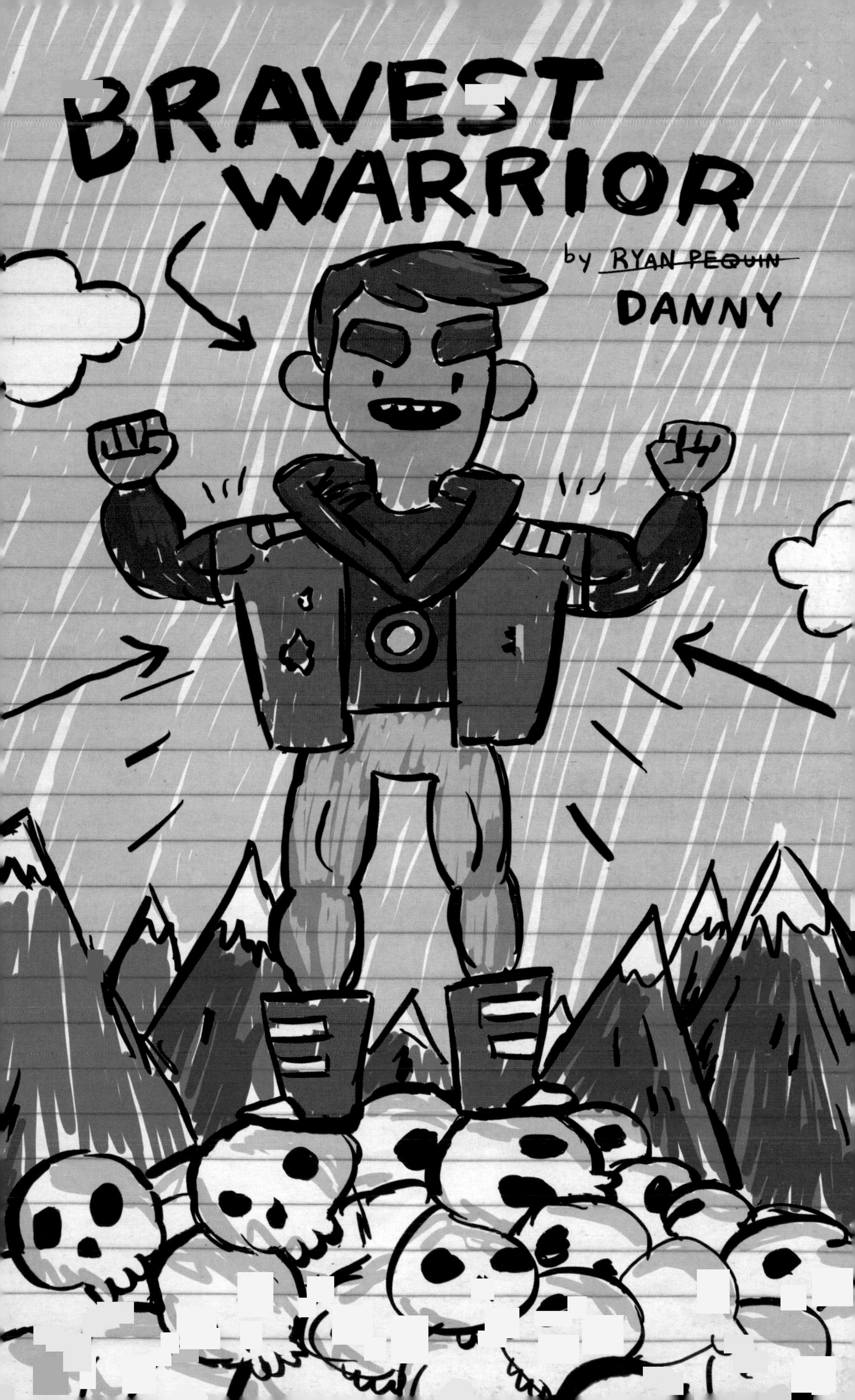
BRAVEST WARRIOR
by ~~RYAN PEQUIN~~
DANNY

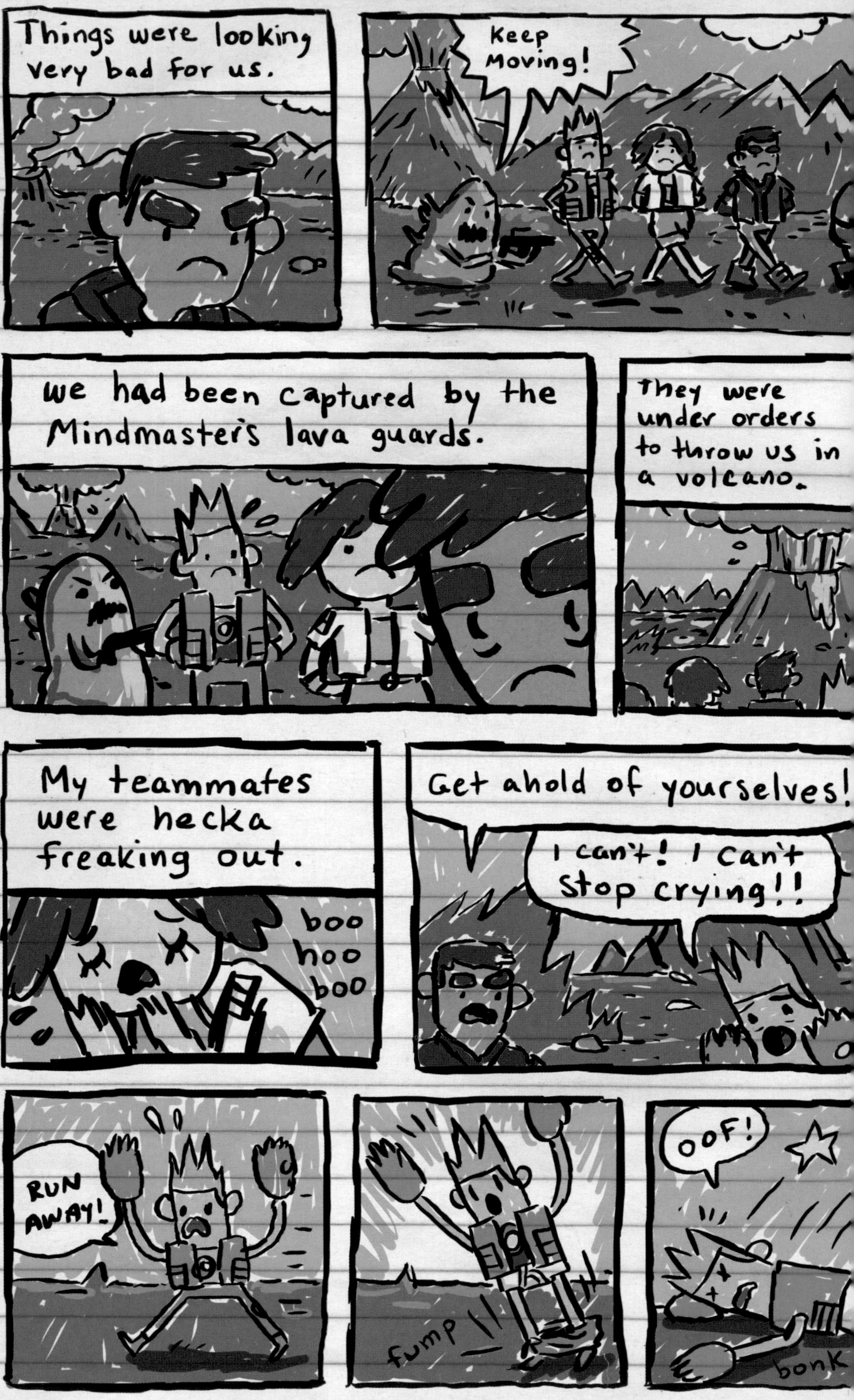
Things were looking very bad for us.
Keep Moving!
we had been captured by the Mindmaster's lava guards.
They were under orders to throw us in a volcano.
My teammates were hecka freaking out.
boo hoo boo
Get ahold of yourselves!
I can't! I can't stop crying!!
RUN AWAY!
fump
OOF!
bonk

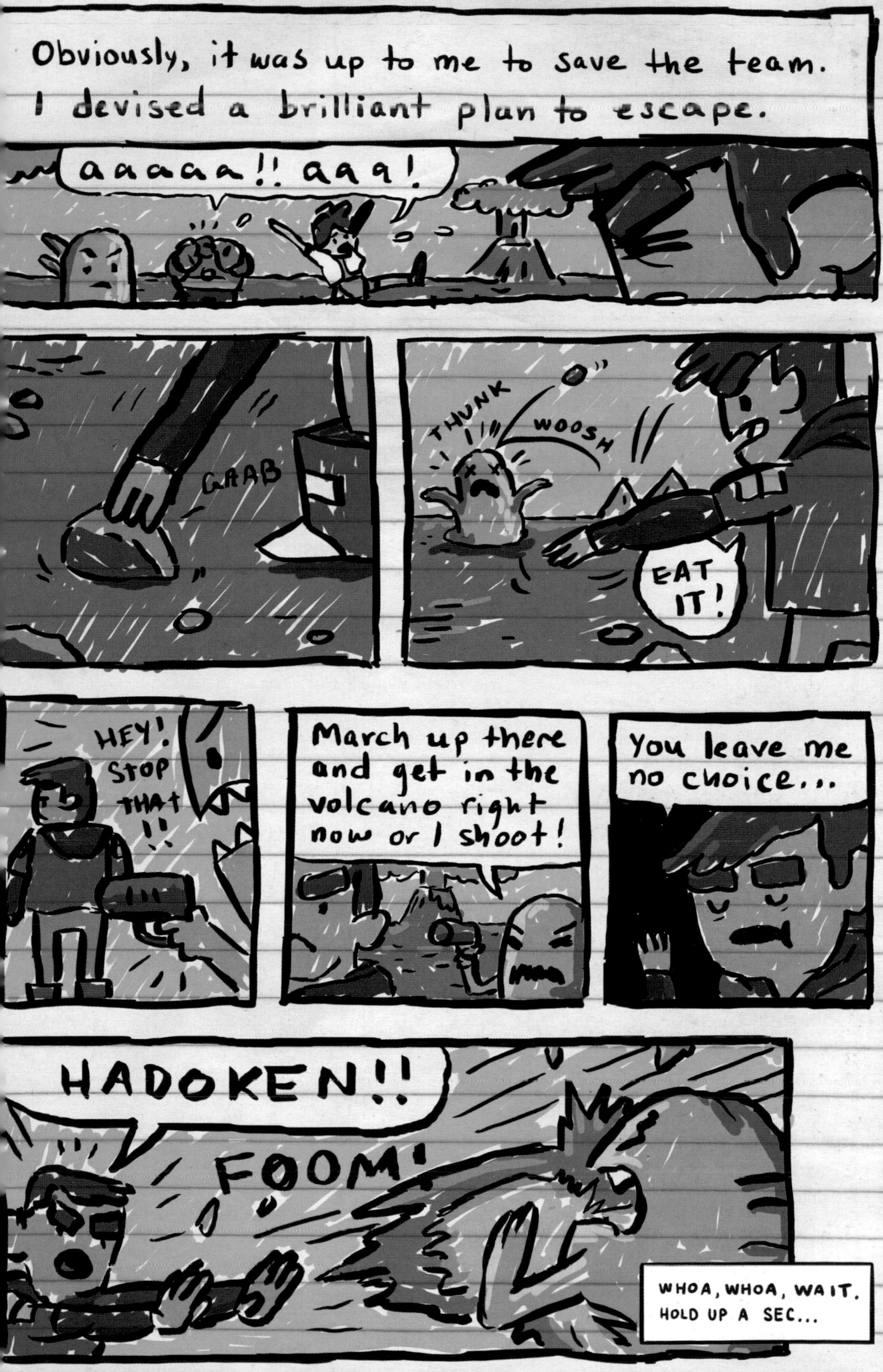
Obviously, it was up to me to save the team. I devised a brilliant plan to escape.
aaaaa!! aaa!
GRAB
THUNK
WOOSH
EAT IT!
HEY! STOP THAT!!
March up there and get in the volcano right now or I shoot!
You leave me no choice...
HADOKEN!!
FOOM!
WHOA, WHOA, WAIT. HOLD UP A SEC...

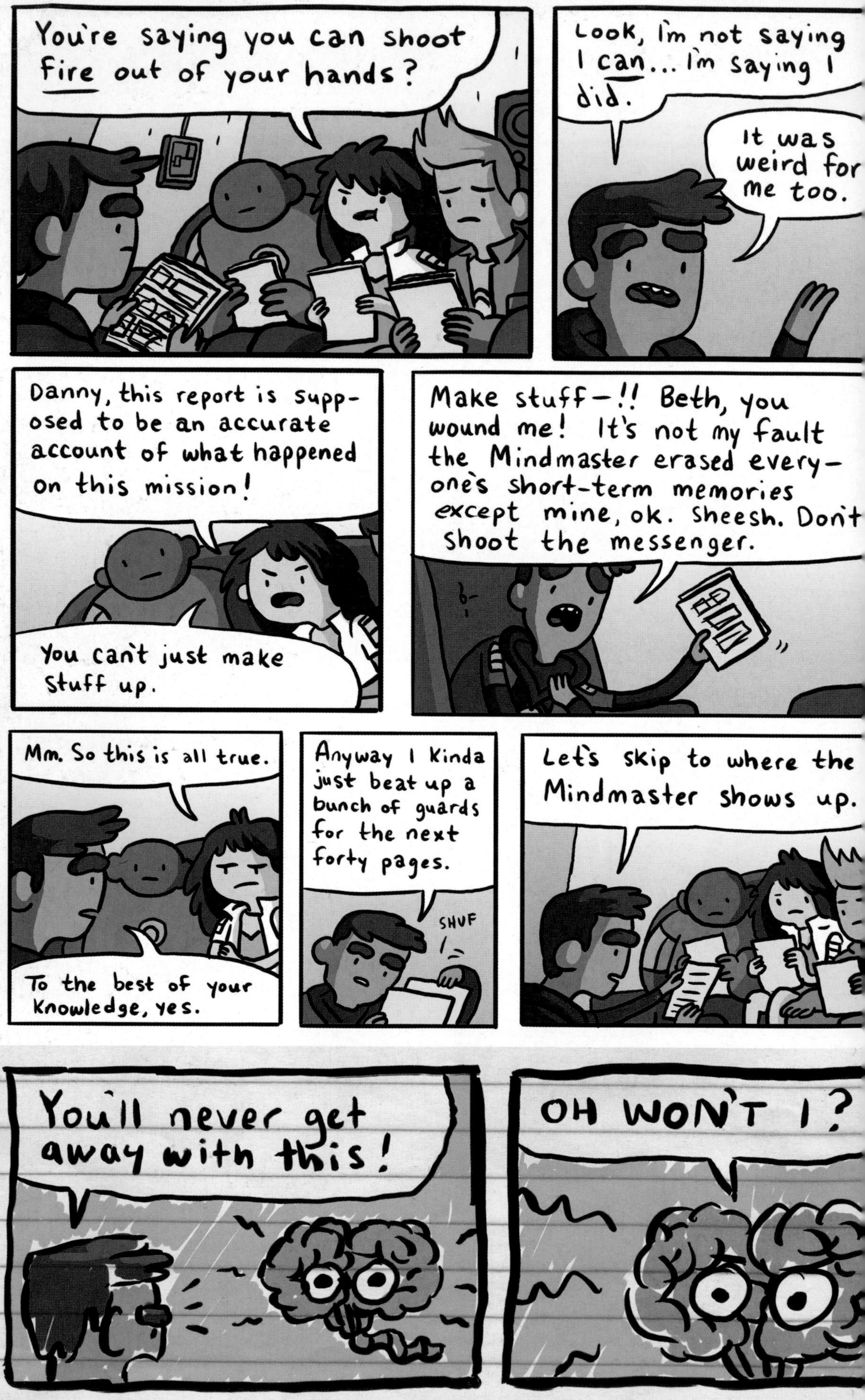
You're saying you can shoot fire out of your hands?
Look, I'm not saying I can... I'm saying I did.
It was weird for me too.
Danny, this report is supposed to be an accurate account of what happened on this mission!
You can't just make stuff up.
Make stuff-!! Beth, you wound me! It's not my fault the Mindmaster erased everyone's short-term memories except mine, ok. Sheesh. Don't shoot the messenger.
Mm. So this is all true.
To the best of your knowledge, yes.
Anyway I kinda just beat up a bunch of guards for the next forty pages.
SHUF
Let's skip to where the Mindmaster shows up.
You'll never get away with this!
OH WON'T I?

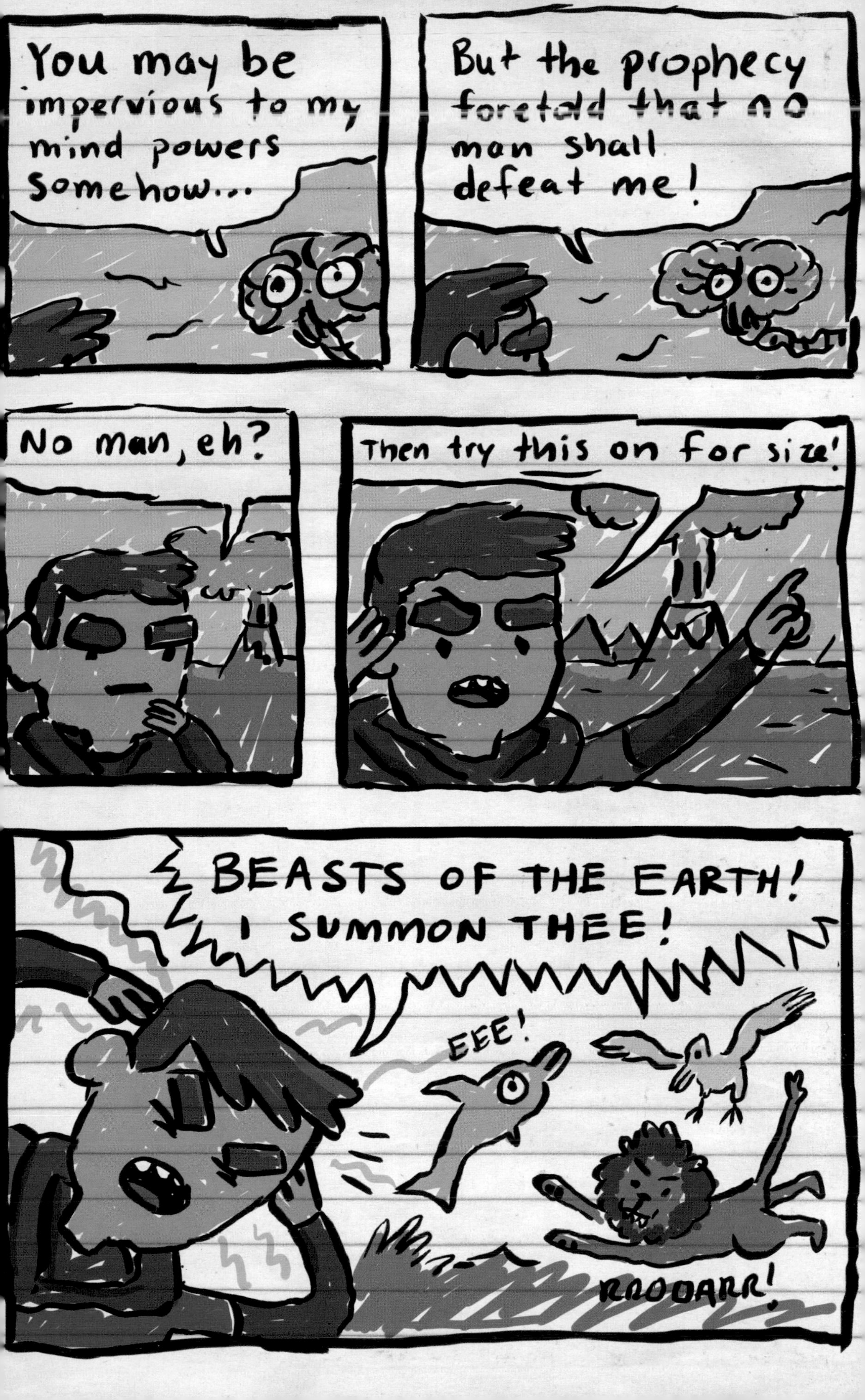
You may be impervious to my mind powers somehow...
But the prophecy foretold that no man shall defeat me!
No man, eh?
Then try this on for size!
BEASTS OF THE EARTH! I SUMMON THEE!
EEE!
RRООARR!

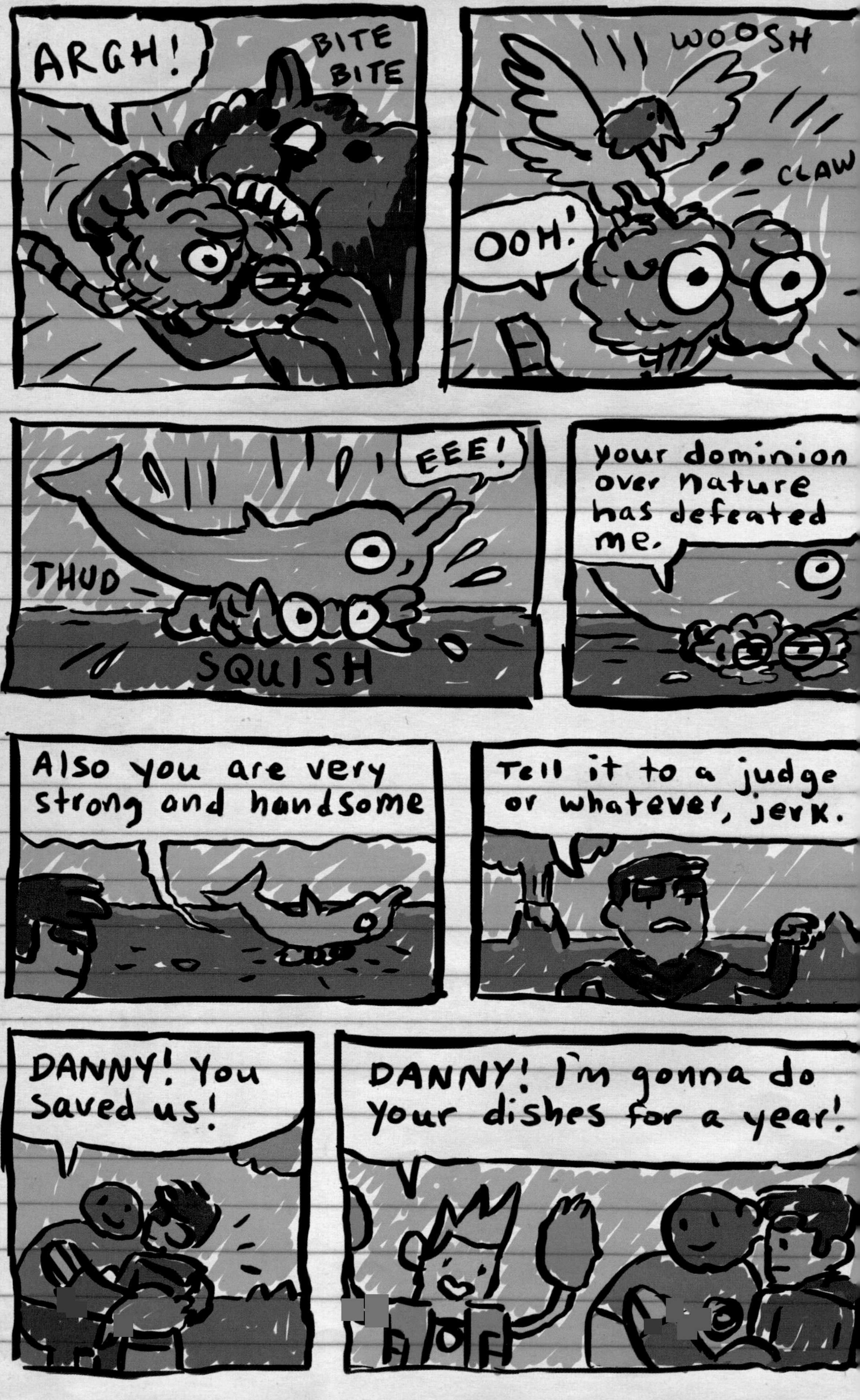
ARGH!
BITE BITE
WOOSH
CLAW
OOH!
EEE!
THUD
SQUISH
your dominion over nature has defeated me.
Also you are very strong and handsome
Tell it to a judge or whatever, jerk.
DANNY! You saved us!
DANNY! I'm gonna do your dishes for a year!

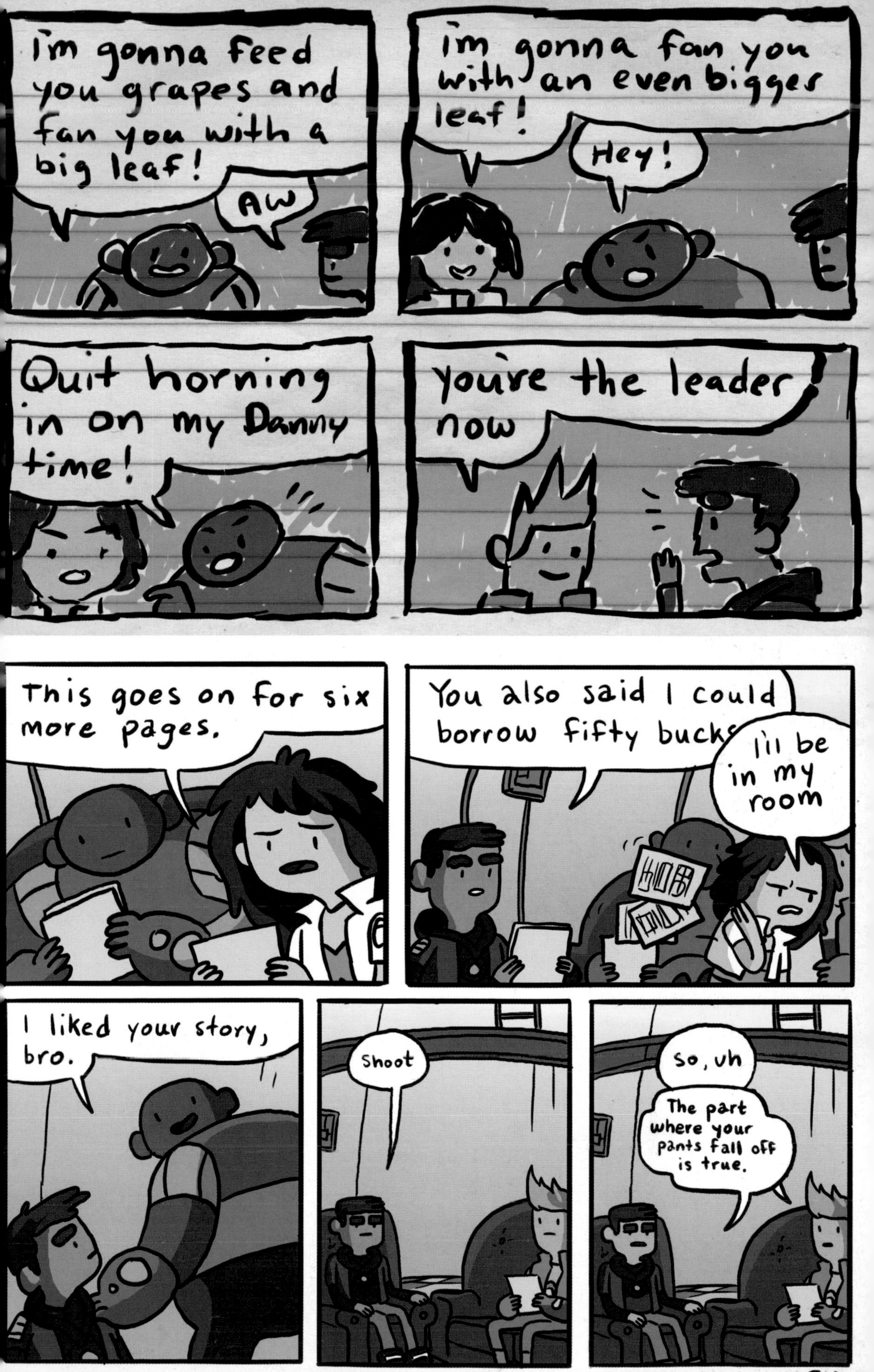
i'm gonna feed you grapes and fan you with a big leaf!
AW
i'm gonna fan you with an even bigger leaf!
Hey!
Quit horning in on my Danny time!
you're the leader now
This goes on for six more pages.
You also said I could borrow fifty bucks
I'll be in my room
I liked your story, bro.
Shoot
so, uh
The part where your pants fall off is true.
FIN

CHAPTER
FOUR

CONTINUE?

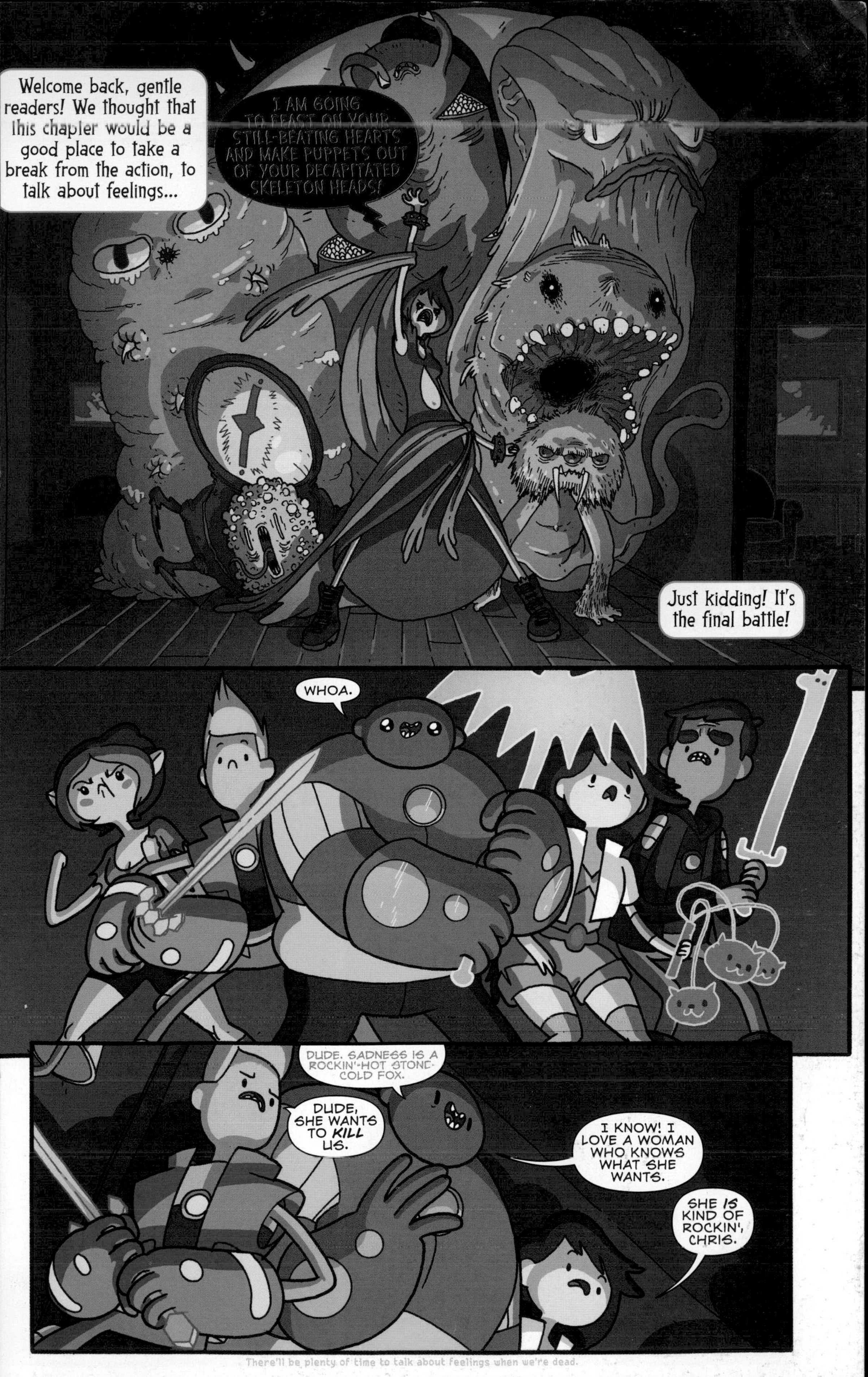

Welcome back, gentle readers! We thought that this chapter would be a good place to take a break from the action, to talk about feelings...
I AM GOING TO FEAST ON YOUR STILL-BEATING HEARTS AND MAKE PUPPETS OUT OF YOUR DECAPITATED SKELETON HEADS!
Just kidding! It's the final battle!
WHOA.
DUDE. SADNESS IS A ROCKIN'-HOT STONE-COLD FOX.
DUDE, SHE WANTS TO ***KILL*** US.
I KNOW! I LOVE A WOMAN WHO KNOWS WHAT SHE WANTS.
SHE ***IS*** KIND OF ROCKIN', CHRIS.

There'll be plenty of time to talk about feelings when we're dead.

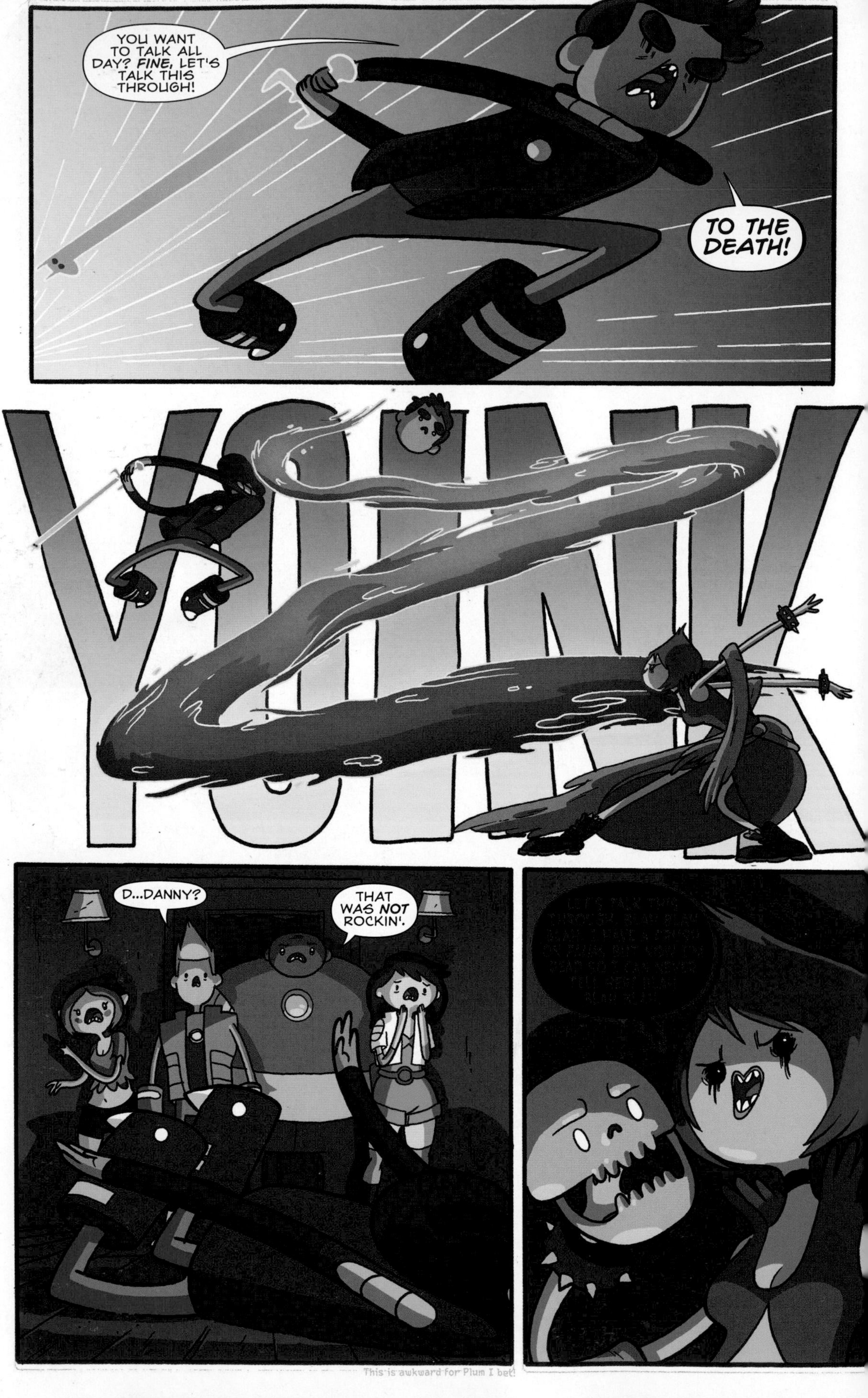
YOU WANT TO TALK ALL DAY? FINE, LET'S TALK THIS THROUGH!
TO THE DEATH!
YOINK
D...DANNY?
THAT WAS NOT ROCKIN'.

This is awkward for Plum I bet!

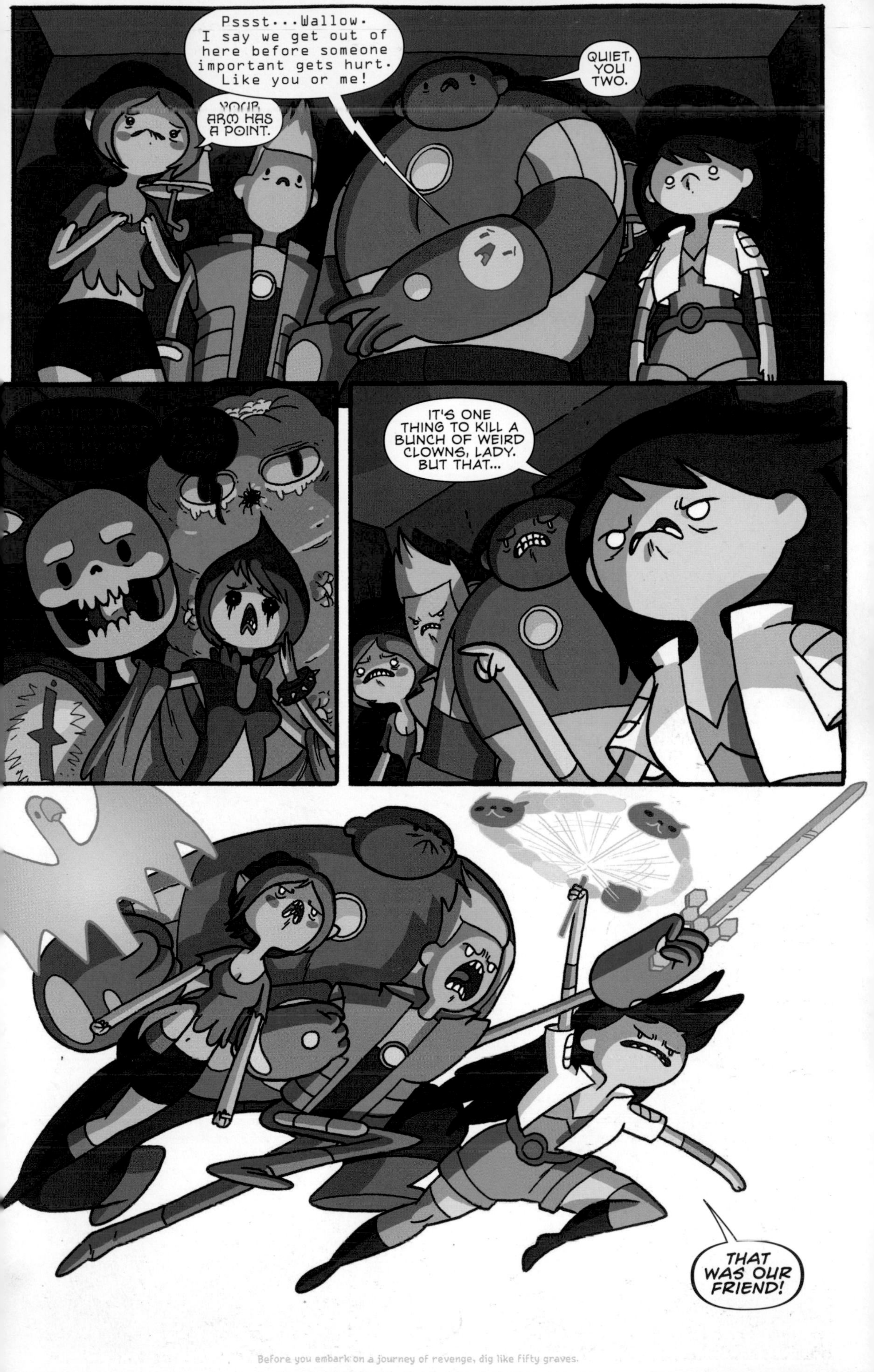
Pssst...Wallow. I say we get out of here before someone important gets hurt. Like you or me!
YOUR ARM HAS A POINT.
QUIET, YOU TWO.
IT'S ONE THING TO KILL A BUNCH OF WEIRD CLOWNS, LADY. BUT THAT...
THAT WAS OUR FRIEND!

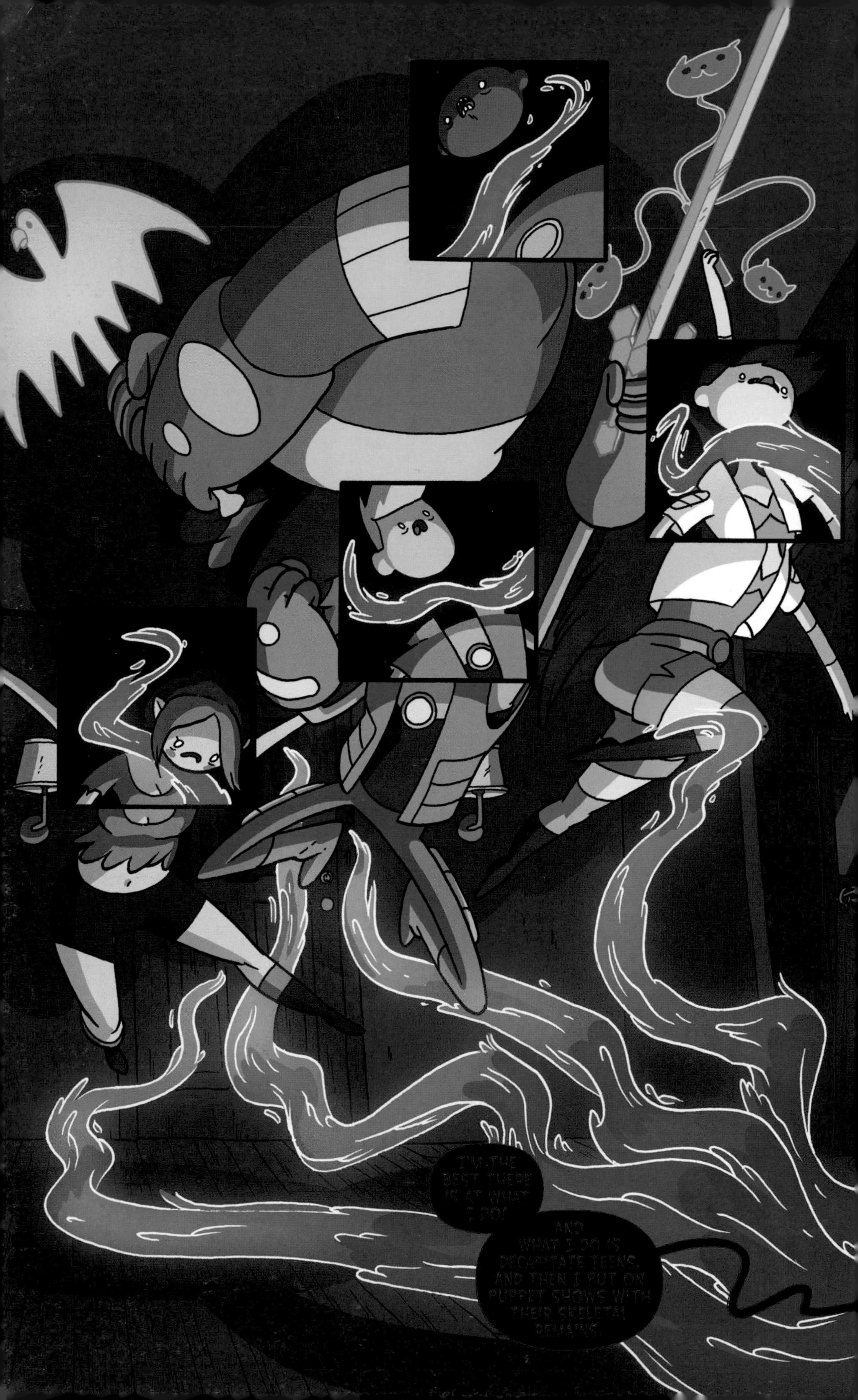
I'M THE BEST THERE IS AT WHAT I DO!
AND WHAT I DO IS DECAPITATE TEENS, AND THEN I PUT ON PUPPET SHOWS WITH THEIR SKELETAL REMAINS.

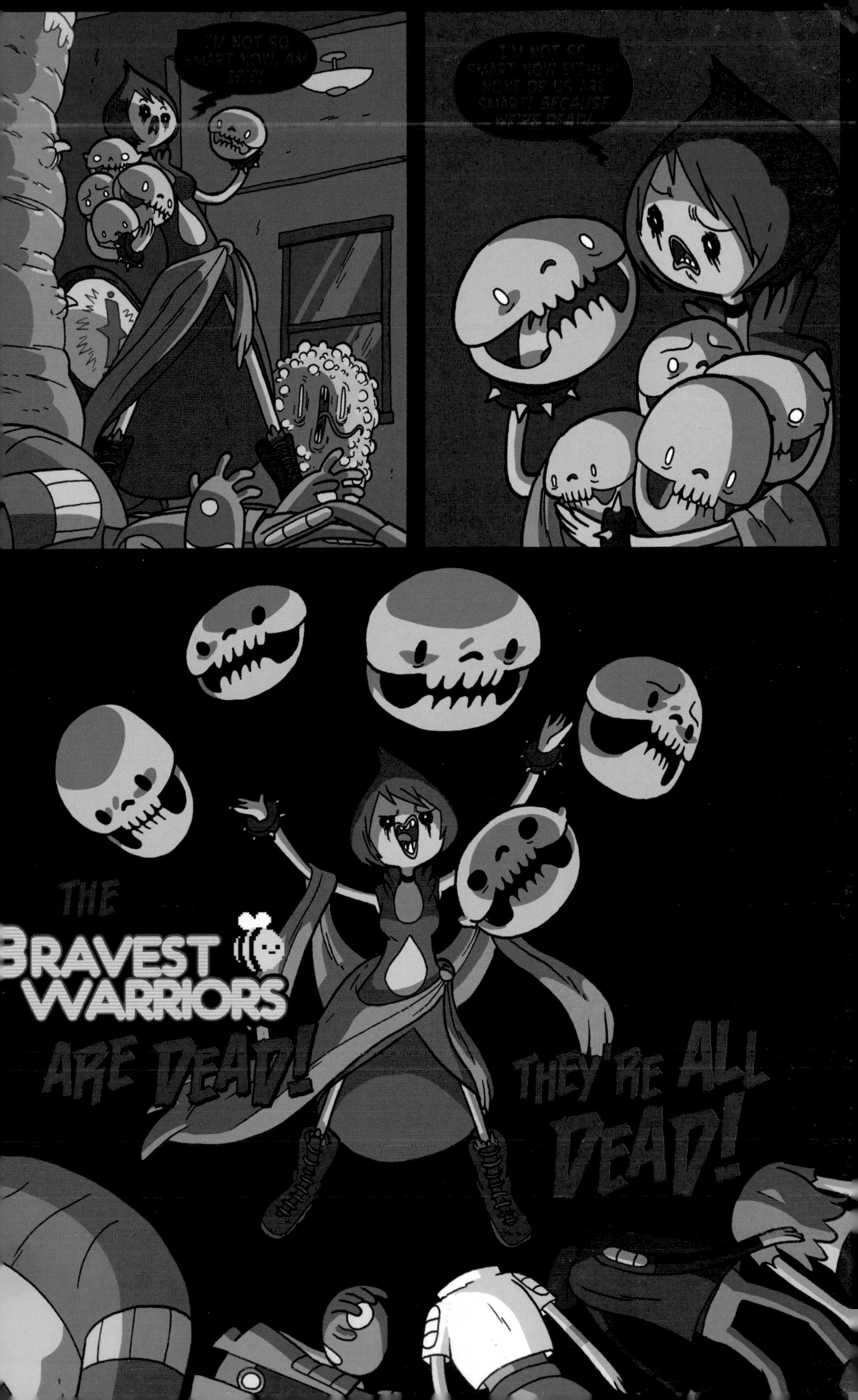
I'M NOT SO SMART NOW, AM I???
I'M NOT SO SMART NOW EITHER! NONE OF US ARE SMART! BECAUSE WE'RE DEAD!
THE BRAVEST WARRIORS ARE DEAD!
THEY'RE ALL DEAD!

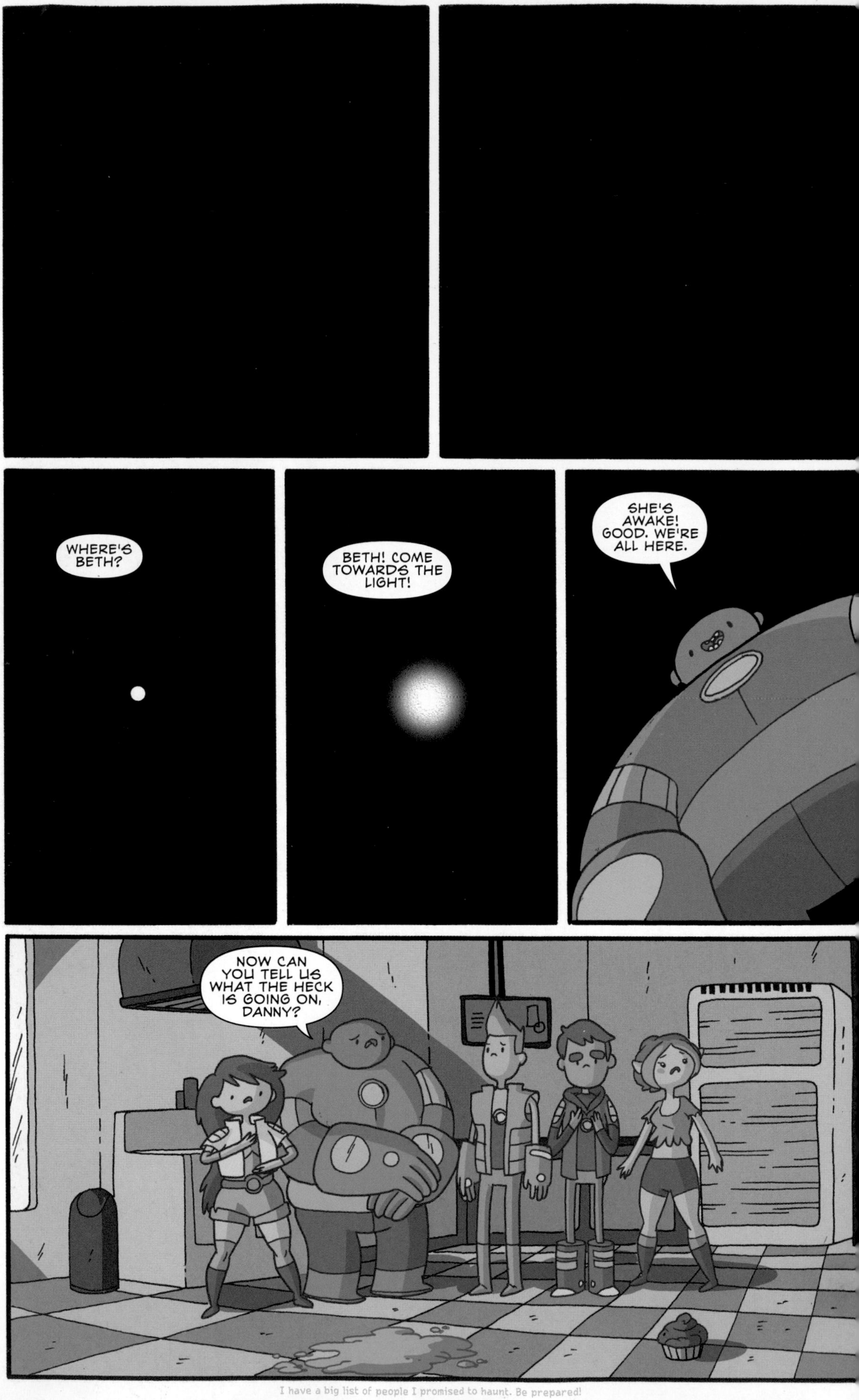
WHERE'S BETH?
BETH! COME TOWARDS THE LIGHT!
SHE'S AWAKE! GOOD. WE'RE ALL HERE.
NOW CAN YOU TELL US WHAT THE HECK IS GOING ON, DANNY?

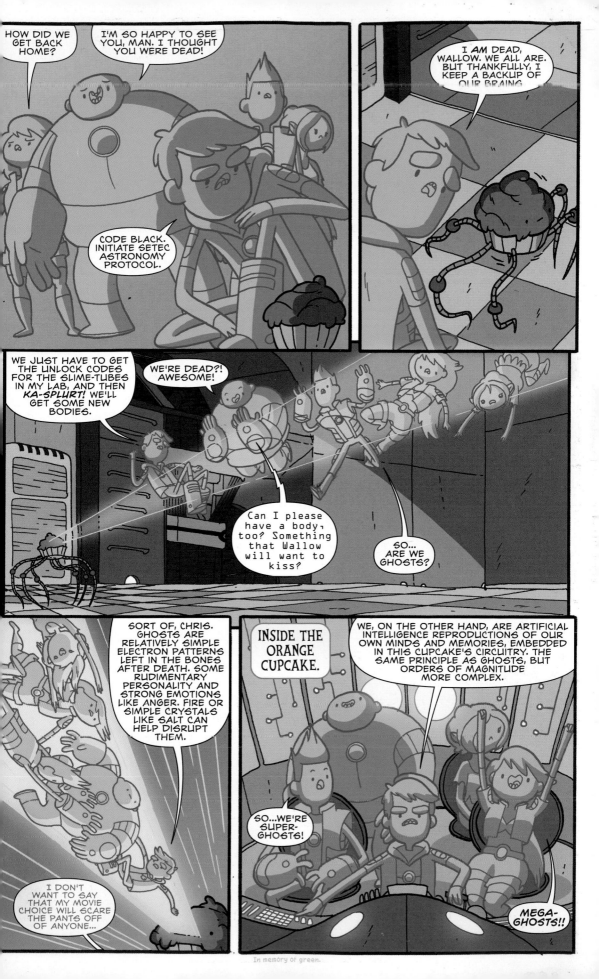

Panel 1:
HOW DID WE GET BACK HOME?

I'M SO HAPPY TO SEE YOU, MAN. I THOUGHT YOU WERE DEAD!

CODE BLACK. INITIATE SETEC ASTRONOMY PROTOCOL.

Panel 2:
I *AM* DEAD, WALLOW. WE ALL ARE. BUT THANKFULLY, I KEEP A BACKUP OF OUR BRAINS.

Panel 3:
WE JUST HAVE TO GET THE UNLOCK CODES FOR THE SLIME-TUBES IN MY LAB, AND THEN *KA-SPLURT!* WE'LL GET SOME NEW BODIES.

WE'RE DEAD?! AWESOME!

Can I please have a body, too? Something that Wallow will want to kiss?

SO... ARE WE GHOSTS?

Panel 4:
SORT OF, CHRIS. GHOSTS ARE RELATIVELY SIMPLE ELECTRON PATTERNS LEFT IN THE BONES AFTER DEATH. SOME RUDIMENTARY PERSONALITY AND STRONG EMOTIONS LIKE ANGER. FIRE OR SIMPLE CRYSTALS LIKE SALT CAN HELP DISRUPT THEM.

I DON'T WANT TO SAY THAT MY MOVIE CHOICE WILL SCARE THE PANTS OFF OF ANYONE...

Panel 5:
INSIDE THE ORANGE CUPCAKE.

WE, ON THE OTHER HAND, ARE ARTIFICIAL INTELLIGENCE REPRODUCTIONS OF OUR OWN MINDS AND MEMORIES, EMBEDDED IN THIS CUPCAKE'S CIRCUITRY. THE SAME PRINCIPLE AS GHOSTS, BUT ORDERS OF MAGNITUDE MORE COMPLEX.

SO...WE'RE SUPER-GHOSTS!

MEGA-GHOSTS!!

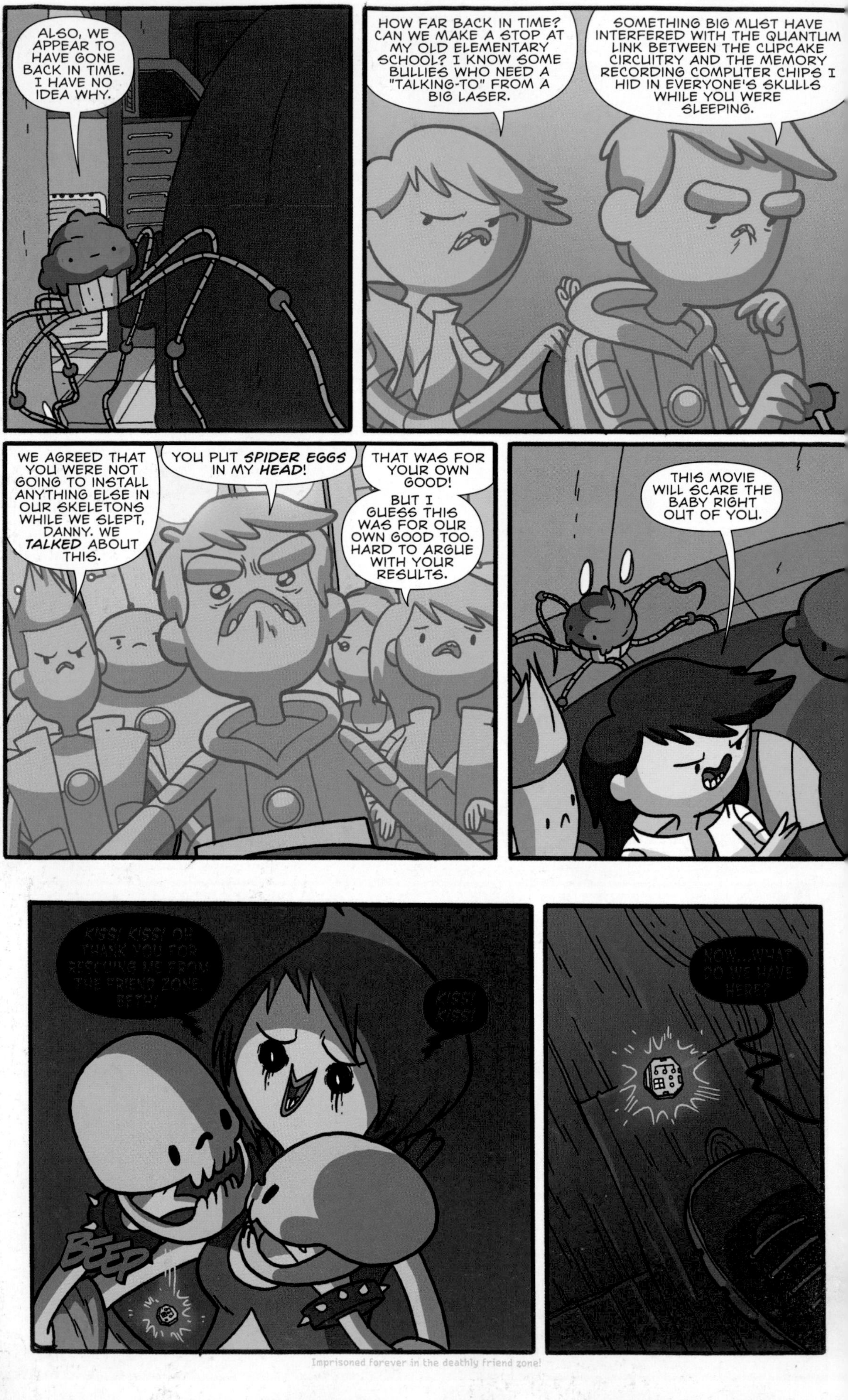
ALSO, WE APPEAR TO HAVE GONE BACK IN TIME. I HAVE NO IDEA WHY.
HOW FAR BACK IN TIME? CAN WE MAKE A STOP AT MY OLD ELEMENTARY SCHOOL? I KNOW SOME BULLIES WHO NEED A "TALKING-TO" FROM A BIG LASER.
SOMETHING BIG MUST HAVE INTERFERED WITH THE QUANTUM LINK BETWEEN THE CUPCAKE CIRCUITRY AND THE MEMORY RECORDING COMPUTER CHIPS I HID IN EVERYONE'S SKULLS WHILE YOU WERE SLEEPING.
WE AGREED THAT YOU WERE NOT GOING TO INSTALL ANYTHING ELSE IN OUR SKELETONS WHILE WE SLEPT, DANNY. WE *TALKED* ABOUT THIS.
YOU PUT *SPIDER EGGS* IN MY *HEAD*!
THAT WAS FOR YOUR OWN GOOD!
BUT I GUESS THIS WAS FOR OUR OWN GOOD TOO. HARD TO ARGUE WITH YOUR RESULTS.
THIS MOVIE WILL SCARE THE BABY RIGHT OUT OF YOU.
KISS! KISS! OH THANK YOU FOR RESCUING ME FROM THE FRIEND ZONE, BETH!
KISS! KISS!
BEEP
NOW... WHAT DO WE HAVE HERE?

Imprisoned forever in the deathly friend zone!

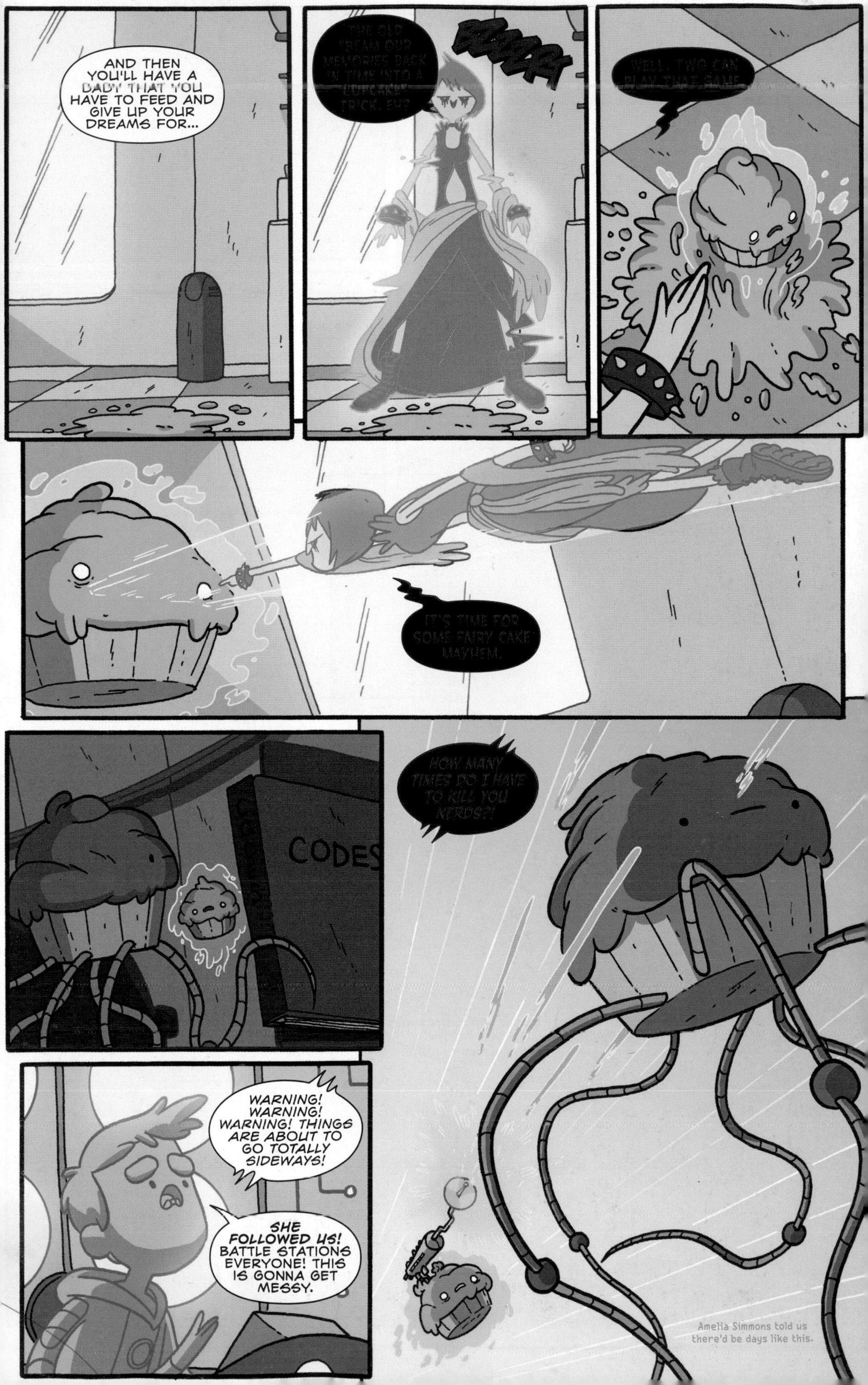
AND THEN YOU'LL HAVE A BABY THAT YOU HAVE TO FEED AND GIVE UP YOUR DREAMS FOR...
THE OLD "BEAM OUR MEMORIES BACK IN TIME INTO A CUPCAKE" TRICK, EH?
WELL, TWO CAN PLAY THAT GAME.
IT'S TIME FOR SOME FAIRY CAKE MAYHEM.
CODES
HOW MANY TIMES DO I HAVE TO KILL YOU NERDS?!
WARNING! WARNING! WARNING! THINGS ARE ABOUT TO GO TOTALLY SIDEWAYS!
SHE FOLLOWED US! BATTLE STATIONS EVERYONE! THIS IS GONNA GET MESSY.
Amelia Simmons told us there'd be days like this.

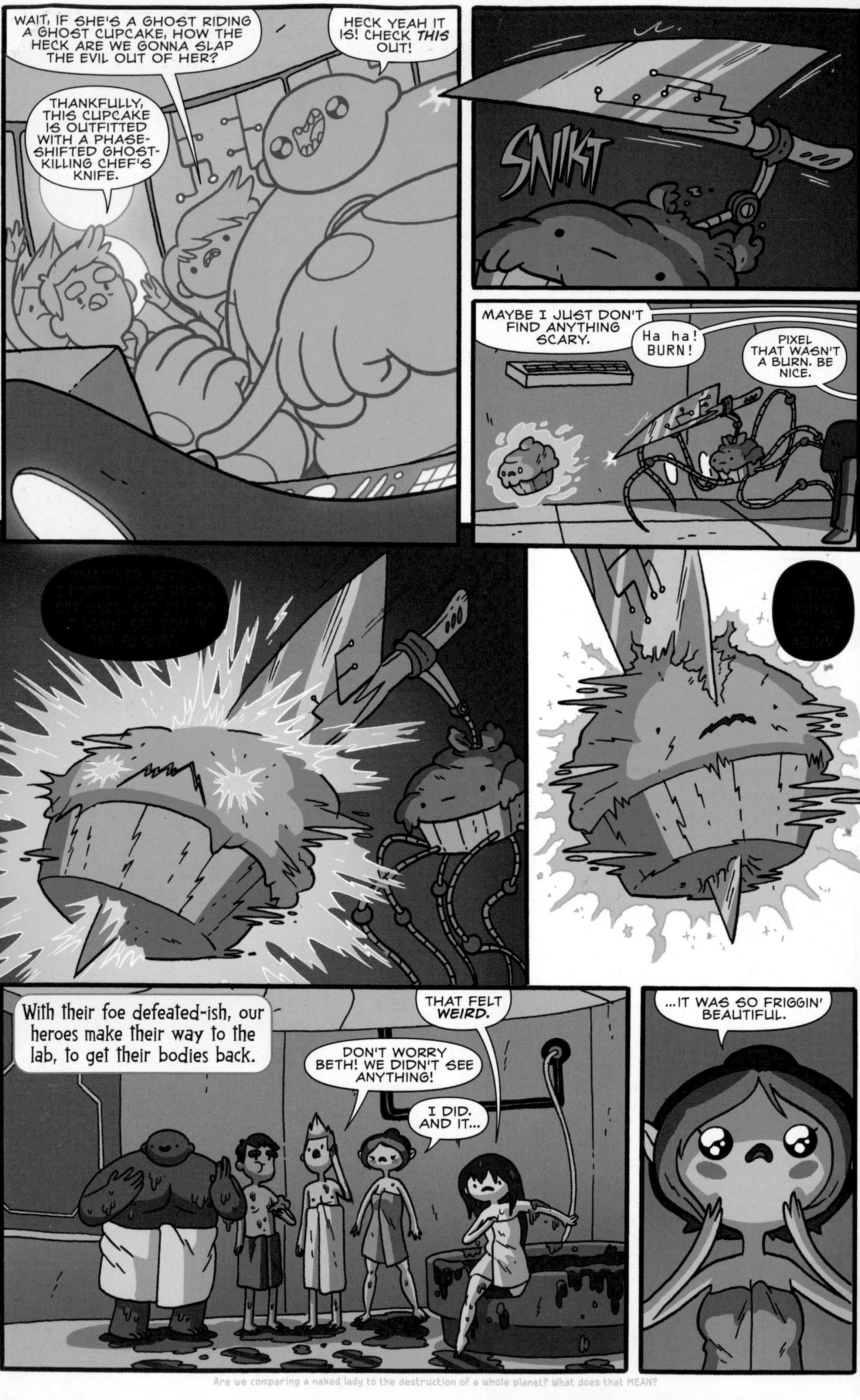
WAIT, IF SHE'S A GHOST RIDING A GHOST CUPCAKE, HOW THE HECK ARE WE GONNA SLAP THE EVIL OUT OF HER?
THANKFULLY, THIS CUPCAKE IS OUTFITTED WITH A PHASE-SHIFTED GHOST-KILLING CHEF'S KNIFE.
HECK YEAH IT IS! CHECK THIS OUT!
SNIKT
MAYBE I JUST DON'T FIND ANYTHING SCARY.
Ha ha! BURN!
PIXEL THAT WASN'T A BURN. BE NICE.
With their foe defeated-ish, our heroes make their way to the lab, to get their bodies back.
THAT FELT WEIRD.
DON'T WORRY BETH! WE DIDN'T SEE ANYTHING!
I DID. AND IT...
...IT WAS SO FRIGGIN' BEAUTIFUL.

Are we comparing a naked lady to the destruction of a whole planet? What does that MEAN?

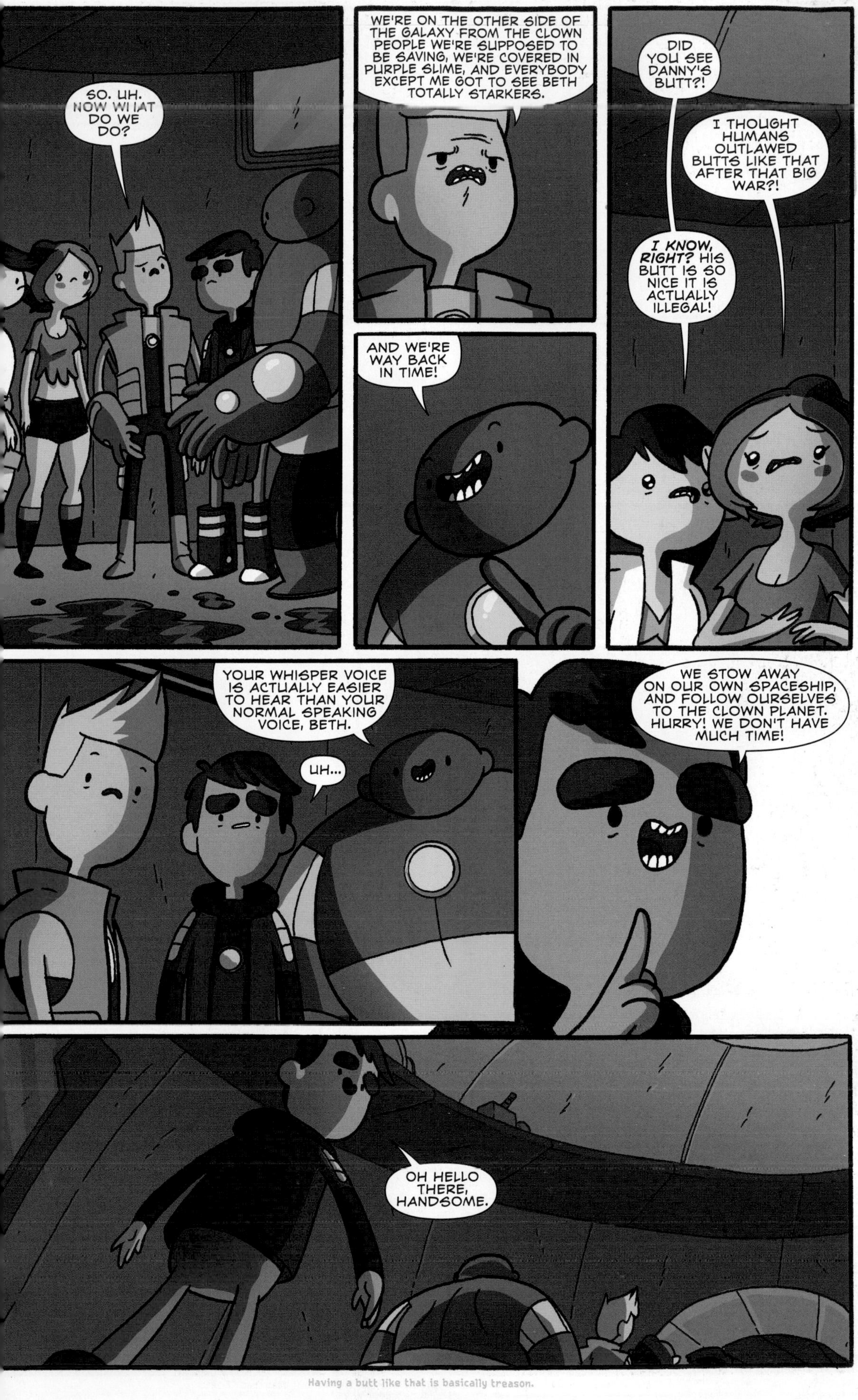
SO. UH. NOW WHAT DO WE DO?
WE'RE ON THE OTHER SIDE OF THE GALAXY FROM THE CLOWN PEOPLE WE'RE SUPPOSED TO BE SAVING, WE'RE COVERED IN PURPLE SLIME, AND EVERYBODY EXCEPT ME GOT TO SEE BETH TOTALLY STARKERS.
AND WE'RE WAY BACK IN TIME!
DID YOU SEE DANNY'S BUTT?!
I THOUGHT HUMANS OUTLAWED BUTTS LIKE THAT AFTER THAT BIG WAR?!
I KNOW, RIGHT? HIS BUTT IS SO NICE IT IS ACTUALLY ILLEGAL!
YOUR WHISPER VOICE IS ACTUALLY EASIER TO HEAR THAN YOUR NORMAL SPEAKING VOICE, BETH.
UH...
WE STOW AWAY ON OUR OWN SPACESHIP, AND FOLLOW OURSELVES TO THE CLOWN PLANET. HURRY! WE DON'T HAVE MUCH TIME!
OH HELLO THERE, HANDSOME.

Having a butt like that is basically treason.

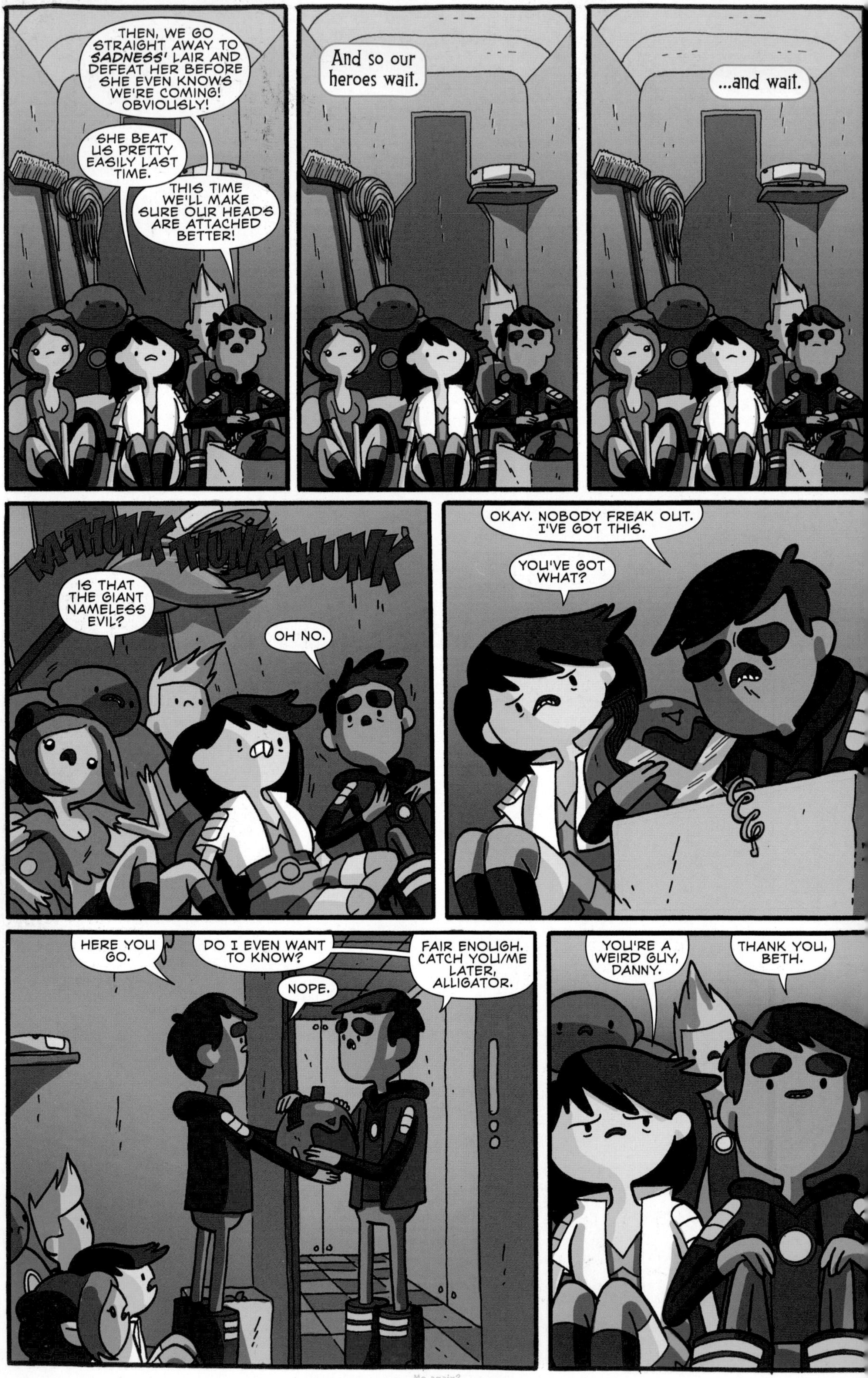
THEN, WE GO STRAIGHT AWAY TO SADNESS' LAIR AND DEFEAT HER BEFORE SHE EVEN KNOWS WE'RE COMING! OBVIOUSLY!
SHE BEAT US PRETTY EASILY LAST TIME.
THIS TIME WE'LL MAKE SURE OUR HEADS ARE ATTACHED BETTER!
And so our heroes wait.
...and wait.
KA-THUNK THUNK THUNK
IS THAT THE GIANT NAMELESS EVIL?
OH NO.
OKAY. NOBODY FREAK OUT. I'VE GOT THIS.
YOU'VE GOT WHAT?
HERE YOU GO.
DO I EVEN WANT TO KNOW?
NOPE.
FAIR ENOUGH. CATCH YOU/ME LATER, ALLIGATOR.
YOU'RE A WEIRD GUY, DANNY.
THANK YOU, BETH.

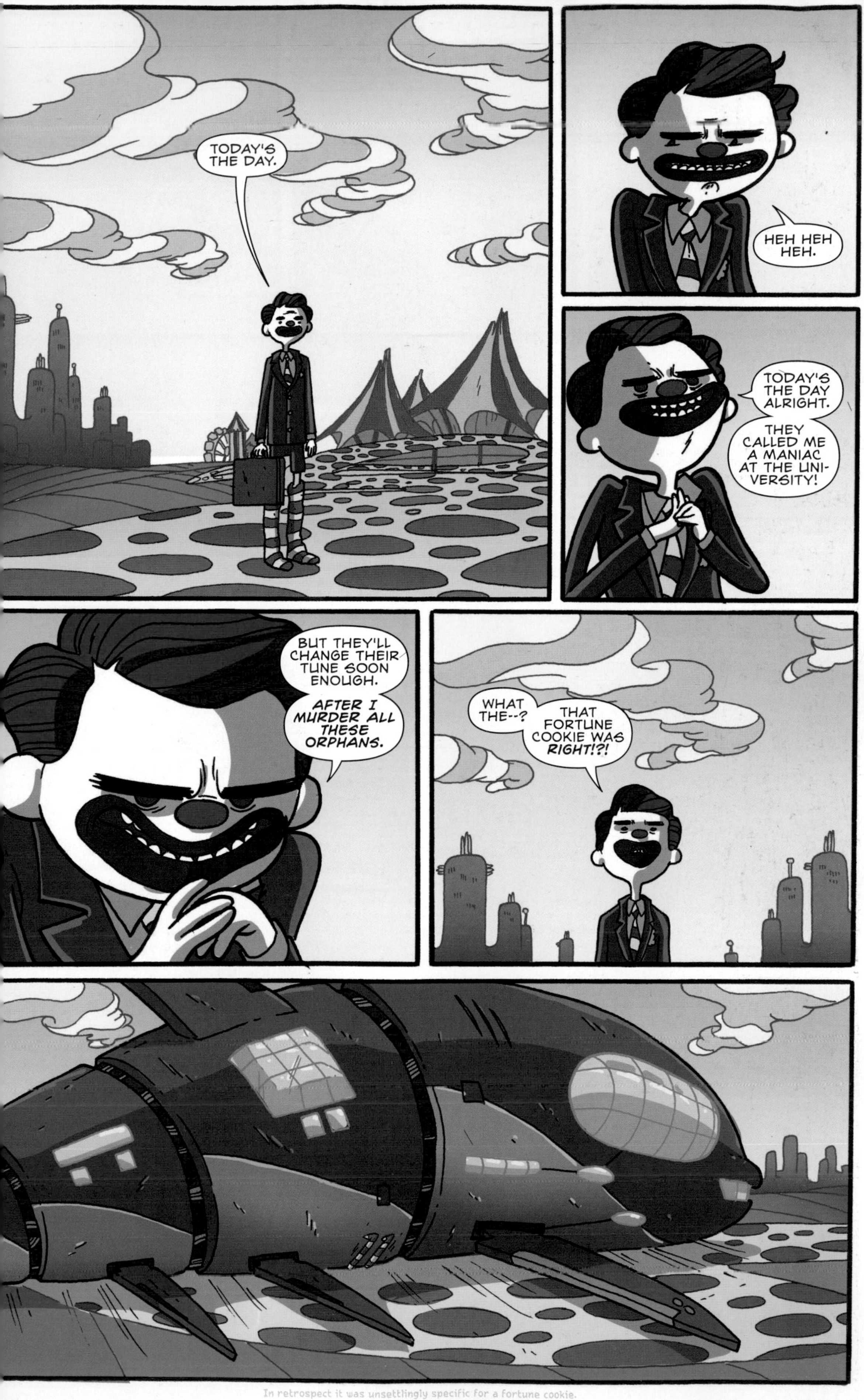
TODAY'S THE DAY.
HEH HEH HEH.
TODAY'S THE DAY ALRIGHT.
THEY CALLED ME A MANIAC AT THE UNI-VERSITY!
BUT THEY'LL CHANGE THEIR TUNE SOON ENOUGH.
AFTER I MURDER ALL THESE ORPHANS.
WHAT THE--?
THAT FORTUNE COOKIE WAS *RIGHT!?!*

In retrospect it was unsettlingly specific for a fortune cookie.

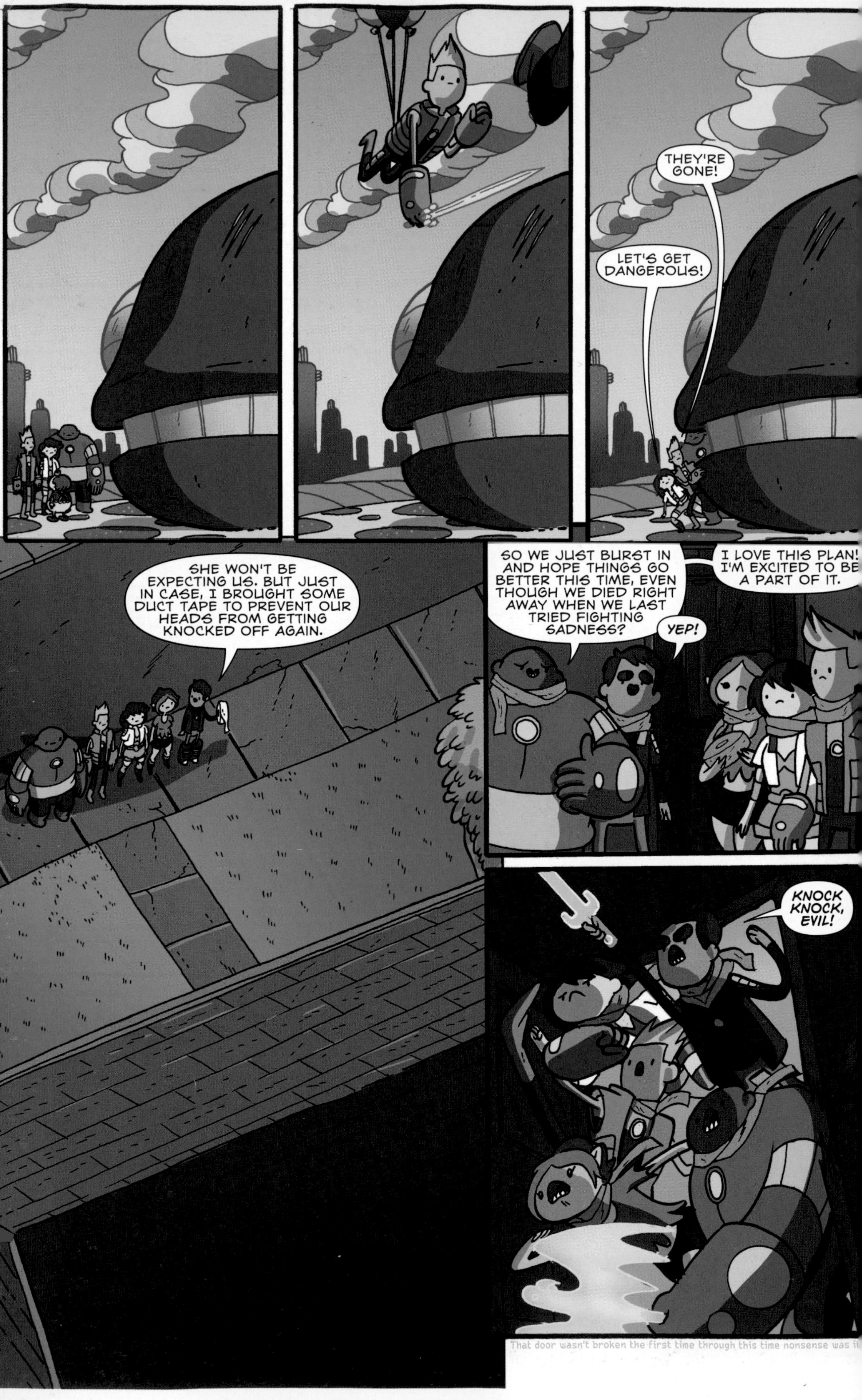
THEY'RE GONE!
LET'S GET DANGEROUS!
SHE WON'T BE EXPECTING US. BUT JUST IN CASE, I BROUGHT SOME DUCT TAPE TO PREVENT OUR HEADS FROM GETTING KNOCKED OFF AGAIN.
SO WE JUST BURST IN AND HOPE THINGS GO BETTER THIS TIME, EVEN THOUGH WE DIED RIGHT AWAY WHEN WE LAST TRIED FIGHTING SADNESS?
I LOVE THIS PLAN! I'M EXCITED TO BE A PART OF IT.
YEP!
KNOCK KNOCK, EVIL!

That door wasn't broken the first time through this time nonsense was i

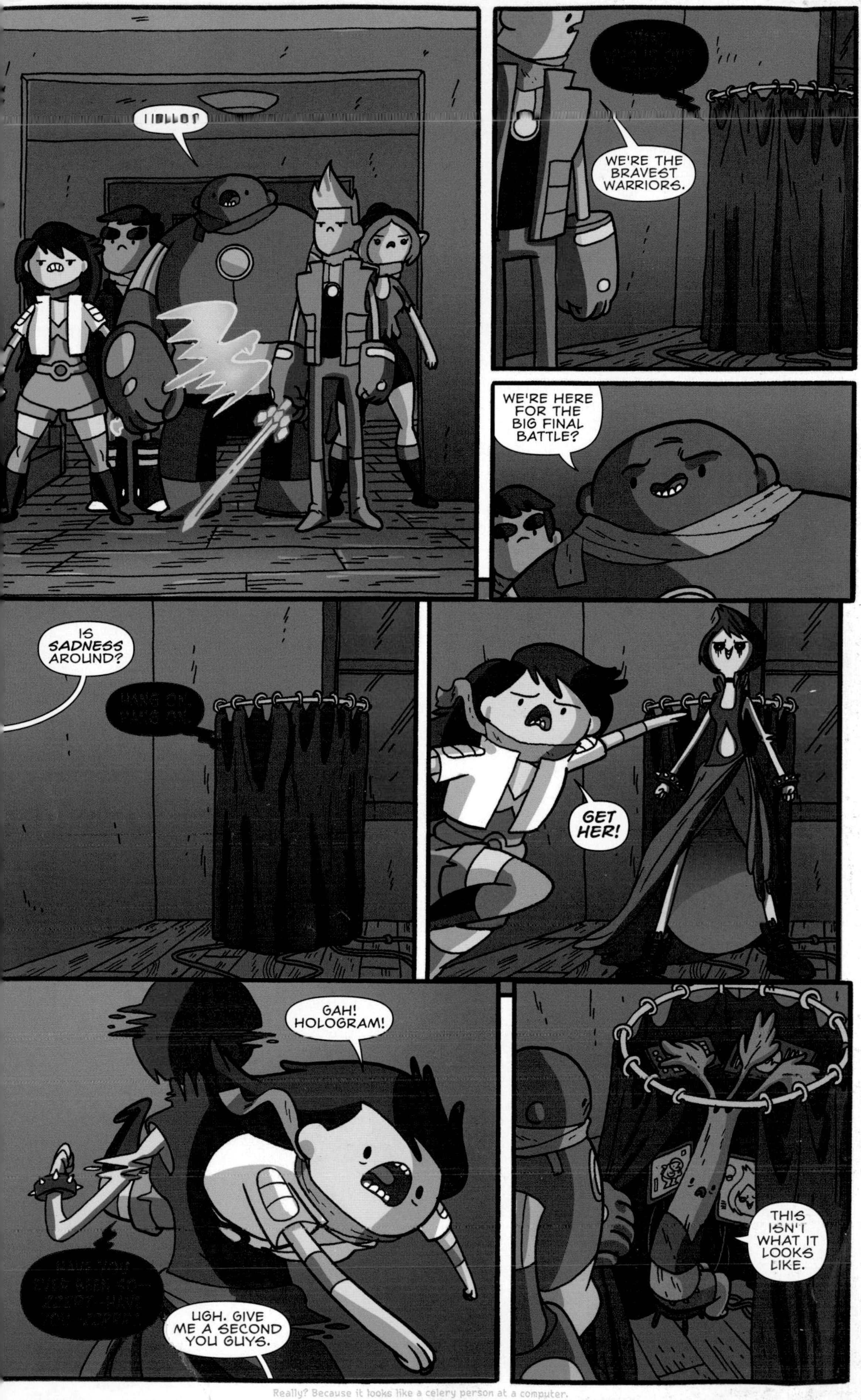

WE'RE THE BRAVEST WARRIORS.
WE'RE HERE FOR THE BIG FINAL BATTLE?
IS SADNESS AROUND?
HANG ON. HANG ON.
GET HER!
GAH! HOLOGRAM!
UGH. GIVE ME A SECOND YOU GUYS.
THIS ISN'T WHAT IT LOOKS LIKE.

Really? Because it looks like a celery person at a computer.

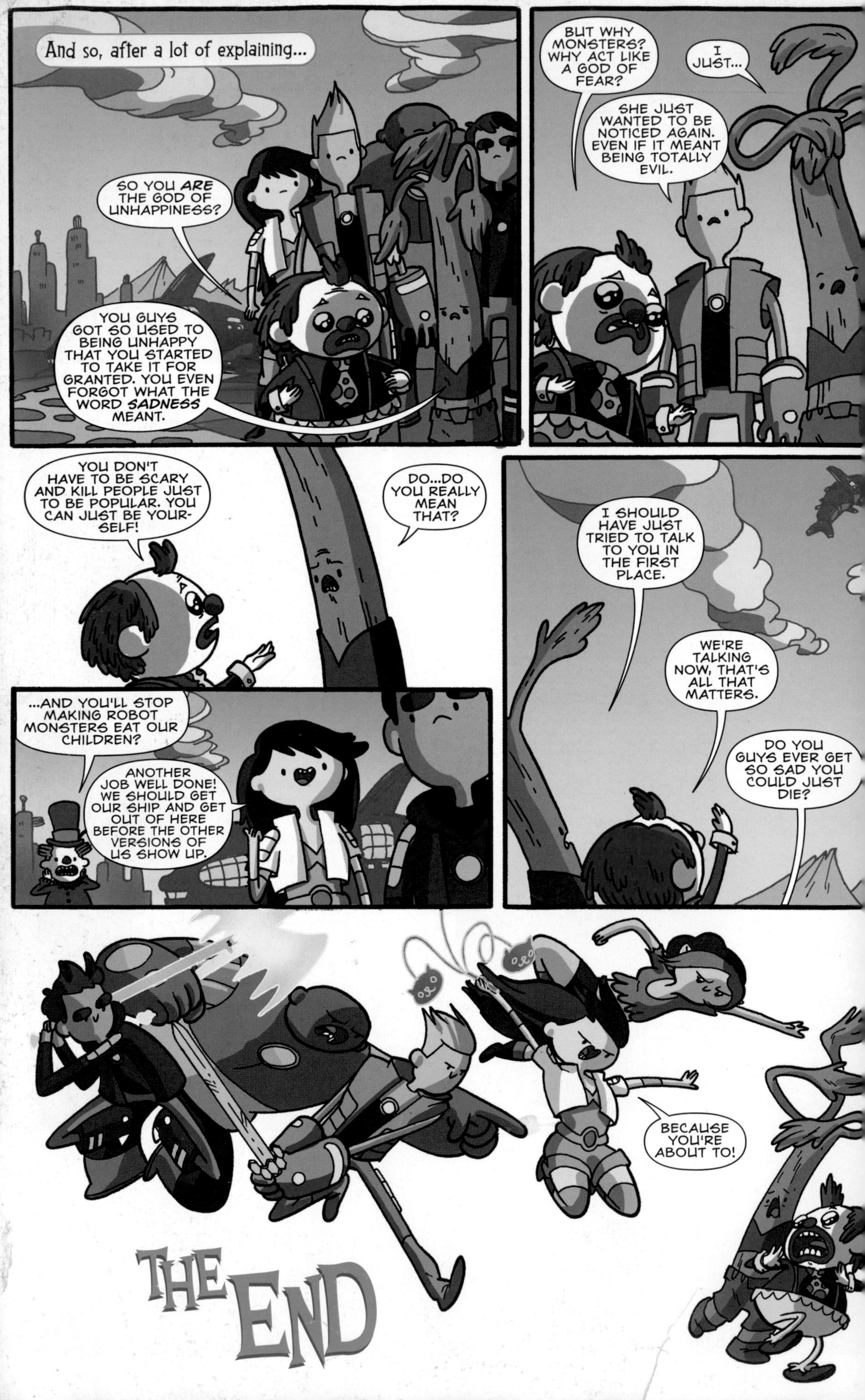
And so, after a lot of explaining...
SO YOU ARE THE GOD OF UNHAPPINESS?
YOU GUYS GOT SO USED TO BEING UNHAPPY THAT YOU STARTED TO TAKE IT FOR GRANTED. YOU EVEN FORGOT WHAT THE WORD SADNESS MEANT.
BUT WHY MONSTERS? WHY ACT LIKE A GOD OF FEAR?
I JUST...
SHE JUST WANTED TO BE NOTICED AGAIN. EVEN IF IT MEANT BEING TOTALLY EVIL.
YOU DON'T HAVE TO BE SCARY AND KILL PEOPLE JUST TO BE POPULAR. YOU CAN JUST BE YOUR-SELF!
DO...DO YOU REALLY MEAN THAT?
I SHOULD HAVE JUST TRIED TO TALK TO YOU IN THE FIRST PLACE.
WE'RE TALKING NOW, THAT'S ALL THAT MATTERS.
...AND YOU'LL STOP MAKING ROBOT MONSTERS EAT OUR CHILDREN?
ANOTHER JOB WELL DONE! WE SHOULD GET OUR SHIP AND GET OUT OF HERE BEFORE THE OTHER VERSIONS OF US SHOW UP.
DO YOU GUYS EVER GET SO SAD YOU COULD JUST DIE?
BECAUSE YOU'RE ABOUT TO!
THE END

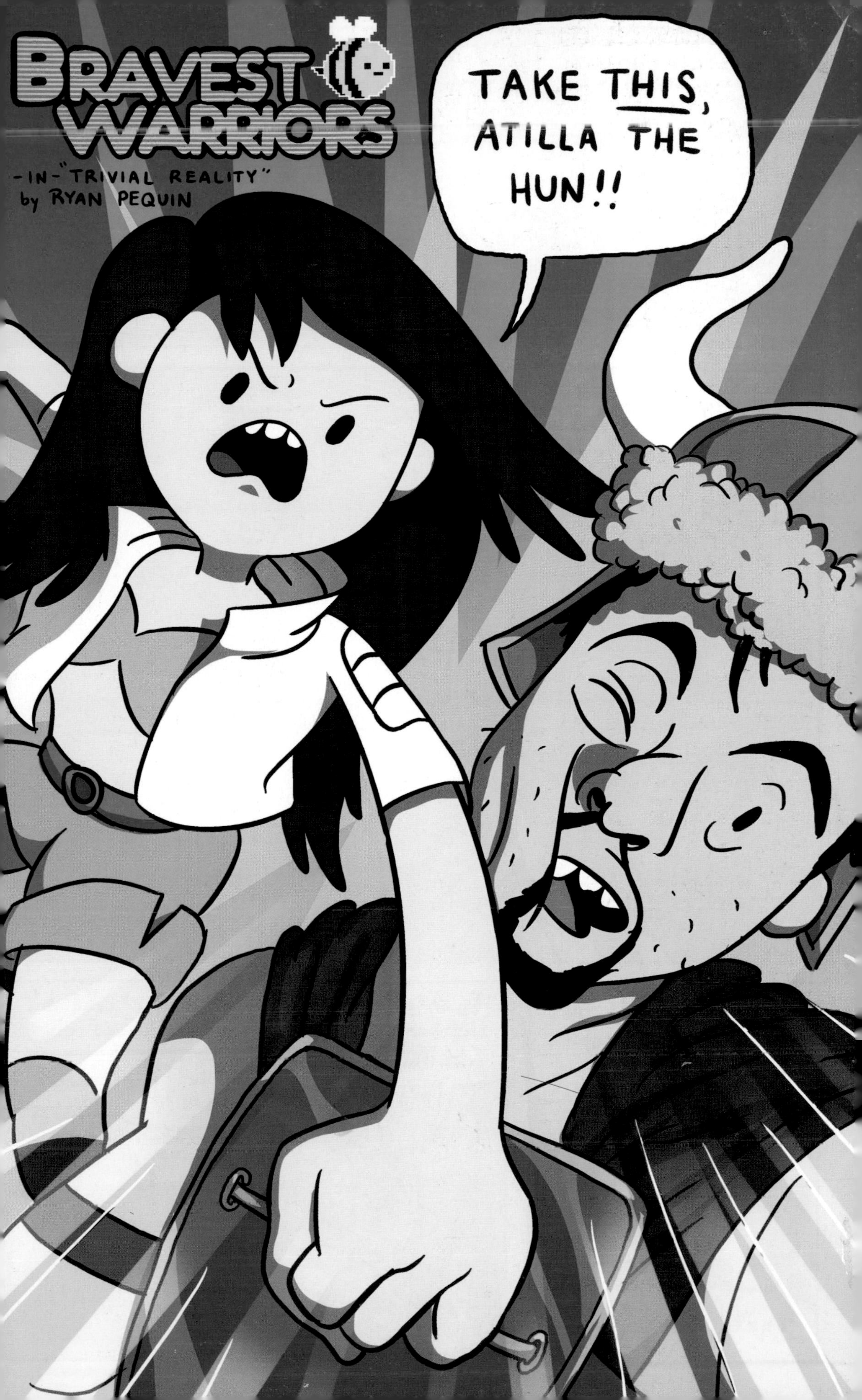
BRAVEST WARRIORS
-IN- "TRIVIAL REALITY"
by RYAN PEQUIN
TAKE THIS, ATILLA THE HUN!!

Mf! By node id bleeding!

CONGRATULATIONS!

POOF!

You figured out the weakness of the mighty conqueror, Atilla the Hun! Level sixteen complete!

BIP!

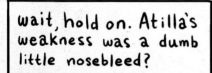

wait, hold on. Atilla's weakness was a dumb little nosebleed?

That can't be right.

It's an educational game, dude! I read on the box that this stuff's all based on true facts.

Really? Facts from where?

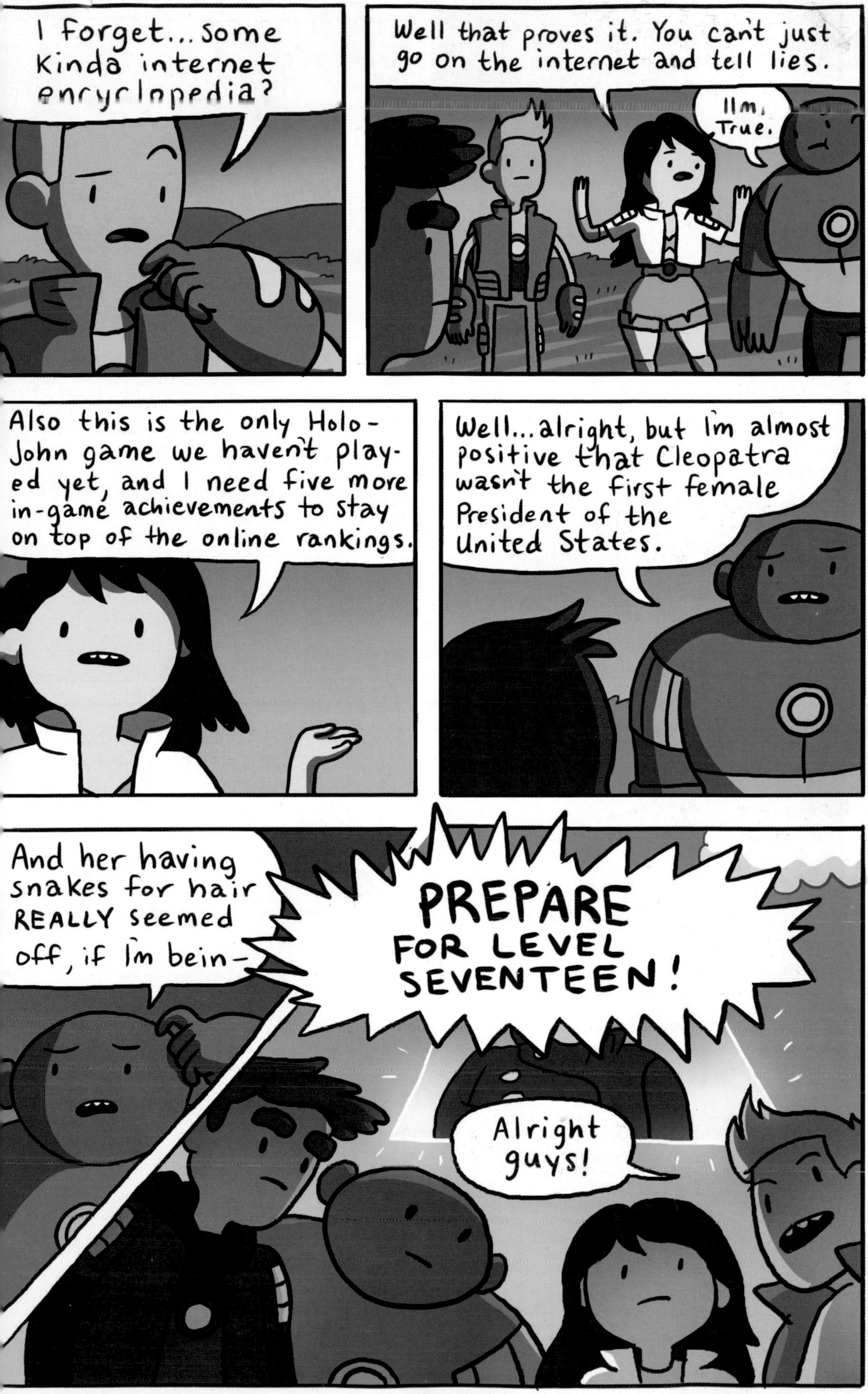
I forget... Some Kinda internet encyclopedia?
Well that proves it. You can't just go on the internet and tell lies.
Um, True.
Also this is the only Holo-John game we haven't played yet, and I need five more in-game achievements to stay on top of the online rankings.
Well... alright, but I'm almost positive that Cleopatra wasn't the first female President of the United States.
And her having snakes for hair REALLY seemed off, if I'm bein-
PREPARE FOR LEVEL SEVENTEEN!
Alright guys!

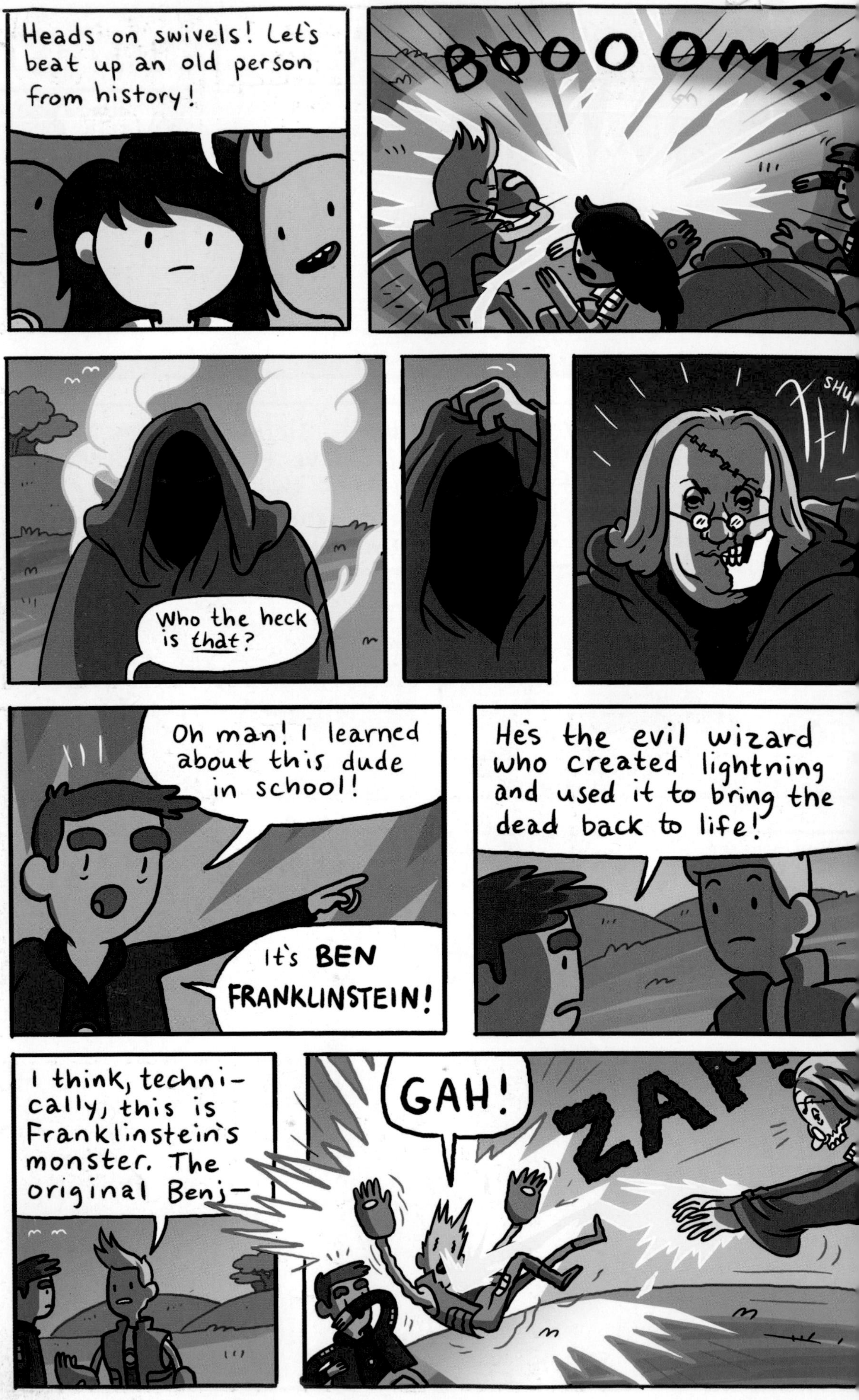
Heads on swivels! Let's beat up an old person from history!
BOOOOM!!
Who the heck is that?
Oh man! I learned about this dude in school!
It's BEN FRANKLINSTEIN!
He's the evil wizard who created lightning and used it to bring the dead back to life!
I think, technically, this is Franklinstein's monster. The original Benj—
GAH!
ZAP

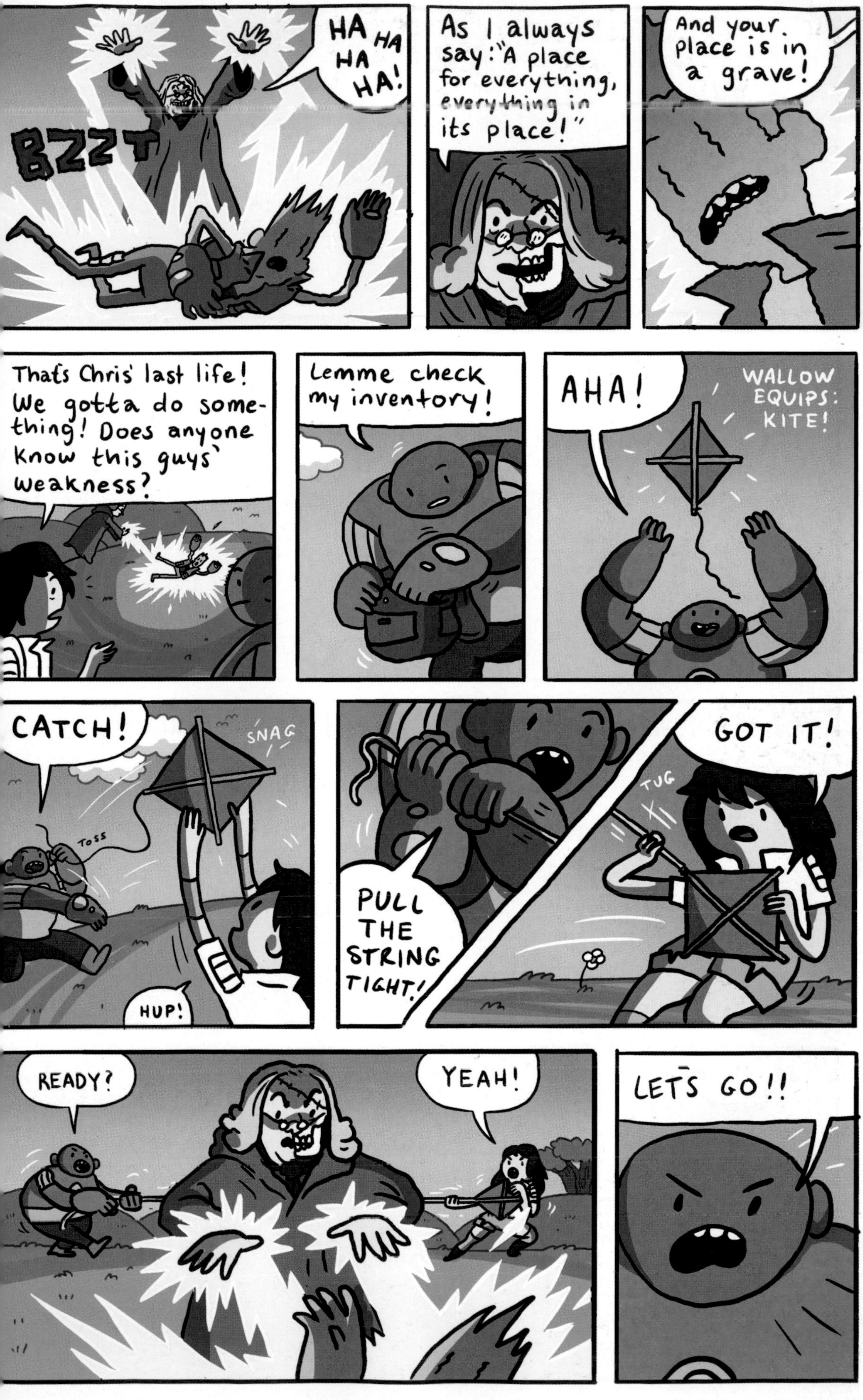
HA HA HA HA!
BZZT
As I always say: "A place for everything, everything in its place!"
And your place is in a grave!
That's Chris' last life! We gotta do something! Does anyone know this guys' weakness?
Lemme check my inventory!
AHA!
WALLOW EQUIPS: KITE!
CATCH!
SNAG
TOSS
HUP!
PULL THE STRING TIGHT!
TUG
GOT IT!
READY?
YEAH!
LET'S GO!!

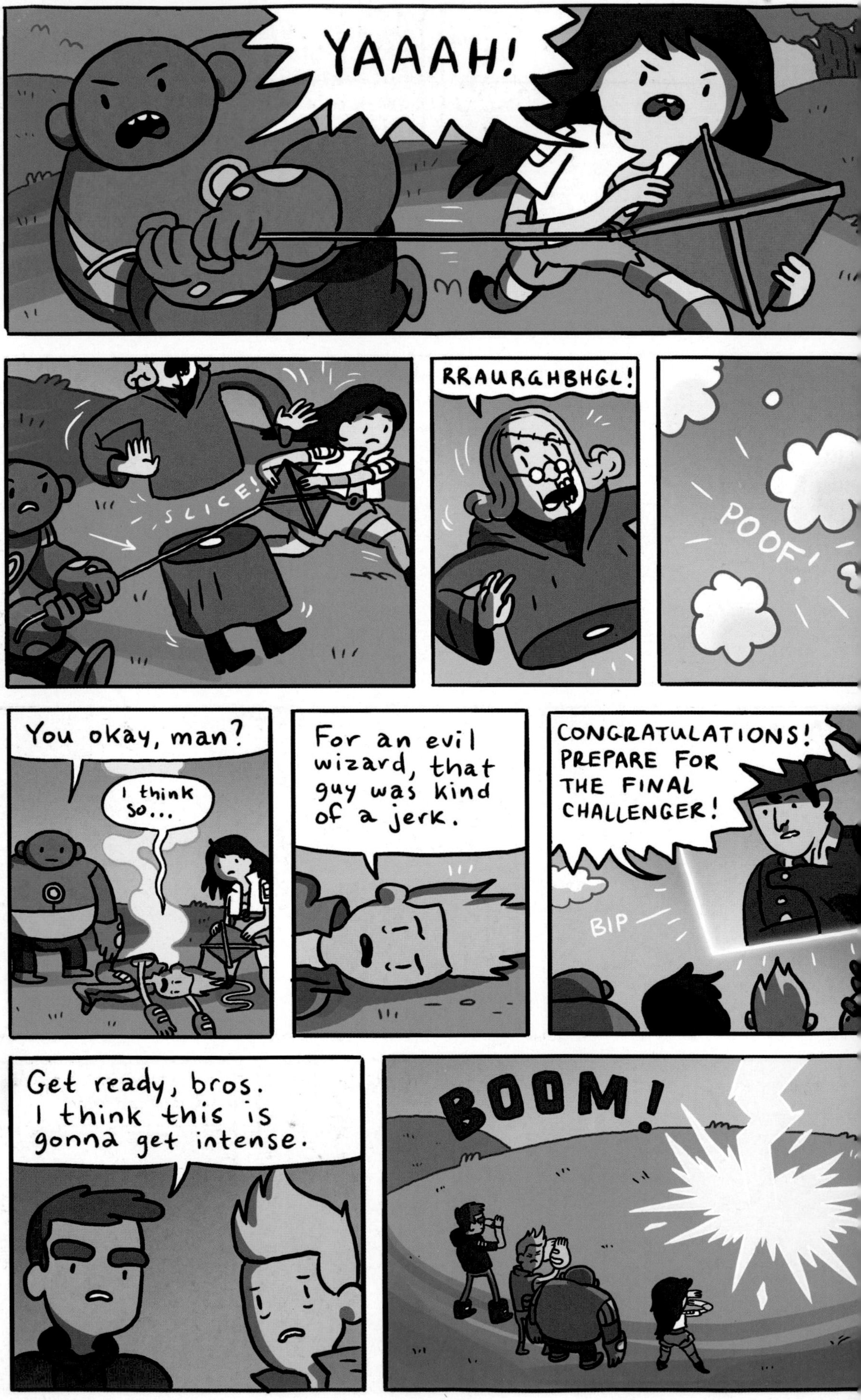
YAAAH!
SLICE!
RRAURGHBHGL!
POOF!
You okay, man?
I think so...
For an evil wizard, that guy was kind of a jerk.
CONGRATULATIONS! PREPARE FOR THE FINAL CHALLENGER!
BIP
Get ready, bros. I think this is gonna get intense.
BOOM!

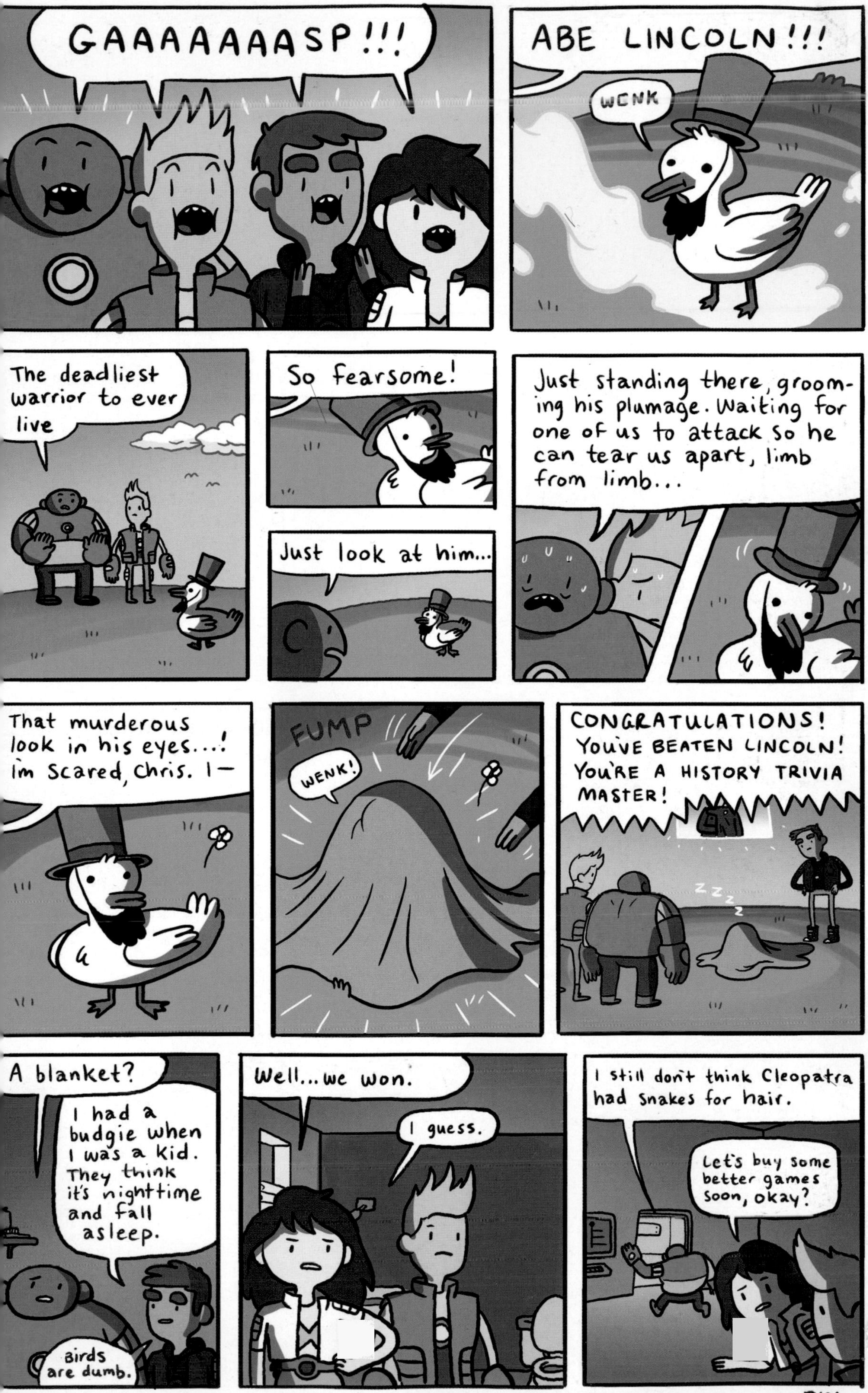
GAAAAAAASP!!!
ABE LINCOLN!!!
WENK
The deadliest warrior to ever live
So fearsome!
Just look at him...
Just standing there, grooming his plumage. Waiting for one of us to attack so he can tear us apart, limb from limb...
That murderous look in his eyes...! I'm scared, Chris. I—
FUMP
WENK!
CONGRATULATIONS! YOU'VE BEATEN LINCOLN! YOU'RE A HISTORY TRIVIA MASTER!
Z Z Z Z
A blanket?
I had a budgie when I was a kid. They think it's nighttime and fall asleep.
Birds are dumb.
Well... we won.
I guess.
I still don't think Cleopatra had snakes for hair.
Let's buy some better games soon, okay?

FIN

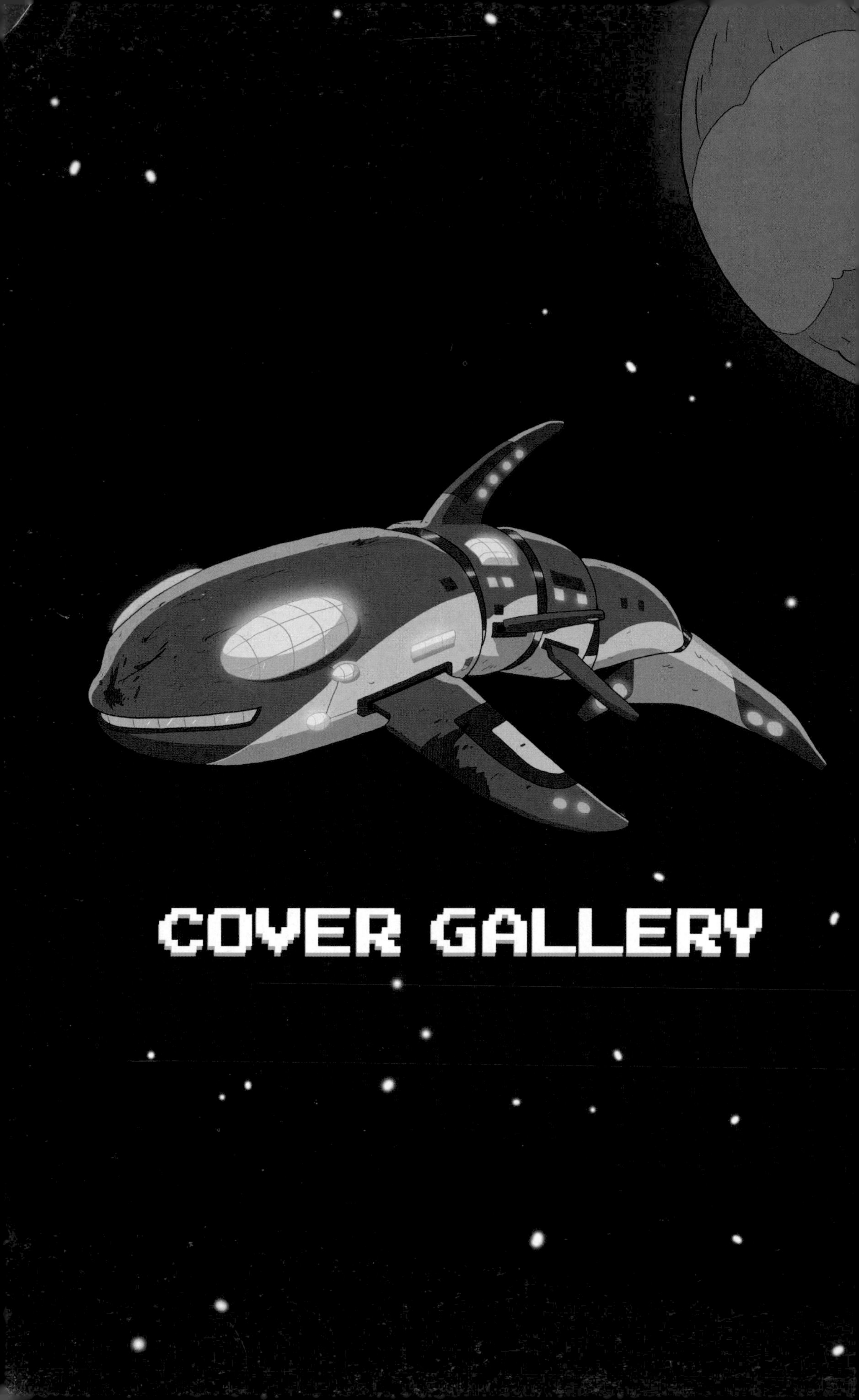

COVER GALLERY

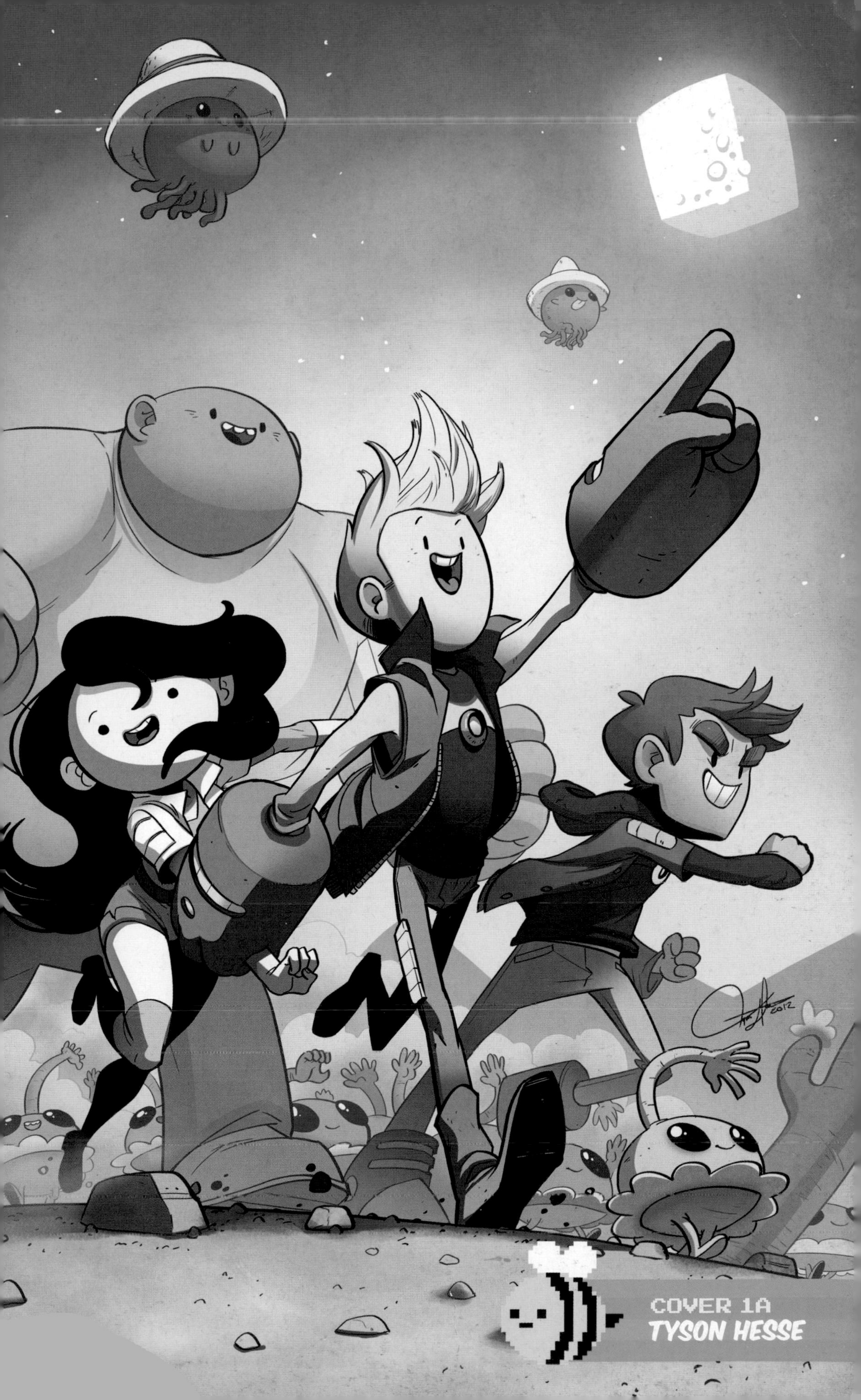
COVER 1A
TYSON HESSE

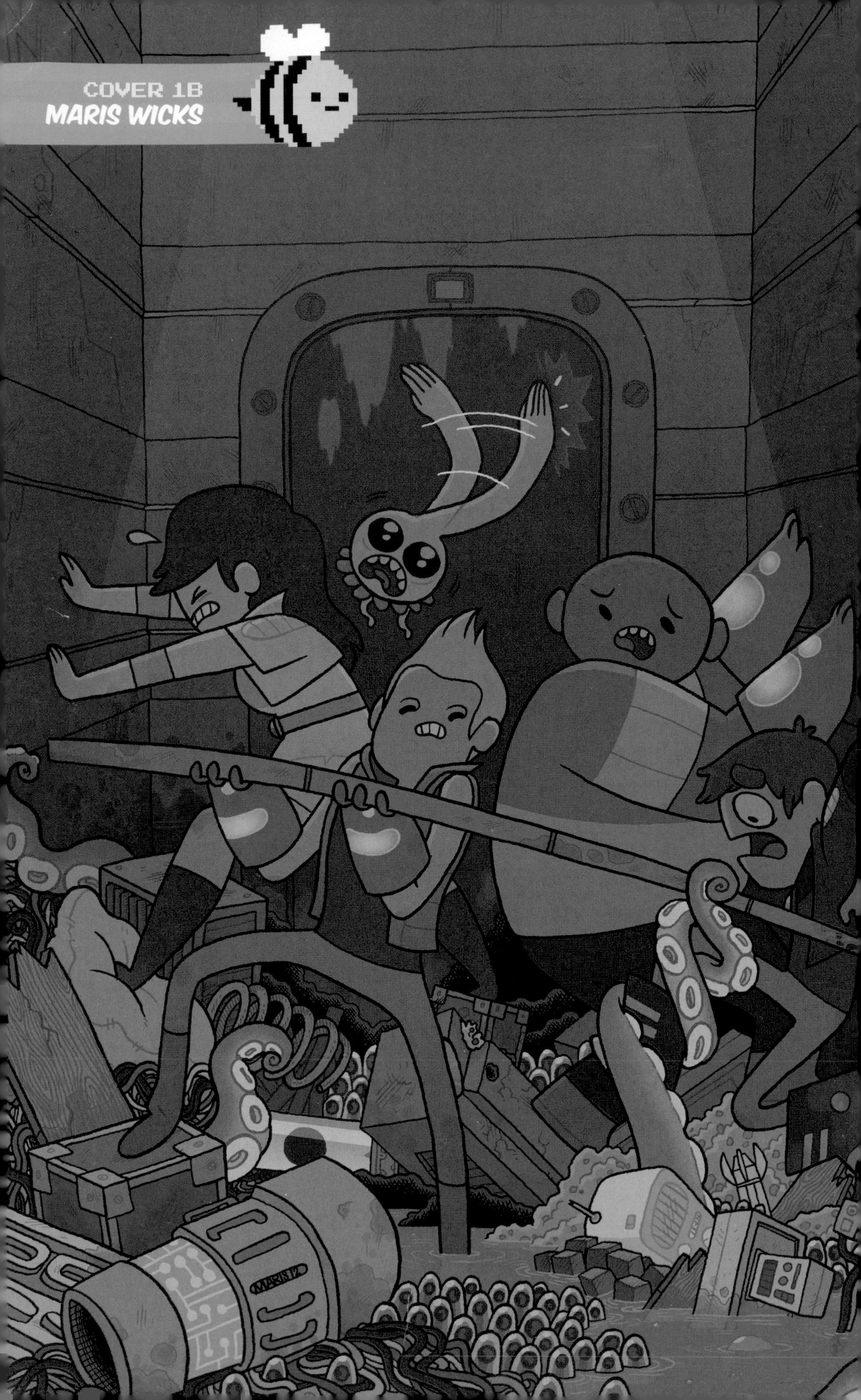

COVER 1B
MARIS WICKS

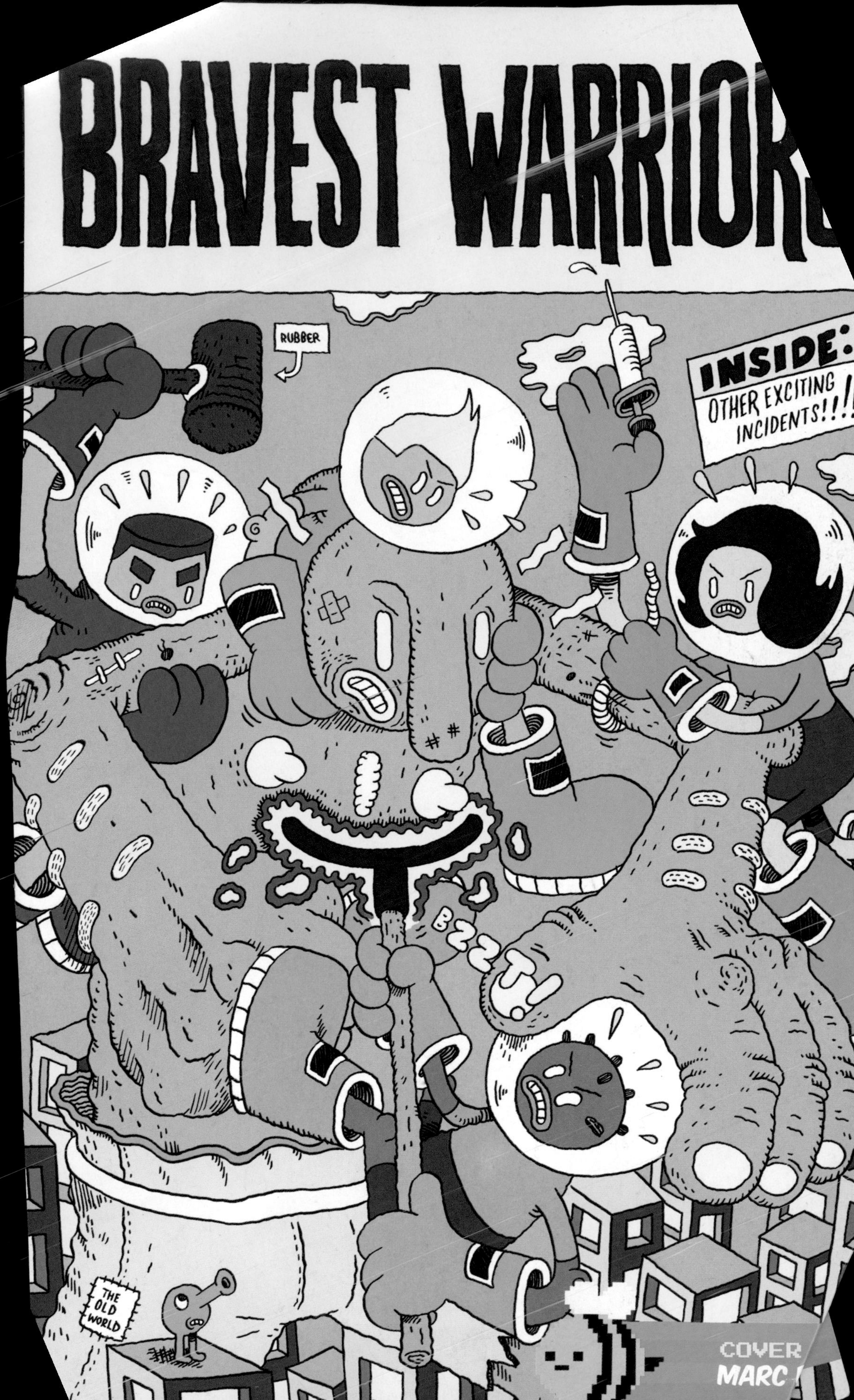

BRAVEST WARRIOR
RUBBER
INSIDE:
OTHER EXCITING INCIDENTS!!!!!
BZZT!
THE OLD WORLD
COVER
MARC

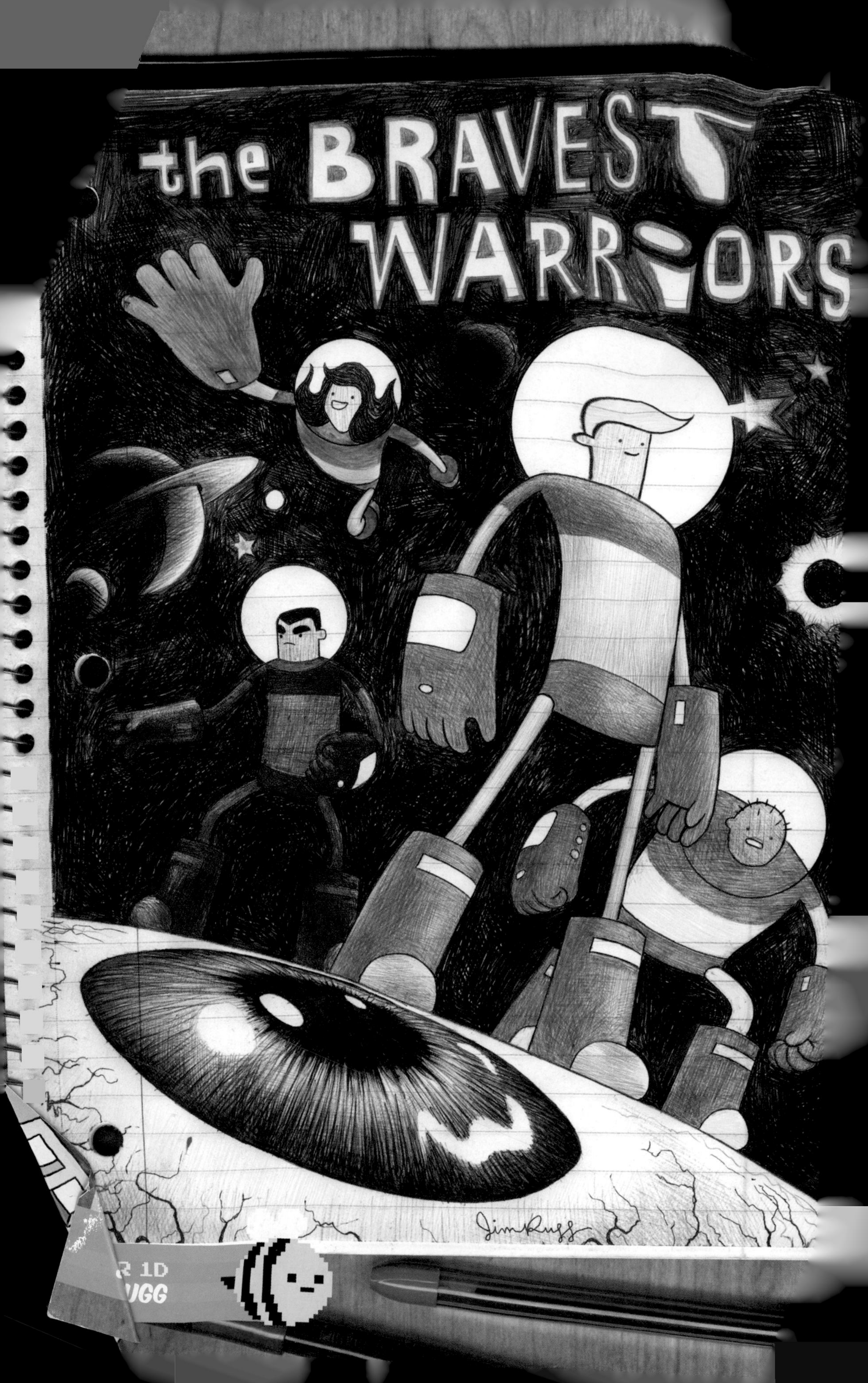
the BRAVEST
WARRIORS
Jim Rugg

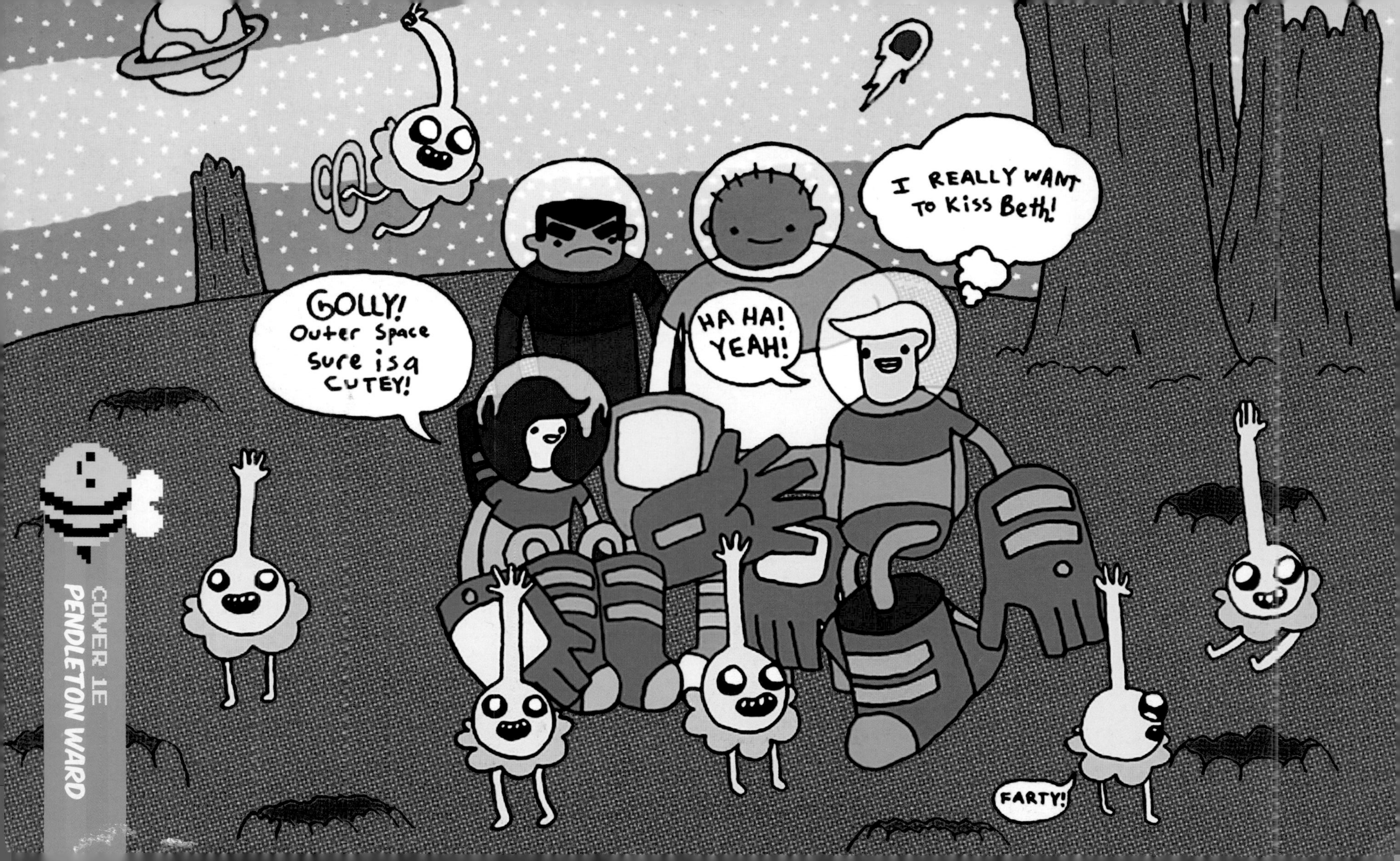
GOLLY! Outer Space sure is a CUTEY!
HA HA! YEAH!
I REALLY WANT TO KISS Beth!
FARTY!

COVER 1E
PENDLETON WARD

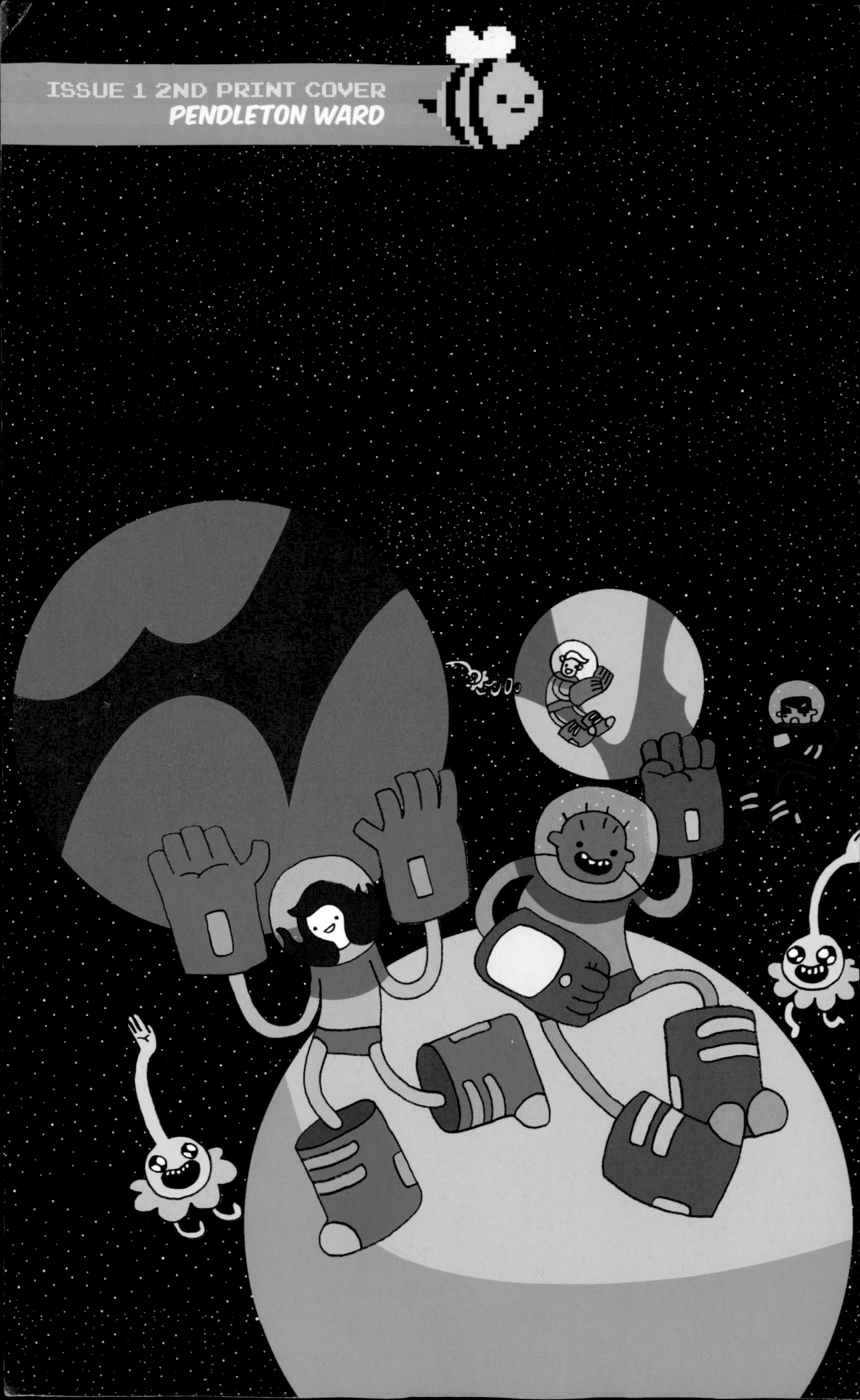
ISSUE 1 2ND PRINT COVER
PENDLETON WARD

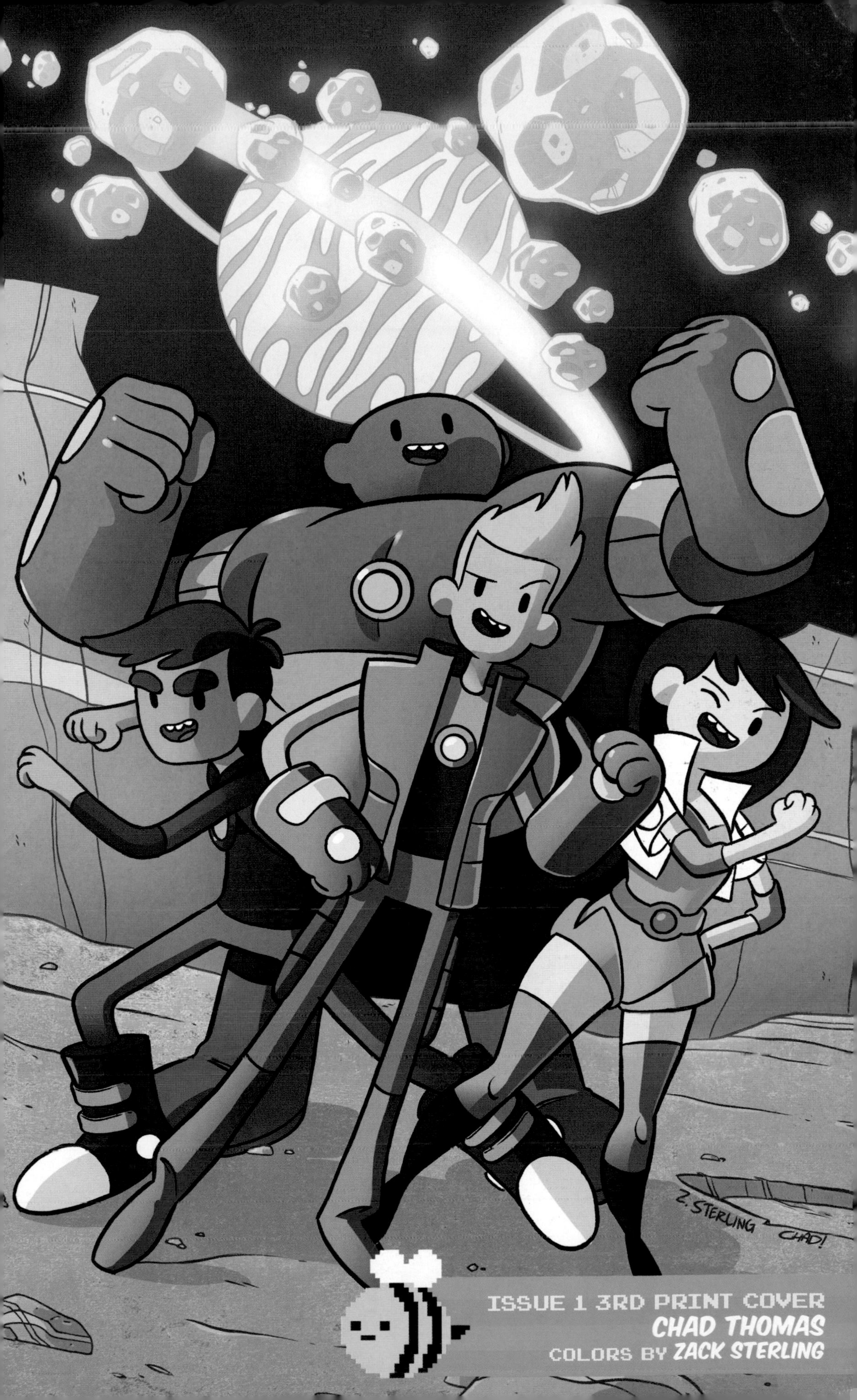
Z. STERLING
CHAD!

ISSUE 1 3RD PRINT COVER
CHAD THOMAS
COLORS BY **ZACK STERLING**

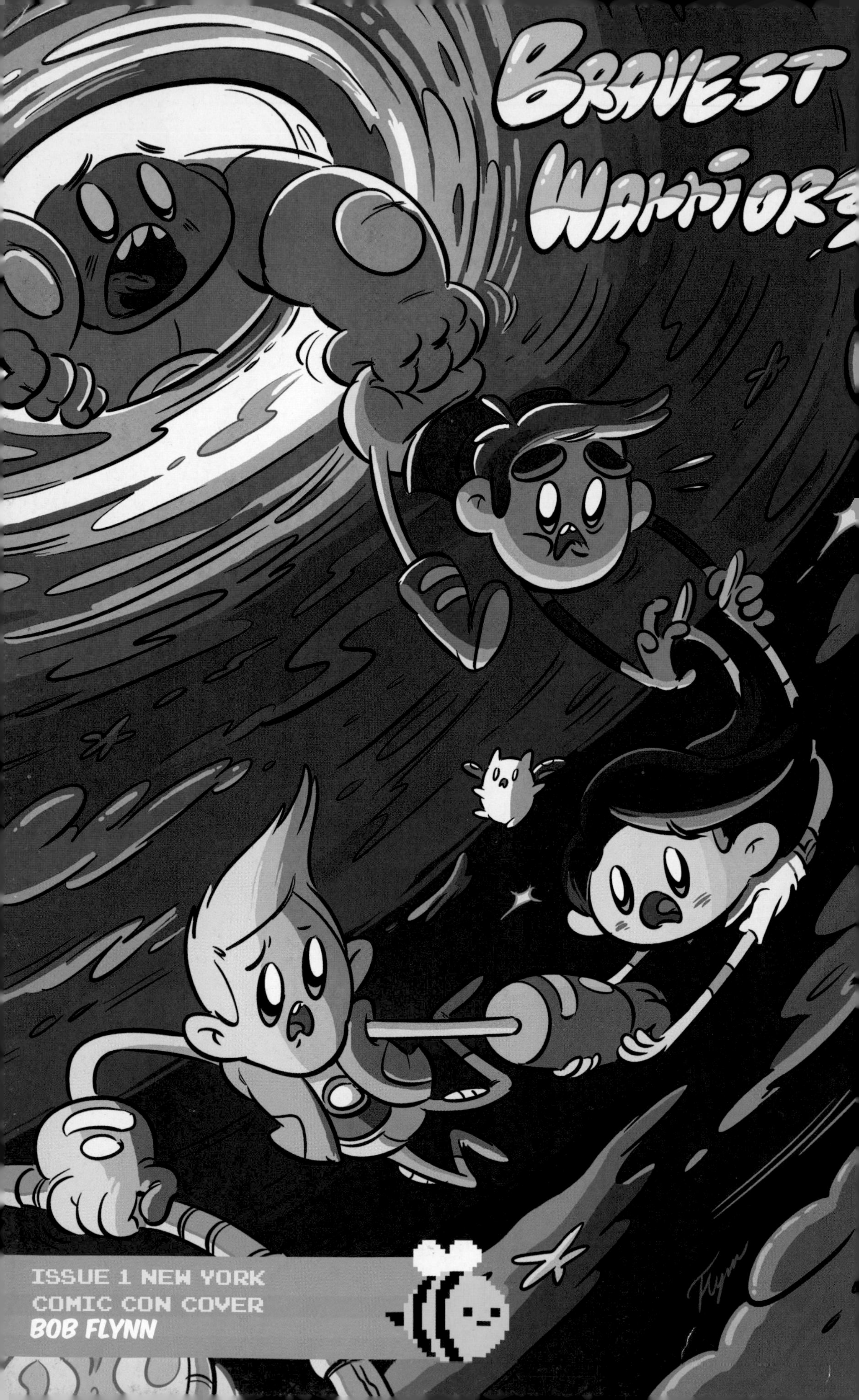
BRAVEST
WARRIORS
Flynn

ISSUE 1 NEW YORK
COMIC CON COVER
BOB FLYNN

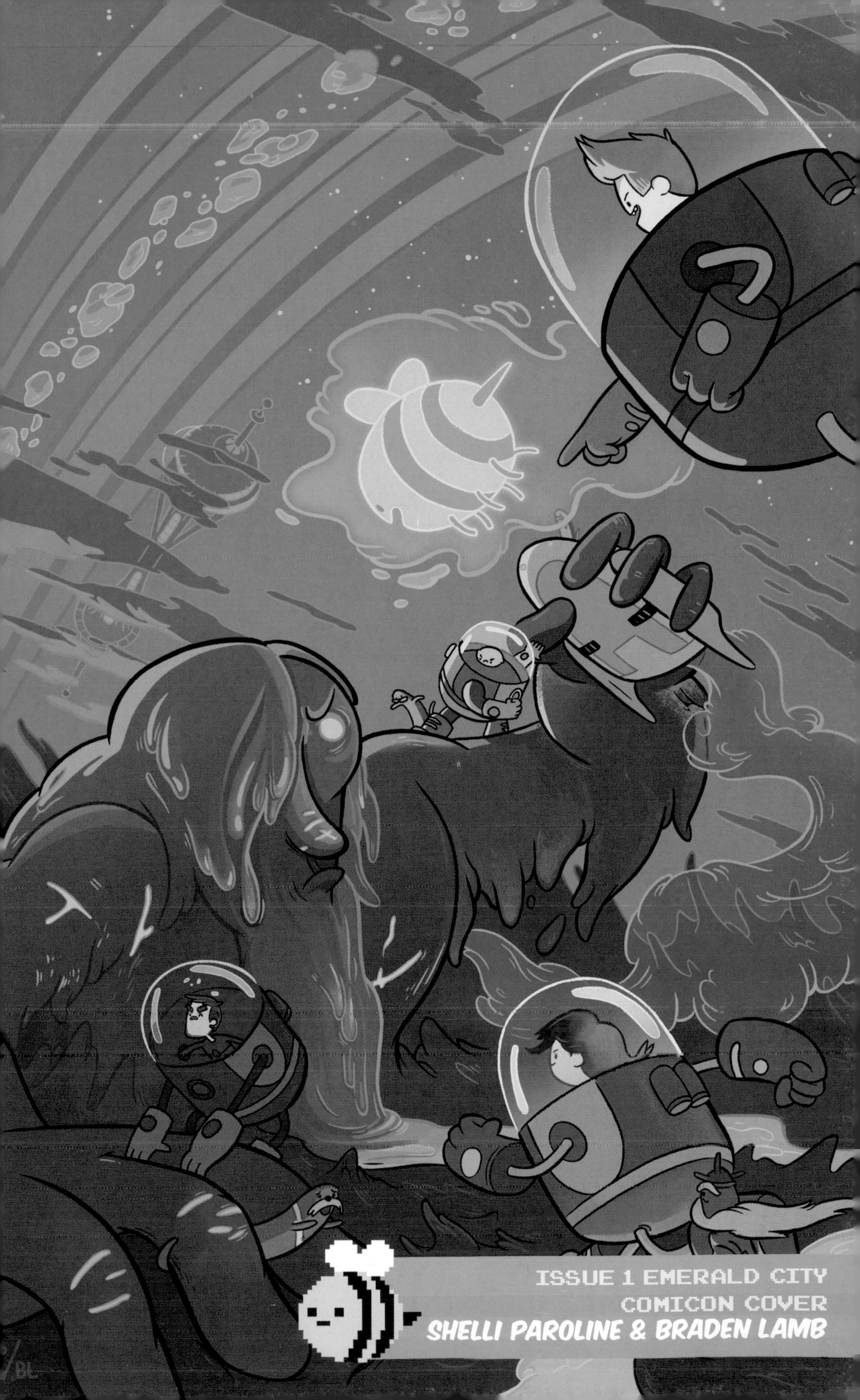
ISSUE 1 EMERALD CITY
COMICON COVER
SHELLI PAROLINE & BRADEN LAMB

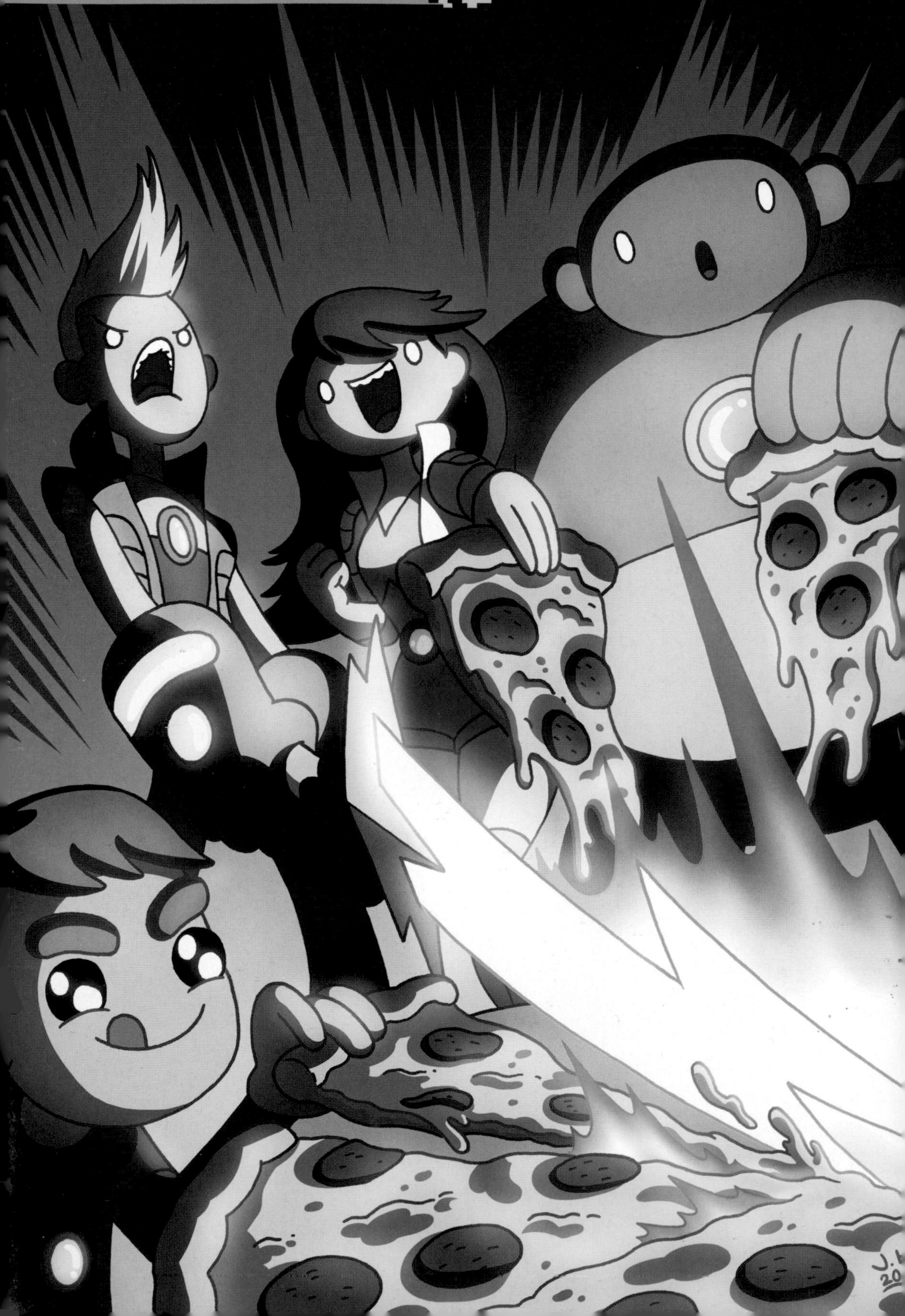

ISSUE 1 LONG BEACH COMIC CON COVER
JASON HO

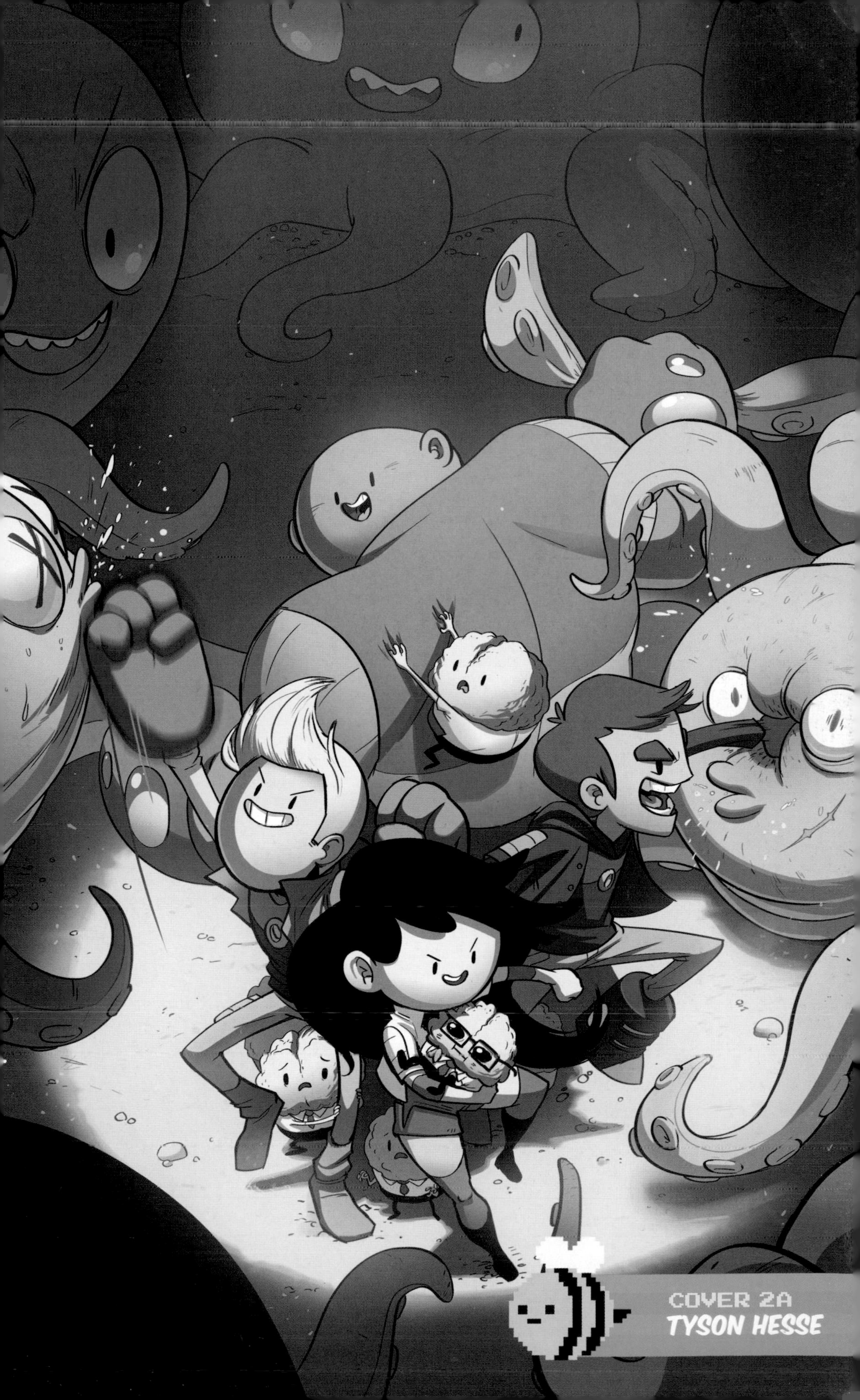
COVER 2A
TYSON HESSE

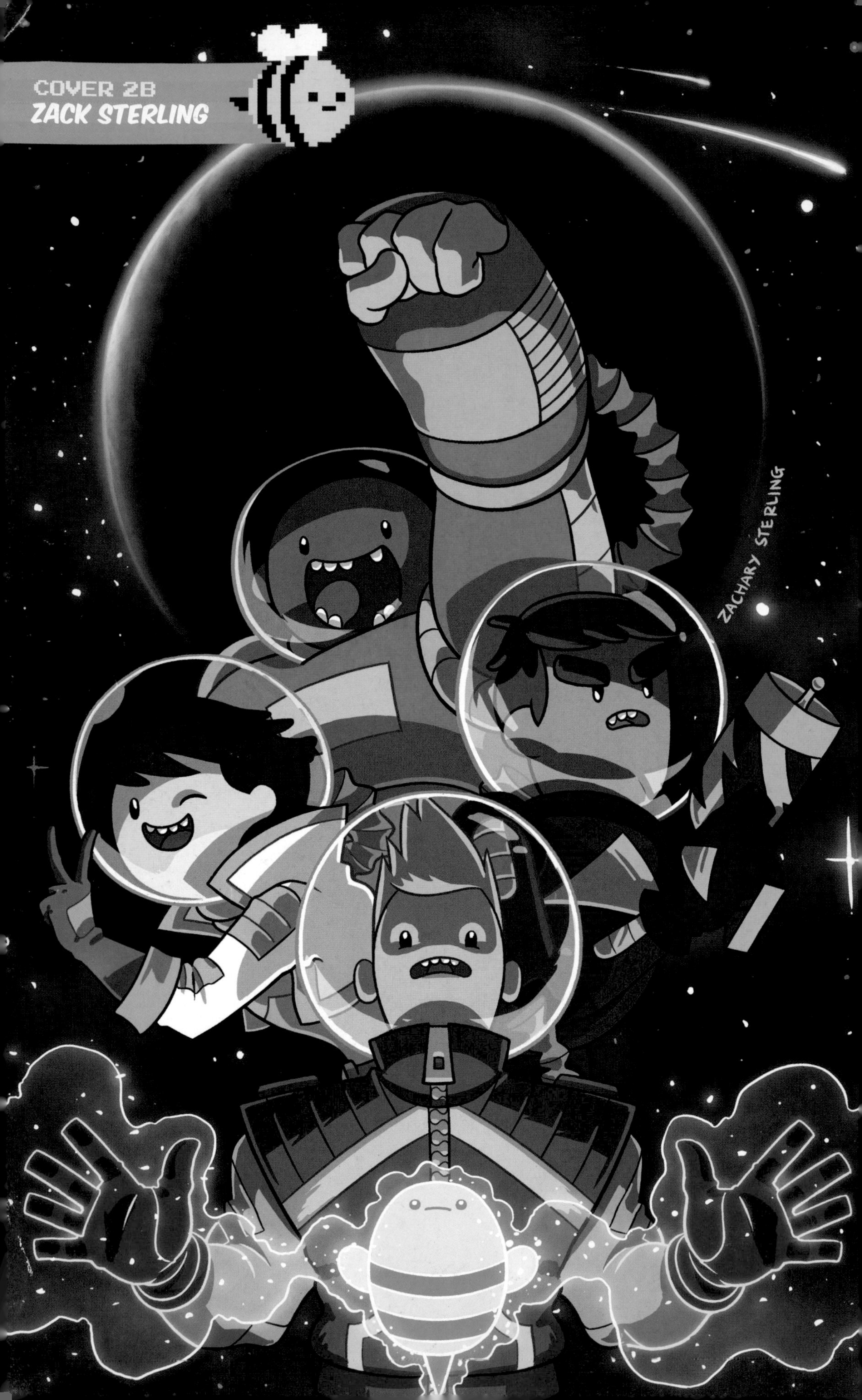
ZACHARY STERLING

COVER 2B
ZACK STERLING

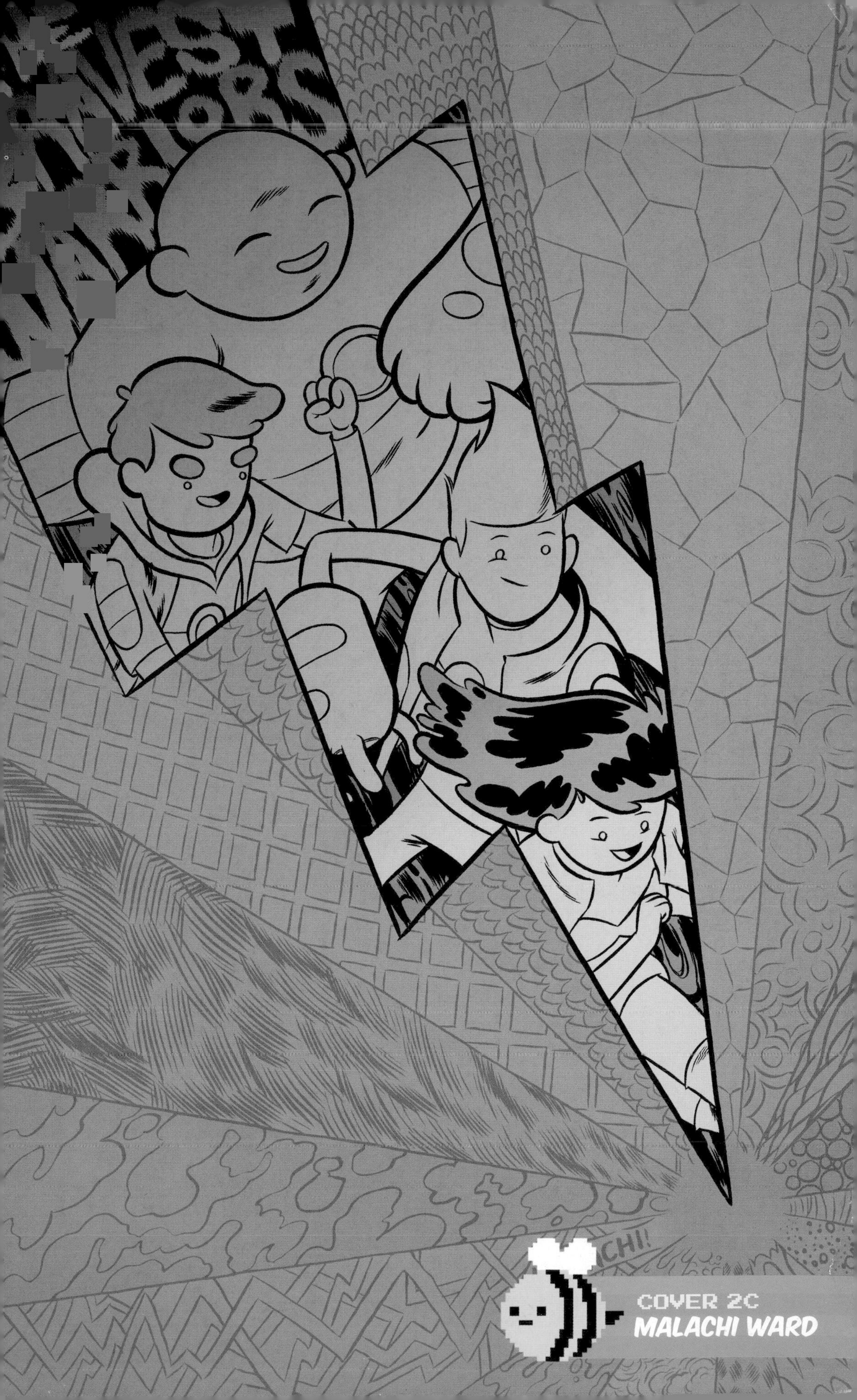

COVER 2C
MALACHI WARD

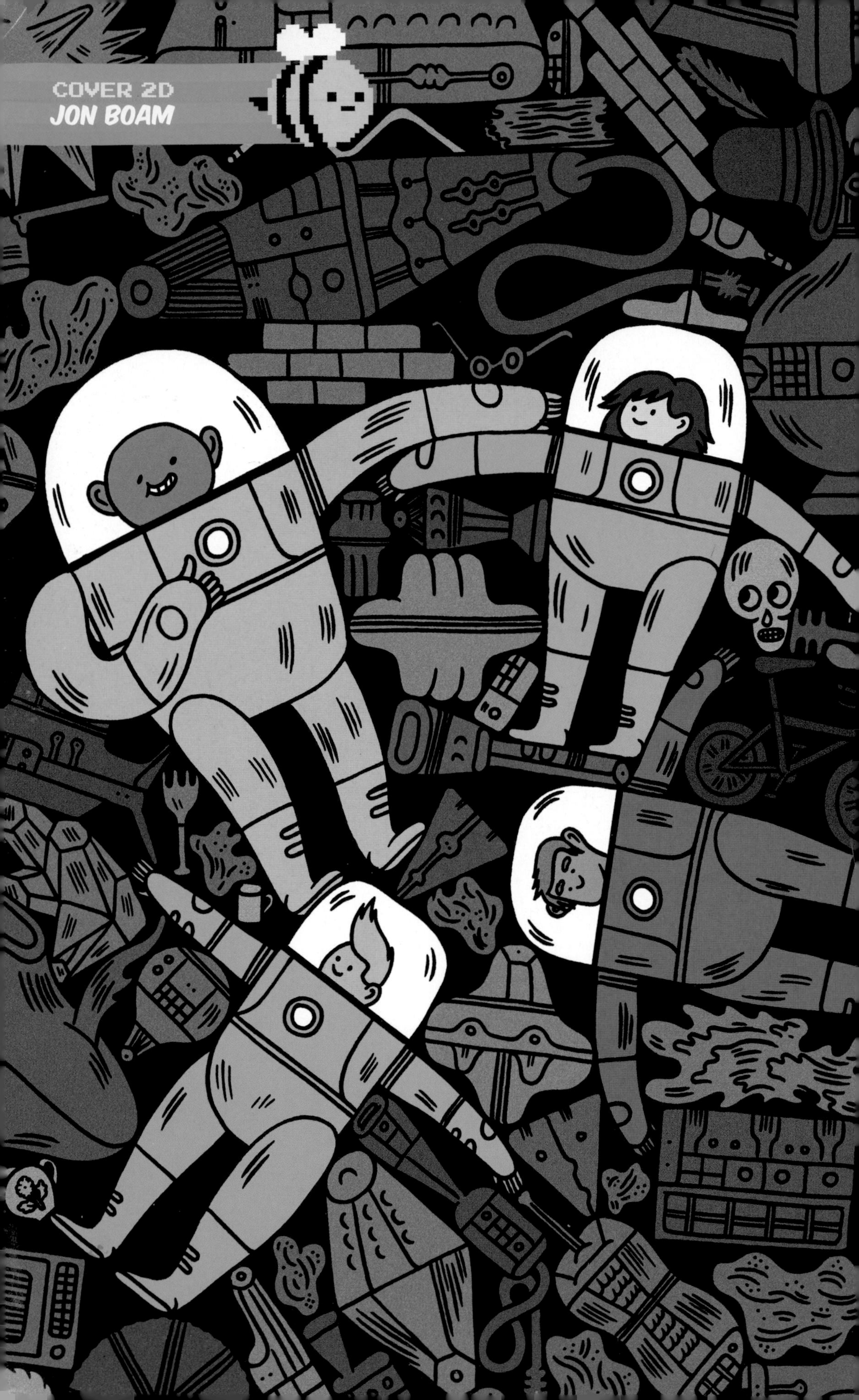

COVER 2D
JON BOAM

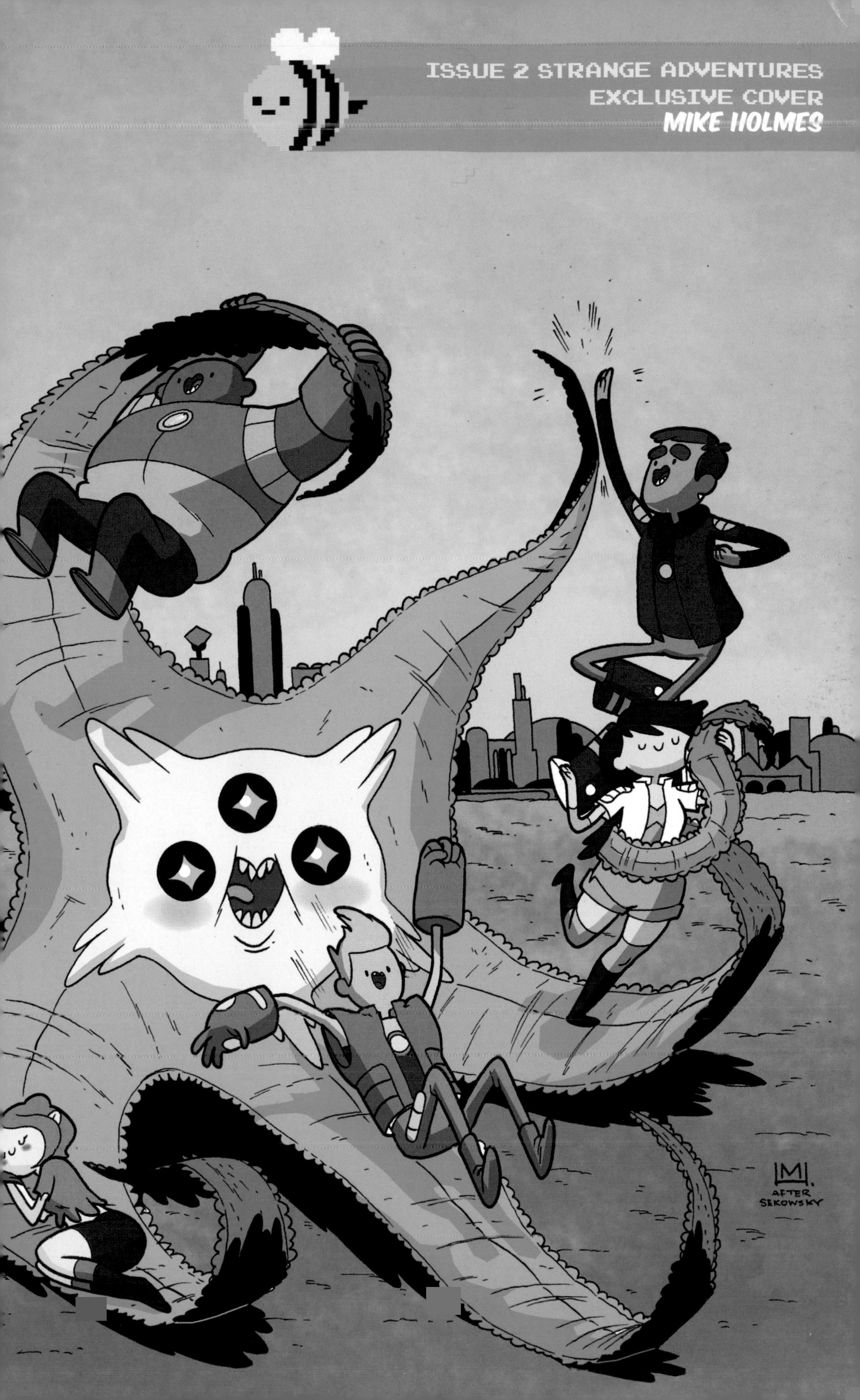
ISSUE 2 STRANGE ADVENTURES
EXCLUSIVE COVER
MIKE HOLMES
AFTER SEKOWSKY

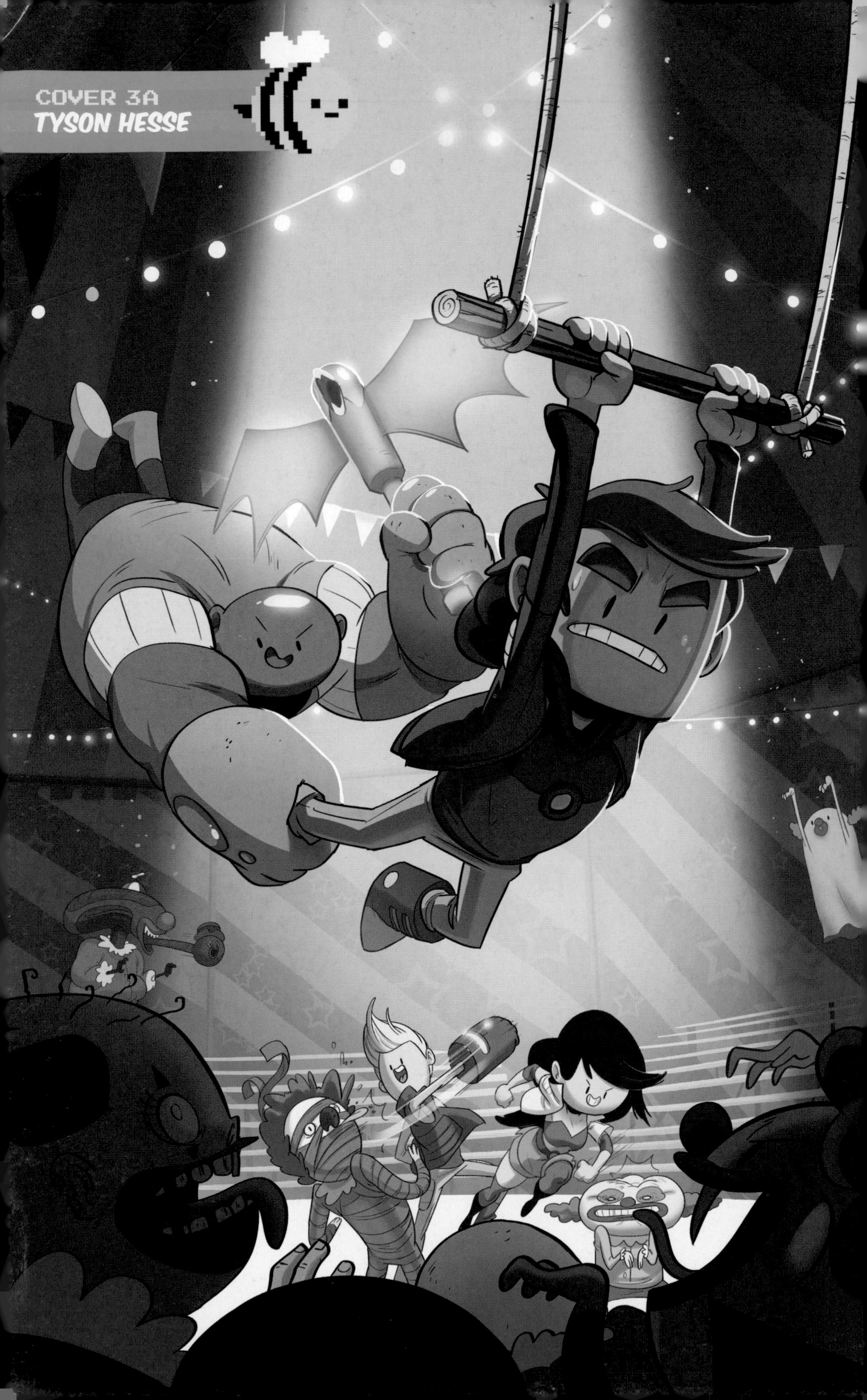
COVER 3A
TYSON HESSE

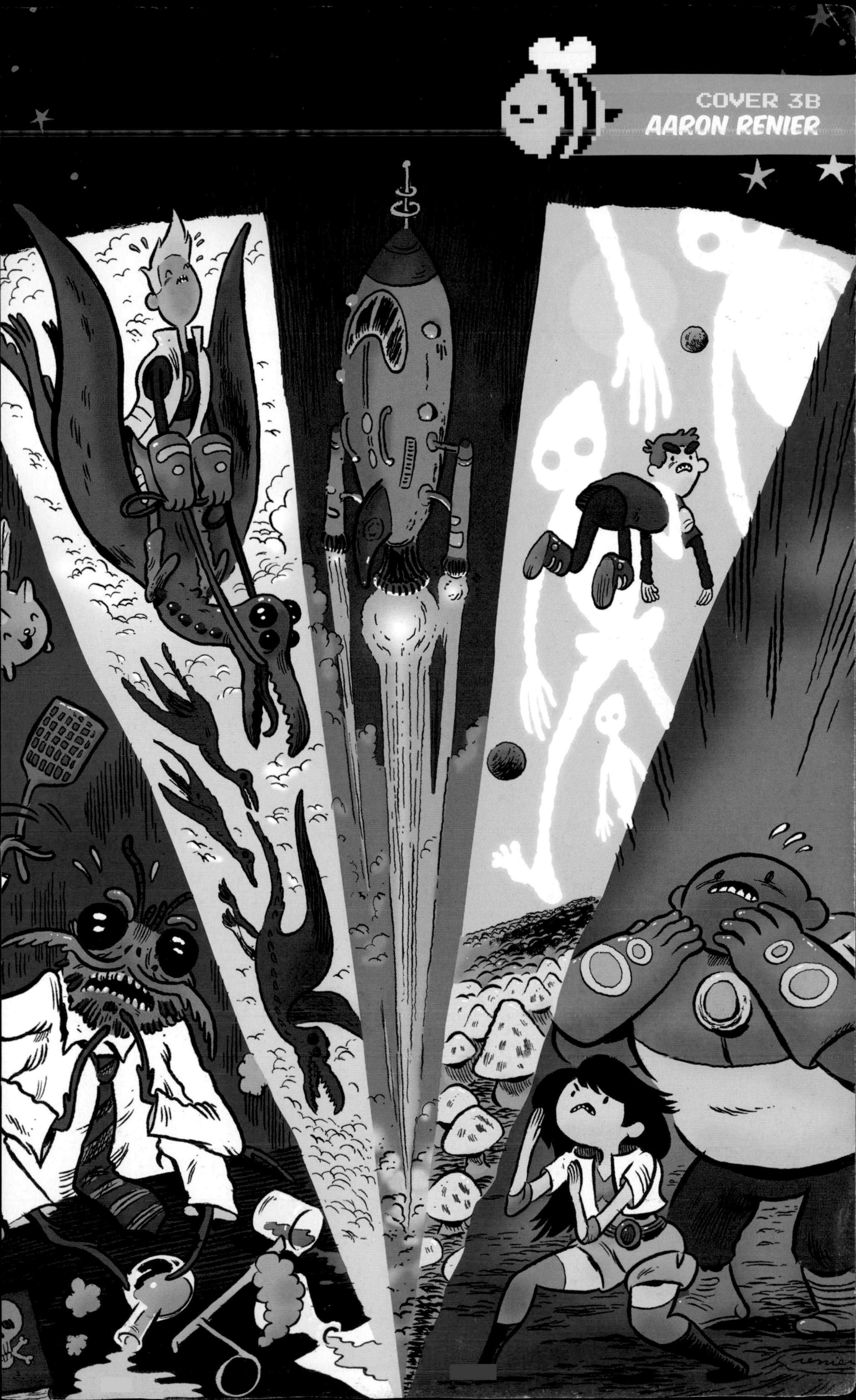
COVER 3B
AARON RENIER

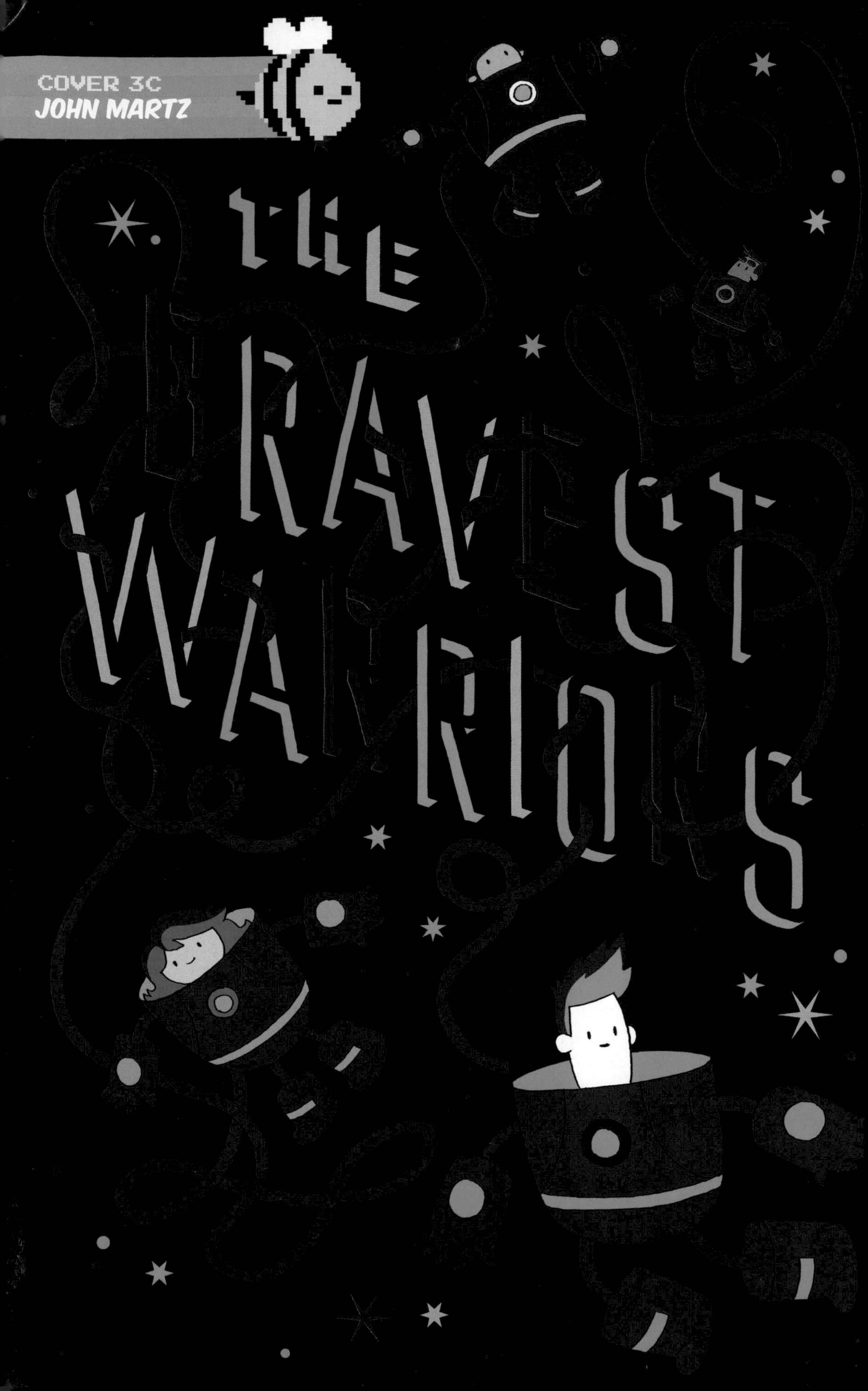
COVER 3C
JOHN MARTZ
THE BRAVEST WARRIORS

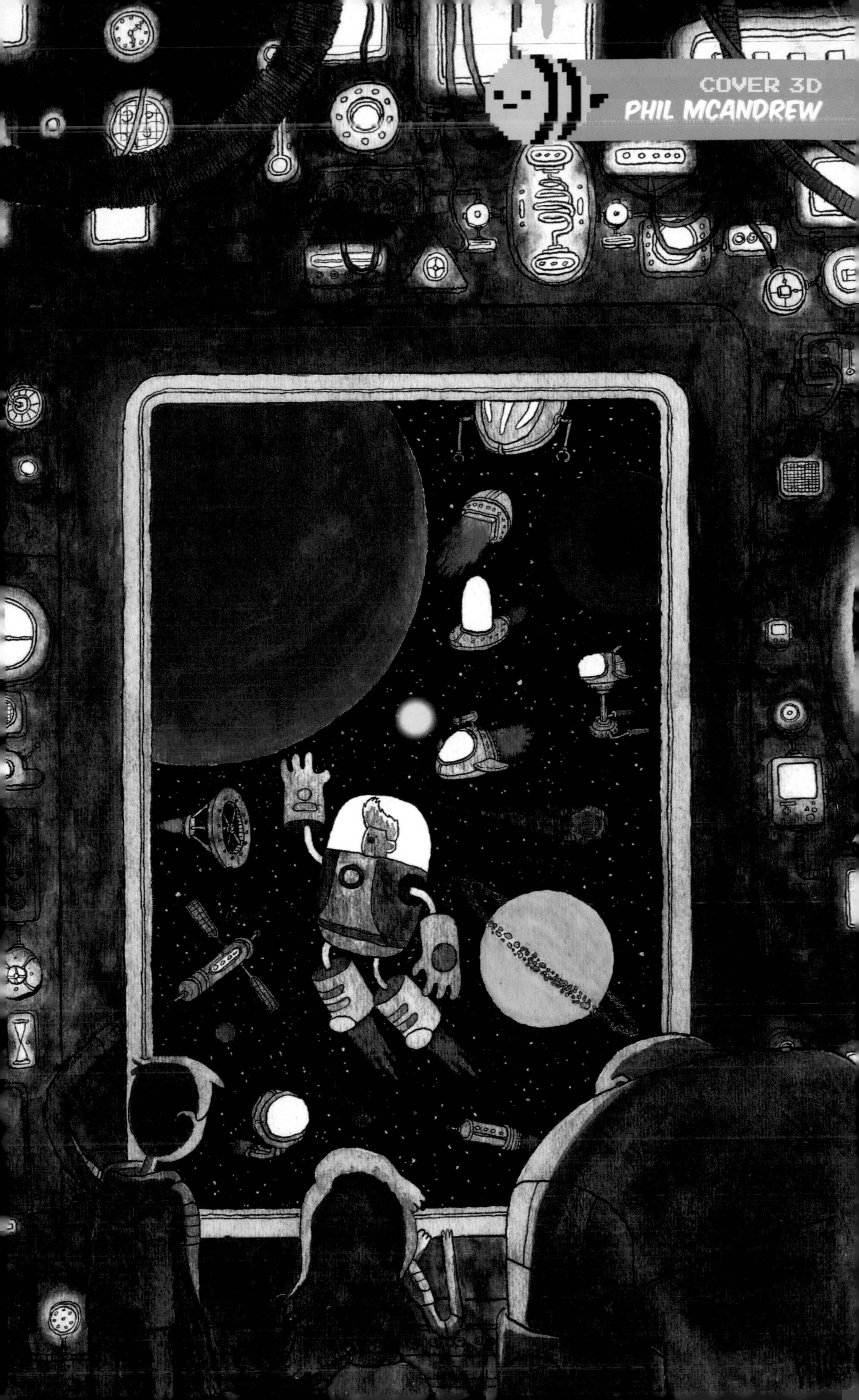
COVER 3D
PHIL MCANDREW

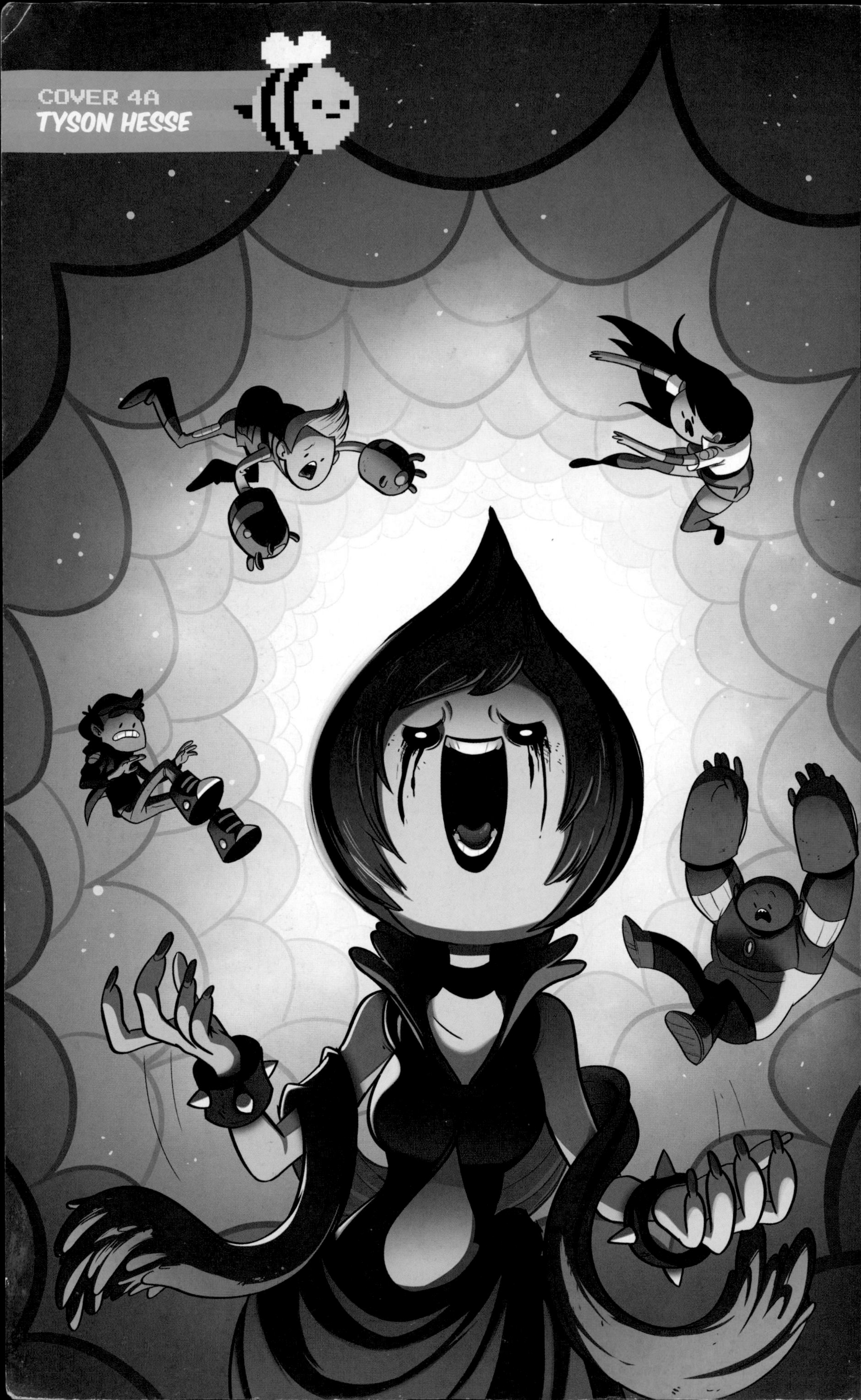
COVER 4A
TYSON HESSE

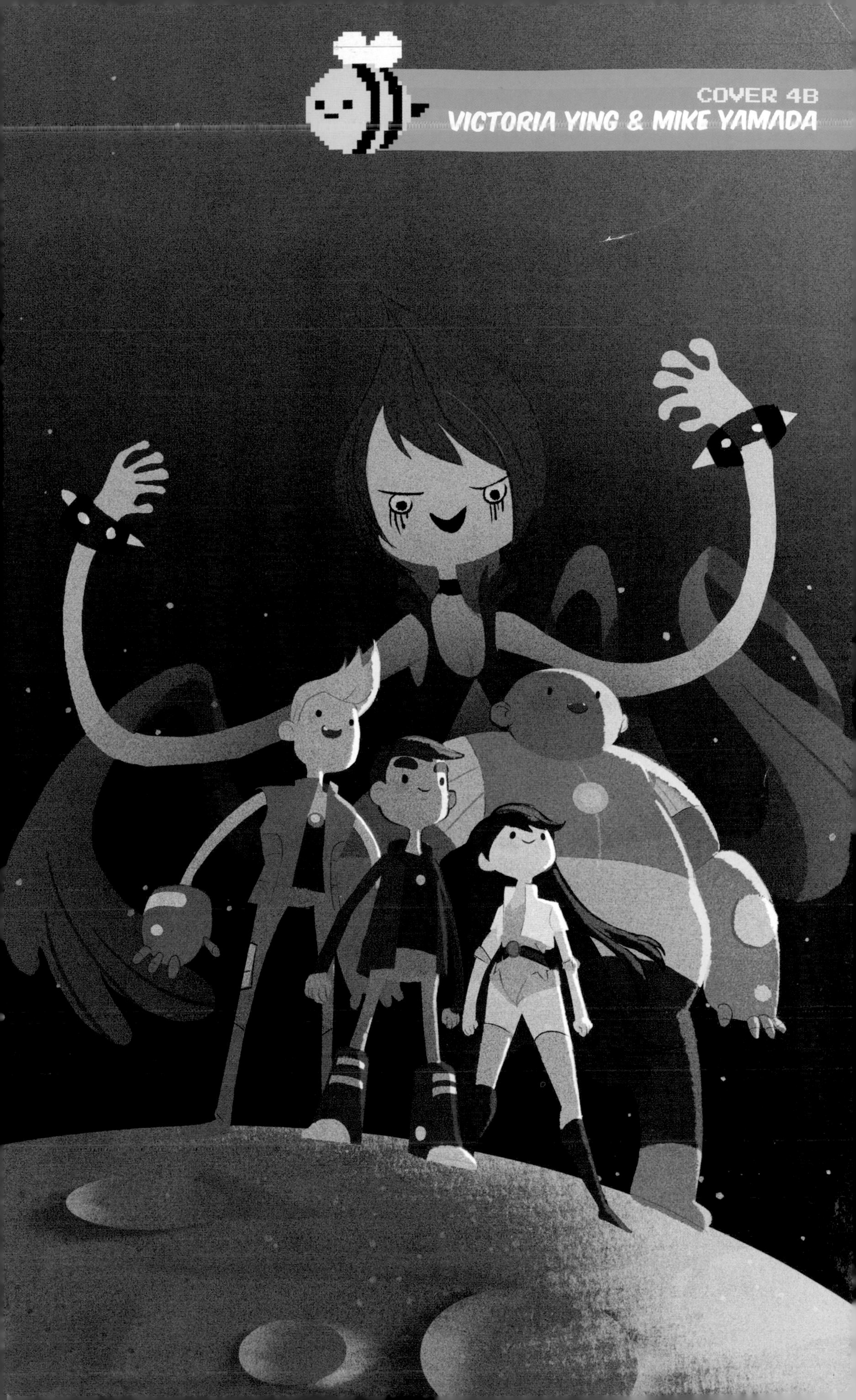
COVER 4B
VICTORIA YING & MIKE YAMADA

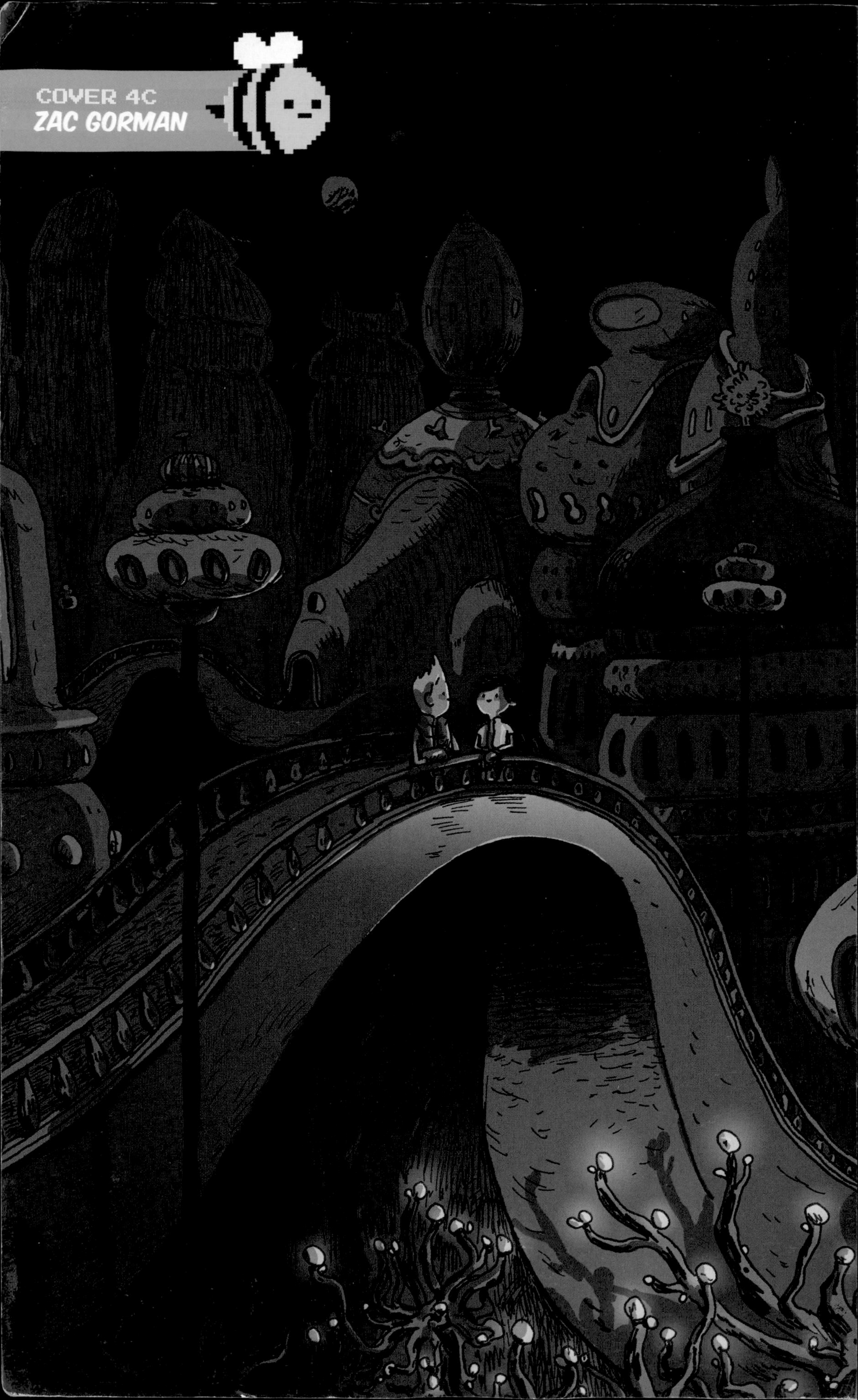

COVER 4C
ZAC GORMAN

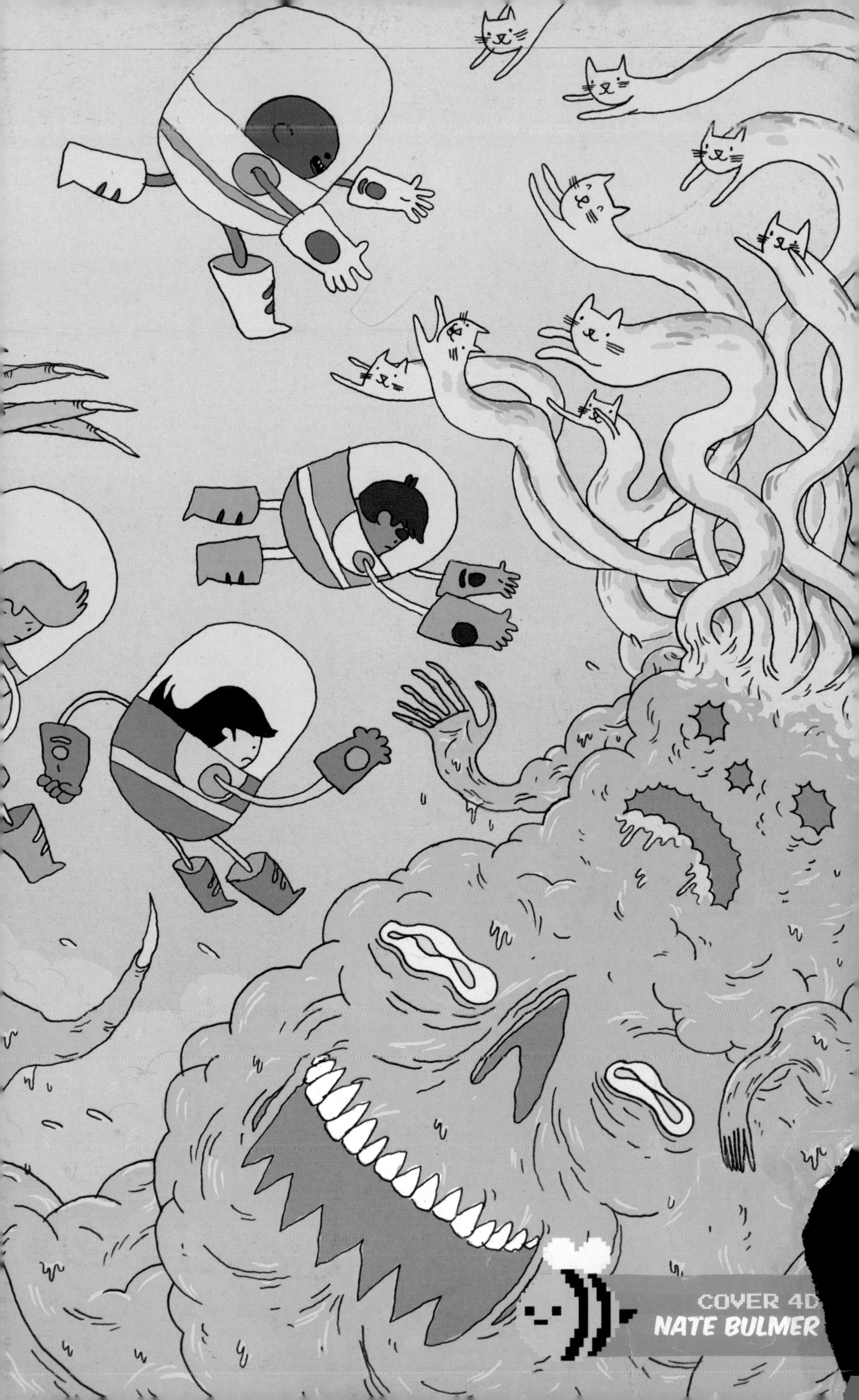
COVER 4D
NATE BULMER

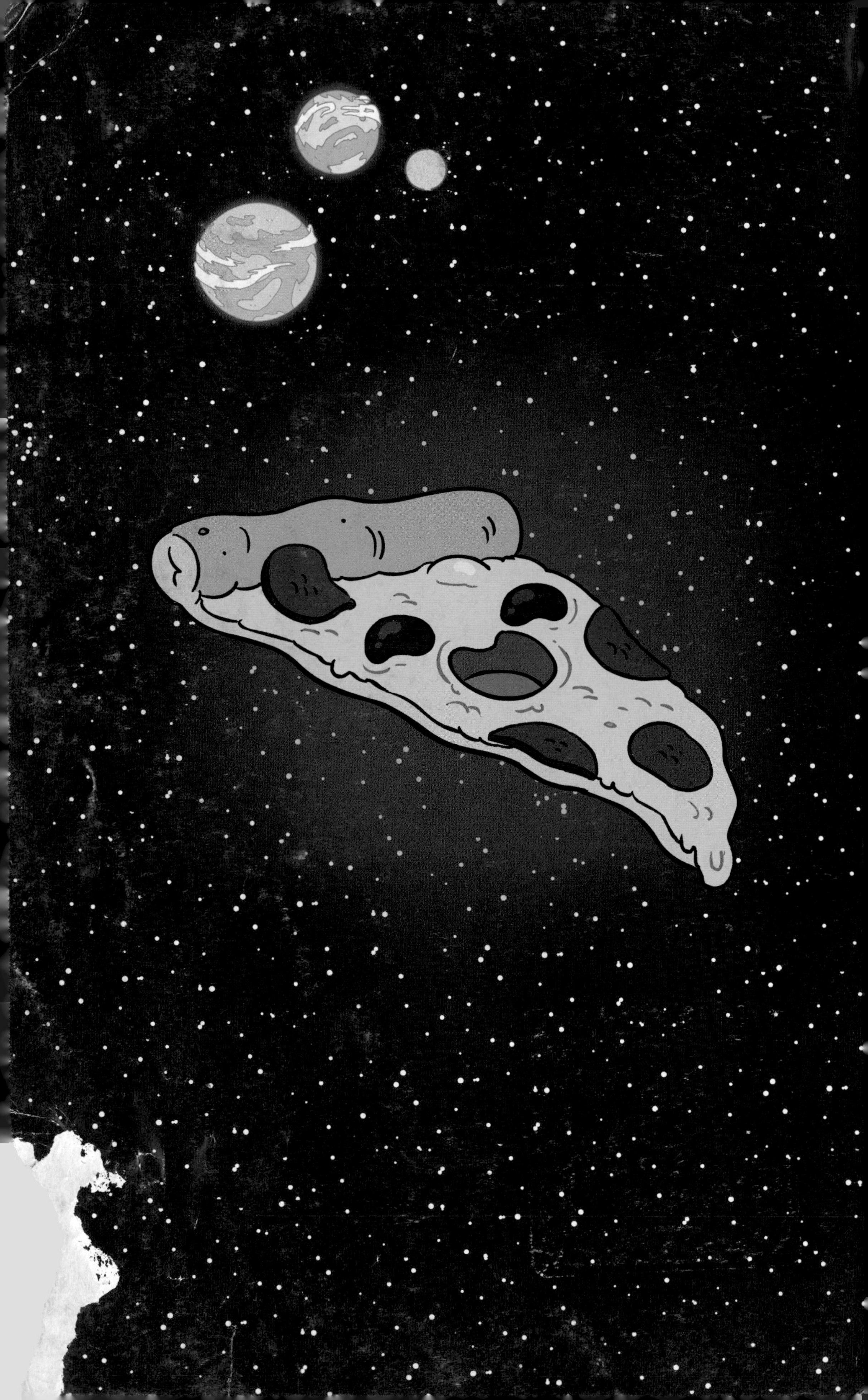